BY THE
NIGHT EXPRESS
AND OTHER TALES

BY THE
NIGHT EXPRESS
AND OTHER TALES

KEITH FLEMING

Edited and with an introduction by
Gina R. Collia

Published by Nezu Press
Queensgate House,
48 Queen Street,
Exeter, Devon,
EX4 3SR,
United Kingdom.

This edition published 2024

By the Night Express (incl. 'By the Night Express', 'Dolores', and 'Love Stronger than Death') first published by George Routledge and Sons, 1889. *"Can Such Things Be?"* first published by George Routledge and Sons, 1890. Short stories: 'So Innocent', *The Idler*, Volume 28, October 1905; 'The Transfiguration of Lettice Willoughby', *The Novel Magazine*, Volume 2, March 1906; 'The Red Skirt', *The Pall Mall Magazine*, Volume 38, September 1906.

ISBN-13: 978-1-917113-03-8

In the interest of preservation, the punctuation and spelling of the original first edition texts have been maintained, and the original formatting has been used wherever possible. Only minor publisher errors and spelling inconsistencies have been silently corrected.

CONTENTS

'Most Unassuming in Demeanour': The Life of K. E. Fitz-Patrick iii

By the Night Express

By the Night Express 1

Dolores 53

Love Stronger Than Death 109

"Can Such Things Be?" or, The Weird of the Beresfords 165

Short Stories

So Innocent 365

The Transfiguration of Lettice Willoughby 380

The Red Skirt 398

'Most Unassuming in Demeanour'
The Life of K. E. Fitz-Patrick

by Gina R. Collia

When I began looking for information about the author Keith Fleming, I had very little to go on. The only thing I knew with any certainty, based on the contents of the publishing contracts she signed with George Routledge, was that her real name was K. E. Fitz-Patrick.[1] It was thought that her first name was Kathleen and that she had been born in Ireland in 1858 or 1859, so I began by searching for a record of Kathleen's birth in Ireland.[2] But I found nothing. This wasn't surprising, as it turned out, as her name wasn't Kathleen, and she wasn't born in Ireland.

Next, I turned to the census books, where I found that Miss Fitz-Patrick had been recorded under four different names. Though it's not unusual to come across errors in census books—generally speaking, the ages given have a tendency to be a bit off—in Miss Fitz-Patrick's case the information is particularly unreliable. Within the 1851 Scotland census, both her name and age are recorded incorrectly. The same is true for the 1891 Wales census, in which her birthplace is also incorrect. The 1901 Wales census has her name down correctly, but it knocks nine years off her age. When presented with so much contradictory information, it can be difficult, without access to the original census forms, to know which is correct.

The main reason for errors being present in Victorian census information is that the records were produced by a third party, based on householder forms that could contain incorrect or illegible information. The average Victorian did not attach quite so much importance to providing accurate details about their own birth as we do nowadays, and it would have been no great surprise to find both men and women knocking several years off their age at census time to recapture their lost youth. In addition to the human tendency towards vanity, a person's exact date of birth was sometimes forgotten by their parents unless recorded somewhere early on (for example, in a family Bible), so guesswork played a much greater role in filling out forms than it does now.

The first national census for England, Scotland and Wales took place in 1801, but the information gathered before 1841 was statistical; for the most part, very few personal details were taken. This changed in 1841, when the first truly modern census was taken. From that point forward a census form was delivered to every property in the land, and the head of each household was responsible for recording the personal details of all individuals residing under his or her roof on a given date. The forms were then collected, and the enumerators transferred the information contained in them to census books. Unfortunately, the original forms were usually destroyed; this changed in 1911, from which time they were retained.

In Ireland, the first national census was taken in 1821. Few early Irish census records still exist—many having been lost when the Public Records Office in Dublin was destroyed in 1922—but those for 1901 and 1911 have survived. And when I looked at the individual householder returns for 1911, I found that 'Kate Elizabeth Fitz-Patrick' filled in and signed 'Form A' as the head of her particular household; she was living at 20 Richmond Hill, Dublin, at the time and recorded the country of her birth as Scotland.[3] Interestingly—and as if to prove beyond doubt how unreliable information recorded by the census enumerators can be—when I turned to the sections of the 1911 form that were filled in by the official enumerator, I found that Kate's name was recorded by him as both 'Kate E. Fitzpatrick' and 'Catherine Fitzpatrick'.

Over the years, various enumerators renamed her Catherine, Katherine, and Kathleen, but she signed herself as Kate. In addition to this, as I later discovered, her name was recorded as Kate in her mother's will, in her own will, and in the records of the cemetery where she was buried.[4] So, based on this small amount of census information—the name and birthplace provided by Kate herself—my search began in earnest, and what follows is the result.

Kate Elizabeth Fitz-Patrick was born in Edinburgh on 12 November 1849.[5] Her father, Peter Fitzpatrick, was born in Dublin in 1813, the third son of Peter Fitzpatrick (c.1768-1819) and his wife, Margaret (née Meighan, 1781-1842).[6] Peter Fitzpatrick Snr was a solicitor, and his son followed in his footsteps, being sworn in as an attorney of the court on 23 June 1838.[7] Peter Jnr's two older brothers, James and O'Keefe, were also solicitors, and the family business was run from 64 Capel Street, Dublin.[8]

On 21 November 1843, Peter Fitzpatrick Jnr married Georgina Elizabeth Queely at St Thomas's Church, Dublin.[9] Georgina was born in Dublin in January 1818, the only daughter of John Queely (c.1790/1–1869) and his wife, Catherine (c.1789/90-1840).[10] Georgina had only one sibling; her brother, Edward, 'a most lovely and interesting boy', died in 1828 at the young age of five, having suffered from hydrocephalus.[11] John Queely operated a 'general agency and discount office', supplying cash to 'persons requiring discounts, or wishing to raise Money on Mortgage, or other securities'; he was a money broker.[12] His premises at the time of his daughter's marriage were at 29 Lower Abbey Street, just half a mile from the Fitzpatricks' office on Capel Street.

Georgina, her brother and mother were involved in a serious

Carlisle Bridge, Dublin, c. 1840.

accident when she was just a child. In December 1825, while crossing Carlisle Bridge in the centre of Dublin—about half a mile from Moore Street, where they lived at the time—Catherine and her children were 'most violently thrown down' by a horse which, ridden by a boy who could not control it, had galloped furiously onto the bridge.[13] Catherine was carried 'in a state of insensibility' to Doctor Butler's Medical Hall—located about four hundred yards away at 54 Lower Sackville Street—along with Georgina, 'a fine and interesting little girl' of seven, and Edward, who was two.[14] Edward escaped 'without receiving the least hurt', but his sister and mother 'received very serious injuries, particularly about their heads'.[15] 'Everything their deplorable condition required' was done for them, and a week later they were pronounced 'out of danger'.[16]

Just one month later, Catherine opened a boarding and day school, 'for the Instruction of Young Ladies in every branch of Polite Literature, &c.', at her home at 22 Moore Street.[17] In 1829, she and her family moved to 15 Hardwick Place, where she re-opened her school and placed advertisements in local newspapers, promising to pay 'unremitting attention to the religious principles and general deportment of her pupils' and offering instruction in French, English, history, geography, 'the Use of Globes', writing, arithmetic, music, dancing, drawing and needlework.[18] 'Mrs. Q.' wished to 'impress on the Public, the peculiar advantages of her School in the Writing and Arithmetic department', as 'Mr. Q.' devoted his entire time to those subjects.[19]

In May 1839, the Queelys moved to 18 Lower Abbey Street, which later became no. 29.[20] When Georgina Queely married Peter Fitzpatrick at the end of 1843, he moved into her family home, and he took an office a short distance away at 53 Middle Abbey Street.[21] But this is the point at which things began to go wrong. By the end of 1846 he was in financial trouble, and six months later insolvency proceedings were initiated against him.[22] His case was set to be heard on 23 June 1847,[23] but he appears to have managed to pay his creditors before the matter got to court, thereby avoiding imprisonment. His father-in-law was not so fortunate.

Catherine Queely died on 5 April 1846,[24] and her husband remarried the following year. In his mid fifties, John Queely married twenty-two-year-old Emily Jessie Dunne on 25 September 1847.[25] Just three months later, in January 1848, notices of his insolvency began to appear in the local newspapers.[26] He was arrested and imprisoned for non-payment of debts, and his case was heard on 17 February; he was in bad health and was allowed out on bail for the sum of £200.[27] More notices followed, warning 'all persons indebted to the insolvent' not to pay him; they were to pay no one but the assignee responsible for the distribution of his assets.[28] He managed to repay his debts and remained in business, and in 1851 he moved his office to 85 Marlborough Street, 'opposite the

Education Board'.[29] But he was insolvent again in May 1860, and again in July 1864.[30] He died on 25 May 1869.[31]

Some time between the summer of 1847 and that of 1849, possibly as a result of financial difficulties, Peter and Georgina left Ireland and moved to Edinburgh, where their only child, Kate, was born at the end of 1849. In 1851, they were living in lodgings at 75 Parkside Street.[32] Around the spring of 1854, Peter started working for the North British Railway Company; he no longer worked as a solicitor and was employed as a clerk in the cashier's office.[33] By the spring of 1855, he and his family had moved to a house belonging to his employer in St Leonard's Hill.[34] Less than two years later he was in prison.

In his capacity as clerk, Peter was responsible for depositing funds into a bank account at the National Banking Company of Scotland on behalf of his employer, but on 5 January 1857 he failed to deposit the amount of £43 16*s* 11*d* into the account, choosing instead to keep the money.[35] He was arrested for theft on 9 January, but he could not be questioned at the time as he was 'labouring under delirium tremens'; he was examined before John Clark, magistrate, a week later and charged with 'wickedly and feloniously, upon the Fifth day of January Eighteen hundred and fifty seven within

St Patrick Square, Edinburgh, by Alfred Henry Rushbrook, 1929, National Library of Scotland.

the premises in Canal Street Edinburgh occupied by The North British Railway Company stealing the sum of Forty three pounds Sixteen shillings and Eleven pence Sterling'.[36]

When the crime was first reported to the police on 6 January, 'criminal officer' Michael Reilly went to Peter's home in St Leonard's Hill to look for him.[37] Finding him not at home, he searched various places around Edinburgh but failed to locate him. It turned out that, on the evening of 5 January, Peter had gone to the house of two drinking companions, Elizabeth and James Baillie, where he had spent the night with their lodger, Mary Ann Goldie; he had remained at that address until he was apprehended by the police.[38] Reilly searched the Baillies' home on 9 January and found Peter 'in a bed in a closet'.[39]

In his defence, Peter claimed that he had no memory of receiving or stealing his employer's money on account of being 'much addicted to drinking'.[40] But according to George Henderson, a witness who had spent time with him on the day the crime took place, Peter had been drinking 'but knew quite well what he was about'.[41] A warrant was issued, and he was committed to prison for further examination on 17 January.[42] Then, on 21 January, he was committed to Calton Prison—the largest and most brutal of Scotland's prisons—pending trial.

Peter's trial took place on 2 March 1857, and he pleaded not guilty, maintaining his claim that he was too inebriated to remember what had happened on 5 January.[43] The jury was unanimous in finding him guilty of breach of trust and embezzlement, and he was sentenced to four years' penal servitude.[44] The sentence of penal servitude consisted of three stages: separate confinement, labour in a 'public works' prison, then release on licence. Peter began the second stage of his sentence at Chatham Convict Prison, the largest prison in England, which had opened the previous year to house prisoners who would hitherto have faced transportation.[45] Cells inside Chatham were 'excellently ventilated, and furnished with a hammock, a bench, a tin water jug and basin, and little else'.[46] The prisoners were well fed, 'to enable them to perform the hard labour they have to undergo.'[47] When Peter arrived at Chatham, in the spring of 1858, he was healthy, but by the spring of 1859 he was an invalid.[48] On 8 March 1859, he was transferred to Dartmoor Prison, which was by that time a light labour or invalid prison, though the work performed by inmates was not in any way light or suitable for invalids.[49] His behaviour throughout his time in prison was 'very good', but he was not released on license; he served his full term and was released on 1 March 1861.[50]

Immediately upon his release, Peter returned to Edinburgh. Perhaps he did so to look for his wife and daughter; he took lodgings at 32 St Patrick Square, in St Leonard's Hill, describing himself at the time as a 'landed proprietor'.[51] As an invalid and ex-convict, he most likely needed someone to look after him. It would appear, however, that he did not find Georgina and Kate; he returned to Ireland alone some time between his release and his death on 30 December 1864.[52] He was buried in the churchyard of Drumcondra Church, Dublin, alongside his father.[53]

Kate was seven years old when her father was sent to prison. Whilst there is much we will never know about her life at the time, or that of her mother, we do know that her father was an alcoholic and thief who mixed with bad company and spent several nights with a woman who was not his wife—the type of woman who, six months after Peter was sent to prison, was charged with 'causing a disturbance, swearing and rioting and fighting' and was sentenced to thirty days imprisonment.[54] We also know that, as a result of

Peter's criminal behaviour, his wife and young daughter were left to fend for themselves and to find new accommodation; they could hardly remain in the house in St Leonard's Hill, the landlord of which was the very company that Peter had stolen from.[55]

According to the various census returns, Georgina and Kate lived on their 'own means' on 'income from land'.[56] Their income must have belonged solely to mother and daughter; otherwise, given the fact that his need for money drove him to crime, it would most certainly have been appropriated by Peter Fitzpatrick. Perhaps, like Mabel and Katharine Arden in *The Sins of the Fathers*, after Peter 'had done his best to shame and beggar both wife and child', Kate and her mother lived on 'the only source of income which her father had been unable to alienate from them'.[57] And perhaps, being to some extent financially independent, Georgina saw Peter's imprisonment as an opportunity to cut ties permanently with a husband who had brought her nothing but shame and pain.

As a result of John Queely's remarriage, Georgina had two half-brothers and a half-sister, and Kate had several half-cousins—one of whom was L. G. Wyndham Shire, chief engineer for the famous Midland Red bus company—but I have found no evidence to suggest that Kate or Georgina resided at any point, for any period of time, with any relative following Peter's imprisonment.[58] Kate and her mother appear to have been entirely self-sufficient and to have gone their own way.

For the years between 1857 and 1887, I have found no record of Georgina and Kate Fitz-Patrick—they always preferred to use this spelling of their name rather than Fitzpatrick. So, we don't know where Kate received her education. That said, given the fact that Catherine Queely ran a school for a number of years, Georgina was most likely educated by her mother, and she most likely passed on what she had learned to Kate who, as is evident from her writing, was well-read. But we know nothing of Kate as a child, adolescent or young woman.

Whilst we don't know when Kate and her mother left Scotland, or where they lived following their departure, we do know that in October 1887, by which time Kate was thirty-seven years old, they were living in Mid Wales. Both the *Aberystwyth Observer* and *Cambrian News and Merionethshire Standard* named them as two of the people involved in elaborately decorating Trinity Church in Aberystwyth for the harvest festival thanksgiving services that year, and the latter gives Georgina's address as Trinity Place.[59] Apparently, the services were so well attended that many parishioners could not find space within the church and had to leave.

By the time Kate's name appeared again, in an announcement in the *Carmarthen Journal and South Wales Weekly Advertiser* on 10 May 1889, it was common knowledge in Aberystwyth that she was the author 'Keith Fleming'.[60] The following day, a review in the *Aberystwyth Observer*, revealed that she had 'been for some time a resident of Aberystwyth.'[61] Kate, described as 'most unassuming in demeanour', was 'well known to the Holy Trinity congregation, which Church has the honour of numbering her amongst her members.'[62] She was a friend of Rev. D. W. Jenkins, the curate of Holy Trinity, and it was he who acted as witness to her signature when she signed a publishing contract with Routledge for "*Can Such Things Be?*" in December 1889. By that time the reverend had taken the living of St Mary's in Pembroke, but, despite his new parish being about seventy miles away from his old church in Aberystwyth, he and Kate had remained friends.[63]

Kate's first volume of fiction, *By the Night Express: A Psychological Romance*, was published by George Routledge and Sons in May 1889.

It contains three novellas—'By the Night Express', 'Dolores', and 'Love Stronger than Death'—in each of which it is 'not easy to mark the line between the real and the supernatural'.[64] Each tale contains 'enough of the horrible to satisfy the reader of morbid tendencies', and there are no happy endings for these characters.[65] In 'By the Night Express', the best of the three stories, Maurice Donovan is travelling to Ireland by train when, having become involved with an attractive fellow traveller, he finds himself mixed up in a gruesome murder mystery and unable to tell the difference between dream and reality. In 'Dolores', when Colonel Frank Oswald is found dead, presumed by most to have committed suicide, Arthur Wilmore receives the solution to the mystery of his death by means of a supernatural vision: 'it was not drowsiness or sleep. I swear it was not sleep'. And in 'Love Stronger than Death', Norah Desmond 'sees' an end to all her hopes and dreams when she suffers a 'terrible mystic revelation'. The book was well received; the *Bookseller* wrote:

> 'The wonderful dreams, which are the groundwork of the plot, might, if they were true, form useful matter for the investigations of the Society for Psychical Research. They will, however, at any rate keep the most sleepy traveller awake for the two or three hours' railway journey he may spend in reading them.'[66]

Announcements for Kate's next book, *"Can Such Things Be?" or, The Weird of the Beresfords: A Study in Occult Will-Power* began appearing just seven months later, in December 1889, and it was issued at the beginning of 1890, in both cloth and 'fancy boards', as part of Routledge's Railway Library series.[67] The decidedly atmospheric tale is that of the fulfilment of the Beresford family curse, in part narrated by Arnold Dysart of Trinity College, Cambridge, based on his father's account of Maxwell and Eunice Beresford and the events surrounding the latter's supernatural experiences and death. As with Kate's first book, *"Can Such things Be?"* received positive reviews for the most part. *Punch*'s 'Baron de Book-Worms' objected to the number of 'twaddling interruptions about "spookikal" research and metaphysical problems', but he seems to have missed the point served by the interjections:[68] to reinforce the idea that the story is based on real events, presented by a man of learning, a Professor of Modern Philosophy, a 'poet and philosopher, dreamer and thinker, imaginist and scientist'.[69] The *Bookseller* wrote:

> 'An old haunted manor-house, a lady who leaves her coffin and re-appears in society, and a violin of "astral" properties, are the main elements of the "Weird of the Beresfords." No one can say that the ingredients of the story are wanting in psychological spiciness. An air of realism is thrown over the tale by the introduction into it of a Cambridge professor, who patiently investigates the mystery and is persuaded of the veraciousness of these occult phenomena. Take it all round, Mr. Fleming's book, for its kind, is distinctly to be recommended.'[70]

Kate's third book, the sensation novel *At the Eleventh Hour*, was published by Routledge a year and a half later, in the summer of 1891. Lionel Hartley Dacre, up-and-coming architect, has been engaged by the Marquis de Vallanelle to design a château on the French Riviera and to make improvements to other properties, so he and his wife, Helen, relocate to Paris with their young son. But the French nobleman's designs are not restricted to his various homes; he has a bad reputation where women are concerned and has set his sights on beautiful Helen Dacre. When Lionel discovers that his wife has gone missing without a trace, he fears the worst: that she has abandoned him, and taken her son with her, to run off with the villainous Frenchman. The mystery of her disappearance is later revealed… at the eleventh hour. *The Scotsman* described *The Eleventh Hour* as 'a novel of conspicuous power and deep interest… that may be read with a great deal of pleasure.'[71] The *Carlisle Patriot* wrote:

> 'The author… here achieves a distinct advance in his art. His previous work proved him an expert in plot and incident; and he has developed a charm of manner and breadth of treatment which add grace to a stirring story. The analysis of character and descriptions are all well done; and altogether the novel takes rank among the best that have been produced of recent months.'[72]

Kate and her mother, like many 'unattached' middle-class women at the time, lived in lodgings, moving from one reputable establishment to another when want or need dictated. By the time that *At the Eleventh Hour* was published, they had left Trinity Place and taken lodgings at 7 Sea View Place, situated just a stone's throw

Aberystwyth, c. 1896.

from the beach in one of the town's most desirable locations.[73]

By the time of Kate and Georgina's residency in the town, Aberystwyth had long been one of the favourite watering places in Wales, praised by fashionable physicians for 'the virtues of its health-giving air'.[74] There were lodging houses all around the main streets of the town, no shortage of hotels, and the local authorities 'spent money freely' to increase its attraction to people in search of health.[75] From 1883, Aberystwyth's water supply came from Llyn Llygad Rheidol reservoir, at base of Pumlumon Fawr, and residents and visitors alike were assured that what they drank was 'pure and unadulterated'.[76] The beach was known to be a good hunting ground for precious pebbles, and every facility was provided for sea bathing. In short, Aberystwyth was an extremely pleasant and attractive place to live.

Kate's final novel, *The Sins of the Fathers*, was never published in book form; it was issued in instalments in several newspapers between 1893 and 1895; its earliest publication appears to have been in the *Forfar Herald* from July 1893.[77] It tells the story of a mysterious disappearance during a party at great, grey Arden Grange on a wild, stormy All Souls' Night. And aside from being a gripping yarn—involving theft, supernatural visions, revenge, kidnapping, and murder—that was popular enough to be picked up by Australian newspapers, *The Sins of the Fathers* provides us with an insight into Kate's views on capitalism and inequality.[78] It also gives us an idea of her views on the hunting of defenceless animals—the victims of 'cruelty and strength' and 'that insatiate, horrible desire to destroy and ruin so strong and rampant in man's evil breast'—in the name of 'sport', perpetrated by 'them cowardly creatures that call themselves "men"'.[79] On the subject of the unfair distribution of 'money and lands and worldly goods' she wrote:

> 'And what are these things? Do they not belong to all alike? Are they not the inheritance of all who know labour? Not the monopoly of a few drones in the world's busy hive. Are they not the natural heritage of civilised, toiling humanity? In the beginning the Great Creator made no distinctions. He gave the earth and the fulness thereof to man, to have dominion over it, and over all things upon it. This was to man in the aggregate—mankind; not to the swollen capitalist—the human sucker of the people's blood.'[80]

Various themes run throughout Kate's work. She seems to have been fascinated by the idea that individuals—people with 'peculiarly organized minds'—who are possessed of 'mesmeric power' could, whether living or dead, influence the thoughts or actions of fellow human beings, even at a great distance.[81] Professor Dysart, in "*Can Such Things Be?*", thinks it possible that the minds of the dead remain active and capable of exerting influence on both people and objects, working as an 'invisible, unimagined force' for good or ill.[82] And Maurice A. Donovan, in 'By the Night Express', suggests that proximity to a severed head, 'that even for one short hour had held the mind… that for all we know, in our dark and groping ignorance, was not then yet dead, though the body was but dust', could account for his uncanny experience.[83]

Kate was a Christian and believed in the survival of the human soul; she also appears to have believed, certainly at the time of writing her supernatural fiction, in the survival of individual human consciousness. As Cyril Raymond explains in *"Can Such Things Be?"*, 'We bury the brain', but 'the immaterial, divine spirit of that mind, the condensed, sublimated essence of the man's being, has surely separate existence'; the soul, he suggests, is 'the spirituality of his mind'.[84] Kate's characters exist in a world where the dead are with us always, 'crowding round us… blessing us as we go', separated from us—imperceptible for the most part by our physical senses—by a 'shrouding veil' that, now and then, becomes 'transparently thin', thin enough to permit us to interact with the 'just beyond' and to 'move amidst a mighty host of the dead'.[85]

As I mentioned before, Kate was described as 'most unassuming in demeanour' by a local journalist. And she may well have been quiet and shy, maybe even painfully shy, like several of her female characters—like Lettice Willoughby, Ula Ferguson, Kathie Ormsby, and Helen Templeton who was 'reserved, shy, almost timid, in the presence of strangers'.[86] But she was an intelligent woman with strong opinions, and she injected those opinions into her writing. And no doubt she did so with less fear of reproach under a male pseudonym; though local journalists appear to have known that *Mr* Fleming was in fact a *Miss*, those working for the national papers thought her to be a man.[87]

Kate opposed war, pointing out the hypocrisy of those who, whilst professing to be Christian, spent their 'highest ingenuity' in 'fashioning devilish instruments, or discovering chemical combinations, that would be most deadly in their slaughter of our fellow-men'.[88] She also opposed capital punishment, that so often, based on little evidence, resulted in the innocent man dying, 'calling God and man to witness that he is murdered'.[89]

With regard to Kate's views on members of the opposite sex, the male protagonists in her stories tend to lack the strength, faith, and determination of her female characters. When their trust in a woman close to them is tested, as is the case with Hugh Denver in *The Sins of the Fathers* or Lionel Dacre—and to a certain extent his son too—in *At the Eleventh Hour*, they are weak and relatively quick to think, and accept, the worst; they lack 'a perfect faith'.[90] In contrast, the women in her stories, such as Mabel Arden's mother, Katharine, in *The Sins of the Fathers* or Helen Dacre's aunt, Dorothy Templeton, in *At the Eleventh Hour*—even Helen's landlady, Mrs. Graham, for that matter—never doubt; they keep perfect, unwavering faith. In the words of Aunt Dorothy:

> 'Oh God! they are all alike, these men—weak, selfish, pitiful cravens where women are concerned; they cannot value any of them, a true, loyal, faithful woman; but are ready to condemn her as vilest of the vile, if but a whisper is breathed by some evil, jealous tongue; ready to think her as false as they are ready to be false themselves, to honour and love and truth.'[91]

Selfishness, Kate explains, 'is essentially man's attribute', and he is very good at keeping things all to himself when he wishes to do so; he 'skilfully arranges it' so that when women encroach upon his 'self-established privileges', if they dispute the 'masculine monopoly in certain directions, they find matters made rather rough for them.'[92]

Following the publication of *The Sins of the Fathers*, no new work by Kate appeared for several years. By August 1895, she and her mother had left Sea View Place and were living at Rossnalee, 2 Trinity Road, a boarding house run by one Mrs W. Bubb.[93] And by the spring of 1901, Kate and her mother had moved again, this time to rooms at 21 Lower Portland Street, about a third of a mile from Holy Trinity Church and their old lodgings in Trinity Placc.[94]

Georgina Fitz-Patrick died, 'after a lingering and distressing illness', on 31 December 1903,[95] leaving the sum of £361 13*s* 7*d* to Kate.[96] At the time of her death, she and her daughter were living at 'Grogwynion', 1 Penglaise Terrace, a short distance from

Holy Trinity Church, but she was buried in Mount Jerome Cemetery, Dublin, alongside her mother, Catherine, on 8 January 1904.[97] Every year for the ten years following Georgina's death, on the anniversary of that event, Kate placed memorial notices in Welsh newspapers 'in ever-mourning memory' of her 'beloved mother': 'Soul of my soul, we *shall* meet again, And with God be the rest.'[98]

It is likely that Kate resided in Ireland for a short time after travelling there to arrange her mother's funeral at the beginning of 1904; she was resident in Dublin in February 1904 when probate was granted.[99] But by the summer of that year she was back in Wales and living again at 'Grogwynion', where she remained until the end of August.[100]

Routledge republished *"Can Such Things Be?"* as a sixpenny novel, under the title *The Weird of the Beresfords*, in the spring of 1905, and it was still available for sale in 1911.[101] But following the death of her mother, Kate appears to have turned her attention entirely to writing short stories, none of which have a supernatural theme. Possibly, all matters concerning death and the supernatural were then too painful for her; or, in order to please newspaper editors and readers, she was forced to shift the focus of her fiction in order to get it published. Whatever the reason, she appears to have given up on all things supernatural, in her writing at least.

The short story 'So Innocent' was published in *The Idler* in October 1905. In it, Fred Glover of the *Western Light* is covering a political speech at Park Hall in Cardiff when his assumptions about a pretty young, and seemingly helpless, girl get him into trouble.

The spring of the following year, 'The Transfiguration of Lettice Willoughby' was published by *The Novel Magazine*. In it, Greville Newcome, rising young politician and Member of Parliament for Blackmore, is looking to marry well in order to advance his career.

When his mother advocates a match between him and the youngest daughter of the Attorney-General, Sir Francis Willoughby, a man of great influence, Greville pooh-poohs the idea. He doesn't want his wife to be 'a limp creature without any backbone'; he wants a woman with character. And 'poor little Letty', according to Greville, is a 'colourless little creep-mouse that is frightened at its own shadow'. But when he makes a bitterly sarcastic speech in the House of Commons that puts his life in danger, Greville discovers that Lettice Willoughby is a woman with character and courage in abundance.

'The Red Skirt' was published in *The Pall Mall Magazine* in September 1906. May Palliser is in love with the poet Percy Wyndall, a man she believes is capable of doing great deeds and of rousing others to 'great and noble action'. He is a man with 'heroic impulses'. Most of all, he is 'a champion and defender of women and children'. But Percy's deeds are not so great when May finds herself stuck up a tree with an angry bull waiting for her in the field below. And he is no champion of children when a little girl becomes the frustrated beast's next target.

The following spring, 'The Courage of Kathie' appeared in *The Sunday Sun*, an Australian newspaper. Its heroine, painfully shy Kathie Ormsby, is travelling by express train from Cardiff, on her way to Llandrindod Wells, when she uncovers and determines to thwart—in order to save the man she secretly loves—a plot to assassinate a Russian aristocrat.

By July 1908, Kate had returned to the boarding house at 21 Portland Street, which was run by Jane Bateman.[102] But some time between then and 1911, she left Aberystwyth and travelled to Ireland, where she took lodgings at 20 Richmond Hill in the Rathmines district of Dublin; she occupied a single room and was still living on 'income from land'.[103] Her short story 'An Audacious Wager' was published in the *Irish Weekly Independent* in February 1912. It is the story of the downfall of Adolphus Treherne, captain of the Lancers, who makes it a rule 'never to look twice at an ugly woman'. Over confident regarding his own irresistibility to the fairer sex, he bets Major Lawrence O'Reardon 'a pony' that he can win over a young woman he barely knows.

By the summer of the following year, Kate had returned to Aberystwyth. In June 1913, a short story entitled 'Garth Austin's Strategy' appeared in the *Weekly Freeman's Journal.* It was the 'Prize Story of the Week' and was written by Keith Fleming of 'Isfryn', Llanbadarn Road, Aberystwyth'.[104] 'Isfryn', not far from the sea and station, was a 'homely' boarding house run by a lady called Mrs Jenkins, who offered 'healthy rooms' and 'every comfort', and Lanbadarn Road was less than half a mile from Kate's previous home at Trinity Place.[105]

In 'Garth Austin's Strategy', Arabella and Eleanor Freeman, both of whom are journalists, are identical twins who 'get themselves up in duplicate fashion'. While cycling at headlong speed through the little village of Creswell, one of the 'Sisters Freeman' is involved in an accident in which an old woman, Mrs. Musgrave, is knocked down and later dies, but nobody can tell the two sisters apart in order to decide which one was responsible. Dr. Garth Austin, who has a deep interest in physiognomy, has 'made brain-study a speciality', and he devises a plan to discern the difference between Nell and Bell.[106]

Of all Kate's short stories, 'Garth Austin's Strategy' is the most like her earlier work, with its male protagonist, a man of science who has dedicated his time to 'brain-study', hatching a plan to solve a mystery. It also marks a return to a subject that seems to have fascinated her: 'that strange mystic affection said to exist between twins'.[107] In addition to the twin sisters Arabella and Eleanor Freeman, in *The Sins of the Fathers* Agatha Hargrave and Walter Oliphant are twins, and Bernard and Brian St. Lawrence are twin brothers in 'Love Stronger Than Death'.

Unlike her earlier short stories, there was no mention of Kate's previous successes alongside 'Garth Austin's Strategy', just the statement that she was awarded two guineas for it. Kate was sixty-three years old when the story was published in the summer of 1913, and I have found no work by her published after that date.

For the years 1913 to her death, I have found no mention of Kate Fitz-Patrick. At some point, she left Wales for the final time and travelled to Dublin, where she lived at 8 Dunville Avenue, Rathmines. Prior to her death, she was a resident of the Home of Rest for Protestant Dying at 20 Camden Row.[108] Kate died at the age of ninety-five on 19 January 1945; she was buried alongside her mother, Georgina, and grandmother, Catherine, in Mount Jerome Cemetery, Dublin.[109]

Notes

1 James Doig, 'Archives of British Publishers/Keith Fleming', online at *Wormwoodiana*, 26 December 2011.

2 Ibid.

3 *Census of Ireland, 1911*, Dublin, Rathmines and Rathgar East.

4 Georgina's will, see *Calendars of Wills and Administrations 1858-1920*. Kate's will, see *Calendar of Grants of Probate of Wills and Letters of Administration, 1945*. Burial records of Mount Jerome Cemetery and Crematorium, Dublin.

5 *Dublin Weekly Nation*, 24 November 1849, p. 14.

6 Peter Fitzpatrick was baptised on 4 May 1913 (see *Ireland, Catholic Parish Registers, 1655-1915*, Dublin, St Mary's). His father died on 22 Jan 1819 and was in the '52nd year of his age' at death, so, assuming that his age was recorded accurately, he was probably born c. 1767 (see *UK and Ireland, Find a Grave Index, 1300s-Current*). Margaret Meighan was baptised on 1 May 1781, see *Ireland, Catholic Parish Registers, 1655-1915*. She died on 11 April 1842, see *Dublin Evening Post*, 14 April 1842, p. 3.

7 *Dublin Morning Register*, 25 June 1838, p. 4.

8 Edward Keane, P. Beryl Phair and Thomas U. Sadleir, *King's Inns Admission Papers, 1607-1867*. Dublin: Irish Manuscripts Commission, pp. 168-169.

9 *Statesman and Dublin Christian Record*, 24 November 1843, p. 3

10 Georgina was baptised on 11 January 1818 (see *Ireland, Catholic Parish Registers, 1655-1915*, Dublin, St Mary's). John Queely's age at death was recorded as 78 when he died on 25 May 1869, so he was probably born in 1790 or 1791 (see *Calendars of Wills and Administrations 1858-1920* and I*reland, Civil Registration Deaths Index, 1864-1958*). Catherine died on 8 April 1846, and her age at death was recorded as 56, so she was probably born in 1789-1790 (burial record at Mount Jerome Cemetery and Crematorium).

11 Edward was born in May 1823 (see *Ireland, Catholic Parish Registers, 1655-1915*, Dublin, St Andrew's), and died 15 April 1828 (see *Dublin Evening Post*, 19 April 1828, p. 3).

12 *Thom's Almanac and Official Directory*. Dublin: Alexander Thom and Sons, 1859, p. 1112, and Saunders's News-Letter, 14 October 1846, p. 4.

13 The accident, *Dublin Morning Register*, 20 December 1825, p. 2. Following its reconstruction it was renamed O'Connell Bridge in 1882. The Queelys' address, see *Dublin Morning Register*, 23 January 1826, p. 1.

14 The accident, *Dublin Morning Register*, 20 December 1825, p. 2. As an aside, Charles Butler, M.D., 'Apothecary and Chemist to his Majesty and the Lord Lieutenant of Ireland', the proprietor of the Medical Hall, produced *Butler's Medical Hall 'Medicine Chest'*, a guide to drugs and doses.

15 Ibid.

16 Ibid.

17 *Dublin Morning Register*, 23 January 1826, p. 1.

18 *Saunders's News-Letter*, 28 September 1829, p. 4.

19 Ibid.

20 *Saunders's News-Letter*, 13 May 1839, p. 3. The numbering was altered in 1844, see *Saunders's News-Letter*, 29 October 1844, p. 4.

21 *Thom's Almanac and Official Directory*. Dublin: Alexander Thom and Sons, 1847, p. 633.

22 'John Byrne v. Peter Fitzpatrick, Gent. Attorney, bill of exchange' (see *Saunders's News-Letter*, 1 December 1846, p. 2)

23 *Dublin Evening Post*, 10 June 1847, p. 3.

24 *Dublin Evening Packet and Correspondent*, 7 April 1846, p. 3.

25 *Ireland, Select Marriages, 1619-1898*. The marriage took place on 25 September 1847.

26 *Freeman's Journal*, 29 January 1848, p. 1.

27 *Freeman's Journal*, 17 February 1848, 4.

28 *General Advertiser for Dublin, and all Ireland*, 15 April 1848, p. 2.

29 *Freeman's Journal*, 6 August 1851, p. 1.

30 *Bankrupt & Insolvency Calendar*, 28 May 1860, p. 2, and 11 July 1864, p. 3.

31 *Ireland, Calendar of Wills and Administrations, 1858-1920.*

32 *1851 Scotland Census.*

33 Declaration of Peter Fitzpatrick, 17 January 1857, AD14/57/313.

34 Valuation Rolls VR010000004-/15, Edinburgh, 1855, p. 15 (National Records of Scotland). Also, John Queely and Peter Fitzpatrick v. John and Edward Harper, 28 August 1856, NRS ref. SC39/8/33.

35 Indictment Against Peter Fitzpatrick, 'Theft; As also, Breach of Trust and Embezzlement', 2 March 1857, JC26/1857/356.

36 Petition of Robert Lockhart Dymock, Procurator Fiscal, 12 January 1857, NRS ref. AD14/57/313.

37 Criminal officer: detective. Statement of Micheal Reilly, 19 January 1857, NRS ref. AD14/57/313.

38 Statements of Elizabeth Baillie (or Fisher) and Mary Ann Goldie, 19 January 1857, NRS ref. AD14/57/313.

39 Closet: a small room. Statement of Micheal Reilly, 19 January 1857, NRS ref. AD14/57/313.

40 Statement made on 17 January 1857 before John Clark, magistrate, NRS ref. AD14/57/313.

41 Statement of George Henderson, 19 January 1857, NRS ref. AD14/57/313.

42 Schedule in precognition, NRS ref. AD14/57/313.

43 High Court Minute Book, NRS ref. JC26/1857/356.

44 Ibid.

45 W. Bayne Ranken, *Prisons and Prisoners*. London: Longmans, Green and Co., 1874, p. 9.

46 Ibid., p. 10. The author's descriptions of prisons were based on his visits to them in 1857.

47 Ibid., pp. 11-12.

48 *Criminal Lunatic Asylum Registers, 1820-1876, Quarterly Returns of Prisoners in Hulks and Convict Prisons*, March 1859.

49 Ranken, op. cit., pp. 9 and 13.

50 *Criminal Lunatic Asylum Registers, 1820-1876, Quarterly Returns of Prisoners in Hulks and Convict Prisons*, March 1861.

51 *1861 Scotland Census.*

52 *UK and Ireland, Find a Grave Index, 1300s-Current.* He was buried in Drumcondra Churchyard and shares a grave with his father.

53 *UK and Ireland, Find a Grave Index, 1300s-Current.*

54 *North British Daily Mail*, 23 September 1857, p.4.

55 Valuation Rolls VR010000004-/15, Edinburgh, 1855, p. 15 (National Records of Scotland).

56 See the Wales census for 1891 and 1901, 'living on own means'. The Ireland 1911 census has 'income from land'.

57 Keith Fleming, *At the Eleventh Hour and Other Tales*, Nezu Press, 2024, pp. 346-347.

58 The Birmingham and Midland Motor Omnibus Company, known colloquially as 'Midland Red'. The company operated in the Midlands from 1905 to 1981, and during L. G. Wyndham Shire's time the vehicles it used were built entirely to his design and specifications.

59 *Aberystwyth Observer*, 22 October 1887, p. 4, and *Cambrian News and Merionethshire Standard*, 28 October 1887, p. 5.

60 *Carmarthen Journal and South Wales Weekly Advertiser*, 10 May 1889, p. 2.

61 *Aberystwyth Observer*, 11 May 1889, p. 4.

62 *Carmarthen Journal and South Wales Weekly Advertiser*, 24 July 1891, p. 3.

63 *Welshman*, 20 September 1889, p. 4.

64 Morning Post, 15 May 1889, p. 2.

65 Ibid.

66 *Bookseller*, 4 May 1889, p. 17.

67 *The Athenaeum*, 21 December 1889, p. 873.

68 *Punch*, 15 February, 1890, p. 75

69 See p. 203.

70 *Bookseller*, 14 December 1889, p. 1365.

71 *The Scotsman*, 22 June 1891, p. 3.

72 *Carlisle Patriot*, 26 June 1891, p. 6.

73 *1891 Wales Census.*

74 Askew Roberts, *Gossiping Guide to Wales*. London: Simpkin, Marshall. Hamilton, Kent & Co., 1894, p. 30.

75 Ibid.

76 Pumlumon Fawr: the highest point of the Cambrian Mountains in Wales. Re the water source: Royal Commission on the Ancient and Historical Monuments of Wales. Quotation: from Roberts, op. cit., p. 30.

77 The first instalment appears in the *Forfar Herald* on 7 July 1893 (p. 2). Its final appearance appears to have been in the *Southern Press*; the final part was published on 25 May 1895, p. 7.

78 *The Sins of the Fathers* was published in Australia in the *Gippsland Times* from the spring of 1894.

79 See Fleming, *Eleventh Hour* (2024), p. 349. (n 57)

80 Ibid., p. 387.

81 See p. 225.

82 Ibid.

83 See p. 48.

84 See p. 226.

85 Fleming, *Eleventh Hour* (2024), p. 37. (n 57)

86 Lettice Willoughby from 'The Transfiguration of Lettice Willoughby', Kathie Ormsby from 'The Courage of Kathie, Ula Ferguson and Helen Templeton from *At the Eleventh Hour*.

87 *Carmarthen Journal and South Wales Weekly Advertiser*, 24 July 1891, p. 3.

88 See p. 264.

89 Ibid., p. 279.

90 Fleming, *Eleventh Hour* (2024), p. 214. (n 57)

91 Ibid., p. 45.

92 See p. 264.

93 *Aberystwyth Observer*, 2 August 1895, p. 4.

94 *1901 Wales Census.*

95 *Aberystwyth Observer*, 7 January 1904, p. 2.

96 *Ireland, Calendar of Wills and Administrations, 1888-1920.*

97 Ibid., and burial records of Mount Jerome Cemetery, Dublin.

98 See *Aberystwyth Observer*, 7 January 1904, p. 2 and 3 January 1907, p. 2; *Cambrian News and Merionethshire Standard*, 29 December 1905, p. 8 and 30 December 1910, p. 8, etc.

99 Probate was granted in Dublin on 6 February 1904, *Ireland, Calendar of Wills and Administrations, 1858-1920*.

100 *Cardigan Bay Visitor*, 30 July 1904, p. 6, 6 August 1904, p. 3, and 20 August 1904, p. 6.

101 *Bookseller*, 9 May 1905, p. 36, and *Wells Journal*, 9 March 1911, p. 7.

102 *Aberystwyth Observer*, 23 July 1908, p. 2.

103 *1911 Ireland Census*.

104 The address is printed incorrectly in the newspaper as 'Is. Fryn, Lanbadarn Road'.

105 Mrs Jenkins advertised in several newspapers, for example the *Runcorn Examiner*, 17 June 1911, p. 6.

106 Physiognomy: the deciphering of character from head and facial characteristics.

107 See p. 117.

108 *Calendar of Grants of Probate of Wills and Letters of Administration, 1945*.

109 Burial records of Mount Jerome Cemetery, Dublin.

BY THE NIGHT EXPRESS

A PSYCHOLOGICAL ROMANCE, IN TWO PARTS

"Is all we see or seem
But a dream within a dream?"
E. A. POE

BY THE NIGHT EXPRESS

PART I

WHAT a horrible murder it was; and what strange possession it took of me, as I leaned back in that comfortable second-class carriage, *en route* from Paddington to Milford. All the way from London to Gloucester it ran riot in my brain, and would not be exorcised. I could literally think of nothing else, not that I was a very sensitive or imaginative fellow in the ordinary way; quite the reverse, I thought to myself; but the peculiar details of this crime seemed to exercise a sort of hideous fascination for me.

And yet I had plenty of pleasant things to think of if only that newspaper, that lay open on my knee, would let me.

I had just got a whole month's holiday, and was speeding away to spend it with those I loved, and who loved me.

I had been nearly three years in London, and was without kindred, friends, I might almost say without acquaintance there. I suppose I was not what you would call a "popular fellow." I know I was somewhat reserved and silent. My fellow clerks at Messrs. Nelson and Oldcastle, Warehouse Street, City, liked me fairly well, and I think respected me; but they would not have broken their hearts if I had not turned up again; in fact, one or two below me might have been rather glad than otherwise, expecting a step. In truth, in all that big city no one would have missed me if I had disappeared; no one was sorry when I left, no one would be glad when I returned.

I grew misanthropical as I lay back in luxurious idleness, gazing out with absent eyes on the lovely summer landscape spread around me; and I forgot to cheer myself with the remembrance of all the loving, welcoming faces awaiting me on the far wild coast of Clare. The dear mother, so fond and foolishly proud of her only boy; the three winsome sisters; with sundry uncles, aunts, cousins, &c.

No, I thought only of my present loneliness; not a soul to see me off, to wish me God speed; no friendly hand-pressure; no pleasant "I'll be glad to see you back, old man." How easy it would be to sink out of life and none be the wiser; to be done away with and no one now.

I was morbid, that was the long and the short of it. I had not been very well of late, slightly depressed and nervous, and I needed a good dose of Atlantic breezes, of the wild ocean winds that circled my Kilkee home. London fog did not agree with me; I was sick with the pathetic *mal du pays*, and these extra gloomy thoughts all came from that confounded paper.[1]

Hurriedly glancing at it while I hastily swallowed my early breakfast, I saw the heading:

"HORRIBLE MURDER NEAR LONDON,
GHASTLY PARTICULARS,"

and did not read it; but when I had comfortably ensconced myself in my carriage for my nine hours' journey, I pulled the paper from my pocket and read that tale of horror.

How terrible it was. That poor, frail woman, supposed to be a lady, and aged, found murdered—barbarously, brutally—on Hampstead Heath on the previous evening, and not one single clue to her identity. Everything had been removed that could in the faintest way lead to recognition. Of all outer garments there was no trace, save a tiny scrap of rich silk—a light summer silk, of

[1] *Mal du pays*: homesickness.

lovely and peculiar design—which was supposed to be a fragment of the dress; the body was clothed only in the under-linen, which was fine and delicate, and from which there were evidences that name or initials had been cut.

But worst, and most horrible of all, the victim's head was missing. A body may be anyone's, but a head and face tells tales, and so the desecrated remains had been cleanly decapitated.

The motive for the crime was still unknown, everything was shrouded in the most complete mystery; the body had been found between nine and ten the previous evening on a lone part of the heath; the doctors who viewed the remains declared that death had taken place fully twenty-four hours before, and up to the time of going to press nothing further had been discovered.

* * * * * *

Well, thank Heaven I was not going to be alone all the way. I had just taken my seat, after stretching my legs a little, the second bell had rung, and in another minute we should be steaming out of Gloucester, with the longest portion of our journey still before us. I should have come down by the night express that meets the boat, but I thought that the run through the country would be pleasant in the daytime and rouse me up; but when I was well started I began to regret my resolve, which would condemn me to kick my heels for some half dozen hours or so in slowest solitude, in that miserably dull terminus of the Great Western—New Milford, when the door opened, and a young girl (a lovely creature I could see at a glance) sprang in, and was quickly followed by a man, young, and not very unlike myself in general *tout ensemble*, I thought, with idle criticism.[2]

---

[2] *Tout ensemble*: overall effect or appearance.

I took up my *Times* again—the train was beginning to move—perhaps behind the shelter I might take stolen glances at that sweet girl's face in the further corner. How winsome she was, how fresh, how young; was there ever so dazzling a complexion? The stale simile of "milk and roses" could give but a poor, pallid idea of that brilliant vivid skin; and then her eyes, what peculiar eyes they were: light grey, but shaded by jet black lashes, and eyebrows in unison, a piquant, challenging contrast to those masses of burnished red-gold hair. It was the girl's intensity of exquisite colouring that made her so greatly attractive.

How quickly and eagerly she and her companion spoke. Were they lovers? I caught myself wondering with interest. Anything nearer and dearer was surely impossible, the girl was but a child, a mere schoolgirl. No, a big brother or a young uncle, that was more likely, a protecting yet unsentimental relationship, or, perhaps, only a friend. Then a big, sudden longing to be that friend possessed me, followed by an irrational pang of—what was it, jealousy! It felt uncommonly like it, yet it was too absurd to knock under ignominiously to a little stranger girl, seen for half-an-hour in a railway carriage, who had only once looked at me, and then with but a sort of inquiring glance.

* * * * * *

I was to be alone again, I reflected dismally, as, on approaching Cardiff, my fellow travellers bustled about boxes, and bags, and railway rugs, but it was not till the train actually stopped that I came to the delighted knowledge that I was to retain one companion.

There was hurried quick speech between them as the train was slackening, but in so low a tone that I could catch no words; then it stopped, and the young man caught up a small black bag and a large hat box (while a large black bag and a small hat box remained), and sprang out upon the platform.

There is a fair stoppage of five or ten minutes at this roomy station, and he seemed not to wish to leave the girl till obliged. He stood just outside the door, sometimes looking in, sometimes glancing hastily along the platform. The noise and hubbub were so great, porters shouting, engine shrieking, passengers hastening backwards and forwards, that the couple were compelled to raise their voices as they spoke; and I, sitting in my quiet corner, had the full benefit of these scraps of conversation.

"Well, Bob, I can't help saying it is a shame that I should have to travel alone; and I did think we'd have such a nice time together. I can't think what cousin Meg will say, when I arrive by myself."

"Don't worry, Popsy, you ought to be so grateful to have done with school and Miss Latimer for ever, as not to mind anything else; it's a beastly shame I know, but I can't neglect this letter." "Horrid letter" (poutingly). "But indeed Bob" (coaxingly) "you might let me get out and stay with you here" (making a feint to open the carriage door). "I'll promise not to be in your way, and I'd like to see what sort of place Cardiff is." "And what would Cousin Meg think, and she expecting us this evening?" responded the young man impatiently.

"Don't be a silly child, Popsy, you are nothing but a great big baby, and I did think I'd got a sensible little sister." How insanely pleased I was to hear that last reassuring word. Then, as the whistle sounded, and the porter came along slamming the carriage doors:

"I'll be so lonely," murmured the poor child, for indeed she was little else, the grey eyes swimming in tears, glancing with eager questioning at Bob, who in his turn, seemed to my newly-developed imagination, to wear in his eyes, a strained anxious look, which he tried to subdue. Doubtless, I thought, that letter is about some "bothering" business, that he does not wish to tell her of.

"No you won't, Popsy," he cried cheerfully, as if trying to reassure the timid little thing. "You'll be no time getting to Tenby; best love to cousin Meg, Sis; and keep up your heart, pet. We'll have a jolly month down there, in spite of this delay. By Monday at latest, I'll be taking a header off my favourite rock; don't you get drowned in the meantime little girl."

And then there was a tearful "Good-bye dear old Bob, make haste to come," and an "All right Pops, take care of yourself." And we were steaming off west again.

The pretty Popsy sank back into her corner, the soft eyes still suffused with tears, that had not yet brimmed over. Would they now I thought, half-scared. To be alone with a pretty girl in tears, was a wee bit terrifying to my reserved, yet somewhat soft-hearted, impressionable Celtic nature; I knew I should not be able to refrain from offering sympathy, and, perhaps, sympathy not sufficiently cold and formal. But the next moment, stealing a look at the troubled face, my mind was at rest on this score; the tears had retreated without staining the delicate cheek, the eyes had a wistful, almost frightened look, but the suspicious moisture was gone.

What a magnificent opportunity it was for making the acquaintance I had longed for; and what an egregious ass I should be if I did not make the most of it, and immediately too. At the very next station we stopped at, some one might get in, perhaps half-a-dozen, and my chance would be gone. But how was I to do it? The little girl was lonely, and possibly might be glad to talk to anybody. And yet, here was I, great blundering idiot, racking my brain in vain, to know what to say. At last I came out with, about the stupidest *bêtise* I could well execute, but at least it served my purpose;[3] I

---

[3] *Bêtise*: foolish or ill-timed remark.

actually asked that simple artless child (she did not look a day more than sixteen) whether she would care to look at the morning paper! What a start she gave, when I propounded my brilliant question; doubtless she had forgotten my insignificant existence, her face seemed a shade paler too, when she turned towards me.

"No, thank you, I hate newspapers," she answered, with a little *moue*, "Nasty dull things, I can't think how anyone likes them, they are so dry and stupid.[4] I do love reading," she continued, after a moment's pause, "but unfortunately, I did not bring a book, not thinking I'd be alone," and the pretty lips quivered.

"Your friend had to leave you?" I inanely remarked.

"My friend?" inquiringly. "Oh! you mean Bob. He's my brother, you know," with a little nod, "we're just us two; we've a dear old uncle though in New York, and Bob went out there to him five years ago to make his fortune, and he did make it," triumphantly.

I expressed satisfaction, and she went on with sweet, artless simplicity.

"We were poor then, but Bob was so good, he put me at one of the very best schools at Bath, Miss Latimer's you know, where I was to learn everything!" opening her eyes very wide, "and left me nearly all our little income, poor dear boy, knowing he'd succeed. But two years ago another uncle died—he loved mamma before papa married her—and for her sake, though he never saw me, he left me a great big fortune, fancy that!" confidingly: "actually left me, a little girl at school, seven thousand pounds! Isn't it a lot of money? We're rich now. Of course I'd share with Bob, only he has plenty of his own, and now he's come home to take me from school, and bring me back with him."

---

[4] *Moue*: pout or grimace.

"You're going to New York?" I exclaimed, with limp dejection in my tones. "Are you and your brother Americans?"

"Oh, no" she laughed, "we're Scotch, and we've got a very Scotch name I think, 'Campbell;' but I'm going over to keep uncle Dick's house for him; and Bob is—you must promise not to tell anyone, for he does not like it spoken of," looking round as if there could be some one within hearing, while I asseverated eagerly that I would be silent as the grave, "he's going to be married very shortly to a beautiful young American, and I'm just dying to see her."

"We chatted on in this familiar, easy, enchanting fashion, I becoming every moment more enslaved by this lovely, bewitching, guileless girl.

What an innocent, unconventional, fearless child she was; and how happily, and yet at the same time, almost dangerously ignorant of the world and its evil ways. How unsafe to let so artless and credulous a creature travel alone, I could not help thinking, as I sat listening to the pretty voice that discoursed so freely of herself, her brother, their means, position, friends, &c., with no thought apparently that such communications were not exactly suited for a stranger's ear. But she had fallen into good hands, I reflected with natural egotism, and sincere gratitude for the happy chance that had sent me such a delightful *compagnon de voyage*.[5]

At an early stage of our intimacy she had drawn from me a brief account of myself, my occupations, my people, my present destination, &c., and I heard how she was going to Tenby for a month to cousin Meg—cousin Meg, with whom she had always spent her holidays; she delighted in Tenby, and she and Bob had planned such fun there, and now he was detained in that horrid

[5] *Compagnon de voyage*: travelling companion.

Cardiff; but it would be only for a couple of days, and then, when they had had a nice holiday and Bob had made all arrangements about her money, they would be off to New York.

How quickly the time sped now that had so wearily lagged before, and ere I could imagine it, we had come to the junction where passengers change for Tenby. By great good fortune (as I then thought) we had been alone all the way, and our acquaintance had progressed with amazing rapidity. We felt already almost like old friends; and I suddenly made the infatuated determination of going on to Tenby with my little companion, letting my luggage sink or swim, sacrificing my through ticket, and running my chance of catching the night mail to Milford; perhaps even hoping that I might be detained, and obliged to remain till to-morrow, or—delicious suggestion—the day after. I could easily telegraph to my friends, accounting for my not turning up, and—Here I had the grace to blush.

Oh, the folly and supreme idiocy of man! Here was I, a tolerably sensible fellow, as fellows go, racing wildly, with blind, mad infatuation, after a little girl whom half a dozen hours ago I did not know existed; whom, most likely after I had conveyed her to her cousin's house at Tenby, I should never see again; and who very probably by to-morrow morning would have forgotten me completely; and yet for her sake I was ready to delay my home-returning indefinitely, for which I had been almost feverishly anxious when I started that morning.

But I did not say a word of my suddenly formed intention till we were actually standing up, preparing to remove her goods and chattels to the Tenby train. She had relegated the large black bag to me, indeed it was much too large and heavy for those small hands; then as I caught up my own hat-box, hand-bag, travelling-rug, &c., I said in the most off-hand way I could assume,—

"I've made up my mind to go on with you to Tenby and see you safely to your cousin's house, Miss Campbell. I hope you don't object? It's getting late" (we left Cardiff at a quarter-past-three, it was then a few minutes after six); "and I don't like the idea of your being in that other train alone."

At my first words she had started, dropping what she had just caught up and looking at me with scared, troubled eyes.

"Go on with me! lose your Milford ticket! Oh, no; I couldn't let you. I'll be all right, never fear. Stow me and my luggage away if you will, and thank you; but you must not lose your train." She spoke nervously, excitedly; the poor child was perhaps beginning to have qualms that she had transgressed *les convenances* in admitting to such familiarity a complete stranger, for she added, somewhat lamely and hastily: "Besides, I fear if you come to Tenby, cousin Meg cannot receive you.[6] She is laid up with neuralgia, and—and—and does not like strangers."

"I don't want to intrude on cousin Meg," I answered, with immediate ireful antagonism to that unknown lady. "I want to see you to your journey's end, and nothing more; and instead of inconveniencing me, I'll be grateful for the delay. I'll go on by the night express, which will be twice as jolly. Come along, and let's find your train."

"Well, if you insist on being so good," her manner altering suddenly; her late-born restraint vanishing as if she was relieved of some weight upon her mind, for she had seemed to be thinking deeply while I spoke, "I really am grateful to you. I did so dread being alone," she said, stooping to pick up what she had let fall,

[6] *Les convenances*: propriety, conventions, social norms.

and hastening to follow me. I was already on the platform, so completely laden that I could not assist her; that black bag of hers was so large and cumbersome, and I'd my own traps besides.[7]

There was a good deal of haste and confusion on the platform: there were many passengers, apparently for Tenby; and we struggled on, making our way with the rest—not that there was any great haste. The train would not start yet a bit, but the Milford engine was snorting and shrieking in an infernal manner, and making nervous people think that they would be late for everything.

We were more than half way, and saw our train waiting patiently for us, its doors invitingly open, its engine blessedly reposeful, when, with a little cry, my companion found she had forgotten a parcel, the only one she had. It contained a present for cousin Meg, and must not be lost. I was about to dash down my heavy load incontinently, and rush off, but, with a swift gesture she arrested me, throwing at the same time the rug and wraps she had been carrying across my arms, and thereby adding to my burden.

"No," she cried, "you go on, and choose a nice carriage. There's lots of time. I shan't be a minute. I know it all so well; I've been so often."

And then, not waiting to listen to my warning shout that the Milford train would be off directly, she darted back through the hurrying crowd, towards the carriage we had left, and I lost sight of her. Hampered as I was, I stood for a moment watching; then seeing the train was not yet moving, and feeling that I was only blocking the way, I went on, found a comfortable empty carriage, and ascertained the train was not to start for five minutes longer. Then getting rid of my *impedimenta*, found that my dear little charge must have made a

---

7 Traps: personal effects.

mistake.[8] There was a parcel carefully put up, certainly not mine, as I carried no small addenda of the kind—presumably the supposed missing one, foolish child. My arms had been so full of wraps, rugs, bags, &c., that I had been serenely unconscious what I was carrying, only having a hazy idea that it was my property or hers; the only thing I was pleasantly aware of, that would not let me forget its presence, was that confoundedly awkward big black bag. Hastily closing the door of the carriage where I had stowed our belongings, I retraced my steps, expecting to see the slim figure running to meet me, breathless from her wild goose chase. I had not gone ten yards when, with much snorting, panting and general offensiveness, the Milford train shrieked itself out of the junction. I stood still, staring at it; I could not tell why—as if something impelled me to do so. I could see all the occupants of the carriages so plainly as it crawled by; there were not a great many, I noticed three or four carriages were quite empty; one of them I thought I recognised, from its position in the train, as the one we lately occupied, and gazed at it somewhat sentimentally; then, hearing a bell that warned me our own departure was at hand, I turned to seek my fellow-traveller—but, where was she? There were but few people on the platform now, I could see right along it, but no trace of her!

I dashed along the way I had come in frantic haste, a panic of sudden fear taking possession of me. She must have met with some accident—fallen between the carriages. No, thank God! my mind was soon at rest on this point, nothing wrong had occurred. I questioned porters with wild incoherency: one thought he saw a young lady, such as I described, jump into a carriage, but he could not say whether she got out again.

---

[8] *Impedimenta*: heavy baggage that is difficult to carry.

I rushed along half-dazed, not knowing what to think. If she had by any chance been still searching for what she thought she missed when the train began to move, it crept along so slowly that she would have had abundance of time to spring out, while it was yet safe to do so; besides, I should have seen her. Any passenger, seated or standing, in any of the carriages was visible to me, and she would have been at the door in distress. No, the suspicion of her being carried off to Milford was untenable; yet where, in Heaven's name, could she be? By this time I had torn through the whole junction, searching over everything, under everything where by any possibility a cat, not to speak of a human creature, could be concealed (though why concealed it would have puzzled me to tell).

And now a final whistle told me the Tenby train was starting. Then a sudden great relief came to me, it was like an inspiration. What a beastly idiot I had been not to think of it before, and what a fool I had made of myself rushing about like a madman. During those few seconds that I stood so imbecilely and watched the Milford train, the girl passed at my back, of course without seeing me, and had doubtless been as much exercised at my mysterious disappearance as I at hers. All that was left for me now was to run for it, and swing myself hap-hazard into the moving train.

Breathless, perspiring, but hopeful, I found myself, by a lucky chance, alone, and in the very carriage I had chosen; the latter not altogether accident, for even at the last moment, as I raced up, a porter (the man I had questioned, and given a trifle to, to have an eye to the things) rushed before me as he saw me coming, dragged open a door—in I sprang, and was on my way to Tenby. For the first minute, seeing I was with the traps, and yet alone, I felt again staggered. How could she have missed the carriage? Looking into each, as she would be sure to do, she could not fail to recognise her own belongings. Then the next moment I again breathed freely; doubtless she found it at once—got in to wait for me—surprised at my non-arrival, jumped out to reconnoitre (when I was making an ass of myself at the far end of the junction)—and then, suddenly startled by the whistle, sprang into the carriage nearest her, and when we reached our destination we would have a good laugh at the cross purposes we had been playing at.

As we slackened into Tenby Station I hauled my portable property together somehow, and before the train stopped, bundled it and myself out upon the platform, determined to be in time to see all passengers alight, and reassure my poor little girl as to the safety of her goods and their custodian.

But surely my eyes must be deceiving me? No dainty girl, with red-gold hair and sweet grey eyes, got out of one of these eagerly-scanned carriages. There were girls, tall and short, fat and lean; portly fathers, blowsy mothers, nondescript brothers, timid maiden aunts, strong-minded specimens of the single sisterhood, children, old people, dogs, old bachelors, young dudes, even a parrot (that immediately set up a hoarse scream of defiance of the engine, which, when he found he could not silence by superior noise, he fell to abusing in language startlingly profane), but no Popsy Campbell.

Was there ever a fellow in so distressing a dilemma? My Milord ticket sacrificed, my luggage gone journeying on its own account, here I found myself at Tenby—a place perfectly strange to me—where I had no earthly business, with another person's property heaped around me, that person having disappeared mysteriously, and on whose account I was devoured by anxiety. The girl for whom I had conceived so sudden a—tenderness, I might almost call it, had vanished, and I was powerless even to make inquiry about her. I knew her name, certainly, but what meaning would that convey to railway officials? Of her friends I knew nothing, though a few minutes ago I should have declared that I knew everything, she had been so frankly communicative.

Her brother was absorbed in the large town of Cardiff; she mentioned no address that would reach him; besides, his stay was short and uncertain. And cousin Meg in Tenby—that was indeed vague. What was I to do? What misery and fright the poor child must be enduring now; for I had at last come to the conviction that she must have been carried off to Milford. Then hastily consulting a railway guide, I saw that she could not return to-night. There she would be, in that dreary miserable place, bereft of everything. Her heavy luggage would of course be marked "Tenby," and have come here; whilst with me there was her large travelling bag, her hat box, the wretched parcel (that caused this awkward, distressing *contretemps*), her rug, and her wraps, everything, in short, save her small hand-bag, which I noticed she still retained as she ran from my side at the junction.[9] It was to be hoped that that held her money.

Poor little lonely girl! my heart ached for her as I sought an hotel, ordered some dinner (which in truth I stood in need of), and sat down to think what would be the best plan. I soon came to the conclusion, with the help of "Bradshaw," that there was nothing for it but to stay quietly where I was, until it was time to meet the night express (down train) which would reach the junction about one in the morning.[10]

To cross by the boat that night, I almost despaired of; for, after getting to Milford, by the time I hunted up my stray lamb (doubtless, poor child, she would be awaiting me in the station,

---

[9] *Contretemps*: unexpected, unfortunate or embarrassing incident.

[10] Bradshaw: a series of railway timetables.

terrified and shivering), and brought her to the hotel (thank Heaven, there was one decent hotel in the benighted place! that was some consolation) and arranged for her return early next day, the boat would most probably have sailed. If such were the case, I determined to telegraph to my friends that urgent business would detain me from crossing till the following night; and then accompany my little friend back here tomorrow morning. How pleasant that would be after our evening's cruel discomfiture, I thought, while a delightful sense of adventure stole over me, for a moment rendering me forgetful in my selfish musings, of the keen wretchedness, anxiety and discomfort, the girl who had so strangely stolen into my heart must be even now enduring. Of missing her at Milford I had no fear, knowing we could not cross each other on the route, as there was no up train till the 2.55 express, and I should be with her before then. And then I heard the newsboys shouting in the street, and I sent out for an evening paper to help to beguile the time during which I must remain inactive.

It was a poor little local affair, the *Evening News*, seemingly much a *réchauffé* of what my morning's paper had informed me.[11] But on turning the sheet, I saw I wronged it. Under the heading,

"THE HAMPSTEAD HEATH TRAGEDY,"

I saw, "LATEST PARTICULARS, THREE O'CLOCK," and composed myself with a weird sort of fascination, to read what further details had been gathered of that ghastly crime during the morning hours.

And the first words struck me with a curious, incomprehensible thrill.

"IDENTITY OF THE VICTIM DISCOVERED."

---

11 *Réchauffé*: dish warmed up, rehash.

So, the poor desecrated remains were not fated to meet that hideous oblivion of impossible recognition, that those hell-loosed fiends had counted on, when they committed that last most sacrilegious outrage.

The murdered woman was proved to be a Miss Marrable, an old maiden lady of large means, living on the outskirts of London; a bachelor brother, dead some twenty years, who had been a man of mark in the mercantile world, having left her all he possessed.

Some five years after his death, she took her little niece, the orphan daughter of an only, and much-loved sister, to live with her. She became much attached to the child, who was then between seven and eight years old, and about a year after her adoption Miss Marrable made a will, leaving everything she possessed to this girl, in the event of her death.

Aunt and niece had lived in perfect harmony until about a year before the present time; when the girl, then nearly two-and-twenty, conceived a frantic affection for a man in every way unworthy, a ne'er-do-well, a *vaurien*, in short, and adventurer, whom her aunt absolutely refused to receive at her house, and whom she sternly forbade her niece to hold communication with;[12] the girl at first was obstinate, but Miss Marrable was firm; if her niece chose to marry this man, she could not prevent her, seeing she was over age; but not one penny of her money should he ever touch.

On the day of the marriage (should it take place), she would make a will, leaving all her property in charity, as she had no relative but her dear niece Janet. But if that niece persisted in disobeying her—to the girl's own everlasting sorrow—she would forget that she had loved her, and act accordingly.

---

[12] *Vaurien*: good-for-nothing, villain

Then the girl submitted, but she pined; the maid said (it was Miss Marrable's own maid, who was devoted to her mistress, and had been with her nearly forty years, since they were both girls) who made these statements.

It was she who recognised the poor outraged body; that scrap of peculiarly patterned silk, and a very slight but very strange and uncommon deformity of the left foot,—of which the old lady was sensitive in the extreme, keeping it carefully concealed from all, none even dreaming of its existence save the faithful maid who kept the secret inviolably, as if it were her own—had been the means of identification.

About six months ago, the niece begged her aunt to let her go and study art in Rome for a while; a friend of hers had lately married an artist, and gone there to live, and she could stay with them; and Miss Marrable, knowing that she had been obliged to grieve her in the other matter, consented at once, though she knew she would feel terribly lonely. She went, and the house had been dull without her.

"The old lady knew Miss Janet's married friend, and she trusted her and her niece implicitly.

"Miss Janet wrote regularly at first, but not quite so often lately.

"Yes, always from the same address. No, Miss Marrable did not correspond with the other lady. She (the maid) had never seen Miss Janet's lover; did not know what he was like.

"Miss Janet was very pale, rather sickly-looking, with dull brown hair, and very quiet manner; some called her pretty. Miss Marrable's household consisted of three female servants, including herself, a butler and a coachman; the latter had been in her mistress's service for years, and when, some weeks ago, he fell ill and had to be taken to a hospital, the old lady, who was somewhat of an oddity, declared her intention of not supplanting him, but of letting her brougham lie idle till he returned to resume his place;[13] she would let no stranger drive her horses; and, in the meantime, she engaged a hired brougham to take her her daily drives. The driver was a very respectable man.

"On last Tuesday her mistress went out as usual; she had a strange fancy for the Heath, and would drive there every other day, she had had this fancy for years; sometimes she would get out and walk, sometimes not; last Tuesday the man drove her there; she got out and walked about a bit, then she got in and he drove away; but they had not been gone far, when a lady—she had a thick veil on, so he could not say whether she was young or old—signed to him to stop, and then she put her head into the carriage window and he thought he heard an exclamation, but did not take particular notice; and, after talking a few moments, the old lady got out, and told him he might return to town, as she would go back in her friend's cab. He saw no cab; thought it must be somewhere about. He then drove off, the ladies walking in the direction of the Heath.

"He thought the stranger looked quite the lady, but had not taken much notice; could not tell how she was dressed; did not think she was what you would call tall, but was not sure. They were about a quarter-of-an-hour's walk from the Heath; the old lady seemed a bit put out, flurried like."

The maid, on being again questioned, stated that when the driver of the brougham said her mistress had met a lady, and was coming home in her cab, she had not thought it anything strange; her mistress had some friends, whom she sometimes went to see, and on rare occasions spent the evening with. There was one lady,

[13] Brougham: light, four-wheeled carriage that could be drawn by one horse.

who lived on quite the other side of London, with whom she was very intimate; they were old and sincere friends, and when she went to her house, which she did pretty often, she always stayed the night, as it was a long way to come back, but never without letting her know. When the evening drew in, and her mistress did not appear, she got a little uneasy, and went round to the livery stables and questioned the driver; then she sent to the few houses pretty near, where Miss Marrable might have gone, and when the messenger returned it was past midnight. She began to feel anxious, and yet was almost certain that her mistress had gone to Mrs. Wright's, the lady who lived so far away; but she thought it strange that she should do so without sending her word. Did not think of doing anything that night, not imagining there could be anything wrong. When her mistress stayed at Mrs. Wright's she did not usually return till late the following afternoon; she did not wait so long to make inquiry; when twelve o'clock came and no signs, she took a cab and drove over to Mrs. Wright's; when she heard that Miss Marrable was not there, and had not been seen at all the day before by Mrs. Wright, she grew really terrified, and communicated immediately with the police. She thought Miss Marrable might have been coming home in the cab alone, after parting with her friend, when there might have been an accident, and she carried off to hospital, unable to speak, or tell her address, or anything. Did not apprehend a fit or sudden illness; for, though her mistress was sixty years old and fragile-looking, she enjoyed excellent health. Was going to telegraph to Miss Fosbrooke at once, but thought there was no use till she knew something definite. Telegraphed immediately on recognising the body of her murdered mistress; did not expect a response for some hours. Ralph Carew, she heard, was the name of Miss Janet's lover, but was told since that he went sometimes by other names; did not know what they were; believed he was an adventurer. Did not know his present whereabouts; before Miss Fosbrooke went to Rome, she said he had gone to Australia, and that her Aunt would never be troubled by him again. Could not say Miss Janet was very fond of her aunt, she was always mild and gentle to her, but it did not seem as if there was any affection in her nature till she went wild about Mr. Carew. Did not think it possible Miss Fosbrooke could be in London without her (Benson's) knowledge; her mistress told her everything, and it was only a week yesterday since Miss Marrable wrote to her niece; it was about three weeks since they had a letter; Miss Janet said nothing of coming home then; it bore the same address.

This ended Benson's examination before the Coroner. No suspicion whatever rested upon the driver of the brougham. Luckily for him, just as the old lady and her friend turned away, and before he had driven a dozen yards on his road to town, a doctor, who sometimes hired the carriage and knew the man well, overtook him, asked him if he was engaged, and on being answered in the negative, entered the brougham and was driven to his own residence, not very far from Miss Marrable's abode. He, the doctor, knew Miss Marrable well by sight, and recognised her as she stepped from the carriage; the other lady he had not noticed, but had a general impression that she was slight in figure, and thickly veiled; he had been in a great hurry, and naturally was not observant.

* * * * * *

This *in extenso*, was the "Latest News" given by my despised little paper.[14]

---

[14] *In extenso*: at full length.

What an immensity of information had been obtained during those few morning hours. The weird mystery attached to that ghastly headless body had been soon unravelled—the identity of the dead woman soon discovered; conjecture there was at an end. But to the murderers there was still no clue.

Where were the guilty wretches, who had slain in so barbarous a manner that defenceless old woman, presumably for the few valuables she had upon her person?

Apparently there was no other motive for the crime. Nothing but commonplace, vulgar robbery; and yet it was still strangely confused. It was about five, or half-past, when they left Hampstead Heath to drive home, the coachman stated—Miss Marrable dined at seven. Why, then, would the lady friend, whoever she might be, leave the old woman alone upon the Heath, and the day drawing in?

Would she not have remained with her, or brought her away in the cab that was spoken of? And who was the mysterious lady? Why had she not come forward, if she was a friend of the unfortunate Miss Marrable's, and declare what she knew? She was the last person seen with the murdered woman. The two figures walking away together in the direction of the heath were observed by both doctor and driver; after that Miss Marrable was never seen again alive! And yet this nameless friend remained undeclared, silent, when she alone of all the thousands that read the account of that appalling tragedy, and thrilled over it, might be able to throw a little light on the thick darkness that gathered round the story.

Was she a friend? that was the question with which I found myself grappling. Or was she a she-fiend, accomplice of the intending murderers, primed and loaded with some tale of misery and want, some petition for the charity that was doubtless never-failing in that kindly old heart; anything, in short, that might entice or lure the victim to the snarer's net?

I worked myself up at last to a pitch of high nervous excitement over that little paper, till I recovered myself with a laugh at my own enthusiasm. It had done one thing, however, that small sheet; it had beguiled me from dwelling unduly on the somewhat distressing, awkward nature of my own dilemma; and then I reproached myself the next moment.

I had been so interested reading the information gleaned about the murder, that I had almost forgotten for the time the dear little girl who had so fascinated me—pretty piquant Popsy Campbell, with the red-gold hair and carnation cheeks, who was alone and desolate in that distant, dreary station.

Poor child, how wretched it was for her, and what a poor beginning to her anticipated delightful holiday!

Then the distracting thought assailed me with inhuman suddenness, and staggered me for the moment: What if I failed to find her at that Milford Terminus? What should I do in the event of such a catastrophe?

But the next instant I scoffed at my own folly for doubting, for feeling the slightest uncertainty. The ground had not opened and swallowed the girl, that was a certain fact; neither, thank Heaven, had there been an accident. The only reasonable supposition was, that she had been carried off in the wrong train; perhaps she had been kneeling down searching for her supposed missing property, and thus I——

*   *   *   *   *   *

Here, my ideas got hazy—I think they had been getting hazy the last few minutes—and I dropped asleep—uneasy, troubled sleep, from which I started half-an-hour later to hear the waiter telling me that I had but just time to catch the train that would meet the Irish night express.

Up I jumped, but half roused, and struggling against a strange feeling of oppression—a dim, helpless sense of dread, of being haunted by some unspeakable horror had come upon me in that unrefreshing slumber, induced possibly by some unremembered dream.

I hastily got my traps together, and, still drowsy, was just stepping from the door of the hotel, when I recollected that I was forgetting the heaviest article of my luggage, and rushed upstairs again to find, with ominously bulging sides, that *bête noir* of my *impedimenta*—Miss Campbell's very full-grown travelling-bag—hiding malevolently behind the door.[15]

I snatched it up and tore down again; was into a fly, out of it, and into the dimly-lit train, which started almost immediately, before I well drew breath. But the hurry had the effect of more or less numbing that unfamiliar sense of nameless apprehension that had been heavy on me during those first few moments of waking.

[15] *Bête noir*: bugbear, bane of one's existence, anathema.

BY THE NIGHT EXPRESS

PART II

AT the junction all was haste, darkness, and confusion; the night mail was late, and when it did tear into the gloomy station—its great red eyes glowing fiercely in the dusky night—I, and the half-dozen silent, sleepy, passengers awaiting its arrival, transferred ourselves and our *etceteras* to it with remarkable celerity.

Seeing the guard standing near me, as I was stowing away my numerous traps, I suddenly thought of telling him in a few hasty words of my misadventure, mentioning how I came by my rather unusual number of packages, and asking, if by any untoward chance I should fail to meet their owner, what would be the best course to pursue. Should I leave them in charge of the Milford Station-master? at the same time placing my hand on the articles not mine. But just as he was about to answer me he had to fly, and in another moment we were again rushing through the midnight obscurity. Although it was August the darkness was profound; thick, low-lying, oppressive, and so still; we were near either a heavy rainfall or a thunderstorm, and I began to feel rather glad that I should not be crossing that night. I felt sure we should have dirty weather before morning, and mentally wrote the message I would flash to my eagerly expectant mother, as soon as I found poor Popsy, and made arrangements for her well-being for the night. "Unavoidably detained: hope to cross to-morrow night: luggage gone, booked through."

There were two quiet elderly ladies in the carriage with me, talking in subdued tones, and glancing at them I suddenly fell to thinking again of that dreadful murder. She was just like one of those, only older and frailer, as little anticipating so hideous a fate. Then like a sudden blow the question struck me, as if it were written in letters of fire on my brain,

"Had the head been found?"

I could not remember what the paper had said, my thoughts grew queerly confused and cloudy, yet with a passionate desire to disentangle this one question, that in an instant had raised my blood to fever-heat, yet at the same time paralyzed my mental energies. What was the matter with me? I asked myself, with a sudden beating heart, as I gazed with blank unseeing eyes at that looming black bag on the seat opposite me. It seemed, even to myself at that startled moment, as if I was under some unaccountable strange influence.

* * * * * *

Before I had shaken myself free of the spell that bound me mentally with such sudden mystic withes, before I could get rid of the eerie mysterious sense of an invisible presence, weird and chilling, we had reached our destination, and my fancies—born, as I thought, of fatigue and worry—vanished before the very accentuated practicalities of the terminus of the Great Western. For the fourth time that day I collected the mutual belongings of myself and Miss Campbell, and seeing a disengaged porter, I flung him everything, save that large black bag, which I looked upon as the article to be chiefly guarded, as judging by its size it ought to be precious, and then, armed with it, I joined the hurrying, weary passengers who were making their way through the dim dreary station, and long ghostly covered passage, to the waiting boat.

But I was not boat bound, as I soon explained to my porter, who was wonderfully affable as porters go in these levelling days, not treating my remarks with haughty contemptuous disregard. I told him in a few words the fix I was in, much as I had told the guard, and how positive I was that the lady who owned the property we carried must be here waiting for me, though to say the truth I already felt a serious qualm as to my certainty of finding her. I had felt so sure that the first thing I should see on springing to the platform would be her pretty frightened face, that its non-appearance staggered me at once.

He made answer, that he had not noticed any lady, such as I described, lingering about the station, if she had been there, he would have been sure to see her; she must have gone straight away to the hotel, he suggested: it was a good many hours since she came, if she *did* come, he interpolated dubiously, and she would never wait all that long time, in a draughty, dismal station; as I inanely darted into a large, bleak, general waiting-room, which was glaringly empty and deserted.

Seeing my limp and helpless aspect, for I really did feel knocked on the head, as if I had been the victim of a monstrously clever conjuring trick, I questioned had I seen and spoken to the girl at all? Was there such a person as Popsy Campbell, and had she travelled with me? Or was she but a figment of the brain, a sensation like him who moralises in Hypatia, on the immaterial nature of all things, even himself?[16]

"I am not I, but I am sensations," he says; "when I see soldiers, that is a sensation," he continues. Perhaps a pretty girl is also a sensation, and a deuced pleasant one I thought, in a sort of dazed bewilderment, until I remembered the very tangible proof of her fair presence, at present dragging out of my right arm; that was a sensation, and no mistake, and a pretty heavy one.

"Perhaps she left a message with one of the other porters,

---

[16] A reference to *Hypatia: Or, New Foes with an Old Face* by Charles Kingsley.

or the station-master, shall I inquire, sir?" with civil alacrity.

"Wait a moment!" I cried, dashing forward quickly, revived by the words "Ladies waiting-room," which that moment caught my eye; "she may be here."

*　　*　　*　　*　　*　　*

"Not quite so fast, sir, if you please; the game is up, the vermin's run to earth, boys; see, will he show the white feather?"

This extraordinary address was accompanied by a heavy hand on my shoulder, and I turned with startled swiftness to find a detective (I guessed his calling even in that scared moment), flanked by two policemen, hemming me in, cutting off my retreat, if I tried to make one, along that wide and friendly platform; shutting me out, by force of that simple but effectual barrier, from those prosaic figures, clad in that fatal blue uniform, those retreating, kindly men and women, from whom I suddenly felt horribly separated, as if a black bottomless gulf yawned between us. Before I could speak, for that strange, nameless feeling of apprehension and dread, had again fallen upon me, the same rasping voice continued:

"Charlie Vaughan, alias Tom Burton, alias a nicer name still, you're my prisoner! It's been a neat job, hasn't it boys? and no one need never say that Bill Symonds hasn't luck."

"Great God! what do you mean?" I at last managed to cry hoarsely. "Who is Charlie Vaughan and Tom Burton? I know nothing of them; and by what right do you thus detain a free man?"

"He's a-comin' the innercent, know-nothing dodge; oh! it won't do this time, Master Charlie, you've slipped from us afore, you're as slippery as an eel, I'm thinkin', but we've got you hard and fast this time, and we don't mean to let you go, do we boys? We've a dead man's grip of you now, as the sayin' is; though, perhaps," with a grim smile, "it would be fitter to say a dead woman's! Back to

Lunnon with me you go by the up-night express, and if you're not in Newgate by this time to-morrow, it will be a queer thing."

"In the name of Almighty God, man! will you explain yourself? It's a horrible mystery, some devilish frightful mistake, and one you'll be sorry for by-and-by. Whom do you take me for? and of what do you accuse me? There's my card, read it, and after that take me into custody if you dare!" Flinging the pasteboard on the platform, which was picked up by one of the policemen, who read aloud my betrayingly national cognomen—

"Maurice A. Donovan."

"Oh! is that the latest? Well, I can't say it's as pretty as some of the others; but you're tryin' new ground when you go in for the Irish, eh, Captain? I believe it was captain you were last, Captain Carew sounded stunnin' well."

"But I am an Irishman," I cried in vehement protestation. "My name is Donovan, and I hold a position of trust in Messrs. Nelson and Oldcastle's, City."

"Whew!" exclaimed the same speaker, unbelievingly. "That's coming it a little too strong, you have not told that tale afore; Messrs. Nelson and Oldcastle to have anythin' to do with the like of you! Now look here, my fine fellow I've a warrant for your arrest, an' let you call yourself 'Donovan,' or 'Vaughan,' or 'Burton,' or the rest of them, back to Lunnon you must come; if you come quietly and make no disturbance, I'll treat you fair; but if you make a fuss, we've the 'bracelets' here, all ready an' comfortable, an'——"

"At least, I suppose I may inquire on what charge—what infamously false charge—you have the audacity to arrest me?" I asked, trying to assume the dignity of despair.

"False? not a bit of it, Charlie; though I didn't think you were quite up to such a black night's work as that; you've done a good many things, in your day, not quite the thing; but I did think you'd stop short of the noose!"

I did not take in this horrible suggestion, and went on, unheeding the low brooding murmur that began to make itself heard from the small crowd around me.

"It must be some hideous mistake, and it will soon be proved. Telegraph to my friends in Ireland, telegraph to my place of business. I've just got my vacation, and am going home to Clare to spend it. I never even heard of the man, or men, you mention. It's infringing on the liberty of the subject to dare to lay a detaining hand on me, a man who has done no wrong."

Here a murmur of approbation swelled from the throats of the easily-swayed listening few.

"Ah! we've only your own word for that, and you've got to prove it, my man. If you're not the fellow we're after, well, 'twill be all the better for you, an' I'll congratulate you. But I think I'd know you, Charlie, even though you've lost them pretty whiskers; besides, we've the description here of the man that's wantin', and I think no one'll say it doesn't tally. Listen, mates," pulling a dirty piece of paper, printed in large type, from his breast pocket, and looking round on the small audience. " 'Above the middle height, broad-shouldered, dark blue eyes, large nose, long brown moustache, clad in dark grey suit with drab overcoat, brown bowler hat, carrying a peculiarly large black traveling bag with brown handles, a small black bag, hat-box, railway rug, &c. Ticket taken through from Paddington to Milford.' I think you'll say that's correct, gentlemen. I never speaks till I'm certain, and there's no manner of doubt that this man, whether he's innocent or guilty, answers to the description of the man I've got to find."

Here a murmur of approval of the other side was heard,

while I remained in a sort of dismayed stupor at the accuracy of the portrait.

"But," and I suddenly again took courage, "But this bag is not mine," I cried, with feverish energy. "It belongs to the young lady that you know I was looking for," looking across at the friendly porter entreatingly.

"Ah! we're coming to the young lady now; that's pleasant," rasped the detective, rubbing his hands cheerfully. "I don't want you to incriminate yourself, but it adds powerful to the case, it does, to hear you mention the lady so glib an' easy like."

"But the lady's no friend of mine. I never saw her till to-day. I know nothing of her," I made haste to add, unmindful in the misery of my position of the intense interest I had felt in the brilliant Popsy.

"Oh, tell that to the marines," scoffed Symonds; and then again I besought him to telegraph to those who could vouch for who I was. But no, he had no instructions to that effect. His orders were to bring me and my traps back to London. He had a warrant for my arrest and a lady's, answering exactly to the description of Popsy Campbell. Good God! I thought, parenthetically. Who was that girl, who seemed a charming simple child, and yet association with whom, for those few short fatal hours, had brought me such destruction? The lady apparently had flown, all the greater reason that he should not lose sight of me for a moment.

"I've a warrant to search that there bag too," he said. "And we can do it at our leisure, as we get back to town. Have an eye on him, mates, whilst I secure a cosy carriage, and a glass of somethin' hot. This sort of travelling's weary work, gentlemen, and takes the grit out of a fellow," turning away with the station-master; whilst two or three clerks, half-a-dozen porters, &c., remained gazing at me in a delicious excitement.

Then the two policemen drew in closer and I was left standing between them, with a horribly confused sense of unreality and vagueness, struggling with my anguish of despair. One of them, an elderly man with a kindly face, said when his chief's back was turned,—

"Cheer up, Guv'nor, don't be downhearted; if you're not the cove as done it, which I do hope, for you looks like an innercent man, tho' things look mighty black again you, I must say you'll have the laugh at us all by-and-by."

"For God's sake," I implored, turning to him with wildly pleading eyes, "you look a humane man, will you take pity on a wretch goaded to madness, and tell me what I am accused of? Before Heaven I swear I am innocent of any act that could bring me within the power of the law; but, at least, tell me what it is foul-mouthed, lying dastards lay at my door."

"Well, Guv'nor, the long and the short of it is, it's murder! There's a lot of things went afore that's down to Charlie Vaughan's account, if you're him you know. But it's murder this time; you're in for the 'Amstead 'Eath affair. God bless me, the man's faintin'; lend a hand, comrade." For I staggered back against the wall, feeling more like dying than fainting; but no blessed unconsciousness came to me, and in a moment or two I could speak again.

"Murder," I gasped—"I, accused of murder? Christ the sinless, yet accursed, help me to endure! Arraigned for murder; may the Almighty God help and pity my miserable old mother!" I moaned scarce above my breath; but my words were heard by that man who seemed to have a heart somewhere under that blur uniform.

"Doan't ye, now doan't," he murmured soothingly. "It'll be all right this time to-morrow; appearances are again you, but ye can easy prove you're not Ralph Carew, him that's also Charlie Vaughan and Tom Burton, an' if not him, why I don't see how they can mix you up with the murder. You see, it looks bad, you're having that 'ere bag an' not able to account satisfactorily for it; an' we think that there same bag will tell a lot of tales. Mr. Symonds is a hard man I know; but when all's said and done, he's only doin' his duty, an' one cannot blame a man much for bein' glad when he's successful, even when that success means the gallows for another; it's the way of the world an' human natur', each one trying to do the best for hisself, tryin' to get promotion by steppin' on them that are thrown down."

And now the station seemed suddenly to grow full of life and bustle again; persons from the boat just in came thronging to the train, persons who had left Waterford at five the evening before, and now touched English, or rather Welsh soil, with glad appreciative feet, though their time had been, indeed, halcyon, compared with that which lay before the unhappy folk just embarked. In these last few minutes the wind had risen suddenly and fiercely, the storm that had been threatening broke. The rain already fell in torrents, and there were occasional flashes of vivid blue lightning.

I was so dazed with horror that I hardly took in anything, except a general impression that even the elements were siding against me, and in angry wrath were proclaiming the guilt that was not mine, but which a diabolical fate had fitted me with, and to which, by-and-by, I must own, for my head was getting a little queer, to a horrified and recoiling world.

A minute later, I found myself in a smoking carriage, a policeman on each side of me, and Mr. Symonds on the seat opposite, puffing away at a short pipe, and eyeing with eager scrutiny that fatal black bag, whose fastenings he had just examined, and which, he was only waiting to open, 'till we started.

And now we were off with a shriek and a roar, rushing again into the night; and the wind wailed and moaned eerily, like a soul in pain, and the rain lashed the panes furiously, while the blue lightning lit up every and anon the inky sky, making the darkness seem more dense, when the angry thunder raised its mighty voice in giant wrath, now muttering hoarsely, now bursting in a sudden, terrific, crackling peal, right overhead. And now, just after Mr. Symonds had demanded the key of that accursed bag, and I had been insultingly searched for it, after wildly declaring with the desperation of despair, that I knew nothing of the bag or its contents, and had never seen the key, when he prepared with a muttered curse, to cut it open—suddenly, like a flash of that lightning, that lit up the murky void beyond those flying windows, I saw it all. The reason for my arrest, the strange incomprehensible accuracy of my description, the mystery that seemed so unaccountable a moment ago, was explained. But for the hopeless confusion of my senses from the appalling shock I had sustained, I should have seen it at once, and now the glare of light suddenly let in was so blinding, that I shrank back in dazed, helpless pain.

I was caught in a mesh, a cruel insinuating mesh, that had seemed such a fair and simple ribbon, and now was binding me with deadly, pitiless iron bands! Yes, I saw it all. That strange chance resemblance, that had even struck myself when at the Gloucester station, my lonely carriage had been invaded by, as I then thought, poor credulous idiot, so pleasant, gracious a presence.

That man! who was he? That man, who in general characteristics was so wonderfully like myself. That man, who got out at Cardiff station; and left his partner in guilt (Oh! to have to think thus of that lovely, seemingly innocent, trusting child) to work my deadly ruin while he escaped. Who was he?

Must not he be the Charlie Vaughan, the Tom Burton, the—Ah! yes, I remember now, the "Ralph Carew," that was the name the paper gave as that of the murdered lady's niece's *vaurien* lover. Suspicion had doubtless fallen upon him, perhaps only too justly, I thought with a cold shiver, and he was fleeing from justice, disguised possibly,—fleeing with whom?—The niece! Great God, was it possible? I could scarcely prevent myself from crying aloud, as the whole horror suggested itself to me. I had been in that carriage alone with the murderers! No; God forgive me. I would not harbour so terrific a thought; that girl at least was innocent; how could she be Janet Fosbrooke? that blooming brilliant creature; and why should that unknown Janet Fosbrooke, be inculpated in that fearful tragedy? And yet, she must have entered into the plot to betray me. I saw it all now; they did not join the train at Gloucester, as I had believed, but had seen me as I walked about the platform, stretching my legs; that fatal similarity of dress and general essentials, had struck the observant watchful eyes, and they had conceived on the spur of the moment the devilish plan they had carried out so successfully "to the bitter end." They had quickly transferred themselves to my carriage, which was otherwise empty; the man got out at Cardiff, a large populous town, and above all a seaport, whence he could ship to any part of the world; the girl coming on farther to an imaginary destination, was if possible, to enter into conversation with me, and compel an interest on my part, which they calculated would not be very improbable in the circumstances. Then in some way or other, she was to manage to deceive and elude me, disappearing, and leaving in my possession those accursed articles, that property which would be damning evidence against an innocent man; for though I could prove with ease, that I was not Charlie Vaughan or Ralph Carew, yet how in the name of God could I prove how I obtained possession of those things; or, that I was not implicated, at least in some remote way with that awful crime? And my heart stood still, and the cold sweat of inexpressible anguish started in great beads on my brow, as I realised the full horror of my position.

These thoughts had rushed through my dazed brain in the few moments that Mr. Symonds was deliberately preparing to cut open the bag. And now again, as the leather gaped and crackled as he cut, that vivid lightning-like flash of instinctive, appalling fore-knowledge pierced me, shrivelling up heart and brain; both lay scorched and quivering beneath that fiery breath of awed and terrified certainty of what that bag contained.

I leant forward breathless, fascinated, yet hideously repulsed. I know not what strange, contradictory, wild feelings surged in my breast as I sat there with aghast eyes riveted on that black bag, and felt for the second time that night that I was under an influence weird, unearthly, mysterious, that had revealed to me already a hidden horror, and would, before the night was gone, reveal more, if I, who was clogged by these bonds of flesh, could comprehend the silent language of the world of shadows.

And now, with an ominous rustling, Mr. Symonds drew from the bag's foul open mouth a woman's dress—a dress of light lustrous silk, a silk with a strange fantastic device running through it, that had been crushed and crumpled and shoved in anyhow, evidently without care for its preservation but only a desire to cram it out of sight, a rich gleaming silk, which was followed by many other articles of feminine clothing, but ah, how differently from the way women pack the things they love and prize. These were thrust in any way, and what meant those odd dark stains, that even here in the dimly-lit carriage flamed dully, sullenly red? Then out of the depths of that devilish interior those rough unsympathetic hands, the owner of which was chuckling with something of a fiendish satisfaction, exhumed a bonnet, torn, battered, bent, a bonnet of rich and handsome materials, but a bonnet that had never framed a young face, it was an old woman's bonnet unmistakably, even to an ignorant masculine eye. And yet this had been the luggage of that girl, who scarcely seemed more than a child, lovely in her youth and innocence; that girl who had fascinated me as woman never did before, and who must have been the possessor of so diabolical and guilty a secret; who looked in my eyes with confiding, trusting simplicity as she told her artless tale invented on the spot, and compassed my ruin, the eternal tainting of my name and reputation, if nothing more, without a qualm. What a heart, what a nerve, what a nature! a weak woman, young and experienced, and yet able—Oh! my God! And then I was conscious of a strange unnatural excitement, almost bordering on exaltation, a sort of frenzied tension, as I gazed at that bag and its disgorged contents with a weird unholy fascination.

That poor maimed bonnet had been laid aside, and other small things had been added to that swelling pile and now these horny hands, trembling with eagerness and fearful expectation, plunged again into that dark interior and drew from one end, that still bulged menacingly, a large shapeless black bundle, which he began to unroll slowly, speaking in lowered tones, awed but exultant. But I heard no words, I was conscious of nothing save an extraordinary instinct that told me what these wrapping folds enclosed. A nameless horror, coupled with an unreal visionary feeling as if my body were chained while my spirit was set free, grew upon me as fold after fold fell away from that shrouded *something*.

That black envelope soon proved to be a woman's cloak, rich

and massive, but disfigured by these same damning stains, large and frequent. And now the last fold falls, and Oh! Great and Merciful God! what I expected—what I knew these aghast eyes were to behold, is at last revealed. A human head! a woman's head is held between the shrinking hands of the detective, and there are excited, loud, vehement exclamations in that flying carriage, but my lips emit no sound. I hear nothing, know nothing, think nothing, feel nothing; my whole being seems to be concentrated in the one act of gazing.

Yes, a woman's head!—an old woman's, judging by the tangled locks of scant grey hair that fall down into piteous vacancy; but the face is mutilated past recognition by those who loved her best.

This was what I had cared for and guarded so faithfully!

And we rushed on through the night, and the rain grew fiercer, and the wild winds wilder, and I sat glaring at that ghastly vision, and, as I gazed, oblivious of all around me, the railway carriage and all my surroundings seemed suddenly to fade away; I was no longer seated, journeying through the hours of darkness, but was alone under the summer stars, on a wide expanse of quiet heath; the storm had ceased, a gentle breeze fanned my face, a faint and ghostly moonlight struggled with the very last departing rays of lingering twilight. I lifted my face to the serene heavens, with a sort of tranquil joy; and then there was borne in upon me the knowledge that I was there, waiting! expecting!—what?

An icy chill crept along that desolate plain, and curdled the blood around my heart, and as I tried to move and shake off the spell that held me fast, voices broke upon my ear, muffled, indistinct; as of the echo of words spoken across a gulf of time or distance, and I raised my eyes to see three figures, somewhat vague and shadowy at first, but gradually assuming form, standing not far from me, but apparently quite unconscious of my presence.

Two—a man and a woman—were close together, but I could not see their faces; the third, also a woman, young, and ghastly pale in the moonlight, stood a little apart, silent, observant, watchful. The light grew stronger as I gazed; yet, somehow, it was not light from the dim heavens, as a cloud now obscured the moon, whose rays, had been but pale and faint; it was as if some mystic light evolved from these three shadowy figures on the heath, so as to reveal them to me, a dumb unseen witness.

And then I saw the faces; saw them as through a haze, but still saw them. The man, tall, broad-shouldered, a fair, cruel face, with large nose, full, light eyes, and long fair whiskers, with a small, peculiar scar upon the shaven upper lip.

The girl, who stood apart, pale now to ghastliness, but naturally sallow, no colouring whatever in the face; hair dull brown. I noticed all this with a strange, keen interest that I could not understand; and then I turned to look at the other woman, whom I now saw was old and frail, but between me and her, as it were a veil fell, and the face was lost in gloom.

And then the man made a swift, fierce movement, and there was a sudden, smothered terrified shriek, a low gurgling sound, and all was still! The old woman lay on the grass motionless, while the other two stood looking down upon her, apparently talking eagerly, but no sound reached me; and I gazed in mute horror chained to the spot as by an invisible force, speechless, stirless, and unseen by these two, now kneeling busy over that silent form; a faint echo of a whisper seemed to waft towards me—"To gain time, time to get away"—and a mist gathered before my appalled eyes, so that I could not rightly see what they were doing, but they worked quickly and noiselessly; the woman seemed to be bundling up clothes and stuffing them into a large bag that stood near, while the man was cutting something, cutting with difficulty, hacking rather than cutting, and I heard the rasp of the knife as against bone; then he sprang to his feet, flinging away the knife, while he caught up what he had cut, rolled it in something, and thrust it into that gaping bag. Then there was a hurried, frantic search through the short, heathy grass. What did they seek? Was it that knife which had fallen almost at my feet?

There I saw it lying, though there seemed to be no light to reveal anything; yet, down amongst that close grass, I saw it as clearly as if I held it in my hand under the noon-day sun: a large clasp knife of rather peculiar shape and design, with a chased silver plate, on which I read, by the same mystic light, the name, "C. Vaughan."

Back and back they came in their frenzied hunt to within a foot of it, but each time escaped to find it. At last, wearied, and fearful of staying longer in the neighbourhood of that awful silent witness of their midnight guilt, they caught up that terrible bag and vanished. I strained my eyes to see them go, but they suddenly seemed absorbed in a cloudy haze and were gone. Then I dropped on my knees to secure the knife, that clue to the crime I had so strangely witnessed; but as I knelt—before I could grasp it—a feeling of death-like swooning came over me, and I became insensible.

* * * * * *

When I opened my eyes I was still in the railway carriage, and the train was slackening for some station. I rubbed my eyes to try and clear my confused senses, while feelings of equal amazement and horror strove for the mastery. I was in the carriage—alone! no trace of either detective or policeman. We ought to be half-way to London by this, yet the night was still profoundly dark. The storm still raged, but there was not the faintest sign of dawn. We did not leave Milford till past three; surely there ought to be light now? How strange the carriage seemed! What had become of that fearful thing that my aghast eyes had last looked on, before I fell into that strange visionary state? Where was that horrible pile of clothing that rose beside it? And where, above all, was that black bag, the cause of my destruction? And, great Heavens! surely we were going the wrong way?

Here the train slowly steamed into a station. What station? By my immortal soul, it was the terminus of New Milford we now entered! the terminus we had left but a couple of hours before, the place grown so familiar during the last three years, so hideously familiar during the past hours.

Mystery of mysteries! "What was the meaning of it?" I asked myself, dazedly, as I looked at my watch and saw it pointed to the hour at which the Irish night express arrives at its destination. I gazed again at the seat opposite me. There was my bag, my hat-box, my overcoat, my rug, but nothing else. Where was the property I had charge of, and which was not mine? Where was that awful bag and its terrible contents? Where, above all, were those officers of the law who had charged me with that heinous crime? Then a thought burst upon me like a shock, yet that brought a feeling of gigantic relief. Was it within the bounds of possibility that I had fallen asleep and dreamed the whole thing? That that terrible ordeal I had been through had been all a vision of the brain? But no, surely not. I could not believe it. I did not at all feel like one who had been asleep. Besides, it was too realistic, too consecutive. And yet—I could swear that this was the carriage I got into at the junction, the carriage in which were two elderly ladies, not an hour ago by my watch. Oh, no; it could not be. Why I had lived through a lifetime of horror since; and where was that black bag? It had been large and looming then on the seat opposite me. Granted even I did fall asleep, and dreamed all those ghastly horrors (thank God for His infinite mercy if it was a vision, and that I was not a suspected murderer!) where had it and those other things not mine vanished to? I reflected wildly. Had I met that girl towards whom I now felt so extraordinary a repulsion? Had I got out at the junction? Had I missed her, and gone on to Tenby with her luggage? Which was real, and which were phantasmagoria?

I fumbled bewilderedly at my pocket, from which I drew my Tenby Hotel bill, and the little evening paper.

Ha! there was proof irrefragable; besides, should I not have been here hours ago had I not been delayed?

The old ladies must have left the carriage at an intermediate station, a station whose existence I had forgotten; but where had those things been spirited to?

Then I grew to think I must have been under some strange inexplicable spell, some influence. I remembered how I felt in the carriage, after I first got in; the weird unaccountable impression of an Invisible Presence! a mysterious influence, before I fell into that visionary state; for that it was no ordinary dream—startlingly vivid and horrible, but still only a dream—I felt convinced. The earlier part, about my own hideous imaginary sufferings, might rank as such; but the latter—was a revelation! and I grew sick and giddy as the mists cleared away that had somewhat dulled remembrance, when I first recovered consciousness, and I recollected all here written with the intense tenacity and clearness of lately acted terrible facts.

Perhaps this was not the same day I left London; perhaps I

had been in that rapt unreal state for a night and a day; perhaps I was brought by that invisible force back through the night's darkness, and had really stood on that desolate plain, and saw!—Great Heavens, what had happened to me? and what could I do now?

The thought of crossing to Ireland then was not to be entertained in my present half-benumbed state; I felt that all I wanted was to rest, and try to think it all out. I stood on the platform, looking at the hurrying figures (so like it all was to the scene I had spirit witnessed once already that night) feeling like a man in a dream, my senses clogged, confused, sometimes not able to disentangle the unreal from the actual. As I thus gazed helplessly about me, the guard came hastening up.

"Well, sir, it's all right about the lady; she got her things safe and sound, and right glad the poor little thing seemed to see them again. I did my best to wake you but could not."

"The lady," I repeated mechanically, my heart instantly beating violently, every nerve in my body tingling, while a feeling of loathing and repulsion, permeated my whole being.

"Yes, sir, and a very young lady she be, to be travelling all alone; she didn't come on here, as you thought, but stopped at the intermediate station. She got such a fright she said, when she found the train a-moving, and she having to go on whether she would or not, silly little lass; she might have cried out, and they'd have let her down, but she thought she'd get out at the first stop, and then be able to go right back, and there she's been ever since a-waiting for you, sir. She said as how she felt sure you'd bring her things, and she begged me not to wake you when she saw you so sound asleep, but to tell you when we got here, that she was much obliged to you for keeping them all so safe, and that she was all right, and would not forget your kindness for many a long day, and then she hauled out what she said belonged to her, and I knew it was all right from what you said, and I shook you again, but it was no good, you only muttered something cross and fierce like, as if you were having a bad dream; begging you pardon, sir, but you're one of the 'Seven Sleepers,' and your eyes were a bit open and glazy like, and it gave you an eerie look; and indeed you're not looking over and above well now sir; you seem scarce up to crossing to-night," concluded the man kindly, and then he turned away, while I remained half-stupefied.[17]

So the whole thing was but a hideous figment of the brain after all? Could it be? Could the girl be really Popsy Campbell? and that she did run back to get something she thought she missed, and had been carried off against her will?

What was the whole horrible mystery in which I took so strange a part? Would it ever be solved? I thought as I tried to shake myself free of the weight of oppression that still clung round me. And I may say here, that it has not been solved yet. The mystery of that midnight revelation still awaits explanation, or rather—I ought to say—that I still watch and wait, though years now have passed, to avenge her, whose spirit hovered round me in that "night express;" a spirit whose presence, whose mystic influence, broke down the barriers that the flesh opposes to the unfettered soul.

I know I am incoherent, vague, unsatisfactory, in my attempt to tell, or rather to explain, this extraordinary experience in my life. The memory of that imaginary journey by the "Irish night express," the unreal and the actual journey having place together,

[17] Seven Sleepers: known as the Seven Sleepers of Ephesus, the heroes of a legend popular in both Christianity and Islam, who, in order to avoid persecution for their faith, fell into a miraculous sleep and didn't wake until many years later.

is indelibly imprinted on my mind; but as a tale it is unfinished, incomplete, because it is not ended yet. I am still watching, waiting; the revelation that was made to me that night, I verily believe, was not made for naught.

* * * * * *

I remained in Milford that night, and the succeeding two or three days, in a state of feverish unrest and uncertainty, as to how I ought to act.

Should I communicate with the police, and tell what I felt I knew? Ay! and be laughed at for a visionary enthusiast, if not supposed to be inculpated in the murder itself, from my suspicious knowledge. And yet, I felt that that one small evidence, which might be dawning proof in the days to come, that peculiar knife with the name so clear, and the blood-stained blade, lay unsuspected amongst the heather where my spiritual feet had trod; and where it had defied the search of those who threw it there, and those who sought a clue to the identity of the murderers.

At last, unable to refrain from testing the truthfulness of that vision, I sent an anonymous notice to the police, directing them to search in a particular spot, that spot burned in upon my brain, and lo! the weapon of my trance was brought to light; but, unlike my dream, "C. Vaughan" told nothing to the police; they connected it not with Ralph Carew, and of Ralph Carew there was no trace; not that any one wanted, or suspected by them, bore his name to their knowledge. To me alone was the revelation made; possibly, because I had sat with the murderer, and consorted even for an hour or two with his accomplice, for of this fact to this day I feel convinced; in my mind it was clear as daylight, when I read in the papers that on the very evening after that fatal night, an accident had happened to the tidal train to Folkestone, a coupling chain broke, one carriage went off the rails, and was smashed, two persons were seriously injured, and a third was killed—a girl answering in every particular to her of the red-gold hair and carnation cheeks, who had been my travelling companion on the day before, for whom I had conceived such a frantic admiration, followed by as fervent a repulsion.

But on further inquiry it was discovered that the deceased was strangely metamorphosed. Those brilliant fuzzy locks covered dull smooth brown hair. The snow and vermillion colouring was laid upon a pale sallow skin, and the eyebrows and eyelashes, naturally fair, had been stained black. Muddy hair, sickly cheeks, colourless face; how well I remembered it, and knew what had to come next. The dead girl was identified as Miss Janet Fosbrooke, niece of the lady murdered a few days previous on Hampstead Heath.

Her luggage chiefly consisted of a large black travelling bag, that bag that had already played so fearful a part in that tragic night's work. Had I not seen it gaping blackly on that dreary plain, must it not have been propinquity with it, actual contact,—that even for one short hour had held the mind, the thinking part of her who was slain, the mind that for all we know, in our dark and groping ignorance, was not then yet dead, though the body was but dust,—that induced in me, a stranger, that ghastly vision of an act, already engulfed in the limitless maw of the past? That bag contained, on examination, only the usual articles of a lady's wardrobe, and gave no clue as to her motive for being secretly in London.

Much surprise was expressed as to the extraordinary fact of her travelling from London without having made her presence known; but I saw nothing strange in it. She was hastening back to the Continent so as to appear to receive the terrible news (a telegram had been sent to the usual address, and the answer came flashing back that she had left Rome for a fortnight's stay in Florence, address not known), and come home heartbroken to be her dear aunt's heiress, for the will, leaving her everything, still stood; that old life had been doubtless crushed out at the proper moment.

Janet Fosbrooke had presumably privately married her lover Ralph Carew. Her friend in Rome proved that she had some such suspicion for a short time back, and then something occurred that made her tax the girl with being secretly married, and she had not denied it, only entreating her not to tell her aunt for a little while, and she, the friend, consented to keep the secret for a month and no longer; but she had never seen the husband, nor heard his name. The girl used to take long, lonely walks, she doubtless then met him, and she felt almost sure he had accompanied her to Florence.

Whether the girl was really going to Tenby on some brief mysterious errand, or whether she came so far to cover the man's retreat, and avert suspicion, avoiding the more recognised routes of flight, and hoping, by being seen with me, to cause confusion, if by some terrible ill-luck they should be pursued, I never knew.

But of one fact I am certain, that, in that crowd pouring to the Tenby train, she saw some one whom she feared might recognise her, even through her disguise, and dashed back on the first pretence that occurred to her, flinging herself on the floor of whatever empty carriage she entered, so as to remain unseen by me, feeling sure that she would not lose her belongings, for that I having to go on would bring them with me, and that she would get them, as she did.

* * * * * *

Is it any wonder, when these two points of my vision have been so startlingly realized—when with my spirit eyes I saw that girl as she was, though in every particular so opposed to her my fleshy eyes had gazed upon; when with my spirit eyes I saw that knife and its inscription that had been fruitlessly searched for in the light of day—is it any wonder, I repeat, that some day or other I feel that these earthly eyes of mine will again gaze on that fair cruel face, with the full blue eyes and the long yellow whiskers, with the strange cut or gash on the upper lip; the whiskers may be gone and the lip shaded by a moustache, as on that day in the railway carriage (for that it was he I am assured); but still I feel that no matter where we meet or when, I would pick out that face seen in my trance—howsoe'er disguised—from among ten thousand.

Ralph Carew has soiled his soul for naught; his wife's death, before the marriage had been made known, before she had been declared her aunt's heiress, above all, her death in such strange—almost *suspicious*—circumstances, forbade his coming forward to claim any portion of that wealth, for which he had bartered his chance of heaven.

Vengeance had soon overtaken his partner in guilt; vengeance swift and sure; but he remains for me!

Why do I talk so wildly—so foolishly? Why should my life be consecrated to revenge? To revenge the death of a poor woman whom I did not know, had never seen, had not the faintest interest in; and yet, I think of that extraordinary vision which must have been the result of some strange, unaccountable force in nature, on whose border-land we are of late dimly wandering, guideless and compassless, for we have not yet found the chart of that mystic country; we have not yet probed the science of the "Power of Will;" dead as well as living will. The subtle influence that one mind may have upon another, distant in life or death.

Or, again, the strange power that is given to some to look into another's brain and see reproduced with mental eyes what runs riot there.

I was out of health, low, depressed, nervous somewhat, perhaps a peculiarly fitting subject for some occult demonstration; and I sat beside Janet Fosbrooke and talked to her while fresh from that ghastly scene upon the heath, with that terrible picture in her mind, and it stamped itself on mine.

* * * * * *

Thus I try to explain to myself the mystery of that weird, unaccountable episode in my life, but never satisfactorily—something always seems wanting.

But still, *I watch and wait.*

DOLORES

A PSYCHOLOGICAL PROBLEM, IN THREE PARTS

"Unknown facts of guilty acts
Are seen in dreams of God."
THOMAS HOOD

DOLORES

PART I

"MURDER or suicide?" This was the pregnant question that had been wildly agitating the pretty, picturesque village of Glenore during the past four weeks.

But at last lingering doubt vanished; conviction forced itself on all, without exception, save myself, that the awful mystery of that strange and terrible death that took place in our peaceful midst, convulsing our small community, and shaking it to its very centre a month before, could be explained only by the second dread term, that made those who used it shrink in memory from him, so beloved in life, compelling them half-unconsciously to substitute horror and reprobation for the infinite sorrow, pity, and rage that filled their hearts to overflowing when first the appalling, tragic story of sudden, violent, unexplained death, on that lovely summer evening was whispered with bated breath from each to each.

"Yes, it must have been suicide," they argued, for the hundredth time, with ominous head-shakes and expressive shudders.

There was no longer any excuse for assuming the possibility of its having been murder. Suspicion had rested on none from the first; in fact, there were none to suspect. No stranger had been seen in the neighbourhood of the village for weeks before the event occurred.

The dead man's servants, but three in number—an elderly housekeeper, well known and respected in Glenore and the surrounding district; a rosy-cheeked village lass, her lieutenant; and the man who, for the last twenty years, had followed the fortunes of Colonel Oswald with the faithfulness and affection so often displayed by soldier servants—were devoted to him. Besides, the usual *raison d'être* of murder—ordinary vulgar murder—was conspicuous by its absence, as robbery there had been none; even the valuables on the dead man's person remained undisturbed; and any other more refined motive for secret, deliberate murder, such as revenge, &c., could not be entertained for a moment.

The genial, kindly Frank Oswald, a good man and true, a staunch and steadfast friend, had not an enemy in the world; of this Glenore felt morally certain, and I, who knew him better, felt thoroughly convinced; and Mills, his trusty servant and adherent, who knew all the circumstances of his master's life for a score of years, declared, with much energy, palliated by grief and humiliation (for after all, when his brave, beloved master was dead, how far better it would be to be able to prove that it was the result of cold-blooded assassination, rather than shameful, cowardly self-murder!) that he knew there was not a creature living wished Colonel Oswald ill; that everyone had loved him elsewhere as at Glenore; and that in all those years whether in the service, or since he sold out, in times of peace or war, action or inaction, his master had never quarrelled with a human being.

And then again, if murdered by some person or persons unknown, there surely should be some trace, however faint and slight, of an intruder's presence in the dead man's home.

That there had been no struggle whatever, was evident from the first; and the supposition that any stranger (always an event of some importance at Glenore) could have walked into the Dingle House in the mellow golden glory of a lovely summer's evening, just at a time when the shadows are thickening, and a dreamy duskiness gathering within doors, though outside the daylight still reigns supreme—and entered the study or library, sacred to the master's use, where that master was wont to repose at that hour, and stab him to the heart, as he lay presumably sleeping; and then out again, without disturbing by a hair's breadth any article in that room, without a sign, a sound to betray that fell presence to the rest of the household, was simply untenable.

The dead man's adopted daughter sat in the drawing-room on the opposite side of the hall, reading by the waning light; and Mills, who generally at this time enjoyed a pipe in the west shrubbery, on which the study windows looked, had been there that evening, and had noticed that the window near the sofa, on which Colonel Oswald lay, was open, and yet he had heard no sound. And he had scarcely returned to the house a quarter of an hour, when Miss Fairfax rang for tea, which he brought to the drawing-room; and while he arranged the table, she crossed the hall to summon her guardian, and opening the study door, her scream of terror and dismay apprised him and the rest of the household of the horror that had happened. That the assassin had deliberately passed out of the house again, into the saffron light of the dying day, through the grounds, out on to the high road, through the village—which he must perforce enter to gain the nearest town, nearly four miles off, as the Dingle House stood beyond Glenore nearer the sea, with a precipitous cliff-wall rising steeply at its rear—and yet succeed in escaping observation, was a practical impossibility, especially at that hour of rest from labour and of general relaxation, when the village folk were gathered at their doors, enjoying the peace and beauty of the summer evening. Besides, would it not argue, on the part of the imaginary assassin, a strange acquaintance with the ways of the Dingle House and its inmates?

No. The theory of murder, after fluctuating mightily for a whole month, now almost expiring, now flaring up into sudden transient life again, was at last finally abandoned by Glenore; and I alone remained true to the memory of my dear dear friend, Frank Oswald, inasmuch as I still refused, in face of the most positive evidence, as my neighbours declared it to be, to dishonour him by doubt. And yet, was it positive? There was one distinct and singular flaw in the suicide theory, which even those most absolutely convinced that it, and it alone, held the solution of the terrible problem of the Dingle House mystery, had to admit was unaccountable—inexplicable. And this was the extraordinary fact—the non-discovery of the weapon that had gone home to its mark with such straight, awful, unerring aim—that had transformed life into death by that small, clean, cruel puncture, which though scarcely the circumference of a quill, yet had proved a door quite wide enough to release the imprisoned soul. No trace of any instrument that could have caused death was found, after the most rigorous and exhaustive search.

The doctors who viewed the wound declared it must have been produced by a weapon of somewhat strange and peculiar design, some exquisitely fine and slender dagger, remarkable and uncommon. But if the blow was self-inflicted, it was quite feasible, they averred, and also possible, that the hand that made that unshrinking thrust might have wrenched the steel from the quivering flesh ere it hung powerless in death; but where was the weapon? It should necessarily be on the floor, or, at least, somewhere in the room, even if thrown from the dying hand. Yet the strictest search revealed nothing. The very sofa on which the body lay was taken to pieces in a last effort to find that one link which, thus wanting, left all in a state of unsatisfactory incompleteness. But, as we have seen, even with this most mysterious disappearance of the cause of the effect, all except myself were fain to accept the belief of self-murder. Confessing there was much mystery in the affair, but still that other explanation was not feasible; and suggesting, as a possible way of accounting for the evanishment of the weapon of death, that, perhaps, when first the alarm was given on that fatal night, and scared confusion reigned within the Dingle House, when friends and villagers alike flocked to the scene of the tragedy, and stood within that room in mute horror and amaze, one of the latter may possibly have unthinkingly picked up the deadly thing, and unconsciously carried it away with him, and have foolishly shrunk since from yielding it up from an ignorant fear that its being found in his possession might in some way implicate him; or, still more likely, that one of the village children had confiscated it as a novel, though dangerous, plaything, had quietly made his own of it, saying nothing but keeping his own counsel with that strange secretiveness that seems so inherent in a child's nature.

This, was, perhaps a plausible mode of trying to explain away the difficult problem of the missing weapon, but it was not sufficient for me; the whole affair was wrapped in impenetrable mystery, but until I received positive, unanswerable proof, that my friend had taken his own life, I should remain firm in the belief that he had been the victim of unimaginable diabolical treachery. It was contrary to all reason and common sense, that the man should have committed suicide.

All motive for so desperate an act was lacking. Frank Oswald, still in the prime of life, joyous-natured, healthy, vigorous; with no troubles domestic or monetary; enjoying the half-sportsman, half-student life he led, in that sweet country home to the full; happy in the society of his ward, Dolores Fairfax, and in that of that dear adopted daughter's betrothed, myself; with a tender, gentle heart, full of love and charity, and kindness for all; a brave soldier;

a true and honourable gentleman; a devout and humble-minded Christian; surely it was not in the nature of things, that such a man would rush thus impiously into the presence of his Maker.

* * * * * *

Some three years before that tragic August night, I, Arthur Wilmore, having just left my thirtieth birthday behind me, and by my father's recent death, became master of the "Manor" (a sad and dreary privilege, as I felt very desolate in my solitary greatness, in that stately grey old house, and a hundred times a day missed my dear old dad, who had been brother and friend, as well as father) met Frank Oswald, who had lately taken "The Dingle House," which had stood empty for years. The acquaintance, begun accidentally, just at the time when my solitude was pressing most heavily, soon ripened into firm and lasting friendship; our tastes were similar, we thought alike on most subjects; were, to put it briefly, congenial. (What better word for friendship's basis? What can so thoroughly insure a true, staunch, mutual liking, whether between man and man, or man and woman?)

"The Dingle House" soon became almost as much my home as "The Manor," and Colonel Oswald and his ward (his "little Grief," as he sometimes playfully called her) my most intimate friends. Dolores Fairfax was at that time but a slender slip of a maiden, little over sixteen.

About a year previous, Frank Oswald, who was then in the East, had been implored, by a very old and much-loved friend, who had married and settled years before in the West Indies, to come to him for God's sake with all speed; it was "a dying man's request," the letter stated, and the urgency was great; his old comrade longed, with an inexpressible sick longing, to place, with his own trembling hands, chill already with the dews of approaching death, his only and beloved child, under the safe and tender guardianship of his dear and trusted friend, before that terrible and relentless foe had chilled for ever the heart that beat with such warm and passionate love for his little daughter.

Colonel Oswald obeyed that summons, and was just in time to hear a murmured blessing, to see a look of glad recognition in the glazing eyes; and then to follow to his grave in that distant land, all that remained of his old friend and comrade, Ronald Fairfax.

Dolores' mother—a West Indian by birth, of Spanish descent—had been dead some years, and the child was literally alone in the world. She had a few friends in Cuba, chiefly amongst the Spanish West Indians, but she apparently felt little regret in bidding them farewell, as she seemed anxiously eager to leave Cuba.

The fifteen-year-old West Indian was but a frail and delicate sapling, when first she saw her father's native land, Colonel Oswald told me; but the year in England had improved and benefitted her greatly, and though when I first saw her, I regarded her still as scarcely more than a child, I thought her very lovely, with something of a strange, singular, silent beauty, but still fascinating in an uncommon puzzling way.

Not that in cataloguing her points of attraction there seemed anything especially peculiar or odd; but it was the indefinable expression of the face, a vague strange abstraction in the manner, that struck one as unfamiliar and novel, and interested one in spite of oneself. Yet, it was rather a singular countenance, with that cloud of rippling yellow hair, framing that coldly clear pale face; no waxen pallor, but a snowy-white purity of complexion, especially remarkable when one remembered her almost tropical birthplace, and her origin on the mother's side; no colouring whatever in the cheeks, and scarcely any in the lips, and yet it did not strike one as the colourlessness of delicacy, but rather as if some rare mental attribute declared itself through the medium of the skin, as well as in those strange great eyes; eyes, beautiful in themselves in form, and in colour deepest, richest brown with jetty fringes; eyes that had centred in themselves all the colouring of the face; but it was not their beauty you noticed, as compare with their unusual, almost startling expression. At times they glowed with a strange luminous light, as if some mystic fire burned in their liquid depths, lit by the yearning soul that was almost visible in that spiritual face.

But this was only seldom; ordinarily they wore a look—what was it? introspective, dreamy, abstracted; or was it rather a singular mysterious expression of looking at something beyond, outside the present person, place or time?

It gave you an odd, slightly shivery impression, and yet attracted strangely. You grew unconsciously to look upon the girl as a psychological problem you vainly and ardently longed to solve; and yet she was simplicity itself in her ways and manners, save for a vague, nameless, silent sense of waiting and watching; an instinctive feeling that there was some latent expectation—of what you could not tell—under that calm, grave, gentle exterior. Here, at least, one saw at a glance that mind predominated over matter; that the soul outweighed the body and left the casket almost transparent enough to see that mysterious Presence at work within.

Yet, in intellectual development, she seemed in no way distinguished from the generality of girls, but probably it was the imaginative, idealistic faculties that were so abnormally accentuated.

As time passed on and she grew into womanhood, my wondering admiration and vivid interest changed by degrees into a warmer feeling. I grew to love this sweetly-grave serious maiden with the mystic eyes; not with the intensity and passion I had hoped and expected to feel when the magical sweetness of that wondrous, inexplicable action of the human heart that men call "love," should visit me; perhaps this arose from the peculiar nature of the woman I loved; she was so cold, and pure, and passionless, that all mere human earthly desires seemed to shrink and pale in her presence. My love for her was calm but steadfast, and was tempered, or rather mingled with a feeling that I could not analyze or account for.

A strange, odd sense of unreality would sometimes suddenly smite me when I was alone with Dolores; a feeling as if a third person were present unseen, or rather, as if I myself were only present spiritually, and that third imaginary presence was really the other person in the dual walk or talk. I would rouse up suddenly with the absurd feeling that I had been straining and listening—for what? that third invisible person's voice I suppose, and used mentally to abuse myself in vigorous language as "a nervous, imaginative, contemptible idiot." But shortly after my father's death I had rather a bad illness, a low nervous fever, and I had never been quite so strong since.

Nearly a year before Frank Oswald's mysterious death Dolores and I became engaged; she was but a little past eighteen then, and it was agreed that we should not marry till she was twenty-one. It was no dowerless bride that would be coming to me; for, though her inheritance from her father was but trifling, Frank Oswald would give her a fortune on her marriage, and at his death she would be—as he told me—his sole heiress, for near relations he had none; and, in any case, he loved the girl so fondly that she was in all things to him as a daughter.

He was utterly pleased and happy in her betrothal to me; delighted to think, if anything should happen to him, that he would leave her in such good hands; she was a fragile sensitive plant, and required to be sheltered from the storms of life; and though in strong, vigorous health himself, and still under fifty, yet all was so fearfully uncertain in this world, that he felt thoroughly glad to know that her future would be so guarded and safe. Dolores herself, too, for the first few months after our engagement, seemed brighter, gayer, happier than I had ever known her. Always undemonstrative, self-contained, reserved to a degree, she yet seemed to live less within herself (if I may use the phrase) than before; she almost appeared for a time like one who had been relieved from some mental burden which oppressed, and which, when flung off for a space, causes a rebound that cannot be quite concealed.

For those first few months she sang and chatted and laughed, and was altogether more like other girls. Her eyes were sweeter, softer, tenderer, with less of the visionary, mystical look that was so puzzling, and that was a wee shade startling, when she seemed to look at some one or something, through or beyond you, and you were tempted involuntarily to turn your head to see whom she regarded, though you knew there was no one there. There was also less of that strange, odd stillness and impression of waiting, listening, watching, in her manner. It was a very pleasant change and flattering; for it was as if her love for myself made her a new creature; but, unfortunately, it did not last, and of late the peculiarities of her nature had been more pronounced than ever, not that her affection for myself seemed at all diminished; nay, rather, she appeared to cling to me more, though her lips grew more silent, and her eyes more absorbed and distant-looking day by day. I sometimes thought she must have unpleasant Cuban reminiscences; that possibly she had experienced some great terror or distress when she was quite a child, and that it had left this strange impress on the sensitive, nervous, highly-organized nature; but though I frequently tried to induce her to speak of her childhood and earliest youth, of Cuba and its associations, she always seemed to shrink from doing so, ever turning the conversation, after answering my questions as briefly as possible.

And now, I shuddered to think of the effect, the lasting effect, this awful event that had convulsed all Glenore would have upon her.

Dolores loved her adopted father devotedly; though undemonstrative, whether in the display of grief or joy, love or hate, yet this sweet, undeclared affection was very perceptible both to me, and to him who evoked it, to whom it had been, as he often averred, the crowning and greatest blessing of his life.

Yes, what a terrible impression it would make upon the girl; what injurious result might it not have upon her, constituted as she was? On the only two occasions she consented to see me, since that fearful night, I was alarmed, awed almost, at the extraordinary unnatural calm and rigidity of her manner: her eyes wore a fixed, stony look, as if they had looked upon a great horror, and were frozen at the sight; her lips had a white look of strain and tension, very painful to witness, she would scarcely speak, and, when she did, not above a whisper.

Hers was a grief that found no relief in blessed tears that so often save the overtaxed brain, and I dreaded to think of the future. She positively and absolutely refused to leave the house, though she had many invitations from kind friends in the neighbourhood to make her home with them, at least for a time. I ardently longed she should do so (to the "Manor," unhappily, she could not come, until she came as mistress, as I was quite alone save for my servants); but she was inflexible, saying, she much preferred staying with Mrs. Joyce (the house-keeper) and Mills, who knew and loved him who was gone, to going amongst strangers.

This evening, just six weeks after that awful tragedy that robbed Dolores of her second father and me of my dear and trusted friend, who had gone out from our midst so silently, inexplicably; just when the long and eagerly-debated question of "Murder or suicide?" had at last been answered by all Glenore to their own entire satisfaction—*I* alone remaining Didymus-like amongst them, awaiting proof incontrovertible[18]—I determined to go up to the Dingle House again and try to have an interview with Dolores, who had so persistently declined to see me, save on the two occasions mentioned, alleging as excuse for what must seem to me (her betrothed husband) somewhat strange (who had a better right to comfort her in her sorrow?) that she was too ill and too suffering to talk; and besides, that seeing me only brought her grief and the horror of its nature more vividly before her.

But to-night I was determined, if possible, to frustrate her growing morbid desire for utter solitude, that would have such an unwholesome effect upon a girl of her visionary, reflective temperament, by stealing on her unawares, and then by dint of much tender persuasion getting her to promise to marry me when six months from her guardian's death should have expired. We had noting to wait for now, and the sooner this unhealthful state of existence ceased for Dolores the better. The girl was quite alone and needed a protector, and who so safe as a husband? And when once my wife, I would take her abroad, and amidst change of scene and surroundings the shock and horror of the bereavement she had sustained would, I trusted, gradually subside leaving but the calm natural sorrow behind; whereas, if the mind were allowed to

[18] Didymus: Doubting Thomas, who, according to the Gospel of John, refused to believe in the resurrection of Jesus without seeing and touching his crucifixion wounds.

prey on itself in this strange seclusion, it might do her serious harm.

Those necessary intervening months I hoped to be able to induce her to spend with cousins of mine, living at the other end of England, where, I trusted, she might begin to forget.

These were my hopes and fears as I wended my way to the Dingle House, on this evening of September the 28th, 188—, just six weeks after Frank Oswald's mysterious death.

DOLORES

PART II

IT had been a dull, cheerless, sad-coloured day, and it was a grey, bleak, dismal evening. When I say evening, it was but little past six o'clock, but it seemed as if the shades of night were already gathering, so gloomy and leaden was the sky. There was a decided chill in the air too, unusual at that season, and unwelcome, and the wind was soughing drearily amongst the hills that clustered in gracious, greenest semicircle round our little village; now it was but a faint distant whisper, a hushed sighing lament, swelling anon into a sobbing moan, a weary, saddening wail, that seemed as if unseen spirits plained and sorrowed round one.

It was an evening to make one creep and shiver slightly, not so much with cold of body as with an eerie sense of desolation and foreboding, as if an actual embodied grief or horror were somewhere abroad, and one shrank from stumbling upon it unawares.

The Dingle House was wrapped in deepest quiet. I saw no one as I crossed the lawn and took my way round the side of the house to that west shrubbery, which the servants already shunned, but which Mrs. Joyce had told me Dolores had grown strangely fond of haunting.

She would pace up and down there for hours together, she said, glancing askance every now and then at that window that had stood open on that fatal night. It was a peculiar fancy, but, perhaps the imaginative girl felt nearer in spirit to the adopted father she so fondly loved, when thus looking on the windows of the room that was so especially his own, but which she had not been able to bring herself as yet to enter.

I hoped to find her here and thus compel her to a meeting. But I was disappointed. All was lonely; solitude reigned supreme, and the wind moaned and sobbed piteously round the gables of the old house, while mingled with it might be heard a sadder, more depressing sound still, the distant, far-away moaning of the ever restless sea, as it beat in sullen swelling cadence on the shore, scarcely half-a-mile off. It was dreary in the extreme, and I felt a sudden inexpressible longing for human companionship. I walked almost mechanically to the farthest window and looked in; all was exactly the same as on that night, six weeks ago, when, in the confidence and security and peace of home the master lay outstretched upon that sofa resting, mayhap sleeping, and fell, treacherous death stole upon him, borne by the assassin's cruel, hideous hand.

He must have been asleep, I argued, else he would have seen that dastardly approach. And yet when the body was discovered the eyes were wide open, with a look of astonished horror and wild dismay in their fixed gaze, very awful to contemplate, and seemed to prove then beyond a doubt that murder had been perpetuated, though public opinion had veered round since, and asserted that that look on the dead face was the instinctive, unconscious awe of the unknown into which the wretched man was about impiously to plunge.

He might have been musing with closed eyes, I thought, but surely some sound, however slight, would have betrayed that fiendish presence, and Oswald, strong and vigorous as he was, would have sprung to his feet and confronted that craven, cruel foe. No, he must have been asleep, but in the death agony, which was simultaneous with that terrible stab, the eyes opened for the last time on earth and gazed for an instant into the murderer's bending face before they glazed in death. And a strange thought struck me as I stood and looked within that familiar room. On the retina of the human eye, it is said, is reflected a photograph in miniature, reversed I believe, of whatever object the eye gazes on.

And if this be so, surely it would not be a very wild or imaginative idea to suppose, that scientifically followed up, this natural picture-gallery, might in cases of crime, possibly lead to detection, to explanation, where all seems wrapt in mystery and doubt. If each object as we look upon it, is pictured on the back part of the eye, then, whatever is the last thing we gaze on consciously before life leaves us, is thus photographed, and it is to be supposed remains so, at least for a time, until chemical changes, forerunners of decay, begin to take place; why should not this hidden microscopic picture be magnified and photographed? If Frank Oswald's eyes had thus been dealt with, a few hours after death, what should we, the gazers on that mystic portrait-painting have seen?

For, it would have been a portrait that his retina would have held. And whose? Should we know then the cause of that anguished horror in the eyes? What diabolical face would look out at us from that wizard-picture, a face that we could follow through the world, of whose identity there could be no possible doubt; and that, when met, or where, we could have no hesitation in avowing, "Thou art the man, for the dead has declared it!"

* * * * * *

It was a strange thought, but one for physicians or scientists, and I was just turning away, to go round to the hall-door, with a vexed impotent feeling that it had not struck me before, when I might have suggested something to Dr. Feversham (our village medico), doubtless only to be laughed at as an imaginative fool—when a faint pecking or scraping noise, somewhere in the shrubbery at my back, attracted my attention. I looked round, and at first saw nothing, but the sound continued, and as I retraced my steps a yard or two, seemed nearer; then, all at once, I saw it was my old friend "Jacko," Colonel Oswald's devoted pet and favourite; a jackdaw of high intellectual powers, wondrous sagacity, loving and faithful, also amusingly pugnacious where he took an inveterate dislike, as in the case of one of my unlucky dogs, whose life was a misery to him from the moment he entered the Dingle House until he quitted it. But there was a spot upon the sun; all these perfections were somewhat marred by one irredeemable vice; Jacko was a thief, unmitigated, irreclaimable, and he gloried in his criminality. It was hopeless to show him the error of his ways; preaching and teaching were without avail; his code of accomplishments (doubtless morals also) ranked robbery, audacious, shameless robbery, or sly cunning robbery, as the highest and best. And yet, we took him as he was, and loved him. I had not seen him since my friend's death, but Mrs. Joyce told me that "the poor bird took on dreadful, missing his master, for all the world like a Christian; he pined and moped and refused his food, and never stole nothing now," which was a sure sign of poor Jacko's depression of spirits. I greeted him now with familiar friendship, but he took no notice of me, he was too busy. It was in one of the densest parts of the shrubbery he was at work, digging rapidly, silently, uttering no little cries of satisfaction, as was his wont; he had evidently stolen something at last, I thought, and was about to bury it, and I stood by to watch the interment.

Once he called out hoarsely, "Who's there?" which seemed so applicable, that I started involuntarily, and then glanced round at that window so near us both; if that miserable unconscious bird had been where he was now that fatal night, and uttered those same words (one of his stock phrases) equally loudly, defiantly, suspiciously, would it not have arrested the guilty hand? would not the intending assassin have fled in terror and amazement, as if challenged by some invisible questioner, some guardian spirit, who saw the premeditated crime? And then my dreamy reflections were cut short by a little cry of triumph from Jacko, and I looked round to see him dragging something glittering from the excavation he had made. Then he was unburying something, not burying, as I had fancied, and I felt interested. What was this spoil that he had appropriated? I stooped down to see better; it was rather dusky there in the shrubbery, amongst all that growth of greenery, as the bird tugged and tugged at his prize. It was something long, slender, shining, it was—yes! surely it was—a dagger! The bird had nearly disinterred it, and I, quickly stretching forth my hand, with some strange, sudden impulse, wrenched it from the soil and from him at one and the same time; he gave one solitary remonstrative croak, and then repeated several times in tones of lively satisfaction, as if relieved of a burden that had weighed upon his mind, "It's all right; it's all right!" Was this again oddly applicable? I thought with a half-scared feeling of instinctive dread, as I grasped that unearthed treasure and stepped out on the gravel path, where the light was stronger, to examine it.

While Jacko marched solemnly off (his mission over) without condescending to notice me further, with frequent contemptuous utterings of, "You're a fool! you're a fool!" which complimentary valediction would at another time have caused a smile.

How strangely apt the creature's speech was this evening; doubtless I was a fool to be so thrilled and moved and excited by that which I held within my hand. I stood where the light was strongest, and, with a quiver of apprehension and repulsion, gazed long and earnestly at that slender weapon.

Yes, I was right, it was a dagger; one of uncommon, peculiar design, evidently of foreign workmanship, looking almost like an ornamental toy, the shaft was so richly and fancifully chased; but the deadly part, that exquisitely fine and slender poignard, was as strong and resistant as the highest tempered steel could make it; if a plaything, surely a dangerous one. It was a damp place rather where Jacko had buried it and the blade or point had become somewhat rusty. Stay! was it rust? I took out my penknife and scratched it slightly; no, even my unscientific eye saw it was not rust, but blood, coagulated blood! and I shivered and let it fall as I realized fully what it meant.

It meant, did it not, that Glenore was right and I was wrong? that suicide was the dark shadow that lay over the Dingle House and my friend's memory after all, and not cruel, treacherous murder. It meant that that erring hand, raised in defiant strength to take its own life, in a last muscular effort, flung the instrument of death through the open window, where Jacko had found and appropriated it. Thus was the puzzle of the missing weapon so easily read; thus cruelly, suddenly died my faith that had been so strong, firm as a rock, in him who was gone.

The reader will naturally say, Why rush to such rapid conclusions? Surely the discovery of the weapon does not prove that murder was not committed? nay, rather the reverse. May not the assassin have been startled by some distant sound, some fancied approach, just as he had completed his hideous work, and in a paroxysm of terror flung from him, through the window, the thing that betrayed him, he himself escaping most likely by the same exit? Yes, that sounds very well and natural, but, unfortunately, it did not betray a stranger's presence, quite the contrary; it belonged to home and those in that home. As it lay there at my feet, I recognised it, as I had failed to do at first. It was one of the many West Indian curios—things of use and beauty, ornamental and the reverse—that adorned Dolores' little private sitting-room in the Dingle House; there were small tables crowded with articles of rare and fanciful design, some lovely and artistic, others slightly odd and bizarre, somewhat unfamiliar to the English eye; amongst these latter was this dagger that the jackdaw had just disinterred. I remembered it now quite well, only that hitherto, I had always seen its dangerousness carefully enclosed in a protecting sheath, chased and ornamented to match the shaft. It was just the instrument to make that small, clean, deadly puncture. How steady, how horribly, wickedly steady had been the hand that guided it.

How incomprehensible it all was! As long as there remained room for doubt, murder—great as seemed the mystery enveloping its accomplishment—seemed to me natural and likely, lacking as was all motive. You never know how, or where, or why, murder may be wrought. An escaped lunatic, with the homicidal thirst for blood strong upon him, had wandered perchance into these grounds, and seeing the sleeping figure, had found temptation too strong to resist.

In my determination not to waver from my trust and belief, I had suggested to myself all possible and impossible theories; but now all were dashed to the ground. Frank Oswald had taken his own life, and God alone knew why. It must have been a very extraordinary case of temporary insanity, I reflected, with a bitterly sorrowing, terribly heavy heart, as I picked up that fearful thing, and took my way round to the front of the house. I felt almost savagely resentful with myself that I had come there this evening, to discover by so strange a chance that link that would confirm Glenore in its belief, and substantiate its right to reprobate the memory of the man I had loved and respected so truly. I should have believed in and honoured

Frank Oswald, though all the world had condemned him: but now I saw that the world was sometimes right in its harsh judgments, and I hated it for its keen, cold, true insight, not him who had earned its censure.

And so, with grief, and love, and yearning pity for the dead—infinite compassion for the state of mind, hidden so carefully and unsuspected, that could in one so good and noble lead to so sinful and desperate a deed—I entered the house, scarcely knowing what I intended.

* * * * * *

I bent my steps half-unconsciously to Dolores' little sitting-room on the first floor, still carrying that baleful thing. How silent and quiet the house was. Though but two storeys in height, it was large, low, and rambling. I heard a faint distant murmur of the servants' voices from their own peculiar region, but all else was stillness profound.

I felt impressed, I knew not why, nervous, strained; a sensation of tension and expectation crept over me, which was strange and uncomfortable. I had not felt so on previous occasions when I had been there since the tragedy. I caught myself glancing about me, hurriedly, dubiously; and I felt glad when I reached that pretty familiar room, Dolores' small sanctum, where I had been allowed to become a privileged intruder. Dolores herself was the first object that met my eye as I entered. A luxurious little divided ottoman stood in the centre of the somewhat fancifully furnished apartment, and in one of the sections sat, or rather reclined, the young mistress of the house—asleep. How weary, how inexpressibly weary and exhausted she looked, as if worn with suffering of either mind or body. How ghastly and wan the spiritual face. Always white and colourless, its livid tint was now almost startling. She had grown thin, even since I saw her last; and robed in her sable garments, she looked more ghost than woman.

My love! my Dolores! she was grieving herself into her grave, I thought, with an agonised contraction of the heart, as I stood and gazed at the girl who lay unconscious, sleeping the sleep of exhaustion. Mrs. Joyce had told me that she feared her young mistress got little rest at night, though she never complained, and here was more or less proof of it. I watched her for a few minutes, my whole being going out with a great throb of pity and sympathy to the frail, tender creature, my darling promised wife, on whom had been laid so terrible a sorrow. I had determined from the first not to wake her; it would be selfish and cruel. Let her sleep, let her have peace and oblivion while she might, and I would wait patiently till she awoke.

I was just about to steal softly from the room, afraid my very presence might disturb that much needed repose, when suddenly the very manner of her sleep changed; the profound unconscious calm that had enfolded her broke, and though she still slept she grew restless, uneasy, distressed, uttering low moans and tossing her hands and head about pitifully.

My first thought was that she was waking; but no, she still slept on, though so differently. Her face now wore a strange look of tension, and the eyes were slightly unclosed, which always gives so unnatural and almost frightful an aspect to the sleeper. The moans grew louder and more frequent, the restless movements more decided, she was evidently dreaming, and dreaming horribly, and it would be only a kindness to arouse her now.

I pronounced her name softly, so as not to startle her, but she took no heed; I spoke louder and even louder, but still she slept on, though the appearances of distress in no way abated. I went over to her and laid my hand upon her forehead (how burning it was), I even gently shook her, but all without avail. How strangely profound was the unconsciousness to external things, that wrapped her round, and yet all so disturbed within.

I grew anxious, a little alarmed, yet what could I do? I shrank from adopting any more violent means of rousing her, in her present state it might be dangerous.

Perhaps my touch might soothe her. Already the great distress seemed somewhat calmed, the anguished moans subsided into a faint sobbing sound, the working hands grew quieter; holding one of the latter which chilled me by its icy touch (my darling must be indeed ill—head so hot, and hands so unnaturally cold), I sat down in the adjoining compartment of the little ottoman. Poor little tender hand! it quivered and trembled, and gave spasmodic jerks as it lay in mine, but I held it fast in my warm clasp while with the other hand I still grasped that fatal dagger; I had almost forgotten it for the moment in my anxiety for Dolores. I retained it unconsciously. Now I looked from her soft slender hand to it and shuddered.

And then, as I sat, a strange feeling came over me; at first a sort of troublous maze of unreality; it was not drowsiness or sleep. I swear it was not sleep; and try as I would I could not banish it. My eyes were wide open, and yet their vision appeared to grow blurred, dim, as if the room and Dolores, and all around me were fading from my gaze; it was more like the sensations of impending faintness without the feeling of illness, or possibly what those feel on whom is creeping a frozen death, a sort of numbing of the faculties, an unconsciousness of surrounding objects.

Two or three times I shook myself free of this spell that seemed to bind me in its mystical embrace. What was the matter with me? I was here to watch over and take care of Dolores, and must not allow myself to yield to this mental lethargy; but each time my efforts to rouse myself were weaker, and at last I gave up trying to struggle against this weird occult influence and let it subjugate me, being conscious at the last moment of increased restlessness and distress on the part of the sleeper, whose hand I still held. Then all grew dark around me, the room and Dolores, and surrounding objects faded from my sight though my eyes were strained wide open, and for a brief space I must have lapsed into unconsciousness; it was as if I were under the influence of opium or Hascheesch, or other brain-intoxicating drug. Then the atmosphere lightened, the grey haziness lifted and all was clear again; but I was no longer in Dolores' room, but in that still more familiar one on the lower storey, whose windows looked on the West shrubbery. I was once more in the library with the master!

* * * * * *

Yes, there on the sofa before me, not three yards off, lay Frank Oswald sleeping, and I felt no surprise, I was conscious of no dismay, no fear, only a sense of waiting. How calmly he slept, how reposeful, how helpless the attitude, with both arms flung above his head, and how kindly and handsome and gentle he looked, I thought meditatively.

Then suddenly a great desire to wake him came upon me, but to my horror I could make no sound, no movement, I sat and gazed at him transfixed, with all power of motion gone, while the feeling of waiting was intensified, accompanied now by a new-born sense of inexpressible dread.

And then, in a moment, I was conscious that a third presence was in the room, though I had heard no one enter. With a supreme effort I turned my head and saw Dolores. Dolores, in her blood-red dress, that ruby gown I had always loved to see her in, that set off her strange beauty to the utmost. Aye, blood-red! that was its colour, though it never struck me so before.

With her face gleaming ashen white, and her eyes open but fixed, like one who moves in a trance she glided towards us, so slowly, so silently, as if impelled forward by some invisible agency, while intense natural reluctance held her back. I watched her spell-bound, but she did not see me, her eyes gazed out beyond the confines of the narrow room, to something or someone outside its narrow limits. And as she drew nearer I saw her face was agonised and drawn with mental torture.

When about half way across the room, that gliding step was arrested, that awful fixed look gave place to a wild, beseeching, imploring glare that still gazed far away, while from those white tightened lips, issued words that seemed breathed from a distance, and that fell like ice upon my heart,—

"I can't, I can't" she moaned in that strange still whisper. "Anything else than this. I will obey in all things; but not this—not this. Monster! Devil! I won't—I can't!"

But even as she concluded, the rigid, stony look returned to the eyes, the whole face became again mask-like, as one who walks in a mesmeric sleep, while from afar off there seemed to whisper through the room some wave of sound, in which my straining ears seemed to hear a murmur of "I command," and on she came, straight to the sofa, and I noticed that her right hand grasped something hid in the fold of her gown. An awful horror grew upon me! I seemed frozen where I sat. I strove with terrible efforts to move, to cry out; but it was as if death lay upon me, and chained me, a living, anguished, bursting soul in a dead inert body. I was helpless as he who lay in sweet peace and security. And now she stood above him, the right hand raised high, and descending swiftly with a gleam of glancing steel. There was a gurgle, a groan—no more!

The sleeping eyes were wide open, and a splash of red upon the coat, like a reflection of that gown that would betray no guilty secrets, that was all. And then, the woman's two hands were raised as if in abjuration or malediction, and the next moment, flinging something from her through the window with a gesture of wild loathing, she stumbled blindly from the room, while suddenly the atmosphere again grew thick and murky. I lost my hold on things around, my brain reeled, my very being seemed absorbed in a great horror of discovery. I felt sinking, falling, dying. It must be death surely, this awful abyss of darkness in which I was being engulfed. And then, quite suddenly, I opened my eyes, which I had closed in that terrible sensation of being drawn down into bottomless depths, opened my eyes to find myself still seated in that same section, of the ottoman in Dolores Fairfax's room. For the first moment or two I stared round me in hopeless bewilderment. To what extraordinary influence had I been subject? What fearful unimagined revelation had been made to me in that unearthly vision? And then I sprang to my feet, while a cold sweat broke from every pore as the whole horror burst upon me. She, Dolores! My promised wife!—His adopted daughter!—She whom we both loved and believed in, as we did in our God! SHE! For, I never for one moment doubted the truth of that mystic revelation that had been made to me.

Great God! Was it possible? She! That frail delicate girl, and yet the heart of a fiend! And for what purpose?

Guilty of murder! Had I not seen it all in that strange trance? The stain of blood on that hand I had been holding.

Ah! I then recollected what went before that singular visionary state I had fallen into. She was sleeping, sleeping miserably, uneasily; evidently dreaming terribly. I sat by her, and held her hand, and with this physical contact, and something in my own nervous temperament that induced it, of which I had hitherto been unaware, but which is doubtless latent in many, unsuspected by themselves, a sort of mental clairvoyance, I saw into that troubled brain beside me; saw that awful hidden picture, which sleep compelled the guilty creature to look on again, and yet again, although it maddened them. Yes! I had held her right hand in my left, while in the other I grasped the instrument that had committed that hideous unnatural crime; its very proximity (that weapon of death) had perhaps acted unconsciously on the sleeping brain, and reproduced the horror for me to read.

I staggered, and groping my way like one struck with sudden blindness, tried to reach the door; to get from under that roof, where crime sat triumphant, unsuspected, was now my sole idea.

That woman who rested at my side so short a time ago, but who had now disappeared, was somewhere in that house, and the same roof could no longer shelter us both; but the horror, the revulsion of feeling was too strong for me; I felt my senses going, and put out my hand to save myself from falling. It was the broad deep window-sill I clutched, and half-sat, half-leaned against it for a minute or two, till I somewhat recovered. Then, raising myself, I looked out across the sweet gardens of the Dingle House, where all was now growing so dusk, though the sky had cleared and brightened since I had been abroad. How peaceful, and calm, and innocent all looked; and how terrible, how frightful was the guilt that was embosomed in the midst of it; all the more terrible from its outward guise of weakness, and fragile softness, and beauty, and youth, and girlishness! How impossible, how incredible it seemed, and devoid of motive. In the first rush of my horror, I ignored and attached no meaning to the strange spell under which the central figure in that mysterious vision appeared to act; I forgot to remember that she seemed urged by some invisible demoniacal agency to the committal of the deed, though struggling against it with an anguished reluctance.

I only knew that to me had been revealed, in some occult, unaccountable manner, the mystery of my friend's death. That girl, his ward, his beloved adopted daughter, my betrothed wife, was the treacherous assassin; and there was apparently no purpose in her guilt.

Unless (and with the thought, the weight of shrinking, blood-curdling horror, that lay so heavy on me, lifted a little), madness was the key to the terrible enigma! Sudden, unexplained madness; or possibly, insanity had lurked all along, unsuspected, in that strange, silent, singular nature, and thus found expression.

Insanity may even have been hereditary; the dead man knew nothing of the girl's antecedents on the mother's side, that Spanish West Indian——

A faint ease stole over my heart—a feeling of relief almost—at this not impossible solution of the meaning of that awful tragedy which I had seen so weirdly reproduced. Insanity was frightful—a crushing, shocking calamity: but still, anything was better than cold-blooded, deliberate, treacherous murder under the circumstances.

I had got so far in my reflections when my absent gaze was caught by some moving object under the belt of trees that shut out all view of the Dingle House lawn and shrubberies from the road. How dark it was growing, and just there the shade was so dense under those spreading chestnuts I could not discern who or what it was; but I kept my eyes riveted on the spot. The object or objects were moving slowly, and I watched with a strange, instinctive watchfulness, my eyes already growing accustomed to the gloom, better able to penetrate the shadow that wrapt them round, whatever and whoever they were.

But I had not to exercise my powers of vision to any straining point; in another minute the dark something I was watching, which I felt rather than knew to be a human figure, stepped out from the shadow of the trees on to the pathway, that just there caught the last slant rays of western twilight, and I saw it was a man—presumably a gentleman from the air and figure; but even at that distance it struck me that there was something foreign in his aspect, though I should have found it difficult to define what, save, perhaps, the wide, soft, low-crowned sombrero-looking hat. And then out of the shadow stepped another figure—a shadow itself, in its clinging, black draperies. Dolores! I knew it; I felt it was coming from the moment I saw that moving something.

Here was the riddle read; the mystery solved; the motive for that heinous crime declared—a lover! a secret, unsuspected lover. And she knew the dispositions of her adopted father's property; she knew, that by his will made on her eighteenth birthday, she was constituted sole heiress of all he should die possessed of. Her apparent agreement to an engagement with me was all a blind to propitiate him, and to hide the real truth. False! False as Hell! both to him and to me. And then she and that unknown man grew impatient of that life that stood between them and what they coveted, and they stamped it out as they would crush a fly.

She may have been urged to that hideous deed by the stranger. Who was he? Where could she have met him? Surely he could not be a Cuban associate? the girl was still such a mere child when she left. But who could fathom the horrible secrecy and depravity of the human heart? Yet she seemed so pure, so guileless, and so young, and I loved her. Oh, my God, how I loved her! I now really knew for the first time how deeply she wound herself around my heart; and she had only used me as a tool to serve her wicked purpose. That young creature, a girl in the first, fresh, earliest dawn of her womanhood, had lived that life of inconceivable deceit and treachery; had kept her guilty secret unsuspected of all (it must be guilty, else why so inviolably hidden?) and now had consummated her end with deliberate, fiendish skill; with diabolical completeness and success; and, triumphant and unsuspected, would have reaped the reward of her labours (was she not reaping them even now, with him at her side, who would not have dared approach while Colonel Oswald lived?) save for that mysterious, Heaven-sent vision which had shown me all.

These thoughts flew through my distracted, maddened brain in the few seconds following my recognising Dolores Fairfax as the second figure in that dual shadow I had watched.

When I came to myself a little my first impulse was to rush forth and confront them both; but I restrained myself. Not thus would I betray my knowledge. Anything like a scene now in the grounds of the Dingle House would inevitably lead to the public disclosure of the whole horrible story, and this I determined to avoid at any cost for the sake of my dear dead friend.

It was better for him to be accused wrongfully of having committed suicide—I knew he would rather have it so—than for it to be known to all the world that the creature whom he had loved and cherished as a beloved child, who had been in all things to him as a daughter, had foully and treacherously murdered him to gain her own wicked ends. Besides, could I give up to justice the woman I had loved, however much that love had turned to loathing?

There might even be some excuse for the wretched creature that we wot not of; some uncontrollable passions inherited from that West Indian mother; some strain of madness; some strong and evil influence.

No; I would keep the terrible secret that had been revealed to me in so extraordinary a way, and none should ever dream of what I had learned save Dolores herself.

I stole quietly from the house. No one knew of my presence there save the girl, who must, when she awoke from the troublous, haunted sleep, have seen me, and, perhaps, frightened at my propinquity—remembering how she had been dreaming, and at my strange, unfamiliar aspect (I must have seemed like one in a mesmeric trance)—fled and left me in a sort of panic. Doubtless it was her departure, the withdrawal of her hand, and of herself, whose tortured brain I had been reading, that restored me to my senses. I got away by a small door in that west shrubbery, that opened into a sweet country lane, without being seen.

Those guilty creatures (for that the man had aided and abetted, and perhaps instigated the crime, I never doubted for a moment) were still on that distant pathway that skirted the lawn, and was only visible from the front of the house. My last glance showed me the two standing close together; the girl with her head drooped, and hands crossed on her breast, an attitude more of grief, despair, resignation, anything rather than satisfied, triumphant love; while the man stood over her with both hands slightly raised, as if invoking a blessing or a curse upon her bowed head.

How I got home I hardly knew. It seemed as if years had elapsed since I had trodden that familiar road, yet it was scarcely more than an hour.

I felt ill and aged, and as if part of me had died. So it had;

my heart, my faith, my trust, had been cruelly slain, and now all that was left to me was to bury my dead out of sight, and live out the remainder of my maimed, broken life as best I could.

I felt dazed and stupid owing to the strange, weird influence to which I had been subjected. What a mystery! What a miracle it was!

But as the hours went by my mind grew clearer and stronger, and I knew exactly what I had to do.

On into the night I sat writing to Dolores Fairfax. It is not necessary to set down what I wrote; it is enough to say that I told her the story of the revelation that had been made to me in so wondrous and inexplicable a manner; told her that I knew all! but that her guilty, hideous secret was safe with me, for the sake of my murdered friend, on the condition that she, and he who shared her sin—perhaps instigated it—left the Dingle House at once and for ever, making no attempt to claim the smallest portion of the heritage she had forfeited, and which to gain immediate possession of she had blackened her soul with guilt so horrible.

This was the only stipulation I made—instant removal of those desecrating presences from the home that had been Colonel Oswald's. For the rest, they might go free. I had no evidence against the man; if I had I doubt whether I should have been so merciful.

In any case, would that mysterious vision be accepted as evidence in a court of law? But I thought not of that then. All seemed to me as clear, and real, and incontrovertible as if I had witnessed the crime in the flesh.

The chill grey dawn of another day was breaking in the east when that letter was finished. It was delivered at the Dingle House before ten o'clock, and through all the long weary hours that followed, I heard nothing, though the whole day was passed by me in a concentrated anguish of suspenseful waiting. For what? I only felt dimly at the time, but now I know, it was for a complete, indignant, yet sorrowful, refutation of the whole thing, denouncing it as a wild nightmare of horror, a hideous phantasy of a diseased brain; and reproaching me in terms of despairing anguish for allowing myself for a moment to be led by a strange, unaccountable, horrible dream to believe her—Dolores—capable of such terrible monstrosity.

This was what I was expecting in a dull, vague, incoherent way. I had been assailed by many torturing doubts.

Was it a vision—a revelation, made through the agency of some mystic power, of which we know but little as yet, which just evades our grasp, but on whose long secret dwellingplace we have at last touched? And though still hovering in ignorant, tremulous, scared confusion on the threshold, we will cross that boundary line by-and-by in serene, calm security—perhaps ere another century is born—and rejoice and give thanks at having wrested still another of nature's solemn secrets from her marvellous storehouse; or was it but some tangled web of dreamland, some insidious, cheating trick of a sleeping fancy? Had some strange potent influence disclosed to me a simulacrum of what really had taken place? Or had I simply dozed as I sat in Dolores' room, and beheld these phantasmagoria of a sleeping brain? I had *not* dreamed that I found the dagger.

That, at least, was a certainty, as I still retained possession of it; but might not its very discovery, and recognising it as belonging to Dolores Fairfax, have induced the horror that followed? It did not seem natural or possible that I could have fallen asleep thus suddenly or mysteriously; but still, was not anything better to think than that to me had been revealed the truth?

* * * * * *

Thus I argued, and doubted, and worked myself into a state of partial frenzy (contending hopes and fears, wild impatience alternating with shrinking dread of news) through that weary, dreadful day. And the night fell, and still no word from that house of mystery and crime.

At last, a little after midnight, a letter was put into my hands from Dolores. The man said a boy left it who did not belong to the village. I opened it with indescribable feelings, but if I were to write for a year I should utterly fail to convey, ever so imperfectly, my sensations on reading the first few lines of that letter.

DOLORES
PART III

"YOU know it all! and I thank God from the very depths of my heart that you do know it. I am guilty, the guiltiest wretch on earth. How it has been revealed to you I know not; I only rejoice.

"Your mysterious vision (I am surrounded and encompassed, God help and pity and forgive me for a despairing, hopeless, helpless sinner, by mystery and devilry) was correct in all details. I am his murderess! I, who loved him better almost even than my own dead father. I, even I! and I can write it and not go mad. My one ray of light in the terrific darkness in which I am plunged, my one hope—if such an outcast as I with the brand of Cain on my brow, dare hope—is, that where he, my guardian is now, he knows all; everything is made clear, and that, consequently, he see that I was but the blind, helpless instrument, the anguished, reluctant agent of one who is more devil than man, of one who is the very incarnation of evil!

"When Heaven revealed to you the circumstances of this horror so miraculously, it seems sad and strange that any links in the tragic chain should have been withheld. You saw me—me, you say, in that mystic vision; I was the acting figure; but, even in your trance, you did not feel that dread and deadly influence that was upon me, compelling, enforcing, under which I might writhe, but never escape?

* * * * * *

"I was but a child of fourteen—a simple, trusting, guileless child, when that withering influence came into my life and blighted it for ever. In Cuba, about a year before my father's death, I met

Gaspar Beccarra, a very distant connection on my mother's side. I had heard of him as a marvellous, wondrous mesmerist, and was curious to know him. He did not exhibit his talents publicly, and so make money honestly and industriously; such a course would be quite too straightforward, too altogether commonplace and aboveboard for him. No! he was a gentleman, though poor, and would not degrade himself by public exhibition. His gift was great, undeniably great and wonderful, but he loved to exercise it secretly, to obtain unholy, iniquitous, horrible power over persons specially adapted to act as mediums for his extraordinary mesmeric force. He mesmerised me at our first meeting, and from that hour I was as clay in the hands of the potter; his influence over me was complete, awful, unbounded; he could do with me as he would.

"At first I thought it all delightful, only fun and frolic; all he required of me were but simple, innocent things, just to prove his power, and I was such an unsuspecting child. But as the months went by I grew to distrust him somewhat, to feel even a little frightened at his strange, unnatural influence over me, which, to my startled mind, I found by-and-by was not limited to when we were together, or in each other's presence, but was just as potent, as compelling, when separated by many miles of distance.

"This first awoke me to the horror I had brought upon myself in my daring, foolish youth. I remembered now having read somewhere that—

" 'When once a person, peculiarly constituted—peculiarly receptive of the mesmeric power—is mesmerised by a certain individual, once brought thoroughly and completely under the power of another will, he can never shake himself free of it again. It will hold him in bonds through life, mastering men's minds as disease masters their bodies.'

"And who was this man to whom I had, in my innocent unconsciousness, given this unnatural, dreadful power over me? Was he one to be trusted with the complete guidance of a young soul?—no, rather with the training of devils? That man, Arthur Wilmore (let me write that beloved name once more, and for the last time on earth! I have loved you, my Arthur, with an intense, true, devoted love, though you have thought me perhaps cold and unemotional; and I will love you so to the last hour of my life, though the idea of love from such as I am now will be doubtless abhorrent to you)—that man was, or rather is, without conscience, principle, or humanity—fiend-like, cruel, remorseless, pitiless! Ambition, self-aggrandisement, and the baser passions of man's nature are his creed! Of course, it was only by degrees that the full and dreadful significance of what I had done grew upon me; in fact, I did not thoroughly realise it while in Cuba, being too young and ignorant. But even there, during the last few months, I became utterly and entirely miserable.

"When I first discovered the strength of this power that Gaspar Beccarra exercised over me, unweakened, unaffected by distance, I begged and implored him to withdraw it; for even then instinct warned me—though he had not yet shown himself in his true colours—of what it might lead to. But he only laughed, and called me 'a foolish child.' Did I think he was 'going to part with his sweet little dual spirit, who was so submissive, obedient, and tractable? No, no; I should be his always in body and mind,' he said.

"At this time I had just completed my fifteenth year, and his manner to me had lately undergone some subtle change; something that made me shrink from him with almost loathing. He told me he loved me, and that I should be his wife, but not quite yet. I said I never should; that I would rather die first. But he only laughed again, saying I could not help myself, that he would never allow me to marry any one else, and would compel me to marry him.

"I grew to hate him as much as I feared him; and yet his power over me was so great that my father, whom I idolized, knew nothing of the unnatural bond between us. I was like the miserable bird or despairing animal fascinated by the wily serpent, conscious of its deadly danger, but helpless, powerless to break the spell that binds it captive.

"Then came those saddest months of my dear father's illness, when I was more in that demon's power than ever, when he had none to guard against; the sick chamber being alone the only sacred spot from that blighting presence. And now I began to see what terrible toils I was caught in; I began to imagine what that utter mastery of one mind over another's mind and being might lead to.

"Three times in the course of as many months I was compelled by that diabolical influence to rob my dying father; each time managing by that wondrous cunning, that extraordinary *clairvoyance* that seems, in truth, like supernatural knowledge, to arrange it so as to appear that it was the act of an old and trusted and dearly-loved servant! My father pardoned and condoned the first two thefts in memory of the past; but, when the third was discovered, the man was discharged, broken-hearted, terrified, believing he was the victim of witchcraft, glad to get away, yet despairing that his protestations of innocence were not believed. I shall never forget my sensations as I stood by and listened, and could not (for I tried) say a word in his defence.

"These commands of my satanic master were always of course performed by me in the mesmeric trance; sometimes I was quite unconscious of what I did when in this state; sometimes I knew. This latter phase was generally when I was aware of the intention beforehand, and struggled against the fate that forced me to comply. Good God! how appalled I used to get when I felt that strange, insidious unconsciousness stealing over me and knew not what it was the prelude to, knew that he was present, though I saw him not, and guessed not what evil might be wrought ere I awoke.

"A month after that last robbery, my father died, and I was alone in the world save for 'him' my guardian (a stranger then), whom I soon grew to love so truly. When I learned that I was to leave Cuba I was overjoyed. I should leave my tormentor, my evil genius behind; I did not dream that that fatal influence could pursue me across the seas; I did not dream, Gaspar Beccarra would seek, or care to retain his unholy power over an insignificant girl, scarcely more than a child, whose heritage was too small to excite even his cupidity, and whose home for the future would be in a distant land. But even then I knew not the man with whom I had to deal.

"Had I been but a beggar on the roadside I know now he would have retained me as his tool; I was too useful to allow to escape. Never again might he meet with one who, from peculiar mental organization, was so strangely receptive of the mesmeric force; never again might he meet with one with whom the relations of master and slave would be so complete. My will was his, to mould and fashion as he would, and he determined to keep his possession.

"Besides, he had managed to ascertain—short as was his stay in Cuba—that he into whose hands I passed on my father's death (my devoted guardian, my best, and truest, and dearest friend) was wealthy, unmarried, and with no near relatives; and I think, even then, there dawned in that hellish mind the first conception of the hideous plot that has been followed out to the bitter end. When we parted he told me he would be constantly with me in spirit; that no matter how great the distance that divided us, yet that his will could always bridge it; that it would be useless for me to try and keep anything secret from him, for that my mind was to him as an open book, and that he should have only to direct his thoughts to me, wherever I might be, and I should perforce answer to the call; that the same compelling power would enforce my obedience here, there, anywhere.

"From this method of communication existing between us there would be no necessity for many letters; but he insisted on a certain amount of correspondence, and I left Cuba with the feeling that has been with me ever since, save during the first few blessed months of my engagement to you, that that fell presence was ever at my side, that my most inner sacred thoughts were no longer my own; I was in a constant, mental attitude of expectation."

(*This* accounted for all I had ever seen peculiar in the girl; the strange stillness and sense of watching, waiting, in her manner; the peculiar expression in her eyes, as of looking at something beyond, outside the present.)

"When we were together, you and I, my Arthur" (so continued this fearful letter) "how often have I felt that third occult presence listening with spirit ears, watching with spirit eyes, dominating over all, yet not subjugating me utterly, not throwing me into the helpless mesmeric trance, only letting me know that he was there always—watching.

"During those four years I have been in England he has forced me to no crime till now. With this foulest, deadliest end in view—as I firmly believe it was from the first—he could afford to wait.

"I began to grow more easy, more sanguine. I grew to think that possibly never in my life should I cease to be linked to this strange, spiritual bondage, yet that the power for evil over me was mitigated; and after our engagement I became so hopeful, so happy, ay, God help me! so blissfully happy, each day, that influence seemed to dwindle and fade, till I got to look on it at last as some fearful dream that was over and past. To account for this I cannot, unless that your dear influence of love and tenderness so encompassed me that for a time it cast out that other. You may have a touch of that mysterious power, unguessed by yourself or others, which you used unconsciously in a dual warfare with that distant will; or, again, which I believe is the true solution, that for a time just then Gaspar Beccarra was engaged with other interests, pursuing some other evil end, which required all his force of will, and that he let me flutter free for a space, only to dominate and master me all the more cruelly after a little. You surely must have seen the terrible change in me. I tried to oppose, to defy, that insidious subjugating power, but I could no more resist its baleful, malignant influence than I could scale the walls of heaven; and when I knew he was coming to England all hope forsook me, the nearer in body the more deadly the mental grip.

"Before he reached London he had made himself fully acquainted with all circumstances connected with my life here, knew that I was constituted Colonel Oswald's sole heiress. You know how I combatted this determination on my beloved guardian's part; from the moment he had decided on thus enriching me, a hideous fear clutched my heart; I instinctively felt what might be the result; though even still my imagination failed to grasp the appalling horror that was coming, that I should be the instrument chosen to——

* * * * * *

"Great God! how can I think of it and live? and I tried my best to die, I swear it, Arthur Wilmore, by all that is most sacred!

"I determined to take my own life when I learned what awful office lay before me. Twice I endeavoured to do so, but each time was plucked from death's welcome embrace by that fatal mesmeric power. He knew my intentions and frustrated them.

"He came to Brenton two months ago, and took up his abode there, and thus, only four miles off, I was more his abject slave than ever. You know the rest—I can write no more.

"I go out from here at your bidding—into the cold, cruel, pitiless world, a despairing, desperate woman, reckless of the future, as the only good it can bring me is death, which I hourly pray may speedily deliver me. May the Almighty God ever bless and keep you, and lead you in the dim, distant days, when she who writes these words has long been dust, to think with pity and clemency—rather than the horror and hatred you now feel—of wretched

"DOLORES FAIRFAX"

Long before I had finished this letter (which I have quoted word for word) my heart yearned over the unhappy, miserable girl on whom so terrible a fate had fallen. Poor, struggling, innocent captive, caught in so diabolical a mesh of mystery and guilt! But she should be freed from such an unnatural, hellish yoke, and I would be her liberator. This letter should be given to the public; the horrible influence under which the girl had acted be made known; I would sacrifice everything to bring his devilries home to him; I would even go to Cuba myself, were it necessary. While he lived and was abroad in the world, Dolores would not be safe. She should be rescued at any cost, and before more evil was wrought.

I read the letter again and again, and pondered long and deeply over it.

The primary conclusion that my meditations reached was that I must take immediate steps to prevent Dolores from leaving Glenore. To keep her where I could watch over her till I could gather evidence enough against Baccarra to warrant his arrest, this must be my first care, and she might purpose leaving the Dingle House at once. Her words seemed to imply as much.

When I roused myself to external things, I found that it was already morning; the night had gone while I was pouring over that strange, terrible letter. I would lose no time. I went to my room, bathed, and changed my dress, which in some degree refreshed me after my sleepless, miserable night, and started for the Dingle House. I was there before half-past seven, but I knew the household would be astir, and I was right; it was not only astir, but dismay and scared uneasiness reigned within. Mills was just about to start for the Manor to seek my help and tell me what had occurred.

"Half an hour previous," panted Mrs. Joyce in breathless agitation, "the housemaid had occasion to pass through the corridor, on which opened the best bedrooms; seeing Miss Fairfax's door partly open, and feeling rather surprised at her being up and about so early, the girl glanced in with a sort of idle curiosity, but was astonished to find the bed had not been slept in, nor the room apparently tenanted since she had tidied it on the previous morning, save that a drawer or two stood open with the contents scattered about, as if something had been hastily looked for, and from the *armoire* was missing Miss Dolores' fur-lined cloak. She would scarce need that for an early morning ramble in the grounds, besides, the fact remained, that she had not been to bed all night.

"And, oh, sir," gasped the good woman in distracted, incoherent conclusion, "what do you think's come to her? Perhaps it's murdered after all Colonel Oswald, my dear master, was, and that now the villains have come and killed my sweet Miss Dolores; but where have they put her? Have they carried off her poor murdered body so that we shan't have even the comfort of burying her decently like a christian lady?"

I could scarcely restrain my impatience while the poor frightened woman raved on thus disjointedly. I knew how it all was. I knew that it was at my bidding Dolores Fairfax had gone out from that sheltering roof; that it was at my bidding she had gone forth to meet the world destitute of all that she had a right to claim; for even her own individual possessions remained behind, as I learned later, save a very few articles of necessary clothing.

That it was at my bidding she went thus out, helpless, unprotected, reckless, despairing, to be at the mercy of that man, who would now, owing to the total wreck and failure of his fiendish scheme, be filled with a deadly vengeance.

She had gone, and I had sent her. But who could think she would have gone so soon? Heaven knows I lost no time after reading that letter. She must have but a very few hours start; I would still be in time to save her. She must be only in Brenton. When had they seen her last, I questioned eagerly, and the housekeeper continued her broken narrative.

"All yesterday Miss Dolores remained in her own little sitting-room, writing all the time. She dined as usual at six o'clock, or at least pretended to dine, it wasn't much more than that with her lately, poor lamb. She hardly ate what would keep a sparrow alive, and then asked that a cup of tea might be brought up to her immediately, as she had a dreadful headache, and would go to her room early, and wished not to be disturbed, and that was the last, sir, any of us saw her. When Bessie brought her that cup of tea at a quarter to seven, she had then gone back to her writing. The house was shut up as usual at ten o'clock, every door and window fastened, and we were all in bed before eleven; but when Mills came down this morning at half-past six, he found one of the drawing-room windows open"—they were but three feet from the ground—"and the door in the west shrubbery, which had been carefully locked, on the latch, and the Lord in Heaven only knows what awful thing has happened to our blessed young lady. If she is alive, and in the power of murdering men, may the good God help and pity the poor desolate lassie, is the earnest prayer of Martha Joyce," sobbed the old woman, and I, knowing all, fervently echoed her supplication.

Mills and I went straight to Brenton, but though we spent the whole day in eager, unremitting search, and engaged the services of the police to help us, we failed to come upon any trace of Dolores. If she entered Brenton, no one seemed to have seen or heard of her; inquiries at the railway-station and at the outlying villages elicited but the same response. It seemed as if the earth had opened and swallowed her.

Gaspar Beccarra we tracked to a quiet lodging in an obscure part of the town; he called himself "Bassanno," but I felt convinced from other particulars that it was the same man. He occupied the rooms for nearly a month but had left these four or five weeks, and nothing was known of his present whereabouts. We returned to Glenore late into the evening, heartsick and exhausted after our fruitless labours. I had telegraphed to —— for a detective, for I despaired of doing anything by myself; he could not be with me before noon next day, and, in the meantime, I was obliged to resign myself to inaction, and to seek the rest I needed so sadly, not having lain down these two nights.

But I had scarcely awoke the next morning, when a sudden

thought flashed upon me like an illumination. I had thought only of Brenton, naturally, on the previous day; but I now remembered that, by walking many miles in another direction, another town might be reached, larger, and that led more directly to London; and any one, very determined to get away, and desiring not to be tracked or traced, might choose this more unlikely route. And yet, was it probable that a tender, delicate girl like Dolores would have the courage, the strength to face ten weary miles alone in the darkness? for she must have travelled through the night, else some one would have seen her on the road; but no one can guess what one driven to desperation may not attempt. Possibly to avoid Beccarra was her great and chief care. He may have been lurking in Brenton unknown to the woman he had formerly lodged with, unknown to any of those whom I had questioned; his presence in the Dingle House gardens on the evening before Dolores' departure, argued his being in the near neighbourhood; and his unfortunate, struggling, trapped victim may have made one last despairing effort to elude his clutches.

I dressed hastily and set off for Durrow, the first village on the road leading to that distant town.

Durrow was just a mile-and-a-half from Glenore, and I hoped to hear something of the wanderer on this first stage of her night journey. And I was rewarded; I did hear something, though not very much.

On the night but one previous, at about a quarter to twelve o'clock, a lady, wrapped in a heavy cloak, and with a thick veil, came into the village which was all shut up save the forge, that was open and alight still. She stopped in the centre of brightness thrown out by it on the dark road, though she did not come near for them to see her rightly, and, in any case, the man I spoke to admitted that he was not familiar with the appearance of the young lady from the Dingle House. She called a young lad who was loitering at the door of the forge, and asked him, would he take a letter for her at once to Glenore, to the Manor House, for which she would give him half-a-sovereign; he delightedly agreed. She said he must go as quickly as possible, that no answer to the letter was needed, that he was not to answer any questions that might be asked, but to run back to her as soon as he delivered the letter, when she would give him the money promised.

"Young Rob was off like the wind," continued the blacksmith, "and the lady sat herself down on that there bench, right away in the shade, so that none could see her, and waited patiently; and I thought it was a lonesome thing for a lady, old or young, and this one seemed young by her voice, to be abroad all by her own self at that time of the night.

"Rob was back again afore a body could scarce think he was there; them three miles were shorter to him then than three miles had ever been afore.

"She thanked him quite sweet and grateful like, and put the gold into his hand (he's been like one crazy since, he'd never so much in his life afore together!) and said good-night, and stepped out into the darkness as brave a little woman as ever walked; and I do hope, sir, that a lady like her is not in any trouble."

Here I found her, without doubt, but here also, I lost her! At none of the other intervening villages had she been seen, which was only to be expected through those small hours of the night; and Grantham was so large and busy and bustling that one quiet woman more or less in its streets or at its railway station would escape observation.

The first London train went at six. By that, the porters present at its departure, stoutly affirmed that no one answering to my description had travelled. There were generally very few going by that train, and the station was deserted, and they remembered those who started the previous morning; but the next train that went at nine there was always a rush for, many travelling by it, and another train just in and emptying itself at the same time, so that it was all fuss and confusion, and no one would be noticed in the general scramble.

Yes; here I was brought up short. That Dolores reached Grantham and went by the London train I had no doubt. Very possibly she purposely waited for that which started at nine, feeling she would be comparatively sure to escape observation then. Poor, lonely, distracted soul wandering about somewhere in the immediate neighbourhood of the town, weary, broken-hearted and exhausted, till it was time to start; how my heart bled for her.

But still I had no proof, and the detective I employed failed as signally as myself. After being seen at midnight at Durrow she had virtually disappeared. It seemed almost like another evidence of the weird, occult, deadly influence that possessed her life. She had vanished and left no sign. Of Beccarra also we could find absolutely no trace. There was mystery surely in such sudden total disappearances. I prosecuted the search for months without avail. I wrote to Cuba, to addresses there that I found amongst my dear murdered friend's papers, but could hear no tidings of those whom I sought.

Beccarra had sailed for Europe more than a year before, but nothing was known of his destination there; he had not returned to the Island, neither had Dolores Fairfax been seen since she left for England with her guardian Colonel Oswald. This was nearly six months after the September night in which I received that memorable terrible letter. All these weary months I had mourned in bitter secret, that mine were the words that had sent the girl out to some horrible, unimaginable fate. I had bidden her go, and she had gone, and been absorbed into some mysterious impenetrable abyss of darkness and unknowingness, where wizard devilry and unearthly power defied all merely human effort to discover her.

What an appalling deadly power was mesmerism! I had never realised before the full horror, the awfulness of any one creature gifted with this strange unnatural force, holding another life and soul in these magnetic bonds, and moulding and fashioning that life, or perhaps lives, as it pleased them. Surely it was contrary to all the laws of God and man. And yet, it could not be reached by the latter. The law was as powerless in matters that skirted the region of what men still call the "supernatural." as is a little child.

* * * * * *

In March I discontinued the search that I had prosecuted without a break through all those long hopeless months. Heart-sick, heart-broken, for I never knew until I lost her how much my life had been bound up in Dolores Fairfax, I returned to my lonely Manor to try to take up the thread of my broken, sorrow-stricken life. I had nothing in the world left to live for now save the good of my people, and I would make an effort, during whatever term of years remained to me, to brighten other lives though my own was sunk in gloom. The owner of a large estate has great and serious responsibilities, and I would take them up and wear them and do my duty though my heart was dead.

The one thing I craved for was certain news of Dolores. To know, absolutely know, that she was no longer amongst the living would be an unspeakable relief. Anything would be a thousand times better than the terrible suspense and dread; imagining her enduring all manner of horrors, being compelled to perpetrate all manner of crimes, unable to escape from that terrible bondage. And this yearning desire of my heart was granted, and in this wise:—

On the morning of the 15th of August, exactly a year and a day since the date of the Dingle House tragedy, as I sat in my study, going over some accounts with my agent, with wandering, absent thoughts—increased depression of spirits on the previous day, the *first* most melancholy anniversary of Frank Oswald's death, being not calculated to stimulate my business faculties—Rawlins, my faithful old butler, entered hastily, flushed and eager looking, to say that a man from the village had just told him that someone must have got into the Dingle House, as, when he passed it by an hour before, feeling curious like to see the place again where that dreadful thing happened just a year ago, he went up the lane, on which that door in the west shrubbery opened, intending to climb up a bit and look over the wall; but to his astonishment the door was ajar. He felt scared like, knowing how the place had been fastened up since Miss Fairfax's disappearance, and was going to run away, when he thought he'd look a little farther first; so, pushing the door open a bit, he saw what really frightened him.

The windows of the study, one of which stood open on that fatal night a year ago, were nearly opposite that small door, and once again that same window was open, the shutters unclosed, the blinds up. Feeling sure there were either robbers or a ghost in the house—he inclined to the latter belief—Rawlins said he ran to the Manor as fast as he could, thinking I ought to know. But though he spoke of ghosts and burglars I could see the trembling, excited old man had been struck with the same thought as myself—that Dolores herself had returned, as I had always hoped and prayed she might; though how she could make a forcible entry into the shut-up house I did not then stop to determine.

I seized my hat, and, delaying only to summon Mills, whom I had taken into my service, as the faithful fellow could not bear to leave the neighbourhood until he had ascertained something definite of the fate of his beloved master's ward—I need not say that he guessed nothing of the real facts; that awful secret was locked for ever in my own breast—I hastened with all speed to the Dingle House, which had remained untenanted during the last year, and was likely to remain so, as few would now care to take it after the unenviable notoriety it had acquired.

It had been let "furnished" to Colonel Oswald, and was now exactly as he occupied it, save that his personal belongings had been removed by me to the Manor, pending the decision of his solicitors as to what was to be done with his property, failing all near relatives, and when they had quite given up its ever being claimed by the legal heir, his ward and legatee, Dolores Fairfax.

Yes, the house remained quite the same, only it had been locked and barred and bolted against all invaders; and how it had been entered now seemed little short of a mystery. There was no evidence of force or violence; that little door in the west shrubbery had been simply opened by someone who possessed a key, that was all.

And it was with a slight catch in my breath, and a sense of eeriness, that I entered the shrubbery, with Mills at my side, practical and indignant, believing only in unlawful intruders. Yes, there were the windows, and one of them with the shutters thrown back, and open!

For a moment I stood irresolute, then, with a few rapid strides, I was by that window and my head within the room.

Ah! it was even so! I now felt that I had been expecting it all along, dimly, shrinkingly, instinctively.

The tragedy was played out to its bitterest end. Within that room, upon that fatal sofa, lay Dolores Fairfax—dead, and dead by her own hand.

"Murder or suicide," Glenore had contended, and now it was both. The shadow of each sin lay upon the Dingle House for evermore. Yes, there Dolores lay dead, in the flower of her youth as to years; a withered, worn, wasted woman as to looks. Great God! what had been the girl's experience during those months—less than a year—to work so terrible a change in one so young? What horrors had those poor, haggard, staring eyes gazed upon? What despairing sorrows and miseries unimaginable had hollowed and wrinkled those soft cheeks, and furrowed that pure, smooth brow? She was worn to a shadow, fearfully, awfully emaciated. And what final desperation of despair induced this last act? The poor, writhing, tortured soul was at last at rest, had at last found peace, had broken defiantly and for ever from the bonds of its hellish tormentor. "Thank God!" was the involuntary exclamation that rose from my heart to my lips as I stood and gazed on the dead girl.

Yes, thank God! and I did not feel afraid to repeat it. If the Great and All-Merciful Father whose knowledge is infinite, and compassion unbounded, the God of the Christian, whose other name is "Love," ever condoned that one daring, unrepentable sin, ever forgave it fully and freely, surely it would be now. This, His creature, a weak, helpless woman, had been goaded beyond endurance; not merely made to endure physical suffering and distress—that she might have little recked—but forced to blackest, deadliest crime; and to escape this hideous network that enclosed and encompassed her, and wound around her as the python's deadly coils, she flew to the one refuge that she knew would not, could not fail her, and was at last free.

There she lay dead at twenty years of age. This was the end of that young life that promised so fairly; and brief as it had been, and early as was its close, what a volume of horrible, unnatural suffering was there written!

And now that awful book was ended; that fearful tale told. The contents of that small phial fallen from the stiffened fingers had written "finis" on the last of those short, dark pages swiftly and well, and all was peace for evermore.

She had recaptured her soul which Beccarra, the mesmerist, had possessed himself of for a space, and gone straight with it to her God, where she knew it and she would be safe for ever. And, as is nearly always the case in this weary, sinful world, she, the innocent, the good, the guiltless (was she not pure as unsullied snow, from even all thought of evil? Had she not been forced to these terrible acts by a power stronger than herself? that she could no more combat with than she could wrestle with and subdue the tempest) had suffered unknown and indescribable torture of body and spirit; while he, that flesh-clad satan, probably knew no evil in his earthly days, and passed on to find fresh victims and bind fresh hellish bonds around them.

* * * * * *

I strained every nerve to find him, to follow him up, so as to bring home to him some of his devilries—those deeds that the dastard caused others to commit so that he might go unsuspected—but I failed utterly and entirely. Gaspar Beccarra was never anything but a name to me. I thought I came upon his track two or three times, but if I did he eluded me, and we have never stood face to face, and I feel convinced never shall. The very insidious horrible power he possesses doubtless warns him of the approach of danger.

It is a power that thus developed, would completely defeat the ends of justice; would allow crime to stalk unsuspected, unpunished through the length and breadth of the land; would allow secret, unaccountable murders to multiply mysteriously. It is a power unholy, horrible, and yet how diligently we seek to cultivate it at the present day, how intensely interested we are in its mildest manifestations. These mild manifestations of the mesmeric power are, we must admit, harmless, perhaps even in some cases good and blessed; as an anodyne it is a boon indeed, and its study ought to be carefully considered by the faculty. But it may lurk in deadly strength in some individuals of which they are themselves unconscious (that almost all temperaments of the nervous imaginative order possess the force in some degree, we are persuaded) and when revealed to them by chance, what unrighteous use may they not make of this weird and terrible influence?

The preceding story puts this very clearly before the reader, and may serve as a slight, though very ineffectual, we fear, warning not to allow anyone to exercise this singular power over them, till they know very thoroughly to whom they are going to give even a temporary mastery over their mind and will.

We none of us know which of us may prove a "Dolores Fairfax" in our dangerous receptivity of, or yielding to, this occult force, or when we may meet a "Gaspar Beccarra" in his unscrupulous use of his deadly gift.

LOVE STRONGER THAN DEATH

A MYSTERY, IN FIVE PARTS

"A spirit passed before my face,
The hair of my flesh rose up."
JOB 4:15

"We are such stuff
As dreams are made of, our little life
Is rounded with a sleep."
WILLIAM SHAKESPEARE

LOVE STRONGER THAN DEATH

PART I

"Love took up the harp of Life and smote
On all the chords with might;
Smote the chord of Self, that trembling,
Pass'd in music out of sight."[19]

YES, it is a great and bitter sorrow to Norah Desmond, for she is a true, pure, high-souled girl, and shrinks with absolute pain and unmerited self-reproach from what woman of less noble nature might perchance glory in.

Norah loves and is beloved, and was utterly content, though, at times of late, a little anxious about him who has her heart in his keeping; but to-day she learned accidentally, with a shock of grieved astonishment, that she has unconsciously won the deep and faithful affection of her lover's twin brother. She has no occasion to feel either remorse or self-reproach, as she never even imagined such a thing could be, much less has she acted in any way to bring it about. She was sweet, and frank, and natural, as was her wont, feeling that Brian's brother was almost her brother too, and now this wretched unhappiness has come, and the girl feels as if all the joy had died out of her life with the suddenly acquired knowledge of Bernard's jealously guarded secret.

Bernard loves Norah, his brother's betrothed; has doubtless loved her all along; though loyalty and devotion to that brother

---

[19] From 'Locksley Hall' by Alfred, Lord Tennyson.

forbade his betraying it even long ago, when she was free to be won by either. From the first hour of their meeting Brian had showed a preference for her, and Bernard seeing this, kept aloof, though of the two, in the beginning of their acquaintance, she had almost been inclined to like him best; he was so true, so steadfast, so self-sacrificing, so altogether and utterly good. But it was otherwise written. Brian carried all before him with his passionate wooing; he was a true Irish lover, ardent, enthusiastic, eager, and thoroughly genuine, and Norah's whole soul went out to the younger brother, younger by half-an-hour, and her little vague, half unconscious fancy for the other died, and was forgotten in the overpowering sweetness of the love story that had come with so vigorous a rush into her life.

But with the light of the discovery she has made to-day, many little things in the past, hardly noticed at the time, but which she now can vividly recall, are made clear; words, and looks, and tones of Bernard's, scarce definable, all bear the one translation: he loves her, has loved her all these long long months, though he has made no sign, and would have made no sign until the end, only for this most wretched accident of this September afternoon.

And she thinks, with a pang of heartfelt sorrow, that since the open avowal of her engagement to Brian, now some eight or nine months since, Bernard's health has seemed to droop; never quite so robust or vigorous as Brian, though apparently strong and well enough before, he has gradually, almost imperceptibly, grown older, weary, worn-looking; the extraordinary likeness between the brothers is no longer quite so startling as of old, a gravity and sadness of expression has grown habitual to the dark interesting face; the kind brown eyes are hollow, and there are grey threads among those close-cut curly locks, for which his two-and-thirty years are scarcely responsible. The tall manly figure too has surely grown a little stooped, and the step slower and less buoyant. Yes, Bernard is changed; either his health is impaired, and he suffers physically, though he breathes no complaint; or mental distress has wrought the difference, and what affects the body so terribly as illness of the mind? Sorrow, disappointment, mind misery of any kind does its deadly work quite effectually, perhaps even more perfectly than bodily ailments. Nature's genial laboratory is blasted, she has neither strength nor care to recuperate her forces, to work her silent mystic operations that tend to the one grand result—health. Disease is in many cases shaken off by the ardent desire for life; with mental trouble disease is induced by the utter failure of this desire, and so comes the end.

* * * * * *

More than a year and a half previously Norah and her father had come to the wild west coast of Ireland from the south. Mr. Desmond is a clergyman: earnest, zealous, devoted to his high and sacred calling, with a lofty, pure ideal of what a minister's life and work ought to be.

He came to this remote western parish—where his flock is but a handful, scattered far and wide—cheerfully and with a glad heart to do his Master's service, however humble the vineyard, though he is fitted by intellectuality of a highly cultivated order to be a "burning and a shining light" in fashionable city churches, where he would be looked upon as a star of the first magnitude in the preaching world. From the damp, enervating climate of the South, with its tame, quiet coast scenery, they came to this home of boisterous, bracing winds, this Connaught fastness, this wondrous seascape.

Wild, grand, majestic, with a sort of savage beauty all its own; our other coast lines seem commonplace as compared with these far western shores of Connemara, these Irish highlands, that look out on those rushing, leaping waters.

An awe fills one's breast, coupled with a passionate joy, if one is a true and earnest lover of the sea, when one climbs the surrounding heights and gazes out upon that vast, tossing, surging ocean. Such waves as the Atlantic alone knows, come racing in; mighty billows, with their snowy crests aloft, and they thunder on the terrible cliffs that lie so far below as to seem dwarfed. Yes, in the fierce, harsh winter and the unruly spring these Western shores stand almost unrivalled for those who love to look on the sea in its wrath, when these storm-tossed waters tear in upon the shrinking coast after mad and furious contests beyond where eyes can see. And even when the gaze is turned inland, this wildest west loses not in originality. Endless rushing rivers; countless lonely lakes; wild ravines; thousands of acres of bog and moor land; and always the shadow of the everlasting hills; sublime, grand, solemn scenery here; bleak, barren desolation there; and anon, sweet, green, fair and peaceful as a tranquil dream.

In this strange yet lovely place, Norah and her father have found a home for nearly two years; and here the clergyman has found the health he had been losing steadily in the relaxing South, and to the girl have come the love and joy and now the sorrow of her young life. Some few months after the Desmonds settled in ——, they made acquaintance with the brothers St. Lawrence. Bernard, the elder, is a doctor, with a large, straggling, unremunerative practice; he is too devoted to his work—too compassionate and unselfish to allow it to be remunerative; he attends the poor—from whom he can hope for no reward whatever—as sedulously, with as much eager zeal and Kindly interest as the best paying patients in the district. He cheerfully and without reproach forgives debts that might fairly be paid with perhaps a little strain on the part of the debtor; and, as the world—his small local world—says of him, with a tinge of disparagement and contemptuous pity in its tones, that "Bernard St. Lawrence has quite too good and kindly a heart ever to be anything but a poor man;" not that he is solely dependent on his profession, if so, he would be poor indeed; both brothers have small independent incomes that would permit them to live without toil of any kind, but they prefer work to idleness, and Bernard's is anxious, arduous work, that entails much self-sacrifice; but he loves it, and until he knew Norah Desmond he was as happy as his sympathetic, tender heart would let him be in a world where pain and sorrow outweigh so grievously the measure of happiness and joy.

Brian is a solicitor with a fairly large clientele; quite lately the exigencies of his increasing business obliged him to establish an office in Dublin, where he placed a trustworthy managing clerk, and all went smoothy for a time. Brian was too much in love, or, at least, too passionately eager and restless while he was still in doubt as to the success of his love, still uncertain as to the state of Norah's feelings towards himself, to care to leave Connemara just then, and so deputed this reliable agent to conduct his Dublin business. But when he had "put it to the touch" and "won all;" when he had assured himself beyond all suspicion of doubt that Norah was his utterly and alone, that the girl had not a wish, thought, hope in life unconnected with him, that he need fear no rivals now or ever, in that pure, true, steadfast heart; why, then, though his love was strong and ardent as ever, yet he felt secure, confident he could afford to relax his somewhat pugnacious, vigilant watchfulness of all men with whom Norah came in contact, he no longer feared a possible favoured suitor turning up suddenly from the South, or anywhere else on the face of the globe! and so, about three months after their betrothal (Norah stipulated for a year's engagement), having an intricate case just then in the Courts, he went up himself to town to conduct it, and in the six months' interval that has passed since then, he has spent the greater portion of his time in Dublin.

And Bernard, in addition to his own private trouble, which none suspected till to-day, when in an unguarded moment he betrayed the secret he hoped would die with him, has had much uneasiness and anxiety about his brother. Brian has fallen unhappily in with a somewhat wild set in town, addicted to gambling, a vice which the St. Lawrences have especial reason to dread, as some ten years ago, their father's brother, an army colonel, a grave, honourable man, nearly sixty years old, who had never gambled in his life, was laid under the diabolical spell of the green tables at Monte Carlo, lost everything he possessed, and blew out his brains in the Kursaal gardens, those lovely gardens that have been the scene of so many a heart-rending self-murder during these latter days. And Brian, though so strong and brave physically, is morally weak, as Bernard knows, easily tempted, easily led, at least where his own inclination may tend; and the unholy fascination exercised by play which dominates the man and subdues him, making him its slave, would be apt to work its Circe-like influence upon his brother's excitable, impetuous nature.

Already Bernard had reason to fear that Brian had plunged somewhat deeply into that fell whirlpool, which so often sucks its victims under, never to reappear. On his last two brief visits to the West he had seemed ill at ease, absent, restless, looked careworn and anxious, like a man who had some mental trouble, and appeared to wish to avoid close communion with his brother. Bernard is terribly grieved, he feels instinctively, even apart from what he has heard from a reliable source, that Brian is involved, perhaps seriously already, and what misery may not this new and overwhelming passion lead to in the end? What sorrow lies in the future, not only for the brother whom he passionately loves, with that strange mystic affection said to exist between twins, but for her, the woman who has come into both their lives, sweetening and blessing and perfecting one, as he has hoped and prayed in his noble self-abnegation; though the same gracious presence has cast the withering shadow of an unconquerable, undying grief and despair over the other.

Is Norah—sweet, trusting, innocent Norah—to have a gambler for a husband? Thus, torn by torturing, conflicting thoughts, he has forgotten himself to-day, forgotten the prudence, the restraint with which he ever armed himself in his intercourse with Norah, forgot all when the woman he loved had been just marvellously spared a terrific death.

Coming over these mighty grass-crowned cliffs together; he, from seeing a distant patient, poor and ungrateful, who only murmured and complained, rebelling against the evil fate that had overtaken them in illness, with never a "thank you" for the man who tried his best with earnest endeavour, and gentle, tender patience to alleviate the suffering for which there was no cure; she, from a long dawdling stroll over those gorse-clad hills, they met and sauntered on together, talking of Brian. Bernard trying to guard two secrets instead of one, for Norah suspected nothing as yet of the cause of the change in her lover.

That there was a change of some kind, vague and indefinite, she had been dimly aware the last month or two. It had made her a little unhappy and anxious; not that he was less loving in his manner when they met, or that his written expressions of affection were cooler. No, nothing of that kind troubled her. His notes were, if possible, more intensely lover-like, his endearing epithets more ardent; but they were brief, and spoke of little but his love. When together he seemed passionately happy in her society, yet he was often absent, silent, and even gloomy, and she felt sure he had something on his mind.

To-day she questioned Bernard; but he, in the unselfish devotion that would spare her all pain, while he bore double tides, laughed off her nervously uttered apprehensions.

Brian had had one or two cases lately that had worried and bothered him a good deal, and when a man has anxious law-business on hand, with the almost certainty of failing to win his client's cause, he may be excused if he seems a little *distrait*, and even gloomy.[20] And then they climbed a still higher shoulder of the hill that they had to scale before they could descend on the other side, and there, on the crown and sloping brow of this giant cliff—sloping for a dozen yards or so, and then a sheer and terrible descent to the sea—grew a belt of delicious greenest grass, unlike the coarse, scant covering of these barren uplands, and here and there scattered on this verdant carpet were rich brilliant patches of wild pansies.

With a little cry of delight Norah flew to that smooth, smiling, sloping edge that seemed so secure. Surely that greenest turf was soft and safe as velvet; surely on that gentle incline, that gradual easy descent, the frail and infirm might walk with security, not to speak of young agile steps; and over that grass-crowned edge Norah walks in perfect confidence.

"For God's sake come back, Norah, that grass is as slippery as ice!" cries Bernard in terrified tones, racing wildly as he speaks, from

[20] *Distrait*: distracted.

the spot where he had lingered a moment, gazing sadly at a little dead thrush, his heart being infinitely tender for all God's creatures.

But the warning comes too late; even as he shouts, the girl's feet glide from under her, she grasps frantically at—nothing! throws herself on the ground, clutching violently, desperately at that treacherous grass that has been her undoing; one wild, awful scream rends the air, and in a moment she has disappeared; disappeared over that distant terrible edge, and Bernard, with a frantic horror in his breast, gazes down that smiling, sun-kissed slope with aghast straining eyes. This instant she was there, so near, and now——

For a moment he feels as if he were dying, so terrible is the shock. He puts his hand involuntarily to his heart, while a strange grey hue spreads itself over his features; but he conquers the awful weakness that nearly subjugates him. He knows well the horribly treacherous nature of those cliff slopes; he knows that to try to follow where Norah has disappeared would be only certainly to incur a similar fate, and so lose any possibility there may be of succouring the girl.

There is one chance still for Norah, and only one. Bernard knows that on this particular cliff, about ten feet below where that sloping, smooth descent suddenly terminates, is a narrow horizontal ledge, or natural path, about seven feet wide, from which the cruel cliff wall falls away in a sheer precipitous descent to the sea, nearly three hundred feet below. If the girl has fallen on this path, if the impetus of her roll was broken sufficiently by her wild clutchings at that glass-like herbage to prevent her pitching off that narrow path with a rebound into the awful void beyond, why then she might have escaped; escaped death at least, though serious injury may be her portion. And with this one frail lingering hope, Bernard starts to reach that ledge as quickly as he can, with still that awful ashen pallor on his face, and a terrible look of tension almost distorting his features.

Swiftly as he speeds, it is a long way he has to go round to attain in safety that perilous path; each moment seems an hour. He is haunted by the terrible fear that even if Norah, by God's infinite mercy, has fallen on that ledge, insensible, as she is sure to be from agonising terror alone, and that she begins to come to herself before he reaches her, in her first half-unconscious movements she may roll over that fearful edge, which she must perforce be so near, and plunge into death and eternity! And with this wild distracting horror in his heart he flies round the curve that reveals to him that little strange cliff path, and there, not twenty yards distant lies the girl on the very brink of that awful gulf—motionless—and safe!

For a few moments Bernard St. Lawrence is almost mad; he scarcely knows what he says or does; the reaction from that ghastly torturing fear is so great, the relief so mighty. He flings himself upon his knees beside the girl in a passion of gratitude, raising the still white face against his shoulder.

"Great God! I thank thee for thy wondrous mercy!" he cries; "she is saved—saved! My Norah, my darling, my love, the one and only love of my life! For these few moments you are all mine; and now that I have held you so, and kissed your lips" (here he bends his head, and with infinite tenderness, presses a lingering kiss on the pale unresponsive lips), "I could die with a happy, grateful heart. Aye! should be glad, glad to die, for the strain is too great and may snap any day. Merciful Father! Thou hast saved her now from a deadly physical peril, save her in the time to come from what may be even worse than——. Thank God, dear, you are all right," with a quick change of manner, pulling himself together with an intense effort, as the lovely grey eyes slowly open, and the wild rose bloom steals back faintly into the soft cheeks. "You've had a marvellous escape, Norah; you're nearly dead with terror, child, and I've been half frantic. I'll carry you round to the open ground, and then you can tell me are you hurt, or only shaken."

The girl shrinks back as he stoops to lift her, but he does not seem to notice, and she feels too weak to make any decided resistance, and along that narrow path at that giddy altitude they go; and the only time the girl dares to unclose her eyes, an overpowering, sickening shudder at that frightful gulf below make her unconsciously cling to him for a brief moment, but it is only for a moment, and then they reach the safe wide green expanse of upland again, and he gently puts her down, asking her whether she feels hurt.

"No, I think not," she responds, in a slow, dazed fashion. "I thought it was death when I felt myself slipping down that fearful place over the edge. Real death could not be half so awful, I think. I might as well have died that moment; it was all the same to me as if I had. I knew nothing more, and if I had gone down all the way to the sea," with a terrible shudder, "I should never have known. I think I owe my life to you. I daresay I should have rolled off that ledge in another minute or so; but I won't try to thank you now, Bernard," with a sickly little smile; "I must wait till I feel a little stronger."

"But have you no pain, Norah? No wrench or twist?"

"This arm feels a good deal strained, and I am generally stiff and bruised, but otherwise I think I'm all right. I'm really sorry to have given you such a scare," and taking her hat and sunshade, which he held, in a hurried, confused, nervous manner, she started off for home abruptly, though she was still trembling and faint from her fall. But Bernard was too utterly unhinged and upset himself to notice the constraint in her manner, or the silence that fell between them as they walked; in fact, he could not talk in the matter-of-course, indifferent fashion of their ordinary intercourse. The strong emotion he had lately yielded to lay upon him heavily, and he walked on as a man in a dream, taking refuge in dumbness, afraid to trust his voice in speech, lest the tide of love, now rushing so strong within (that terribly sweet kiss, that clasping of the woman he loved to his breast, had sadly weakened his self-control) should again find utterance, to the eternal death of his honour. He was already shocked and ashamed of the weakness that had betrayed him into speech, even though that speech was addressed to an unconscious creature; that he should have spoken words of love and tenderness to his brother's betrothed, even though her ears were deaf to all around, would be a source of unending reproach to his loyal, sensitive nature; the man's moral rectitude was of so high an order, that he positively shrank from himself as if he had betrayed a trust.

He must exercise a terrible watch over himself for the future; he felt he was no longer safe in his confidence in himself. He must avoid the girl as much as possible without exciting suspicion. What would Brian, his beloved brother Brian, say if he knew? How he would despise and distrust him. Thus thought the good and noble man who had wronged no one by a thought; who had only given way to the natural human weakness of letting the hidden, strangled love find exit through his lips for a brief moment, when the creature so beloved was just snatched from a terrible death.

How could he have been so base as to kiss her? He thought. Her lips should have been sacred to him. Would she ever forgive him if she only knew? Yet in spite of his fierce condemnation of himself, there was a strange, wild joy in his heart that he could not kill. The memory of that kiss is a sweetness that will abide with him unto the end.

Such were Bernard St. Lawrence's reflections as he walked at Norah's side, and noticed not her embarrassed silence; the nervous twitching of her fingers; her half-scared, half-pitying, furtive glances at himself.

The girl was evidently greatly troubled, astonished, and shamed; but in his absorption he saw it not; and when they reached the point where their roads diverged, she bade him "good-bye" hastily, flushing and paling as she spoke, while the great, luminous eyes drooped and quivered, and hardly dared to meet his own; but if he saw any difference, he attributed it to the weakness consequent of her fall and terror. He offered to go with her to her father's door, but not very urgently, and she negatived the proposal eagerly.

"She was nearly all right again," she declared, "and would not be a minute running home. I feel quite dazed and queer, as if I had been asleep in the middle of the day," she said, with a little ghost of a laugh. "Swooning is not at all a pleasant sensation. I would rather bear the hurt of a good honest fall twice over than become totally insensible that way; one feels so strange and helpless, anything might happen, and you'd know nothing about it." Then, fearing that she had overdone it, she paused suddenly, glancing at him with frightened eyes; but he was not looking at her, he was living over again those few moments on that wild cliff path. "Why some one might have come along there, say a madman, and thrown me over that awful edge, and I should have been none the wiser; think how horrible," she added, with a strange little catch in her breath, while her fair face suddenly flushed all over a deep burning red.

Then feeling that she had done what she wanted, that she had conveyed the impression of her own utter unconsciousness during those few miserable never-to-be-forgotten moments (not that her hearer required to be so impressed, as he had no doubt upon that point), and that if she stayed longer she might undo her own work by blurting out some fearful *bêtise*, she said a hurried good-bye and turned away quickly, walking with rapid steps that never paused until she reached the large, roomy, quaint old parsonage, that had been the Desmonds' home during the past two years, and that stood just in the protecting shadow of a mighty cliff.[21] She rushed straight to her own room, where she locked herself in, and then threw herself, in a whirl of dismay, upon her bed, forgetful of her stiff, sore bones, her wrenched arm and aching head, forgetful of all physical distress, in the grieved distraction of her mind. When Norah felt herself slipping over that terrible edge she cried aloud in ghastly fear, and then her senses suddenly left her, and she became unconscious; but the period of utter insensibility was comparatively brief, although still her body seemed stricken as by some strange numbness, that precluded all motion, even to the raising of the eyelids, though still she lay to all appearance deaf, mute, unknowing of all; yet the brain had partly aroused itself from its fainting torpor; her thoughts were dazed and confused, but the mind was awake, and the ear no longer dulled.

She heard, and understood to a certain extent, Bernard's words; she felt his kiss, and she was in no way discomposed or shocked. There were two or three things he said seemed misty and meaningless, but otherwise it was all sweet and pleasant, and she lay in her enforced quietude, and listened dreamily and happily,

---

[21] *Bêtise*: foolish remark.

though she could make no sign. The fact was, that out of her brief swoon the girl awoke to the belief that Brian was beside her, watching and guarding her from some great peril, and his loving words were so comforting and reassuring, (the brothers' voices are almost identical), only there were some things she did not understand, and then those strange ominous words, that sounded like a prayer, that she might be delivered from some greater danger or sorrow that loomed in the future, rung in her startled ear, and dispelled the mist of confusion, still locking her senses. She recollected all now clearly, with a shock of amazed horror.

It was Bernard who was speaking, not Brian. Brian was far away in Dublin. Bernard had kissed her, and spoke those words of wild passionate love. Bernard! How artful it was! what should she do? He must not continue talking thus, and yet he must never know she heard him. And then, with a great effort, the dismayed girl brought herself back to movement and speech. Of a peculiarly frank, open, candid nature, it was terribly hard to feign, but she must do her best for all their sakes, and she succeeded pretty well as we have seen, though she feels now distractedly that never was there pretence so clumsy; anyone with a grain of penetration would have seen by her flurried, embarrassed, nervous manner that she knew, for she did feel so fearfully ashamed. But he did not guess, she feels certain, and he must never, never know, that she has surprised his secret.

Bernard loves her; oh, how sad it is, and how terrible her heart aches for the solitary man, bearing the burden of a hopeless, unsuspected, unrequited love. "Oh! what am I," she wails, "that they should both love me? And he so good, so utterly and entirely good; I love Brian, of course; he is the only man in all the world for me, yet I know no one is so good, and noble, and unselfish as

Bernard, and I have blighted his life. He said he'd be glad and happy to die now. What ought I do? Ought I to go away and hide myself, and never see either of them again? But my father would never consent to that, and the whole wretched thing would come out; and yet, to cause unhappiness, discord, unkind feeling between twin brothers, and such brothers, is terrible. But I need not fear that any pain or sorrow that reaches Bernard, either directly or indirectly, through Brian, will make any difference in his love for him, he is faithful and true. What an unlucky, miserable girl I am to have brought sorrow into so good a man's life; and he does look so ill, and worn, and weary lately, and I cannot breathe a hint to Brian, for he must never guess his brother's secret. I should be horribly dishonourable and wicked if I ever betrayed it, and yet it will be so hard to be as usual with that in one's mind always. And what—what did he mean by those strange words?" Reverting for the first time to that ominous speech that seemed to prophesy a shadow brooding over her own future life. "Could he have meant anything about Brian? Surely, surely, there is nothing gone wrong with him; and yet he is changed of late." Perhaps it was knowing and fretting about Brian made Bernard look so ill and aged, not as she egotistically thought, love for herself. "Oh, how unhappy and wretched it all is, and life seemed so fair and bright, and altogether goodly this morning."

And so for an hour or two she grieves and worries, and speculates, until at last she lays aside her personal sorrows, and weary, sick, aching as she is, joins her father at dinner. He must not be made lonely and miserable because she is unhappy, and she feels it is fortunate that she has her fall and swoon to make bear the brunt of his anxious comments on the pale sad face, with the faint lines of care traced on the smooth broad brow, the troubled eyes and drooping mouth, that encounter him at that meal; but her father must never guess, any more than Brian, of this misery that has arisen, and so she exerts herself bravely to talk naturally, telling him, without scaring him too horribly, about the wonderful escape she has had to-day, and Mr. Desmond, never dreaming there is aught behind, returns heartfelt thanks to God for His great and marvellous mercies.

LOVE STRONGER THAN DEATH

PART II

> "Upon this narrow strait
> And promontory of our mortal life,
> We stand between what was, and is not yet."[22]

NEARLY three months have passed away since the lovely September afternoon when Norah Desmond made the two startling simultaneous discoveries that have sobered and saddened her bright inconsequent youth. Already she feels that she has lived long, and that life is full of trouble! Her three-and-twenty years seem to the girl herself to be weighted with the experience of age. She has known sorrow and anxiety; is not this enough to blur the fair landscape of youth, to dull its radiant colours and to blot out, for a time at least, all the subtle, ineffable beauty of the golden halo with which it unconsciously surrounds itself. That halo in which youth imaginatively wraps itself, must surely be the nimbus of hope; and we are told that when "hope" itself lies dead, a pallid corpse, why then the man dies also. And if hope of some kind is thus necessary at every stage of life, if it is the natural attitude of man's spirit, even to the end, and that, bereft of it, all the rest is but a barren husk that soon lies shrivelled and lifeless; how much more necessary is it to the perfection of youth, which, deprived of its potent glamour even temporarily, loses its gladness, its joy, its very meaning, and becomes in very truth a human anachronism.

---

22 From 'Clytemnestra' by Edward Robert Bulwer-Lytton.

The line of anxious care on Norah's white forehead is now habitual; the dark-grey lustrous eyes have a world of sorrow in their earnest depths, while the soft cheeks have lost something of their roundness and are nearly always pale. Yes, Norah Desmond's winsome youth has had a blight.

Sorrow to the young seems unending; they find it almost impossible to think that the cloud now brooding so loweringly can ever be lifted, revealing the light beyond; and we question whether it ever is lifted completely; the radiance of early untroubled youth once quenched, is it not extinguished for ever? Life's lamp of hope may be rekindled, but has it not lost that dazzling brilliance that shed a glory over all things?

These three months have been a time of real sorrow and secret care to Norah; the very fact of her distress being hidden, having none to whom she can confide her great causes of uneasiness and grief, makes the burden harder to bear. Had she a sister, or were her mother living, she would not feel thus so terribly alone in her sorrow. And the burden is much heavier than when first she felt its weight, that September day when she so narrowly escaped a frightful death. A month since she learned beyond all doubt that Bernard's mysterious words held only too sad and true a meaning. That Brian had within the last year become passionately addicted to gambling, that he was neglecting his profession, and was yielding himself up to the horrible fascination of this deadly, soul-ensnaring vice, which exercises something of the effect of a sort of moral "Hascheesch" or opium-eating, intoxicating, false and fatal.

She has this confirmation of her fears from two sources, both thoroughly reliable. One, a friend in Dublin, who is aware of her engagement to Brian St. Lawrence, though having no knowledge of him personally.

Kitty Trevor and she have known each other all their lives, and, in fact, were scarcely ever separated till Norah came to the West with her father, and Kitty married and settled in Dublin. The two girls are true, thorough, loving friends, and when Kitty (Mrs. Halpin) wrote to tell her the sad tidings of Brian's lamentable infatuation which she learned through her husband, Dick Halpin, who never speaks of anything until he is quite sure he is correct, Norah felt no longer any doubt that trouble, serious, grievous trouble, was looming for her in the future.

The Halpins have not written to her father, for which she is most thankful. Her other informant is Mrs. Brady, Bernard's housekeeper, a good, faithful, true-hearted woman, who has lived long in the St. Lawrence family, and loves and serves the brothers with true Irish devotion. In one of her many late talks with Norah about her dear Mr. Bernard's strangely failing health—talks which are so many stabs to poor Norah's sensitive tender heart (how horribly rapidly Bernard's health has seemed to decline since that memorable day three months ago!), she admitted incautiously, oblivious for the moment that she had been charged by her master not to speak of it to Miss Desmond, that he had such cause for trouble and anxiety lately about Mister Brian, that he had taken fearfully to gambling, and had involved himself very seriously already; that not all Mister Bernard's prayers and entreaties could turn him from it. That he almost went down on his knees to him the last time he was home, a fortnight since, beseeching him, by all he held most sacred, to give it up before it was too late.

"They were in the library, Miss Norah, and I was in the dining-room, seeing had Molly laid the table right, for she's a careless colleen, and forgets more nor she remembers; an' I heard, without manin' to hear, an' faith it's meself's had the sore, scalded heart ever since.[23] An' I know well what me dear masther fears, Miss Norah; I know it's always in his mind about his uncle the Colonel, may God have mercy on his soul!

"A finer an' a grander man you couldn't wish to see, Miss, nor a better, for the matther of that, until he went mad like about the play, unless it be Misther Bernard himself; he's the best man in all the earth, I'm thinkin'; never thinks of himself at all, at all, only of others; an' yet, glory be to God, it does seem a bit contrairy, alannah, that when a body is raal good, they're sure to've trouble, while the black, bad sinners have it all their own way.[24] The onfairness of it bates me intirely. But Mr. Bernard, God bless him, is mortal bad, I'm fearin'; it's just the way his poor mother, God rest her soul! was took. She got worse an' worse, without any raison that a body could see, an' then went off quite sudden. An' I know he's grievin' a power about Mr. Brian, who he loves just as a mother loves her sick babby; an' Misther Brian (I don't want for to say a word agin' him, I loves the pair o' them, though Misther Bernard was always the one for me, manin' no disrespect to you, ashore) he was just dogged like, an' Misther Bernard pleadin' with him as for his life, an' niver a word to say as how he'd give up his devil's play or nothin'. Sorra a bit of me knows what black an' bitther trouble may be comin' to the St. Lawrences; but I do say, that them that does no wrong have no call to suffer for them that do! Don't cry, avick;[25] 'troth, I'm a pratin' ould woman to have brought tears to your sweet eyes. The Lord send it'll be all right! I was ordered not to say a word to

[23] Colleen: girl.

[24] Alannah: child.

[25] Avick: my girl. Presumably used in error instead of a term for 'my girl'.

you about it, an' the masther'll niver forgive me if he knows; but, shure, Miss Norah, I took it into my foolish head that if you were to write a letter to Misther Brian, sweet an' pretty like, as you always do, but sayin' as how you'd heard all this sorrow (niver namin' me, agra![26] for that might make Misther Brian bitther agin the dear Masther, thinkin' he'd bethrayed him) an' implorin' him for the love of heaven an' of you to give up the play, that it's breakin' your heart, an' that you know it'll be the death of his brother, an'——"

"Oh, no! Mrs. Brady don't say that, he's not so bad, surely; why I saw him passing your house yesterday, and he did not look much worse than usual," interrupted Norah, looking with eager questioning at the woman through tear-drowned eyes.

"Begorra, he's worse, Miss, nor no one dreams of! He won't nurse himself nor stay in doors, but goes off curin' them as is twice as well as himself, an' ongrateful into the bargain, bad cess to them! but he can't decave me, that has known him since he was a little bit of a boy;[27] he doesn't sleep, an' he doesn't eat, an' he's just consumin' himself away in a fever night an' day! It's the mind, Miss, is doin' it, more nor the body; steady grief an' sorrow that niver dies is worse nor consumption or small-pox, an' Misther Bernard has had somethin' troublin' him this time back, long afore he heard tell of Misther Brian's doin's in Dublin. The Lord love ye, my lamb, an' keep ye from all trouble! I must be goin'." And Hannah Brady turned away, leaving Norah indeed sore smitten.

This more than ample confirmation of Kitty Halpin's written words a month ago, makes her heart sink despairingly. She has never dared to question Bernard. Seeing him but seldom since that

[26] Agra: dear.

[27] Bad cess: bad luck.

miserable September day, an awkwardness has insensibly sprung up; she cannot help feeling *gêné* and embarrassed in his presence, and at the same time stricken with self-reproach while she gazes on his worn, altered face.[28]

After this conversation with Mrs. Brady, which takes place just ten days before Christmas, she tries to believe that it is altogether anxiety for his brother that has wrought this change in Bernard; though this, God knows, brings her no comfort, only adds misery of another kind; but she cannot quite make herself think so, as even in their few meetings, she has surprised two or three glances from Bernard that have dumbly told her that those passionate love words, spoken to her apparently unconscious ear, were truth welling straight from that noble, unselfish heart. Brian himself she has only seen once since she has had positive reason to know from Mrs. Halpin's letter that Bernard's strange words alluded to him.

A fortnight since he was down for a few days, and she was so utterly happy in his society that she had not the courage to introduce the wretched subject always in her mind, and which might, for all she knew, mar all their loving delicious time together. He had seemed different too, she thought, not gloomy and pre-occupied as of late, but strangely bright and cheerful, either feverish or assumed gaiety, she now feels it must have been, with this new light thrown on that last visit by Mrs. Brady.

Seriously involved? Bernard pleading with him as for life, to give up the accursed thing before it was too late?—That was the undercurrent of those few days, and yet he seemed gay!

She begins to feel dismayed, frightened even. That suggestive allusion of Mrs. Brady's to the Colonel's awful, self-inflicted death,

[28] *Gêné*: awkward, uncomfortable.

instituting as it did even the slightest similarity between the cases, fills her with terror. What if such horrors repeated themselves?

Mania of a certain kind may run in families, as well as more orthodox madness, and surely the unaccountable, terrible gambling passion is insanity pure and simple?

Yes, she will write to Brian, she will write this very night; she will plead with hm with her very heart's blood—on paper. She can do so better thus than by speech, where one is so apt to forget the very thing one wishes most to say. And he will read the letter, whereas he might stop her uttered entreaties, either by growing angry or laughing them off. When at home, a fortnight ago, she had hoped to coax him not to go back again before Christmas; but he said he was compelled to return, that urgent business would detain him in town till Christmas eve, when he hoped to come down again for a good long spell. Now she guesses what that urgent business really is.

"And I shan't disguise the truth about Bernard's health," she murmurs to herself; "at least, I shall just repeat what Mrs. Brady said, and surely that will move him, and bring him down at once, and when he sees that his brother is really ill, for he has grown worse lately I am sure. Mrs. Brady, of course, exaggerates, when she speaks of dying; but still, I don't know what to think, he seems to have no special ailment; he goes out as usual and makes no complaint, but I saw a look in his eyes yesterday that startled me, like one who had done with this world, and was looking beyond, and my father said only last week that he did not know what had come over Bernard St. Lawrence; that he did not seem ill, yet that he appeared like a man who was fast losing his hold on life. And oh, my God! I feel in my heart that if he were only happy, he would be just as he was a year ago.

"I feel so guilty, so cruel; yet what can I do? And what a terrible misfortune that he should have all this grief to bear about Brian just at the same time. No wonder the thought of his uncle's awful end is ever with him. Oh, Brian, my darling, how can you break both our hearts? And if my father once suspects how it is with him, he'll break it all off for ever between us. A gambler! why the very word is a horror to him; and I am afraid he must have heard a something, a whisper in the town, from the strange way he questioned me this morning at breakfast. It will be three lives broken and blighted then instead of one, for Brian loves me as strongly as ever, I know, and if we are separated he will only drift on quicker to——. No, I won't let myself think of such misery. Nothing shall separate me from Brian now, unless he himself wishes it, and I *will* wean him from this dreadful vice."

And with this solemn determination, that almost sounds like a vow, Norah sits down and writes the letter that she hopes will bear such good fruit. For three days she gets no response, and she grows wretched, watchful and uneasy. He may be angry at her having ventured to remonstrate so urgently, in such eager, passionate terms; at her daring to allude to Colonel St. Lawrence, as if for a moment suggesting any comparison; or again he may be torn with distress and remorse at her appeal to him for his brother's sake, shocked and ashamed to think he is partly responsible for Bernard's rapidly breaking health; or, worst of all, he may not write, owing to being plunged in some still deeper current of the fell whirlpool in which he is caught; some crisis of misfortune may have overtaken him; he has been losing heavily, Mrs. Brady said, perhaps—God knows what may have happened; he may have borrowed a large sum, lost it, and be in despair. One does not need the green tables of Monaco to play fast and loose with fortune. In any gambling hell in any large city, as well as on the shores of the Riviera, you may stake your all and lose it, and become a desperate man.

The surroundings may be very different, and the setting less attractive; also the game may be something you have a hand in yourself, not merely watching in frantic inaction the rolling balls of fate, something in which a little may seem to depend on your own skill, not altogether on the diablerie of chance.

Still, the result in each case is very much the same. Many miserable thoughts are Norah's companions through those three days of silence, and then the response comes; 'tis but one line, yet those two or three words utterly satisfy the girl: "Grieve no more, my darling, when we meet again, on Christmas eve, all will be well."

* * * * * *

And then another week speeds quickly away; and now to-day is the 23rd of December, and to-morrow will be Christmas eve, when Brian must come down, when he can no longer have any possible excuse for staying away. Only another day and she will have him again at her side, and the ice once broken by her letter, she will not hesitate to beg and pray, and implore him by his love for her to give up what must lead to such awful unhappiness, and he will listen to her she feels sure. Yes, please God, it will be all right, and there will be no more sorrow or wrong; she will strain every nerve, if need be, to pluck him from the jaws of this moral death, and they will be happy, so happy; he says himself "All will be well."

And as the day wears itself away into the early twilight, she gradually shakes off the depression that has rested on her so much of late, and grows to feel hopeful and even buoyant, as she repeats over and over again to herself "This time to-morrow he will be here."

Of Bernard too she has had better news, which helps to cheer her. Only this morning she saw Mrs. Brady again, who reported her master as brighter, stronger, more like himself than of late; which she attributed to having no ill news from Misther Brian, and expecting him down on the morrow for a lengthened stay. She was sure, after all, she concluded, that they were going to have, "a raal happy Christmas, shure with the dear masther well again an' glory be to God, he seems on the high road to it these few days—an' Mr. Brian got to give up that cursed play, an' you'll make that your work, won't you, acushla?[29] Now ye've put out your hand you won't draw it back, an' then with the weddin' comin' on in a month or two," with a little nod and smile that brought the bright blushes to Norah's fair cheeks, "why, we'll all be as happy as a cat in a dairy;" and though the metaphor seemed a little morally unsound, the happiness of the fictional feline being based upon the unstable foundation of thievery, still Norah was not captious, and happiness even stolen is sometimes sweet.

And now, as the evening draws in, a strange feeling as of exaltation fills her breast; she feels excited and almost gay, as if on the brink of some new experience; yet that surely must be pleasurable, else she would not feel as she does. She sings for her father song after song that he loves, chiefly Moore's matchless melodies. She laughs and chats, and makes little foolish jests that amuse them both, and she is altogether the bright sweet Norah of old. The Rev. Eustace Desmond marvels somewhat, but he is wise, and says no word of the change he notes; his little girl has not been herself of late, sad-eyed and sorrowful, and he feels only too thankful at her renewed lightheartedness, and carefully avoids any ill-judged remark that might frighten it away.

---

[29] Acushla: darling.

She has been in some trouble about Brian, he guesses, though he is very far from imagining the real cause; in spite of Norah's reading of his questioning a week ago, he does not dream that his child's betrothed has turned gambler. If he did, though it might be his daughter's death-warrant, he would separate them at once and for ever. Years ago he solemnly declared, in Norah's presence, that he would rather with his own hands lay his child in her coffin than marry her to a drunkard or a gambler, and that of the two he would have more hope of the former, as in a gambler's reformation he had no faith; and Norah vividly remembers those portentous words.

* * * * * *

But as the hour grows later, and the night draws on apace, though Norah's restlessness and excitement increase, yet the strange, unaccountable, happiness vanishes, giving place to a singular attitude of mind, as if of waiting.

As she parts with her father for the night, and bends her steps to her own room, a sudden inexplicable desire not to go to bed at all, to remain active, waking, helpful, fills her breast. An immeasurable restlessness is upon her, and she longs to wander, and to watch—for what she knows not—the long winter's night through; but with a little laugh at her own excited folly, and a furtive glance behind her, she shuts herself into her pretty bedroom, looking so cosy and inviting with its bright fire and small shaded lamp already lit, saying as she does so: "If it were to-morrow night, and Christmas eve, the received time for all weird manifestations, I'd say something uncanny was abroad."

LOVE STRONGER THAN DEATH
PART III

"A still, small voice spake unto me
Thou art so full of misery,
Were it not better not to be?"[30]

AND what of Brian St. Lawrence, far away in Dublin, on this evening of the 23rd of December?

He is filled with remorse and terrible self-reproach, and is a frantic desperate man. A week ago he received Norah's letter, which cut him to the very heart with its pathetic, loving, earnest expostulation and appeal. What a brute he was to bring such sorrow and misery to his darling, and to Bernard his noble-hearted brother.

And then he vowed a great and solemn vow, that after the week he was then entering on was over he would never play again; but during those few days between him and Christmas eve he must try to retrieve his fearful losses. The luck must surely turn; it could not always be so diabolical; besides his honour was at stake, having exhausted his own ready money, he had borrowed a large sum wherewith to recuperate his continued losses; secure in the belief, that is the gambler's creed, that the luck must change, and that by-and-by he would be as great a winner as hitherto he had been a loser.

Of this large sum of money but £200 remained, but with this he would play wisely and well, and he must—be must retrieve himself, or else—"O God, I am a ruined man!"

* * * * * *

[30] From 'The Two Voices' by Alfred, Lord Tennyson.

These were Brian's reflections on the day he got Norah Desmond's letter. How does he feel now, on this 23rd night of December, as a few minutes after twelve o'clock he leaves what has been a veritable mental "hell" to him these last few days, and steps out into the cold, clear, brilliant moonlight.

He feels wild, frenzied, a dishonoured desperate man. He has staked all (his own, that which he borrowed, and certain moneys entrusted to him by his clients, so sure he felt that the luck must turn) and all has gone, absorbed into that hideous maëlstrom that never cries "Hold, enough!" All lost, and he disgraced and dishonoured. Oh! that he had only died before this night. What is there for him now but death, he thinks in feverish despair.

The sum of money that brings him in at £5 per cent, his small independent income of £150, is, thank God, still untouched. That realised will redeem the honour he has smirched, it will pay all debts and keep his name clear from actual disgrace; but otherwise, what is there for him in life? His business going to the dogs—he has been neglecting it horribly; and of course when his late acts get wind, he will lose caste in the profession, and people will hesitate to trust him, him—Brian St. Lawrence—O God! it is too bitter! The St. Lawrences who have ever been so honourable and honoured, to be disgraced by him! His uncle Ambrose committed a desperate act, but still his honour was untouched, he had lost no one's money but his own.

And Norah (and when he thinks of her, he feels an actual blow on his heart; in the first rush of his horror and reprobation of himself, as he fully realised what the last few weeks' madness really meant, he had forgotten the girl, who is more to him than all beside), Norah, his darling, his almost wife! She can never be anything to him now, even if her father would let her marry a pauper (and he will be little more now; his capital and small patrimony gone; his business dwindling daily, as it must and will, and above all his good name sullied), he would never consent to let her become a gambler's wife.

He had heard the Rev, Eustace Desmond express himself once on the subject of gambling, and his words return to him now with a sudden terrible clearness. Yes, all stripped from him at a blow. Wife—ambition—reputation—means. What more remains? Nothing! Death would be infinitely preferable to life with such a future.

His uncle committed a rash and daring act; he went forth to meet his God with the awful sin of self-murder on his soul—for which there can be no repentance—but God was wondrously merciful and pitiful, and of infinite compassion. "His nature is ever to have mercy and to forgive."

His uncle, at least, had wronged no one by his desperate deed but himself; he took his life because he did not choose to live a beggar, and he, Brian, would not only be a beggar but disgraced; his good and honourable name soiled and smirched. It would be better, even for those he left behind, to end all now, with one mad leap in the dark, than to live on with a shadow on his name that might cast a reflection ever so faint on theirs. And so, with wild, confused, conflicting thoughts, the distracted man tramps on and on, scarce heeding how he goes, until by-and-by he finds himself in the Phoenix Park, that loveliest park in Europe; wild, romantic, embracing in its vast circumference almost every phase of meadow and woodland scenery, grassy nooks and mossy dells, tangled thickets, open plain, winding shadowed glades 'neath patriarchal trees; cultivated perfection here, wild, picturesque beauty there, all within that wide radius. And the calm, restful, almost unearthly loveliness and stillness of the scene, as seen thus, bathed in the glorious flood of moonlight at midnight, unconsciously enters his soul; a sort of peaceful weariness steals over him, and his thoughts are no longer so cruelly clear and distinct as awhile ago. He will rest awhile, and then he will try to think what he ought to do. Shall he go back to life and the world, or——

This is the question he wants to decide, but all seems so strangely vague and misty, and he cannot think clearly . . . . Somehow life seems to have slipped away a little from him these last few minutes, and he feels as if it would be a heavy burden to take it up again. How good and sweet it would be to have done with all here now. It is a dead world surely he has entered; grand, lovely, majestic, but without one throb of life. It is the stillness of death itself that is round him, wrapped in that glittering mantle of regal light.

He lifts his gaze to the distant wintry stars, and death seems to reign everywhere, even to the remotest region of space. He drops it earthwards again to the desolate, leafless trees, standing motionless, like sentinels frozen at their post. How strange and weird and densely black the shadows? how intense and white the light, and yet no life anywhere except his own. It is death's very kingdom, he thinks dreamily, silent, cold, and shadowy, and surely none may enter it and return again to life and warmth and human love.

He has wandered by chance into "the valley of the shadow," and he must keep on now, and not turn back, until he gains the light beyond that valley; not that weird, mystical moonlight that is now around him, but the "Light that shineth more and more unto the perfect day,"[31] that "Light that never was on sea or shore;"[32] that

[31] Proverbs 4:18.

[32] Based on a line from 'Elegiac Stanzas' by William Wordsworth: 'The light that never was, on sea or land'.

city that hath "No need of the sun, neither of the moon to shine in it, for the Lamb is the light thereof."[33]

He has aimlessly sunk down on a bank at the side of the white, winding road, his thoughts are strangely wandering and confused. He has unconsciously drawn a revolver from his pocket, which he turns about in his hand and stares at blankly with eyes that see it not. Opposite him is a dark dense belt of thicket enclosing, as he knows, a deep, still pool.

Water and fire, man's marvellously submissive servants, his terribly tyrannic masters, both to his hand; which shall it be?

* * * * * *

Thus in a dazed, bewildered, helpless fashion, Brian St. Lawrence tries to argue the problem of life or death. But his ideas are singularly misty and incoherent. Wild fantastic images, passages from Holy Writ, all seemed jumbled in his head, with the dire question at issue. What's the matter with him? he cannot think properly, surely his mind is wandering? He feels as if under some strange influence, all seems so unreal.

He stands up suddenly, putting his hand to his head, his hat has fallen off, and the deadly weapon he has slipped back into his breast-pocket. He gazes long, with an undecided wavering look in his absent eyes, at that shrouding barrier of thicket. Is he trying to decide for the water, so still, so cold, that lies beyond? Then, with a long-drawn sigh, he turns his head slowly, while a strange, creeping shudder passes over his entire frame.

* * * * * *

"Bernard!" he cries, in a hoarse terrible whisper, starting horribly, but the next moment outstretching a trembling hand of

[33] Revelation 21:23.

greeting, while a softened eased look gradually dispels the fixed distracted expression of his features. "How did you come, old fellow? Why did you think you'd find me here?" with a nervous tremor in the voice, as the mute motionless figure before him, so startlingly like his own, slowly extends the right arm, as if to clasp Brian's outstretched hand; the hands appear to touch, but Brian feels nothing, he is, as it were, greeting a shadow.

And still the figure stands there, silent, stirless, awful in its calm and unearthly repose!

"Is it Bernard?" he thinks, while the cold sweat of a ghastly terror bursts on his brow, and he shrinks back, gazing on that face scarcely two yards distant, that face so marvellously like his own. "Yes, surely it is Bernard looking at him with such a gaze of mute, pathetic, reproachful love. How ill and weary he looks, and in God's name why doesn't he speak and not stand looking at him with those terribly sad eyes?"

* * * * * *

Then he pulls himself together, and tries to think rationally; he feels he is the victim of some strange optical delusion. It must be himself he is looking on, and not as he thought his twin brother.

How could Bernard be here at this time of night, and without a hat? No, either some singular affection of the eye, or the half-maddened brain, has conjured up this life-like vision; or, in some extraordinary way, he sees his own reflection mirrored and refracted by that unseen pool.

These thoughts dash through his brain with lightning speed, in the few seconds that pass after that shadowy hand-clasp. In his heart is a great and unspeakable terror, though he scarcely acknowledges it.

* * * * * *

"Bernard, my brother, speak!" he whispers with white and palsied lips. "Why did you come all this long way? It is late and cold, and you have no hat, and I am coming home to-morrow, you know."

Trying to speak naturally, but the dumb motionlessness of that mystic form appals him, and those last words are almost frozen in his throat.

How terrible is the silence! Then suddenly the figure raises its hand and points solemnly to the ground at Brian's feet, and he finds, with a thrill of horror, that he is standing on the very brink of a precipice, a black, bottomless gulf yawning at his feet, and into which he gazes spell-bound; it stretches between him and his brother, widening, ever widening. Then he hears, like the echo of a voice, breathe the words as from a terrible distance, "Farewell, dear Brian!" and looking up with a start, the figure has gone! The moonlight is brilliant, intense as ever, throwing out in a strange distinctness and relief each tiny twig on those leafless trees; every object is clearly revealed along that white, winding road, but no figure of a man is visible. He glances again at the ground at his feet; where is that gaping abyss into which he looked this moment? Gone too! Nothing but the hard, white, level road, unbroken, unchanged. To what extraordinary influence has he been subject? Who and what was that figure that stood so near and bore the likeness of his brother, that came and went without a sign, a sound? He sinks back on the bank at his side, weak, nerveless, almost unconscious for a few moments.

Then rousing himself, he looks at his watch: ten minutes to one.

"He is dead, I know it, I feel it; and I have killed him!" he murmurs in desperate tones of terrible conviction. "He has loved me with a boundless love, and I have broken his heart! I am accursed; his murder—the murder of the best and noblest man on earth is on my soul; we are divided for ever; that gulf he pointed to separates us for all eternity!"

* * * * * *

He pauses for a few moments, with an awful look of maddening despair. Then suddenly that aspect changes. The strange, terrible smile of insanity steals over the anguished features, a vacant look creeps into the haggard eyes. "I am coming, Bernard!" he mutters, as if answering a call, raising himself and gazing out straight before him fixedly, "Coming fast, so fast; you called me, and I am ready. We were born together, and we must die together—wait but a moment, brother; do not leave me, I cannot go alone; I am coming now—now!"

And with a ghastly, frightful smile spreading and deepening on the livid face, he puts his hand again into his breast-pocket; there is a click, a short, sharp report, and all is still again.

And the brilliant moonlight pours down upon the face of a dead man upturned to the sky, with that terrible smile of madness fixed for ever on the rigid features, and the blood welling slowly, slowly into the soft, green, innocent grass, from that small fatal wound on the temple.

* * * * * *

Yes, Brian St. Lawrence is dead by his own hand!

Tragic calamities repeat themselves singularly in families! Ambrose St. Lawrence blew out his brains ten years ago in the Kursaal Gardens at Monaco, and now his nephew Brian has committed a similar desperate deed in the beautiful Phoenix Park; but his sin is the result of a paroxysm of madness, following upon a great horror and despair!

LOVE STRONGER THAN DEATH

PART IV

"The wide world sunk in dreams and death,
With guilt and wrong upon its breast,
Like nightmares choking up its breath,
And murdering all its holy rest."[34]

WHEN Norah Desmond shut her bedroom-door, almost the first thing she did was to light two small dainty candles, standing in a pretty little candelabrum, and extinguish the lamp; for though the latter gave a better light, yet, being a reading-lamp, it was a condensed and shadowed one—if one may be allowed the term—and threw the further and upper parts of the room into a sort of mysterious gloom, especially uncongenial to the girl in her present excitable, restless, watchful mood. Then she stirred the fire till it blazed brightly; drew up a soft, low chair to the side of it, and sat herself down with her pet pussy purring at her feet for companionship, and a new novel on her knee.

"It is barely a quarter-past ten; it would be ridiculous to go to bed now, I couldn't possibly sleep," she murmurs. "I'll have a good read and tire myself out, and then I'll tumble in as fast as I can and pray that I shan't wake till morning. How horribly long the nights are now; the honest, friendly daylight seems as if it wouldn't be here again for ages, and I do so dread the darkness to-night. I don't feel as if I could face it."

---

[34] From 'Brothers, Arise!' by George Phillips, written to the Irish Nationalists during the Monster Meetings of 1843.

But the novel remained unopened on her knee, and pussy laid soft, pleading paws against her young mistress's gown, wistfully craving a little notice, which she never before asked in vain, and, to her extreme wonderment, received no answering caress.

Norah sat gazing into the fire with dreamy, abstracted eyes for a while. Bernard was strangely in her thoughts these few minutes back. She found herself dwelling much on his last visit to them, now nearly three weeks ago; these once so frequent visits had grown sadly rare and brief of late. She remembered with singular and startling clearness every word of that last conversation they had had together, though she had not thought of it again until now. It was a somewhat strange and uncommon subject.

Bernard and Mr. Desmond had drifted into discussing a rather peculiar work by a French writer that appeared some years ago, and which bore the somewhat original and striking title "The Day of Death."[35] Not approving its speculative tendencies the clergyman had but cursorily glanced through it, but Bernard seemed to know it well. She recollects his saying, with a strange vibration in his voice,—

"What a weird fascination, and inexpressible attraction there is in aught that treats of the 'just beyond.' I devoured that book, Mr. Desmond, as if it, or any other written by man, could tell us anything definitely of 'the Unknowable and His mysteries'; and yet," he continued, "it does seem a wonderfully rational theory, though, of course, you may make answer 'What has the rational to do with the Infinite?' But to our human, and necessarily narrow, understandings, it appears more just, more reasonable, more merciful—I trust I

[35] *The Day After Death: Or, Our Future Life, According to Science* by Louis Figuier, French scientist and writer.

am not irreverent—that we poor, weak, erring, mortal creatures should be given a second—aye, and a third and fourth—chance before being punished for ever for what our sinful natures, in ninety-nine cases out of a hundred, cannot help."

"Yes," responded the Rev. Eustace Desmond, thoughtfully; "but if you grant that by having another chance the man in his second earthly life improves his moral condition, why, then you must admit that memory of the former life and death are with him. And then, what are we?"

"We meet none that actually remember a previous state of existence, certainly," replied Bernard, quickly; "but one often has queer, unaccountable impressions of having done and said the same thing before in some other state of being."

And then Norah, who had dipped into the book and been fascinated by it, recollects chiming in,—

"But what a lovely idea it is, that after our single, double or treble lives here—single, I hope," and Brian was not by to reproach her with apostasy, "we go through various purifying stages of spiritual being to fit us for the final one; in each stage we become less material, more etherealised, until at last we drop all remaining fragments of earthly grossness. The only thing is, one shrinks terribly from the idea of so many deaths; but each grows less awful than the last, I suppose."

"There is no death! What seems so is transition.
This life of mortal breath
Is but a suburb of the life elysian,
Whose portal we call death."[36]

[36] From 'By the Fireside: Resignation' by Henry Wadsworth Longfellow.

Bernard quoted softly, with so strange, distant and wrapt a look in his dark eyes, as if he saw what no one else could see; and then she had been led on to continue a little wildly and dreamily, encouraged by his peculiar absorption in the mystic subject.

"I think there was one perfectly beautiful theory advanced, solidified poetry as one might say. Do you remember where it says that a divine voice is never lost upon the earth; but that the moment a great singer dies his or her voice enters a newborn baby, and so is handed down through all the ages; and I have thought sometimes if that singular idea could be true about each person having so many lives with the same soul—earthly lives I mean—that perhaps, in the beginning, there were only a certain number of souls created by God, not the enormous number we imagine, that frightens and appals us at its multitude, and that these repeat themselves with different bodies through the centuries, and that though there have been many, many men, enough to daze and set one mad to think of God hearkening to any one creature amidst such a terrible number; yet that there will not be such a countless host of spirits or liberated souls hereafter—I mean liberated from the flesh, which has been their prison in various forms since the beginning. How curious it would be to think that souls on the earth now walked and talked, and thought and worshipped in the days of the patriarchs, only under different presentments.

"Norah, Norah, my child, you grow abstruse and foggy; you are plunging altogether too deeply into the fathomless sea of mystic speculation. You seem also to forget, dear, the 'great multitude that no man can number,' or again, 'the number of whom is as the sand of the sea,' " had chided the clergyman gently;[37] and then again,

---

[37] Revelation 7:9 and 20:8.

softly and dreamily, as if his mind had never wandered from the thought engendered by those loveliest lines, penned by that prince of pure and reverent song writers, the noble poet of the West, whose voice is now hushed for ever. Bernard repeated the words, "There is no death," &c.

And these are the words which haunted Norah so strangely to-night, for the first half hour or so after she retired to her room. It seemed to her as if Bernard's very tones as he spoke them sounded in her ear in the silence, and how sad his eyes looked, and strange, with that distant, rapt, visionary gaze.

"Why does it all come back to me to-night so vividly?" she thought, with a queer little thrill; and then that tiresome restlessness got the better of her again, and she began softly to pace the room up and down, up and down; then she went to the window, drew back the curtain and raised the blind. Ah, that was comforting, a flood of intense, brilliant moonlight poured into the room, contending with fire and candles for supremacy.

She gazed out long and earnestly. What did she expect? What was she looking for? she asked herself with a little nervous laugh, as she seated herself again at the fire, her hands twisting and twining themselves together, as if under pressure of some strong mental strain or tension.

It really seemed when at the window as if she were anxiously watching for something.

"I think I am bewitched to-night. What's the matter with me that I cannot rest? But I'll force myself to stay quiet, I'll control this absurd desire for movement and watchfulness;" and suiting the action to the word, she locked her slender hands in her lap in enforced motionlessness, and lay back in her chair, still gazing at the fire. And by-the-by, this very compulsory quietude of body induced mental restfulness. After a while her thoughts grew less clear, became by degrees confused, misty, vague, and at last she fell asleep—profound, untroubled sleep, her last conscious act being to glance at the little clock on the mantel-piece, the hands of which pointed to half-past eleven.

* * * * * *

Nearly an hour and a half later Norah woke suddenly, broadly, an intense, vivid, instant wakefulness, accompanied by a strong, shuddering chill.

The fire had burned to red embers, one candle was out, the other flickering low in the socket. How intensely cold it had grown? And then, as if affected by a sudden draught, the expiring candle gave one last flickering leap and went out instantly. In that momentary flare, Norah saw that the hands of the little clock pointed to ten minutes to one.

What an icy air rushed through the room! The girl's teeth chattered in her head, and she was suddenly possessed by the horrible idea that there was some mystic, unearthly presence near. An awful impalpable something seemed to glide and hover somewhere in the gloom. With fearfully dilated eyes she strove to pierce that brooding darkness; and then, unable to bear the agony of unreasoning terror any longer, yet shrinking from disturbing the sleeping household for what she tells herself must be only nervous imaginings, she rushes softly over to the window, through which the welcome moonlight still streams, though nearly all the room is in profound shadow; anything is better than that shrouding darkness behind her. To look out on the lovely, wild, yet now familiar scene outside, will surely banish these terrifying fancies, and so thinking she throws wide open the window, and leans far out into the night. For a moment or two she breathes more freely; how sweet and calm and still it is; all the great, heaving, panting, sinful world sunk in slumber; and the mysterious never-resting ocean, embracing and holding all within the wondrous circle of its moving waters—out away there it is, moaning and tossing and sighing, a wail of unending sorrow in its mystic voice. But then suddenly this feeling of relief and returning tranquility is followed by a singular sense of unreality; a strange awful feeling of some extraordinary phenomenal change taking place in herself. It is as if her spirit and body were being separated by some occult mysterious power. Her physical self is leaning on the window-sill of her room, and yet she is floating away, away, leaving all behind! Her spirit eyes seem to look back and behold that motionless form—her own—looking out into the moonlight, and then on and on, with a rush through haze and vague misty shadows she is compelled to go, without volition on her own part.

And now she is still again, but where she knows not. It is a place strange and foreign to her in which she stands. It seems to be a great, shadowy, moonlit glade; she has never seen anything like it; vast, beautiful, silent, it stretches away in the dim mysterious distance. The light somehow grows stronger as she looks, and now in the foreground she sees the indistinct figure of a man seated on the bank at the roadside. Alone in that great solitude, in the dead of night, with elbow on his knee and head upon his hand, she cannot see the down-bent face. With a strange intentness she watches that scene so mystically revealed to her, her whole being concentrated in the one act of gazing. She must see that face. Who is that man so fearfully alone? What is he doing? What is he meditating? And as she looks the light grows stronger still, the brooding form is clearly revealed. With a sudden gesture of despair the man raises his head, and she recognises her lover, Brian St. Lawrence.

Brian, with a wild, fixed, desperate look on his face, which presently gives place to an awful unnatural smile. She frantically tries to approach him, to speak, to make some sign, but human sound and human movement are denied her, and she must powerlessly wait for the terrible end which she feels already coming.

She sees a revolver drawn forth, she sees it placed to the temple, while that maniac smile grows ever wider, wilder. One cry she feels would save both life and reason, she makes a last horrible desperate effort and becomes unconscious.

LOVE STRONGER THAN DEATH

PART V

> "The shores where tideless sleep the seas of time,
> Soft by the city of the saints of God."[38]

WHEN Norah recovers from her swoon she finds herself lying beneath the open window. She had fortunately fallen back into the room, instead of falling out. The chamber is in perfect darkness; the moon has set, and the wintry stars diffuse no soft glimmering radiance as in the summer sky. All is impenetrable gloom. For a few moments she lies wondering how she came there, trying to remember, to collect her scattered senses. Then she hears a violent, hurried knocking at the hall door; that alarming unfamiliar sound at that hour helps to restore her to full consciousness. With a rush the memory of that awful visionary state she has been in comes back to her. To what weird, occult influence has she been subject? Was it trance or reality? or could it by any possibility have been only a dream?

Yet her spirit certainly seemed to go forth from the flesh. She felt herself borne along, in that extraordinary movement that was neither walking nor being carried; but a sense of floating swiftly through dusky nothingness until she reached that distant place, where she saw——

Great God! what did she see? and now the full horror of that terrible mystic revelation bursts upon her and almost stuns her.

---

[38] From *Tanhäuser; Or, The Battle of the Bards. A Poem* by Neville Temple and Edward Trevor.

It was Brian she saw in that trance of the soul. Brian! and he—he!——

*　　*　　*　　*　　*　　*

And then that strange, loud, peremptory knocking is repeated, she starts to her feet in wild alarm, and strikes a light with trembling fingers. Her first glance at the clock shows her that it is more than an hour since she fell into that awful trance; it was then ten minutes to one, it is now five minutes to two. And once again the knocking resounds with a hollow sound of grim foreboding through the silent house, and this time it is heard, as she hears soft-moving footsteps; the servants are aroused, and she waits in frantic fear, incapable of motion, waits for the message that she feels is coming. The returning steps pass her door; they are going to her father first. She hears an exclamation, some hurried words, and still she cannot stir. Then a minute or two of breathless silence elapses, and she hears his steps approaching.

He knocks softly; in an instant the strange sense of numbness is gone, she flies to the door, unlocks it, and looks at his agitated face with speechless appeal. "My child!" he exclaims, "have you not been to bed? or did the knocking startle you? I feared it would rouse you, and thought it best to come and tell you at once."

"He—is—dead!" she gasps, in a horrified whisper, "I know it—I saw it all!"

"Norah!" he cries, frightened at her strange manner and stranger words. "What do you mean, dear? What did you see? Poor Bernard—he is indeed dead, though how you knew I cannot tell. I thought he was better, so much better; but Mrs. Brady has just sent here in a frenzy of grief and fright, to say he seemed to pass away suddenly at a few minutes to one o'clock, but that she cannot believe he is dead! She has sent for the doctor and for me, and I——"

"Bernard! Bernard dead?" the girl breathes, in astonished, questioning tones. "Did you say Bernard was dead, not Brian?" And there is a sound of immense relief as well as incredulity in her voice.

"Brian," repeats her father carelessly, "what should happen to Brian? he's all right, of course. Poor Bernard, he seemed so much more like himself when I was speaking to him three days ago; it must have been the heart."

"Yes, the heart indeed," thinks Norah, with a pang of keen sorrow.

When the weight of intolerable, suspenseful anguish and awed certainty that her mysterious vision had been real was lifted off, the girl's first instinctive feeling had been of gigantic relief; but now that she has had time to realize the truth, to understand that Bernard St. Lawrence is dead, dead of a broken heart, as she knows too well (she and Brian being the two people on earth who have consummated that end), she is seized by a feeling of terrible remorse.

Bernard, whom she had forgotten in her panic of unspeakable fear for his brother—Bernard, who is dead for love of her, and grief for Brian's wild persistence in wrong doing? Hurriedly she dons some heavy wraps.

"I am coming with you, father," she cries, as the Reverend Eustace Desmond turns to the door.

He tries to dissuade her from her purpose, fearing that in her present excitable, strange state, to come face to face with death may prove highly injurious to those overwrought nerves; but she is determined to go, to remain in that room, that house seems horrible now. To her excited fancy it is as if it were charged with some unearthly presence. The marvellous experience she has so lately gone through, the remembrance of that extraordinary aerial journey, freed from the bonds of flesh, while she actually saw her physical self left behind, is too fresh, too vivid, with the awful vision at the end, to admit of her laying it aside mentally just as a dream that was dreamt and nothing more.

There was some weird, mystic meaning in it, if nothing else, she feels sure, as she follows her father downstairs and out into the bitter cold of this earliest morning of Christmas eve.

The car that brought the messenger is waiting for them. It is a drive of more than two miles, but the horse is young and fresh, and they make the distance in a brief time. As they go Norah tries to calm her highly-strung nerves by reflecting that she has been thinking much lately of Colonel St. Lawrence's melancholy end, thinking of it with a sort of dread and apprehension; and these thoughts may have possibly induced that weird, life-like vision she saw to-night.

She awoke in her chair startled, nervous, full of unreasoning terror. She ran over to the window, perhaps not properly awake, and it was possible (yet was it possible?) that she fell asleep again leaning on the sill. Had she not read somewhere that to sleep in the full light of the moon induced ghastly, horrible phantasmagoria of the brain? And it may have been so with her.

* * * * * *

And now they reach Wild-Cliffe House, the home of the St. Lawrences, and there is a sound of mourning within. Honest, faithful, tender Hannah Brady is grieving loudly for the master she so truly loved.

The doctor has just arrived, an old friend and *confrère* of poor Bernard's, and he declares positively that death, owing to failure of the heart's action, took place an hour ago or more.[39] His friend's

[39] *Confrère*: colleague.

heart was weak, he says, and he must have had some strong mental distress lately, either some shock to the nervous system, or else brooding, cankering care or sorrow, that undermined the health and weakened the hold on life. Bernard had seemed strangely exalted the previous afternoon he goes on to say.

He (Dr. Blake) had called on him to discuss a case they were both much interested in, and it seemed to him more than once during the interview as if his friend was not quite himself, inclined to wander a little, to smile oddly and unmeaningly, and he had a bright, feverish, restless light in his eyes, and at the same time an absent distant one that he did not like. He questioned him about his health and he answered indifferently that he was feeling better than a while ago, that he was only "waiting for the signal, he would soon be called now."

"That was one of the queer things he said," continues Dr. Blake. "It struck me as strange, and I determined to look after him. Then for a while he talked quite pleasantly and sensibly as usual, yet there was an air about him all the time that produced on me the singular sensation as if he was watching for something, something invisible, intangible, unreal; something outside the ordinary finite range of man's surroundings, some sign, in fact, from the unseen world. A very wrong and absurd idea you'll doubtless say, Mr. Desmond?" feeling that the clergyman might be apt to condemn such speculations as irreverent and unsound. "Yet this was exactly the impression poor St. Lawrence's manner made on me, and I am anything but an imaginative fellow.

"And then, just as we were parting, he said another strange thing. 'I shall be wanted to-night,' he muttered, with that strange far-away look in his eyes; and at first I thought he alluded to being summoned in his professional capacity; but as I rode away I saw it was another of the singular wandering speeches, and I fully resolved to come back late in the evening, and perhaps stay with him if he still continued strange; but unfortunately an old woman, five miles away, was dying, and I got home only half-an-hour ago, in time to hear that my poor friend was gone.

"That he had some strange prescience of his coming end I have no doubt; or perhaps he had some morbid presentiment that he was to die to-night, and that the very imagination produced the result, as in many cases on record. However it may be, there seems some touch of mystery concerning it. It will be a terrible shock to Brian; with that strange affinity there is between twins, I should think it would almost crush him. I must send a telegram as I ride back."

"Ah, sir, you're right, an' so it ought to crush him," sobs Mrs. Brady, who has been listening eagerly to the doctor's speech, while Norah and her father have been gazing with tear-drowned eyes and grieving hearts at the still, white face of the dead man. There is a look of startled horror on his features, which is rather awful to look upon, and for which it is very hard to account. Dr. Blake cannot explain it, as he says the deceased could have suffered no pain; besides, it is not an expression of physical suffering, it is rather as if the dying eyes looked on some sight that shocked, and that the look froze in death.

"Ah, sir, an' so it ought, when his death may be laid at Mr. Brian's door; God forgive me for having to say such a thing, but it's the blessed truth," repeats Mrs. Brady. "I didn't tell ye, Mr. Desmond, sir, that the dear masther's last word was 'Brian,' an' said so sudden an' awful, an' scared like, an' he startin' from his chair an' starin' at something beyant me that I nearly dropt with the fright of it, and looked round to see could Mr. Brian have come unknownst to me, but, glory be to God, there was not a craythur there.

"An' then he sank back in the chair, lookin', lookin all the time with just that look on his blessed face that he has now, God rest his soul! And then he seemed all to drop to pieces someway, an' he was gone in a moment, though I thought it must be only a faint. An' when he called out that way it was just ten minutes to one, for I'd been lookin' at the clock the second afore, hoping to coax him to bed."

"Ten minutes to one?" repeats Norah, gazing at the woman with dilated, fearful eyes. "That was the time I saw that awful thing!" she murmurs, but no one heeds her.

"Yes, ten minutes to one," reiterates Mrs. Brady. "He had been queer in himself all the evening, just as Dr. Blake says, wanderin' like, an' smilin' to himself one moment, an' then sighin' so awful sad the next, an' he kep' readin' in that there book," pointing to one that lay open on the table, "on an' off all the time, an' I think as how it was always the same little piece he read, for he'd sometimes look off an' say it soft like to himself, as if he loved it, God rest his soul, an' may the Heavens be his bed, my dear, dear masther!"

Here the poor woman breaks into uncontrollable, desperate sobbing, and Mr. Desmond and Norah both simultaneously turn to that book left open, where the dead man had been reading. It was a volume of Tennyson, and one short passage heavily scored, seemed to indicate that meant by Mrs. Brady, only those well-known three or four lines from "Maud," which are so intensely, pathetically tender:—

"She is coming, my own, my sweet;
Were it ever so airy a tread,
My heart would hear her and beat

Were it earth in an earthy bed;
My dust would hear her and beat,
Had I lain for a century dead;
Would start and tremble, under her feet,
And blossom in purple and red."

"Poor fellow," murmurs Mr. Desmond, in tones of infinite sorrow and compassion. "I did not know he had a love story, and an unhappy one, in his life. What a noble, loving, tender soul his was, and how strange that he should have had a grief of this kind to bear; surely any woman ought to have been proud to win his love." And Norah, understanding all, is torn with despairing self-reproach.

It is between nine and ten o'clock before the Desmonds find themselves at home again. They enter the breakfast room, the letters and papers have come and are on the table. Norah looks eagerly for a note from Brian, forgetting for the moment that there could not be one in the time; then when she remembers, she is inclined to wonder that he has not telegraphed in response to that terrible telegram of last night. But why would he, after all, when he is coming so immediately; a very few hours must see him here now, unless, and her heart flutters strangely, he is too ill from the shock to travel. Dr. Blake should have only summoned him, saying that Bernard was ill, very ill, but not that—that—awful word "dead."

And then her father takes up the morning paper to try to divert his mind somewhat after the long night's sorrow and agitation; but he has scarcely opened his *Irish Times* when a horrified exclamation bursts from him, and he starts up with a ghastly face, muttering. "Oh! my God, no, it can't be, it's too horrible, impossible!" He has for the moment forgotten Norah; now he looks at her with aghast eyes, crumpling the paper up in his hand.

But she has heard those muttered words, she sees the appalled face, and in a moment she is round the table trying to draw the paper from his grasp.

"No, no, child, it is nothing, nothing at all; I am nervous this morning and easily upset," with a horrible effort to smile, "and these papers make such fearful mistakes. Norah, my child, my darling," in terrified, imploring tones, as the girl has snatched the fatal sheet, "don't read it, for the love of God don't read it; it is all some hideous mistake."

But Norah's eyes already devour the dread paragraph, that he would have given so much to conceal from her, and this is what she reads:—

"STRANGE AND MYSTERIOUS SUICIDE IN THE PHOENIX PARK

"Last night, between one and two o'clock, as two gentlemen were crossing a secluded portion of the Park, from the Lucan Road, they came upon the body of a man lying full in the moonlight, with a small wound in the temple, from which blood was still flowing; life was quite extinct. Death was evidently self-inflicted, as the right hand grasped a revolver, five barrels of which were still loaded. No particulars as yet are known, or any reason assigned for the desperate act. There is a ghastly smile on the dead face very awful to look upon, and which seems to indicate insanity.

"It has just transpired that the deceased is a Mr. Brian St. Lawrence, a member of a good old Galway family, himself a solicitor, practising in Dublin, prosperous, happy, and about to be married; this wraps the affair in greater mystery."

But Norah reads only the first few lines; are they not enough for her? does she not know the rest? was she not there in that lonely park herself last night? did she not see with her spirit eyes the tragedy enacted? and with a low groan she sinks to the floor.

For many months she lies between life and death, and even at last, when life has conquered the grim tyrant, there is a long battle for the reason which seems scarcely a blessing to her. At last, for she is young, she regains both bodily and mental health, but life and its interests, its hopes, its joys, is for her virtually over. Hers has been blighted, blasted, broken, and she cannot take up the severed threads and knit them into fresh shape and design. She enters the Anglican Sisterhood, which gives her work to do; noble, arduous, unselfish work, and for the rest, her heart goes in mourning all its days for the brothers St. Lawrence, whose mysterious dual with death seems to argue that between twins exists some strange esoteric bond, some mystic, indissoluble link, at least in some temperaments, not sufficiently recognised by the world at large, or the medical faculty. Science has explored so many singular remote paths recently, and with such splendid success, that it seems odd she does not seek to unravel the mental problem of "brain rapport" between human creatures born of the same parent at the same time. It surely is a subject full of infinite suggestiveness.

THE END

"CAN SUCH THINGS BE?"

OR

THE WEIRD OF THE BERESFORDS

A STUDY IN OCCULT WILL-POWER

"Our birth is but a sleep and a forgetting;
The soul that rises with us (our Life's star)
Hath had elsewhere its setting,
And cometh from afar."
WILLIAM WORDSWORTH

"There are more things in heaven and earth
Than are dreamt of in our philosophy."
WILLIAM SHAKESPEARE

"CAN SUCH THINGS BE?"

PREFACE

I CANNOT pretend to account for, or in any way attempt to explain, the extraordinary mystery of the following tale. I only try to tell the mere facts of a marvellous unearthly experience in all the same as here related, save that she who went through this great horror lived—though but for a brief week or two—and told the story of that terrible night.

Many will, doubtless, assert that it must have been a dream, an hallucination, or the phantasmagoria of a diseased fancy; that either insanity, or the strange optical delusions and imaginations engendered by opiates when they fail as sleep inducers, must be the true solution of this weird problem. And possibly they may be right; but one or two unalterable, inexplicable facts remain.

The mysterious music was heard by others besides her to whom the ghastly manifestation was made; and above all, the singular disappearance of the violin, its reappearance a year later, and its still more marvellous and weirdly-mystic vanishing at the moment of death, are inexplicable phenomena.

I think it necessary to say this little word of deprecation, as apology for offering to the world a tale almost too wild for belief.

ARNOLD DYSART, M.A., F.R.S.,
Fellow of Trinity College, Cambridge,
and Professor of Modern Philosophy.

CAMBRIDGE,
June 17th, 1883.

PART I
HIS VIOLIN

> "There are more things in heaven and earth
> Than are dreamt of in our philosophy."
> WILLIAM SHAKESPEARE

CHAPTER I

ALONE!

AS the last stroke of midnight sounds on the still, frosty air, and the sweet Christmas bells ring out in a burst of glad triumphant harmony, old Maxwell Beresford's spirit passes away unto the God who gave it, and his daughter Eunice is indeed alone—a desolate, friendless loneliness, very terrible to contemplate.

These two have been so thoroughly all in all to each other, have lived so utterly in and for one another, for such a number of years now, that the daughter can scarcely remember or imagine any other state of being. Her mother died when she was but ten years of age. She is now some years past forty; and in all that long time, save for a brief halcyon interlude, more than twenty years ago (but her lover had to travel to distant lands, and for long, long years his bones have been bleaching under an Indian sun), none have come into this father's and daughter's life, to disturb its even, monotonous current, to cheer or sadden, or in any way break the long union of these two, connected by that closest of all ties—parent and child.

And now—she is alone! Alone in the cold, cruel, pitiless world, with no one hand outstretched across that awful silence, in friendship or compassion; alone and poor (for her father's means died with him), with youth and hope behind her, and an open grave in front.

Maxwell Beresford was in all things a disappointed man. Life with him had been a failure in those things that men hold dear. Success had been denied him; the ambitions, hopes, and aspirations of his earlier years had never reached fruition. His marriage, also, had been somewhat unfortunate, and had not yielded him the happiness he craved. Worldly prosperity was not his, and all his love and dreams and hopes centred in his little daughter; in her bright and radiant future he would live and be glad again. But the cloud had darkened his own life, that cast its brooding shadow o'er his child's. A brilliant, happy future seemed suddenly to open to his Eunice, but only to close up again into the grey dreary blank, that became all the gloomier when shorn of hope, and sorrow-laden. Yes, his girl's life was blighted at its outset; she grew old and grave and sad, while the bloom of freshest, loveliest youth was on her brow. And so these two maimed and narrowed lives grew closer, each finding in the other the solace, the sympathy, the happiness which the outside world denied them—"the world forgetting, by the world forgot."[40]

Such was the story of the Beresfords' lives during those latter years. And now, for all time, they are divided. One has gone forth into the great unknown, and has left the other behind, to mourn in a desperate, infinite loneliness.

And what makes this solitariness and isolation seem more awful is, that Eunice must, perforce, go forth and face that hard, unsympathetic world; she must leave her home—the home of her race, the home in which she has spent her whole existence, save for three or four baby years. Even now, as she gazes down in a passion of unutterable grief on that dear dead face—even now, it is no longer her own, but has already, with that spent breath, passed away into the possession of aliens and strangers.

This great grey old Manor House, in which Eunice has lived her life, is the last remnant of the Beresford property, once vast

[40] From 'Eloisa to Abelard' by Alexander Pope.

and flourishing; but now even the name is extinct, and Eunice, the last of her race, must go forth in a few days, not only to face the world, but to fight it single-handed; to try and add to the miserable pittance of some £30 a year, which is about all she will be able to call her own. To increase this scanty store, she must work—alas! poor Eunice! at her age, and having lived such a life of refined seclusion, with no rough-rubbing or sharp contact with the callous world to prepare her for the fray. But though timid, shrinking, and sensitive, Eunice Beresford is true to the instincts of her race. She has a faithful, unselfish heart, coupled with infinite endurance and unending patience; she accepts her fate with resigned and Christian spirit. And by-and-by, when she bids an eternal farewell to that dear old Manor, with which all memories of him whom she has lost are so indissolubly connected, that the familiar house and grounds seem like a part of her own very being, she does so through blinding tears, but not with a bitter, rebellious spirit. An infinite trust, rather, is the attitude of her broken heart—trust in God's goodness and mercy; He will not leave her desolate. And deep down in her breast, unconfessed even to herself, but yet there, is the hope, the longing, that this desolation will soon be broken, in the only one way that can give her reunion with that beloved lost father. It cannot be for long, that she feels—this blank, cold barrier of separation. Life has naught to offer her, death has much. She will live on as long as God wills, unmurmuringly, patiently waiting for the end that will bring her joy and peace ineffable; but surely that end will not be very long in coming. And, in the meantime, she will struggle bravely, and try to bear meekly, without impious repining, her heavy burden of sorrow, taking up the broken threads of her life, and essaying to weave them into as goodly a garment of Christian fortitude and endurance as she may.

These are desolate Eunice's thoughts and yearnings and resolutions, as she drives away alone from the only home she remembers—away to that distant cheap lodging, in a respectable, though somewhat humble neighbourhood of the busy city, a few miles outside of which she has lived her life.

It seems singular—some might say, almost impossible—how any one could be so completely alone as Eunice Beresford, not being a stranger in a strange place—a circumstance which always accounts for intensest solitariness; but it is easily explained. When Maxwell Beresford succeeded his father as squire of the Manor, and took possession of his barren heritage, he was even then a weary, world-worn, disappointed man, though his little daughter was but four years of age. He shrank from meeting strangers, and gave himself up somewhat to the life of a morbid recluse, living in and with his music and his books.

His wife, a gay and frivolous woman of fashion, had become already a confined invalid; and, between physical suffering and seriously crippled means, she also shrank from the world during the half-dozen years she lived; and, save her attendant physician, no stranger entered the doors of the Manor House.

Gradually this isolated mode of life grew so on Mr. Beresford, that he could contemplate no other; and through all the days of his daughter's childhood there was no alteration.

The little girl had governesses, therefore she had not even the chance of making school friends.

By-and-by, when she was grown, she made a few acquaintances—one could hardly call them by the stronger term—as youth must and will; but when her own life was shattered, and all its sweet promise buried in a far-away grave, she too withdrew from the small world that had been hers for a brief space. Shunning those whom she knew and mingled with during the short sunshine of her life, she drew back into the shadow which seemed her portion, as well as her beloved father's; and none cared to follow into its drear duskiness. And so the years rolled on, and the few young people she had known in life's glad morning are now dead, or scattered, or faded into unknowingness, and Eunice, as we see, it utterly alone.

* * * * * *

To increase the miserable yearly sum that would barely save her from actual starvation, she determines to get a little teaching. She loves music with all her heart and soul. Dear as are her books to her, yet her piano has been still more of a solace—a faithful friend that cheered and comforted and soothed in the long years of her shadowed life. Music was a passion with the Beresfords, both father and child; and old Maxwell's violin and Eunice's piano led a wedded life of truest concord, and were continually blent in sweetest harmony and union.

Both loved the divine art for its own sake, and not for the sake of shining before others, as it was only the unresponsive walls of their lonely home heard the wild, sweet, wailing music that they delighted in. Yes, Eunice is fortunate, and possesses a speciality; and when some few months are gone by, and the first fresh torturing anguish of her sorrow has somewhat spent itself, she awakes to the knowledge that there is business as well as grief in the world for her; awakes to the knowledge that she has already four pupils, all girls over fifteen, each of whom pays her two guineas a month. And the knowledge that she can earn the bread that is necessary to life—though that life she would gladly lay down—is pleasant, even though that bread must ever be mixed for her with tears and sorrow.

And now a sort of saddened peace, a dreary, desolate restfulness, comes to Eunice, after those first few months of active, agonized sorrow. During those first days of her mourning, after she had left her old home, life seemed insupportable. Pray as she might for resignation, for strength to endure, the hideous, awful loneliness was so terrible, the sudden complete severance from that one friend, who had never failed her since she was born, was so frightful, so impossible to realize, and yet such a soul-crushing fact, that she felt she must either go mad or die. She and her father, who had scarcely been apart a day; from whom, looking forward, she felt she could never be separated, they loved each other so well,—now to be divided for ever! at least, for all time; and to know nothing of him—*where was he*, or *what was he*! Was he no longer the loved parent, whose intangible presence seemed ever near her? Or must she think of him only as an ethereal essence, a spirit, cold, passionless, sublimated, purified from all mortal dross, with no remnant or memory of the humanity that was so dear to her?

The thought of meeting him again in that guise brought no satisfaction or comfort, but, rather, dismay and shrinking—a disembodied soul!

> "When, leaving the body, out to the free ether thou reachest,
> A god undying thou shalt be, no longer a mortal."[41]

These lines were ever in her mind during those first days, and brought her desolation instead of solace. She longed and craved and yearned for the father she had known, the earthly being she had loved so well; and these wild, speculative thoughts, that would intrude themselves, only made her faint with shuddering scepticism and despair. But "Time the consoler" lays its softening healing hand

[41] Based on the theory of the Greek philosopher Empedocles, who held that human existence is a penal state; having served a sufficient period of penance in mortal form, man returns to his former godlike existence.

on this wounded heart, and when some six months have glided into the past since that terribly sad Christmas Eve, Eunice Beresford has regained her calm, steadfast faith and trust, that never wavered, until half-stunned by the force of a paralyzing blow; and she has also regained, in a measure, the noble endurance, the sweet, serene patience, that have been hers through life. "All will be right in the end," she whispers to herself. She, and *he*, so lately gone out into the darkness of nothingness, and that other *he*, she "loved long since and lost awhile," will all be reunited in God's own good time—reunited for all eternity.[42] The unshakable conviction grows each day stronger in her breast, that the great and wise Creator never implanted in the human heart the capability of such true, intense, unchanging love, merely to serve our little span on earth. These unsearchable mysteries of love, these unfathomable depths of man's heart, were fashioned for everlasting, and not for a day. "For what is your life? It is even a vapour, that appeareth for a little time, and then vanisheth away."[43] So the apostle speaks of the life, the breath; but so he does not speak of that God-like attribute in man—*love*. "Many waters cannot quench love;"[44] no, not even the Lethe of death.[45]

The order of her life is changed to an extent; she has new duties and responsibilities—duties that infuse a faint flavour of interest in the performing; Eunice being not merely a painstaking

---

[42] From the poem 'The Pillar of the Cloud' by John Henry Newman which, when set to music, became the hymn 'Lead, Kindly Light'.

[43] James 4:14.

[44] Song of Solomon 8:7.

[45] In Greek mythology, one of the rivers of the underworld of Hades.

automatic teacher, bent only on bringing on her pupils, but one who feels an individual regard and interest in each young life thus brought into contact with her own.

Thus her mornings are passed in work that occupies without fatiguing, and is consequently healthful. Her late afternoons and evenings are her own, to spend with the books she delights in, or the music that is her second self. Her beloved piano from the Manor has accompanied her in her exile; that, and her father's violin, her dearest, most treasured possession, are almost the only visible links in her present obscure home that connect her with the past.

When she brings herself to play again, which is not for months, she always opens that dear violin case, leaving the enclosed silent inmate within sight; and somehow she fancies she feels less lonely thus.

That same violin has somewhat of a strange history of its own. It is old, very old, and has been in the family for generations, belonging to a far-away ancestor of Maxwell's, whose life history had been a shadowed one, according to tradition; which said that his wife had played him false, and had murdered either him or her lover somewhere in the eastern gable of the Manor House, which was declared to be haunted by her unresting spirit. This, at least, was the popular legend attached to Eunice's home; but she thought little of it. The phantom presence had never made any sign during her time or her father's, and she often forgot the strange old story connected with the house, of which there was no record whatever among the family papers; but she did know of the violin's antiquity, and had, in consequence, a sort of veneration, almost verging on reverence, for it. It seemed a part of themselves, as if it bore a mystic life that somehow linked it with the family. Of course it was only imagination, but it sometimes seemed to her a sentient creature, with a human wail of sorrow in its wondrous voice. It had been her father's best and dearest friend, save herself—his "familiar," as she would laughingly say; and for this reason, if for no other, she loved and treasured it.

And so the year wanes and wastes for Eunice Beresford in the calm, uneventful, monotonous routine of this new life—routine that is so often as a bulwark to saddened, broken-hearted women; a moral defence, entrenched behind which they struggle on, hopeless but enduring, deprived of which they would collapse and die.

Though her pupils increase, and her income improves, yet still she remains on in the obscure home she has made for herself. The street is respectable, though situated in a somewhat humble neighbourhood, and the house quiet in the extreme; the only occupants being the owner, a lady, elderly, frail, and partly deaf, but gentle and kind-hearted, and her servant, a cheerful, obliging young woman, who seems to think it a pleasure to do Eunice's small behests.

A house in which the only lodger can be as secluded, as utterly alone, solitary, and quiet, as if it were her own,—this is what Eunice craves, and this is the reason why she remains. She shrinks from the idea of the stir of gay young life, noise, bustle, excitement.

When her day's duties are over, she likes to creep to her quiet rooms, and there, with those inanimate intellectual companions, pass her long hours of leisure; though it would be much more wholesome for her if she were compelled to mingle more, if she were not thus enabled to indulge her love of solitude, and so perhaps foster singular mystic thoughts and imaginings.

CHAPTER II

VANISHED!

THE year has worn almost to its close; Christmas Eve has again come round—Christmas Eve, so glad, so joyous a season for nearly all; the saddest day in the year for Eunice Beresford. Was it not with its expiring breath, and the new-born moment of the holy morning, that Maxwell Beresford passed into the "silent land," and left his daughter desolate?

Yesterday Eunice bade her pupils "good-bye" for a fortnight, and this most melancholy anniversary is the first day of her liberty. All those long, sad hours she spends in unbroken solitude, and sorrow that forbids all occupation. Better for her were she compelled to work till she almost dropped, than thus to muse and grieve and yearn.

She feels tired—so tired—towards evening, and half determines to go to bed early (quite contrary to her habitual custom, as in no circumstances does she leave her sitting-room till past twelve), and try to forget her troubles in sleep; but she changes her mind suddenly. To-night, of all nights in the year, she must remain up and awake. Must she not live, in spirit, over again that moment of anguish last year? Would it be even respectful or reverential to that dear memory to pass in sleep the first return of the time when soul and body underwent their mystic parting? Besides, she feels involuntarily that it would be yielding to a sort of cowardice; for as the hour grows later, she is half-conscious of an eerie sense of expectation—a watchful, nervous, half-formed dread, for which she despises and condemns herself.

So she heaps coal upon her fire, turns up the lamp, to give a brighter light, and, for the first time that day, tries to seek in occupation a refuge from unhappy thoughts.

The piano—she cannot touch it—and the violin in its case, which rests upon it, are closed and mute. She has been trying to rub up her German lately, which has got somewhat rusted. Some of Heine's poems in the original she is studying with much delight; and now she brings out her books, and settles herself for an hour or two's work. The poem that presents itself for to-night's reading (she is going through her small selection regularly) is, by a strange chance, the singular legend of "Geoffry Rudèl and Melisanda of Tripoli." Doubtless, all know the story of how the Countess Melisanda saw Geoffry dying on the beach; they kissed and loved; he died, and she worked the scene into the tapestry. And Eunice dwells long, with a strange thrill at her heart, on these two verses, which are rendered thus in an English translation:—

"In the Château Blay at night-time,
Comes a rushing, crackling, shaking;
On the tapestry the figures
Suddenly to life are waking.

"Troubadour and lady stretch their
Drowsy ghost-like members yonder,
And, from out the wall advancing,
Up and down the hall they wander."[46]

The whole weird poem has a sort of fascination for her, and she lingers over it, until at last the fatigue and drowsiness that oppressed her earlier in the evening overcome her, and she drops

[46] Based on the poem 'Geofroy Rudèl und Melisande von Tripoli' from *Romanzero*, Book I: 'Historien', by Heinrich Heine.

asleep about eleven o'clock—profound, dreamless sleep, from which she starts suddenly, vividly, to hear the neighbouring church clock strike twelve; and, with the last stroke of midnight, and just as the bells in a glad, sweet jangle break upon the still, cold air, a loud startling knock resounds through the silent house.

Now, one of Maxwell Beresford's most decided characteristics was his mode of demanding ingress; his knock was long, loud, peremptory, even when he was broken in health and spirits. And Eunice now recognizes it—first (out of her sleep, before she remembers) with a thrill of delirious joy; then, as the steps move swiftly, in answer to that imperative summons, a feeling of awe, fear, astonished expectation steals over her, as she hearkens to the beloved familiar footfall ascending! What mystery is she on the brink of penetrating? . . . Then the step pauses, the door-handle is softly turned, while she remains transfixed, immovable, with dilated eyes gazing at that slowly opening door. How horribly slowly it moves! . . . And what will be revealed in the void beyond? . . . Then, with a cry of rapturous delight, she starts to her feet, and speeds across the room, for there on the threshold stands Maxwell Beresford!

Yes, it is he, and no other—even himself; no mocking semblance or optical delusion. For one instant she pauses, gazing in frenzied, non-comprehending joy and wonder at the dear face for which she has hungered. The next moment her arms are round his neck. Ah! thank Heaven, all lingering doubt vanishes. This is no spirit, no ghost, but warm, living humanity.

How she clings, and cries, and gasps incoherent questions, the answers to which, seem to reach her through a fog! It is as if a mist enveloped her brain, her thoughts and ideas are so hazy and unreal. But through the confusion there is the one grand dominant feeling of thanksgiving and gratitude unutterable. Her father "was dead, and is alive again," "was lost, and is found." Time enough by-and-by to try and understand how it all is; now she can only rejoice with an exceeding great joy.

How wonderful it is to look on that beloved face again!—that noble, grand old head, with the long, snowy hair resting on the coat collar; the great dark, dreamy eyes that age or sorrow could not dim. She leads him over to the easy-chair by the fire, and brings wine, for he looks weary and worn, and kneels at his feet in a transport of speechless gladness and content. And then after a little he explains to her the mystery of his presence,—how when he had appeared to die, it was but a trance, which left him conscious, though, to all seeming, dead; and then, when, on the last night before the coffin was closed, he regained the power of movement—the fearful catalepsy that had bound him in iron chains falling suddenly away, and leaving him free in the dead of night—he rose out that awful thing which would have closed on him for ever on the morrow, made a semblance of a figure beneath that terrible winding-sheet (in the early winter daylight the change would escape observation), and then stole away—away, so that none might know. And when Eunice asks in astonished query, why the secrecy, the concealment, that gave her such agony of grief? why he had not come straight to her, that they might give thanks together for the marvellous blessing of life restored, he speaks vaguely of motives, strong motives, that necessitated his acting as he did, compelling him all this time to refrain from making any sign. But all seems wrapped in mystery incomprehensible; her head is dazed and bewildered, she cannot think or understand properly, and his talk is vague, dreamy, misty. But, after all, what matters anything but the one grand fact? Her father is not dead! It was all a mistake, a horrible mistake. He has come back to her! Great and sudden joy sometimes kills, but she has survived the shock; and they will be happy once more in the old quiet way, and look back upon all this past misery as only a vivid, terrible dream. Perhaps it has been only a dream, she thinks; her mind feels so clouded and obscure, that all seems unreal and visionary.

* * * * * *

The long hours of the night pass away in loving reunion. They take up the thread where it snapped a year ago, so easily that no break is discernible; and by-and-by he plays. The violin that has been so long mute (mourning the hand that made it laugh or weep as that hand dictated) once more speaks, and sighs, and shrieks, and groans, in a tumult of wailing, tempestuous sorrow; and Eunice sits in a trance of wondering dismay. Why is the violin not glad? It ought to be glad—so glad! It surely *is* an independent creature, a spirit, a voice, a living, palpitating something, that is sighing and sobbing through the room. It is sorrow and despair embodied thus in sound—wild, wailing, terribly sad sound—and it ought to be all joy to-night.

How wondrously he plays, she thinks, as she looks at the great rapt eyes of the old man, and the streaming white hair; he seems music's very soul! Never in past years has he played like this. Wild, strange harmonies he has always affected; but these weird, singular strains seem unearthly, laden with mysterious, wordless sorrow. She shivers with an undefined dread as she listens. And then the theme suddenly changes, and soars to higher, purer regions. Sublimated, exalted, majestic, it grows more and more, until at last she is, as it were, hearkening to the "Song of the Redeemed" in heaven. *A Violin's Voice?* Surely not, but the echo of an angelic choir.

As he ceases, she notices that the first faint grey streaks of the late winter dawn show sickly pale through the window-blinds.

He rises, with a shudder, still holding the violin, and moves to the door; he will come back soon, very soon—come back for her; but he must go now. When he comes again he will take her with him. She cries, entreating him not to leave her, but to take her now. He quietly disengages her clinging, detaining arms; he cannot wait, but he will come again soon—soon! And, so saying, he reaches the door, still holding the violin pressed close to his side. On the threshold he turns and looks back. Spell-bound, she gazes in silence on those dark, sad eyes, that seem to have gained a strange, new, unfathomable light. And then, as she looks, *he is no longer there!* Out into the void beyond the threshold she gazes on blank nothingness!

She is conscious at the same moment of the room having become in an instant dark and chill. Lamp and fire seem suddenly extinguished! With a cry of instinctive terror, she tries to reach that open door way, and with that cry she awakes—awakes in perfect darkness, save for the gleam of a street lamp just opposite her window, that diffuses a ghost-like glimmer of light through the room; awakes cold, scared, bewildered, on the very spot on the sofa where she had established herself with her books at ten o'clock!

There is the little table beside her—the light is strong enough to discern it dimly; and the book that her hand rests on, as she stretches it out, it Heine, open at the poem of "Geoffry Rudèl." She had fallen asleep, she knows and remembers; but was it possible that she never waked from that sleep till now; that when she appeared to herself to start suddenly from profound slumber into vivid, instant wakefulness, to hear the church clock strike twelve, and the bells ring out in a clashing peal, that she only then passed into dreamland—dreamland that very possibly she was ushered into by those pealing, jangling bells striking on the sleeping ear, and inducing that weird, realistic vision from their connection in her mind with her sorrow of a year ago? *Only a dream!* she thinks, as she rises, with stiff, cramped limbs, and nervous, frightened glances into the duskiness around her. The rapture, the delight, the joy in that wondrous reunion was but a figment of the brain, after all. Her father has not come back to her; she is solitary and alone as ever. And yet it was so awfully vivid, realistic, consecutive. It is hard, oh, so hard, to think it but a dream!

And then, with groping fingers, she strikes a light. The ashes in the grate are cold and grey, the fire has long been dead. She looks at her watch. Four o'clock—and she has been sleeping since eleven! She had slept, though she determined not, through the time when we cross at midnight the boundary 'twixt night and morning, and when he had crossed the boundary 'twixt life and death. And yet, at the very same moment when he left her a year ago, he returned to-night in sleep. Was it sleep? she again questions, with a strange thrill at her heart. She has dreamt of her father often, since he died—dreamed that he was living, dreamed that he was dead, but never of his having been given back to her from the grave; and it is a cruel disappointment to find it all a baseless vision.

Again she looks lingeringly round the room, almost finding it hard to understand why the armchair does not stand near the hearth, as in her dream, with the little table close by, holding wine and glasses. The chair is back in its accustomed corner, the table stands by her sofa, and the wine is invisible in her cabinet; but as her eyes range slowly round, they are caught and held by one startling difference. The violin-case on the piano, that was closed when she fell asleep, is open, *and the violin gone!*

For an instant she believes her sight deceives her; but when she realizes that it is indeed a fact, her heart gives one wild throb, and then stands still; her brain reels, and she clutches a chair to support herself.

The violin gone!

All round the chamber her appalled eyes travel, hoping that by some strange, unaccountable freak she may have removed it from its case in her sleep, and placed it elsewhere. But this one hope of a natural solution of the weird problem soon fades. The violin is, indeed, incontrovertibly gone! And *how did it go?*

That no earthly hands removed it, she at once feels certain. Her landlady and her servant are every night in bed, and the house is securely fastened up before eleven o'clock; besides, say it were possible that any one could have entered the room while she slept with felonious intent—is it likely that they would have contented themselves with the violin, or touched it at all, when her purse lay on the mantelshelf, and her watch rested in a little stand close by, besides scattered trifles, more or less of value, relics of her old home?

No; another presence besides her own has been in that room to-night; but that presence has been an unearthly one! A guest from shadow-land has sat by her hearth, and that guest her father!

She now firmly believes that the extraordinary experience she has been through was no dream, but that in her sleep her spirit partly freed itself from the trammels of the flesh, and caught a glimpse "behind the veil." *He* had come, and her eyes had been opened, and she saw him as he is in the world of shades. But still there must have been some phantasy of the sleeping brain mingled with the spirit sight and sense, else why the strange, incomprehensible confusion of his not having died, and being still in the flesh? He may have often come to her before, but her eyes had not been opened, her ears had not caught the sound of that wondrous music that was not of this earth.

And the violin is gone! She remembers how he appeared to hold it closer, closer, as he vanished through the doorway!

What weird mystery has this night held in its sacred bosom? Is it—as she once read—that, when asleep, we are strangely, awfully near the confines of the other world—just hovering on the boundary between the real and the unreal; that between the visible and the invisible the veil is then so thin as to be almost transparent; and that in some phases of temperament, health, or circumstance, the spirit actually goes forth from the sleeping body, and has separate existence, touching mysteries unapproachable by the awake understanding, imprisoned in its fleshy tabernacle?

Sometimes, for all our finite humanity knows, soul and body lead thus a dual and distinct life; and in some peculiar organizations, where the nerve and brain-power outweigh the carnal nature, and the man lives more in his mind than in his body, during the hours of darkness, sleep, and silence, the spirit escapes from its earthly bondage, and wanders free and unfettered; and, possibly, the singular impressions so many have at times of other experience outside of the present life—faint, shadowy remembrances that one cannot grasp; illusive, yet penetrating—may be traced to this double life of the soul, and not to a pre-existent state in another sphere, as many assert that these unaccountable impressions prove.

Possibly also the "mesmeric sleep" into which individuals of a certain highly-strung, nervous, sensitive organism can be thrown by those possessing the marvellous magnetic power, and in which the eyes of the spirit are opened, while their earthly eyes are close in unconsciousness, and they see what the natural eye could never see, also annihilating time and space, seeing and hearing and feeling what is distant, still in futurity, or absorbed into the past, is another proof of the soul's dual life.

Such a theory has been advanced; and Eunice, having read on the subject, thinks of it now, with an irrepressible shudder, though she feels a strange glad, exultant joy within. She may be allowed by-and-by to hold communion with her beloved dead, not through the medium of sleep or vision, but spirit actually touching spirit. And ought she not to rejoice instead of to fear? And yet the weak humanity cannot be altogether exorcised, and she shudders again.

* * * * * *

For many days and weeks the remembrance of this singular experience, the strange mystery of Christmas Eve, remains ever present with Eunice. She goes about as one under some introspective spell, while she is always conscious of a feeling of expectation, unrest, apprehension. But as time passes the impression becomes less vivid, less intense; she grows to believe it was a dream, realistic and startling, but still only a dream; natural enough, considering how her thoughts were saturated with the one subject. The problem of the missing violin remains unsolved, and is a mystery which she seeks no longer to unravel; it is beyond her skill, and she must perforce let it rest as it is. It is gone, and its disappearance cannot be accounted for; but she will try to struggle against the supernatural dread that has laid hold of her. And if it is ever given to the flesh to see the things of the spirit; if her father should return to her in dream or vision, surely, she ought to rejoice, not fear.

And so, about eight or nine weeks later, striving against a singular foreboding of some strange manifestation, she forces herself to play again in the evening, as is her wont.

The empty violin-case has a sort of fascination for her, and she cannot withdraw her gaze from it as she plays. The first two nights all is as usual, but on the third she is scarcely playing ten minutes—a wild, sweet, plaintive melody, a favourite in the olden time—when she suddenly becomes conscious that she is *accompanied by a violin!* It is as if there were half a dozen rooms on the same level, and that in the farthest, with the door half-closed, was the violin-player! Clear, distinct, yet low and softened by distance, come the vibrating notes. Eunice's blood turns to ice as she hears the familiar strains—the voice she knows so well, *the* violin's voice, the missing violin—and knows whose shadowy hand is making it speak! . . . It was no dream, then, after all. He did come, and took the violin with him. And though she feels half-dead with supernatural terror, her heart beating to suffocation, the moisture of a deadly awe upon her brow, she continues playing, as if compelled by some power outside her own. Her hands feel weak, nerveless, helpless; yet her fingers weave these subtle, intricate minor harmonies unerringly, unbrokenly . . . . And still the wailing voice of the violin comes to her ear, now softer, now louder, sighing, sobbing through the room in melancholy cadence!

*   *   *   *   *   *

At last, after about an hour, she is released from the mystic spell that bound her, and rises, white and weary and worn, from the unnatural ordeal. And yet when that unearthly music ceases, she feels a strange void; the sudden silence oppresses her with a sense of desertion and intense solitude, as if she were alone in some new dumb world. And this feeling develops into so strong and irrepressible a yearning to hear once more, if she may, those phantom strains, that on the following evening, at the same hour, she is impelled to play again, though a sickening terror possesses her; and, as before, after a little, that weird violin's voice is heard clear and low.

And so, as the weeks go on, Eunice Beresford grows to lead a sort of double life: through the daytime, in the world and of it to an extent; while in the night she seems to have a partnership with the land of spirits, through the medium of that mysterious music.

She grows to love it with an absorbing love, hardly feeling to live save in its presence. For, every evening now, those strange occult harmonies are to be heard. Sometimes the strains are sweet, soothing, familiar; at others, weird, startling, blood-curdling, like that night of her vision; or again, soaring into empyrean heights of heavenly melody.

This phantom music is not now heard only by Eunice in ghostly accompaniment to her own playing, but long after she ceases wild bursts of strange, wonderful harmonies float through the room!

CHAPTER III
HER VISION

"And till my ghastly tale is told,
This heart within me burns."[47]

AS the months roll on, this unearthly influence, this invisible companionship of the dead (for that the mysterious violinist is her father, she has no doubt) leaves its impress on Eunice Beresford. She becomes strangely silent, wrapt in abstracted reverie; her attention wanders from her pupils during her working hours. Her eyes have gained such a dreamy introspective light, and, withal, there is such an aspect at times of watching, straining, listening, in the worn face, that these fresh, young, happy creatures grow to shrink almost, with a sort of fear, from the gentle woman whom they had loved. She seems so strange and visionary and changed. And as the year glides away into the dreary, dank, cheerless days of late autumn, when all nature seems mourning for her shorn joys, and sorrowful human life is at its saddest; when the rapidly shortening days remind one so pitilessly of the shortening life, that each hour draws nearer to the darkness, unfathomable, of the end,—that "night" when "no man can work," that is stealing surely on all and each; when it wants but a month or so of another Christmas,—Eunice finds herself without a pupil.[48] By degrees, all have fallen off, chilled by the singular absorption, the eerie

---

[47] From *The Rime of the Ancient Mariner* by Samuel Taylor Coleridge.

[48] John 9:4.

silence, and far-away gaze of their teacher. Her instruction was excellent, all that could be desired. In fact, on two or three of the few occasions she had played for her pupils during these latter months, they, and others who had heard, marvelled at her music. It seemed as if a spirit, not of this world, had entered into the quiet, sad-faced woman's fingers, and spoke of divine mysteries or demoniacal horrors through them. When asked what she had played (the mystic, wondrous strains being unfamiliar), she had each time passed her hand wearily across her brow, and replied vaguely that she did not know! . . . So they got afraid of her, these young people and their friends; and now, as Christmas approaches, she is more alone than ever, with that stern, relentless foe, grim poverty, facing her, as her future life companion.

But just at this juncture an old and dear friend of her father's, who had been long abroad, but whom she had known well in her childhood and girlhood—in fact, almost the only visitor to whom the Manor House opened its doors in those far-away days—returned to England, sought her out, heard with grief of his old friend's death, and was pained and shocked at the terrible change in Eunice;—the bright, beautiful girl he remembers so well, to see her again thus! How sad, how dreadful it is! To see her old before her time, broken-hearted, lonely, and desperately poor, would be grievous enough when he recalls the brilliant, lovely dawn of this greyest afternoon; but he is still more distressed to discover the strange absorption of her mind in what he considers wild, visionary hallucinations. It seems like the shadow of coming insanity, he thinks, with a pang. However, he does his best for her: he makes arrangements with the gentleman into whose hands the Manor passed on her father's death for her return there for a few months, hoping that the old familiar surroundings will break this weird attitude of waiting and watching that seems to have settled upon her; will dispel those wild fancies of an ever phantom-presence and unearthly music in which she lives.

It is late in October, just two months from Christmas, when he gets her transferred to the Manor House, back to the same half-dozen rooms on the one level that she and her father occupied almost altogether of late years, seldom using any other of the multitude of apartments—many falling into mournful decay—in that great, rambling old pile.

Mrs. Hancock, the faithful old housekeeper, who loved and honoured the Beresfords, both father and daughter, is still at her post, the new owner having temporarily retained her and the two or three other servants who formed old Maxwell's sole household. She is delighted to welcome back her beloved Miss Eunice.

But Eunice herself hardly realizes the change in her circumstances, although her manner is always sweet and graceful. All that she cares for in life now, or almost thinks of, is that ghostly music which has become a necessary part of her being. All day long she sits and dreams of it in rapt ecstasy. She has almost ceased, during those long months which were void of any further manifestation, to hope for, or fear, any vision, or more personal communion with the dead. But that music, played by the spirit hand of him whom she mourns, is her very life.

And thus Christmas Eve again comes round, and finds Eunice by her old hearth, not quite so desolate and alone as a year ago, and not so sad or grieving. Instead of passing the day in bitter, hopeless weeping, she is filled with a strange tremor of expectancy. She insists on passing the day and evening utterly alone, absolutely refusing to allow him who is her friend—and in whom she has confided the singular mystic phenomena of the past year—to share her vigil.

A thrill of unutterable awe and terror passes over her, as she notes the dwindling daylight; but, mingled with the fear, there is an indefinite sense of hope. She feels as if *release* were at hand.

*　*　*　*　*　*

She is oppressed by no stupor or drowsiness to-night as the hour grows late, but is painfully, vividly, alertly awake, every nerve tingling, every pulse throbbing wildly.

"Will *he* come?" she asks herself in feverish apprehension.

But, after all, it was in sleep she saw him last year, whether dream or vision; and she cannot sleep to-night, not if her life depended on it. She feels as if she could never sleep again!

She makes no pretence of occupation, but walks restlessly to and fro, stopping to listen every moment. The strain and tension of nerve and brain are horrible. She sometimes feels as if she had become suddenly deaf, and that the mightiest thunder-peal could not penetrate her dulled ears. Again the silence feels full of maddening, indefinite sound . . . For three nights past she has not heard the phantom music, and she distracts herself wondering fearfully what its cessation presages.

Then she grows weary of the monotonous, restricted pacing, and sits down, with hands folded, in enforced quiet, while the terrible throbs of her heart seem to fill all the air around.

Again she starts to her feet, unable to sit still and bear the awful suspense of watching for she knows not what—of waiting for some mystic revelation from the unseen world.

But at last, as *the* hour draws near, she sinks into her easy-chair, her limbs suddenly collapsing, and refusing to support her from excess of nervous trembling; her lips white and bloodless; while her eyes, dilated unnaturally, seek the door and rest there. It is a large room, and decidedly a long one, in which she sits; and her chair near the hearth, and the doorway in the opposite end wall leave the whole space of shadowed room between—shadowed because her lamp, a reading one, though throwing a circle of brilliant light in a circumscribed radius, leaves the further and upper parts of the apartment in a sort of gloomy duskiness. Just outside that circle of shining light sits Eunice, gazing with fascinated eyes into the suggestive dimness.

* * * * * *

And now, slowly and solemnly, the clock in the roomy, deserted, tumble-down stables of the Manor House strikes twelve; and just as the last stroke dies away on the still air, and the sweet-toned bells of the old country church, half a mile off, clash forth in gladsome peal, announcing with triumphant joy the birth of another Christmas morning, the same loud, startling knock of a year ago resounds through the great echoing mansion. But not, as in her dream, is it followed by swiftly moving steps answering that imperious summons; no familiar footfall sounds upon the stair. Deathly silence follows that crash of sound; but still her eyes are riveted on the door . . . And presently—slowly, noiselessly—it opens wide!

Into the space beyond her eyes glare wildly, and see—nothing! Yet, as she looks, it closes again softly, and she is conscious, with an instinctive, horrified thrill, of a *presence* in the room beside her own!

An irrepressible scream of terror rises to her lips, but is petrified, ere it finds utterance, by still greater awe.

Staring into that shadowed gloom, she sees nothing; and yet *something*—an impalpable, indefinable something—seems to be gathering form there,—a shadow, a degree deeper than the rest, a breath of icy air that sweeps across to her!

Paralysed with a fearful horror, she slips from her chair, and, crouching to the floor, shrinks back close to the wall behind, perhaps with a half-instinctive effort to gain the door that communicates with an inner room, and that is but a foot or two distant.

But as she moves, that awful something seems to move too! Is it but a wreathing vapour, or is it a gliding shape?

A long mirror fills the space between two of the three large windows—the space most distant from her. Across this the *thing* must pass as it advances, and she gazes in a trance of terror. What will she see reflected there? And, even as she looks, an awful formless grey mist seems to steal across the shining surface! . . . And still the air grows colder, and that terrible shadow in her room becomes denser and more tangible, as slowly, slowly, it glides ever onwards to the hearth.

And now it is there—a black, spectral, brooding, as yet indistinguishable form; but the human shape is evolving itself from that floating, awful vapour! And the fire burns dimly, and the light from the lamp, though clear, is bluish and ghastly; and gradually the shrouding mist appears to melt, and a human figure is revealed in the midst thereof—shadowy, unearthly, awful; a face livid, ashen; a face of the long-buried dead. And, once again, with her living, waking eyes, Eunice Beresford looks on the face of her father, Maxwell Beresford—gazes on that simulacrum of embodied death, which is yet but a phantom, a shade, as, through that awful form and ghastly corpse-like face, she can see the light and room beyond! And still she lives, still she crouches, with rigid muscles and fixed stony eyes, gazing in transfixed horror . . . And the mist grows clearer that envelopes that terrible form, though still a sort of luminous haze palpitates around it, through which those great dark eyes now gleam with a shining, unearthly lustre. It is as if life suddenly entered that awful phantom of death—

spirit-life, that is but an essence, and requires no substance for its dwelling-place.

Yes; more and more like the human creature, the father she knew and loved, that mystic shadow grows. Clearly defined now is the whole tall, stooping figure; distinct the noble head and snowy hair. And now the long, shadowy hands are moved and raised; and the cowering woman, who retains consciousness and life, as it were through some inscrutable mesmeric power that holds her spell-bound, sees that those spectral hands clasp *a violin*—or rather, the semblance of a violin, as it, too, it shadowy and wraith-like;—and once more that awful unearthly music reverberates through the room—now, as the voices of angels singing; again, as demons wrestling in despair!

And now *it*—*he*—that ghastly vision on her hearth, is playing a dirge-like, mysterious melody, the burthen of which is madness, despair, and death, laden with unutterable woe, full of wild, hopeless, inexplicable trouble. It suddenly changes into a rapid measure, weirdly horrible, morbidly terrible. The wondrous transitions and complex developments, shifting phases of beauty and deformity, might be likened to the phantasia of life itself—and played by a shadowy, spectral hand; by one who has passed out of life into the "great beyond;" a sublimity of awfulness is reached, which imagination fails to conceive.

*　*　*　*　*　*

And the wretched woman, crouching on the floor, still hearkens with starting eyes, from which the reason has almost fled!

*　*　*　*　*　*

And now all is silence again, and the shadow thickens once more round that unearthly figure. Formless, shapeless, it again grows, as it glides to where she cowers . . . And from out that awful floating mist comes a voice; and yet it seems far off—so far!

"*Eunice*," it says, "*I have come for you! I promised, and I have come! Take this token of my presence, and follow me!*"

Something is pressed into her shrinking hands, and the terrible shadow floats onward to the door. There it pauses and vibrates, with a strange quivering motion; then for an instant it parts, and she sees again the face she loved, gazing back at her, with mournful, yearning eyes. The next instant all is vanished! The room is in darkness, profound, impenetrable, while the angry swirl of rain against the windows, and the low moaning of the wind are the only sounds that break the stillness.

* * * * * *

And the hours of the night creep away; and by-and-by, in the chill, late daylight of the Christmas morning, the maid who waits upon her, finds Eunice Beresford on her face, by that door communicating with the inner room—unconscious, but still breathing; while grasped between the stiffened fingers is *the missing violin!*

* * * * * *

For two days she remains thus, life being manifest only by the laboured, struggling breath; in all other respects she is as one already dead. The muscles never relax their grim clasp of the violin. Without force it could not be remove; and so it is left in the dying woman's hands. By-and-by, when death has supervened, and the rigid stage in passed, it will drop from the lifeless fingers, says the doctor.

And on the morning of the third day, before the late grey wintry dawn is born in the east, that terrible panting breath suddenly ceases, and all is still!

The friend who had brought her from her obscure lodging back to the Manor House, which seems to have killed her with some wizard devilry, is present—has never left the house for a moment, night or day, since he was hastily summoned by the terrified housekeeper. He has got a skilled nurse from one of the great London hospitals; but he feels it is useless, that the hour has almost struck that will call the last of her race home. He feels an unending reproach in his breast that he had not remained at the Manor on Christmas Eve, despite her urgently expressed desire to be alone.

Tired and worn out with watching, anxiety, and nervous dread, he had dozed for a few minutes when the night is insensibly blending into day. Mrs. Hancock is there too, seated with her back to the bed, grieving, scared, alert; but she is slightly deaf, and notices not the cessation of that panting breath.

The nurse, who had been absent but for a few minutes, returns at this juncture. The strange, sudden silence strikes her; she moves quickly to the bed, and sees at a glance that all is over. And, mystery awful and terrifying, the *violin is gone!!* gone out of the dead woman's hands—vanished—a second time inexplicably! And never again is it seen by mortal man! . . . Has she brought it with her, as directed? . . . Or did *he* who gave it come for both? . . . None may say. All remains in darkness, profound, inscrutable.

CHAPTER IV
A PSYCHOLOGIST

"WELL, gentlemen, it is nearly five-and-twenty years now since Eunice Beresford passed through that awful ordeal and the gate of death," continues Professor Dysart, the narrator of the preceding ghastly experience.

Arnold Dysart, Fellow of Cambridge, is a man who has travelled much and read immensely; whose mind runs in certain grooves—grooves bordering on the mystic line stretched between the real and the ideal, between the natural and what men still call the supernatural. He is both poet and philosopher, dreamer and thinker, imaginist and scientist—a combination, apparently, of opposites; but the line of demarcation between the two is often so faintly traced, that we lose ourselves on that border-land, trying to define the exact point where idealism ends and philosophy begins; the dreamy, wild, impassioned soarings of the one merging almost insensibly into the consecrated calm, the sublime and lofty region of the other.

He lectures on modern philosophy in the University; but the subjects that lie really nearest his heart, in which he takes an untiring, unsleeping interest, are others than this.

He is somewhat of a theosophist, believing, to a certain extent, in the doctrine of metempsychosis, and the utter purification of man from all remaining earthy dross, by his being born again and yet again after this earthly life, ever more selfless, more etherealized, more spiritualized, until at last he is absorbed into the Deity from which all life emanates, and of which it is a part; each individual existence being but a ray, or throb, of that great central Divine

Life that is the universe and God in one, and back into which great sun of life these tiny radiating sparks must be again absorbed, when loosed from the fleshy trammels that have held them prisoners for a little space.

Such, at least, is the doctrine of "Buddha." And the votaries of "Esoteric Buddhism"—who are so numerous in our midst, growing quite a power in our land; whether for good or ill, of course, it remains to be determined—teach, we believe, much the same theories, only, perhaps, incorporated with others still more startling and difficult of conception.

There are fashions in religion, we know, as well as in all other things in this sad, bad world; and the present day is peculiarly ripe in originating "fads"—for, in truth, they are little else.

Some one starts an idea more or less novel, original, startling, if possible, whether in morals or religion, and there is immediately a crowd of worshippers—or perhaps, rather, "would-be initiates" is the better term. The originator is the hero or heroine of the hour, and they at once feel themselves apostles of the new light; preaching a crusade against the superstitious darkness that still wraps most of the world. But thank Heaven for the gloom that shuts our eyes to those will-o'-the-wisps that dance over the marsh and morass, and are soon engulfed therein; and thank Heaven still more for the light that is from above, that is in our hearts—"the light of the world" that "passeth not away;" and he that followeth that light "shall not walk in darkness, but shall have the light of life."[49]

But, to return to Professor Dysart; he is a student of occultism, and takes an ardent interest in all psychical phenomena, whether

[49] John 8:12.

they take the form of singular dreams, presentiments, coincidences, hypnotism, thought transference, etc.; in fact, "will-power" of any or all kinds; holding the rather peculiar doctrine, which he is fond of promulgating in the words of some modern writer, "that the power of will and the principle of life are fundamentally identical; and he who can control his own will, becomes thereby able to direct currents of life within his own organism, and to transfer them upon others for the purpose of giving health, strength, etc. Also," he will continue, still quoting the same author, "it is believed that those who have obtained the power to control their own thoughts, may thereby become able to read the thoughts of others; because the mental images created by the latter become reflected and mirrored in the minds of those whose souls are tranquil, and such images may enter their consciousness."[50]

He has faith in the power of will distant in life, and also in the power of will distant in death! He holds the belief, that though the body be dead, yet that the spirit of thought, the very essence of life itself, still has being somewhere, and can influence living minds, possibly even more forcibly than when that liberated will was encased in flesh itself; and also he believes that in sleep the soul sometimes escapes, and leads a dual life—a theory that would account for many strange, inexplicable impressions, and seems as mystical as it is marvellous.

But, in spite of his being so very advanced a thinker and enthusiastic psychologist, there is nothing at all terrible or mysterious about Arnold Dysart. He is a tall slightly-built man, with a pale, thoughtful, worn face, but with the kindest eyes and sweetest smile imaginable, and with a manner as kind as are his eyes.

---

[50] From *The Life of Joshua, the Prophet of Nazareth* by Franz Hartmann.

The two gentlemen to whom he has just read the foregoing singular and most weird story are old and valued college friends, whose bent of mind and thought are not very unlike his own.

The younger, Cyril Raymond, is a clergyman, and somewhat of a visionary enthusiast, dreamy and spiritual; while the other, Harvard Fenton, is a barrister of brilliant renown, famous in the conduct of great criminal cases, and whose persuasive, fervid eloquence, when retained for the defence, almost inevitably turns the scale of popular sympathy; and the accused, who had seemed wrapped in garments of an inky darkness, suddenly issues forth from beneath that cleansing stream of sparkling, impressive oratory, pure and white as an angel's wing.

For besides possessing a clear, logical, forensic mind, there is a strong vein of poetry and idealism in Fenton's mental nature, and the two united combine to make him one of the very first counsel of the day.

"My father, who made the notes from which I elaborated the horrible story I have just read to you," continues the Professor, after a short pause, "was an old and intimate friend of Maxwell Beresford's, although many years his junior; in fact, he was the friend of whom I allude in the tale. Eunice he had known well in her girlhood, but during the last twenty years of her life he had seen very little of her, being almost constantly absent from England; and it was owing to this fact that he was unaware of old Beresford's death, and his daughter's sad change of circumstances. When he did return, he at once sought her out. It was he who effected her return to the old Manor House, the home of her race. He did all he could for her, seeking to rouse her out of the singular absorbed, apathetic, and yet at the same time, unnaturally exalted, frame of mind which had become normal with her; but to no purpose.

She was too utterly withdrawn into the visionary world ever really to belong to the things of earth again; the 'Hidden Life' had opened its mystic doors a little way to her dazed, yearning eyes, and she only waited for it to open wider still, when she might cross those shadowy portals, and know what lies beyond.

"It was just two months before the end that my father met her again. He was one of those to whom I allude in the little preface to my sketch as having heard the mysterious music; Mrs. Hancock, the housekeeper, was the other.

"Eunice told him everything, and though rapt, dreamy, ecstatic, she was sane as I am.

"On that last terrible Christmas Eve he urged her strongly either to come to his hotel or allow him to be with her at the Manor, but she refused to hearken to either proposal. She felt, she declared, that some added revelation would be made to her from the unseen world, and that if her father did come for her, she desired to be alone to meet him. And so she passed through that awful experience in self-elected solitude."

"Yes, Dysart, it's very horrible; indeed, the most ghastly thing I ever heard," says Fenton. "And this extraordinary narrative of yours impresses one peculiarly, owing to one's having such undoubted testimony of its absolute authenticity. But you say in the preface that the unfortunate lady lived to tell the horror of that last night, whilst in the story, as you have written it, she never recovers consciousness. How is that?"

"My dear Fenton, ever practical—which, I suppose, is the natural outcome of the legal mind. A lawyer's 'occupation's gone' if he may not ask the 'how' and 'why'—eh, Raymond?"—glancing at the clergyman with a smile, who is sunk in profound reverie upon the mystical tale just concluded. "I made that slight departure from the actual, merely for the sake of dramatic effect. Two days after that awful night, Eunice recovered speech and consciousness, and, though evidently dying, her mind was clear. She sent for my father, who had never left the house, and told him all. He was inclined to think that she was the victim, either of hallucination, or some monstrously clever trick, although he had heard that phantom music with his own ears, although with his own eyes he now gazed on the restored violin. The grasp that had clutched it so firmly as to defy its being removed without force had relaxed with renewed consciousness, but she would not allow it to be touched; it lay on the bed beside her, just where her hand could rest on it, and it was thus she told the ghastly sequel of her tale to my father.

"For two or three days she remained in this state—weak, panting, conscious, but with the dying eyes ever fixed as on some unseen presence. It was a strange and awful experience, my father said, to see her as she lay thus, waiting for the prison bars to burst, that she might go free; yet, even while still caged, looking on the road she was about to travel.

"During all those days my father never left the Manor; and I, a boy of thirteen or so, remember well tremblingly crawling to that dreaded door and gazing in with awed, horror-struck eyes at that mysterious wizard violin, and the pale, drawn, visionary face upon the pillow. Even to my child's understanding I knew she gazed on what was not visible to mortal eyes, and I shrank away, shuddering and terrified.

"Then, by degrees, she sank again into the state of torpor or insensibility that first held her, body and brain apparently paralyzed, and life only evident by the struggling breath; her last conscious act being once again to clasp the violin to her heart.

"Thus she remained for forty-eight hours, and then came the end, exactly as I have written it.

"My father had dozed but for a few minutes, in the chill early dawn, when the nurse's exclamation roused him. The laboured breath had ceased. He started to his feet, and saw that Eunice's spirit had fled and the violin with it, and, strong man as he was, the awe of so weird a manifestation almost overcame him.

"Then, after a little, he grew again to think that possibly the whole eerie marvel was the result of some diabolical trickery, practised for some unimagined sinful end—possibly to rid the Manor House of inhabitants; and with this view, he determined to have it thoroughly and systematically searched."

"Yes," speaks Fenton, again interpolating, "that would be a most natural solution for him to arrive at, save that the first manifestation was made in the lodging which Miss Beresford occupied in Westerham; it was there the violin disappeared, so how would that account for——"

"My dear fellow, you are rational and logical, of course; but a man, after going through such an experience as my father just had, is not quite so cool-headed; he felt he must unravel the mystery by which they seemed to be surrounded, or at least make some attempt to solve the weird problem, and the first thing that suggested itself to his half-dazed brain was to examine the servants, and search the great old rambling house. The first step did not take long; they were but two or three in number, faithful old retainers, who had loved and honoured the last of the Beresfords, and mourned her dead deeply and sincerely.

"They and my father both knew that the house had the reputation of being haunted; that there was an old story or legend attached to it, of a murder having been wrought somewhere under that many gabled roof, in days long past and gone, and that the spirit of the guilty creature could not rest, but constantly revisited the scene of her crime.

"Strange and unaccountable sounds were reported at long intervals, as proceeding from that disused east wing; but in the last generation or two they had been heard but seldom, and the restless phantom who, if tradition were to be believed, had intruded her unwished-for presence at all inopportune times and seasons upon her ungrateful descendants, left these two, the last of the line, in peace.

"Superstition said that her actual appearance always boded ill to the house of Beresford; but she was seen so often during the lifetime of the late squire's grandfather—the last baronet—all the evil almost that could be wrought following in her train, that I suppose that is the reason she left these two last representatives of the race unvisited.

"To Eunice, at least, that shadowy *she* was nothing but a name, and my father said that she seemed to attach no importance whatever to the legend. Of course, up to that date, this wild tale of a haunting presence had never been actually verified; and these things are so very generally only folly. Some absurdity is started, originally, perhaps, but in jest, or by some ignorant, superstitious folk, whose crazed fancies are not worthy of the slightest regard by sane people; but the thing grows and grows, and in the end assumes giant proportions, man, on the whole, being so credulous an animal.

"But tradition in this instance spoke truth, apparently. And that strange, weird story of a past sin, and an abiding shadow ever brooding over the house of Beresford, was to be confirmed in a singular and startling manner. In fact, there is so strong an air of exaggerated mysticism about the sequel of my story, that I almost fear you two will fancy I am drawing on my imagination."

"No, Dysart, we shan't; say on," says Cyril Raymond, with rapt, dreamy eyes fixed intently on the Professor's face. "For my part," he continues earnestly. "I believe that man knows little as yet of the mysteries that surround him, and especially little of the greatest mystery of all, his own thinking self. 'The highest study of mankind is man,' we are told; but I should word it differently, and say, 'The highest and most important study of mankind is the *brain* of man.'

"Amongst all the marvels of creation, the wondrous works of the Infinite, *it*—that small portion of white and grey thinking stuff in each human head—is the acme, the crown, the very apex. It is a mystery ungraspable by the most learned. Man has wrested many strange secrets from Nature's storehouse, but of the most terrible secret of all, that awful mystery of his own being, he knows absolutely nothing.

"Of late, certainly, he has begun to recongize this ignorance, and to make little abortive attempts to render it less profound; but what has he discovered as yet? Nothing, except the startling depth of his want of knowledge.

"He is on the threshold of the most marvellous mine of mysteries that the world holds, but he has not yet crossed it. When he does—as doubtless he will by-and-by, when the time is ripe—stepping even ever so little a way within that mystic chamber, he will know what we call wonderful, mysterious, weird, supernatural, arises only from certain conditions of that complex, extraordinary, wizard organism, in peculiar temperaments, where the body is subordinate to that mighty magician, the brain, and that——"

"Raymond, my friend, shut up! If once we let you mount your peculiar hobby, you'll be sure to ride full tilt, and will 'let nothing you dismay,' laughs Fenton good-humouredly, who knows the clergyman's weakness for this one absorbing subject. "Let the Professor finish his horrors, and then you can treat us to a dissertation on the brain, if you feel disposed; though, I fear, between Dysart's *diablerie* and your metaphysics, *my* poor 'thinking stuff' will be *ex curia* to-morrow, and I shall lose my case.[51] Go on, Arnold, like a good fellow, and I'll engage to keep this enthusiast in order."

---

[51] *Ex curia*: out of court.

CHAPTER V
THE DISCOVERY

THUS adjured, the Professor continues:—

"That day my father did nothing; he was too thoroughly shaken for action of any kind, besides feeling that there would be a sort of want of reverence for the newly dead to institute anything of a regular search immediately.

"He felt really grieved for Eunice, the woman that he remembered so well as a child, and as a bright, beautiful girl; and mingled with his sorrow were both horror and awe at the manner of her death, and its attendant incomprehensible circumstances. So through that day he grieved and pondered, determining to do all that lay in his power to clear up the mystery on the morrow.

"But before the morrow came, there was still another little link of mystery added to the chain that had already grown so strong and was so binding.

"When the night and sleep and silence fell on the Manor House, my father, tossing in restless wakefulness on his bed, with a dim sense of an unearthly presence brooding somewhere beneath that wide old roof, heard clearly, yet faint and low, as if coming from a great distance, the vibrating notes of the spectral violin! At first he thought that his senses must be deceiving him. He sprang up and listened intently at the door of his room, while a strange supernatural awe grew strong upon him.

"That mystic music had been silent for many days; yet now, once again, those phantom strains breathed, as it were, low amongst the rafters of the Manor roof.

"The weird sounds no longer appeared to proceed from any

portion of the great rambling old house in the neighbourhood of the rooms Eunice had occupied, but stole, and crept, and sighed, away far up above one's head, away in some distant, remote untenanted region of the old dwelling. And as my father stood and hearkened, rooted to the spot, as if by some singular magnetic power, he seemed to know instinctively that they proceeded from that lonely east wing, that desolate gable which tradition pointed to as the scene of the murder in the Long Ago.

* * * * * *

"How strange and wild and unearthly seemed that mysterious harmony! Where did it come from, and who was the player? The very nature of the music seemed to declare its supernatural character; the distance it appeared to travel seemed so vast, with numberless closed and locked doors shutting it off and off; and yet the sounds, as they reached the ear, though low, were intensely, vibratingly clear.

"And through the hours of darkness the ghostly strains sighed and sobbed and plained in eerie lament through that haunted gable, and my father lay and listened; but, brave man as he was, he had not courage to trace it to its source.

* * * * * *

"With the reassuring daylight returned both courage and unbelief in larger measure than before. That it was some devilish trickery, he felt convinced; and if cunning or conjuring had devised or perpetrated the previous horrors—horrors that had compassed the death of poor helpless Eunice—why, this last little bit of simple jugglery would be but child's play.

"And, with this conviction, he organized a proper and efficient searching party, numbering in its ranks of half a dozen or so a police officer, as representing the power of the law.

"But the latter's impressiveness was quite thrown away; no

delinquent was discovered who would shrink appalled by the awful authority of the 'man in blue;' no one, or nothing that could be arrested, prosecuted, and punished, was found beneath the Manor House roof. A few scurrying, belated rats; a timorous, peeping mouse or two; aggressive, bloated spiders,—these alone held the fortress of the eastern gable.

"And now to continue in my father's very words, for he wrote out a minute account of this day's proceedings; though the notes from which I wrote Eunice's story, and these papers I now hold in my hands, were not discovered by me till less than a year ago, in a secret drawer of my poor father's writing-table:—

Nothing else, either earthly or unearthly, was to be seen, no strange music to be heard. The undisturbed dust of ages lay thick upon these lone, drear passages and echoing staircases; dust so dense, as almost to form a carpet for the foot, and which was proof incontrovertible that no human presence had penetrated this haunted gable, to practice wizardry of any sort.

How eerie and terrible now to think of that midnight music! How impossible almost to realize it, and still more the ghastly, awful facts of the last week or two!

That mystic violin—where was it? *What* was it? Could it be that *she*, that haunting spirit of evil, whose phantom presence was said to dwell in this shunned east wing, had entered it, and spoke in the weird music of its wailing breath?

Yes, it was a violin bewitched; or rather, that beloved old Straduarius of poor Maxwell Beresford's had become possessed by the lost soul of *her* to whom tradition pointed as the sinful, ever-brooding shadow of the house; it was co-existent with her, and now they were one.

I know not what wild, fantastic thoughts took vivid hold upon me as, after exhaustively searching every part of that strange, eccentric old gable, we stood at last within the room at its remotest end—the room reputed to be the scene of the tragedy in the olden time.

The threshold evidently had not been crossed for a great number of years; possibly a century and more had elapsed since any one stood within these mouldering walls. And it was this fact, I thought at first, that accounted for the strange stifling sense of oppression that struck me with a queer foreboding chill of dread expectancy.

* * * * * *

It seemed to my excited imagination as if this room we now had entered was surcharged with some subtle influence—was dominated by some invisible presence . . . I had felt nothing of this in those many other rooms and passages and stairways; and this impalpable influence appeared to reveal to my quickened senses that a clue to some mystery was at hand . . . I looked about me in vague bewilderment . . . I felt strange, odd, unlike myself, as if drawn to some hidden end by some invisible force . . . I verily believe I was the subject of some sort of weird mesmerism, emanating from the long dead will that reigned in that desolate chamber.

* * * * * *

I looked round on those that accompanied me; they were unmoved, unaffected; they felt no unseen presence in the air; the room held for them nothing but dust and decay. I bade them leave me; my voice sounded strange and distant. I seemed to speak and move as one who was locked in some paralyzing dream.

When they were gone, I moved across the room with mechanical steps, as if guided by some unseen hand . . . It contained three or four pieces of very ancient crumbling furniture; one was a sort of old-world bureau, an article with numberless drawers. To this I went direct, without hesitation. What did I expect to find? I did not know. I had no thought in the matter. All I did was automatic. I moved and acted without volition of my own. A sort of numbness, as it were, bound my faculties. I was a machine, not a man. Of course, I do not insist that all this was so; it may have been only some extraordinary phase of an overwrought imagination, and that I only fancied I was influenced.

But though I moved to the bureau with such strange directness, the great number of the drawers seemed to puzzle me, and for a minute or two I stood uncertain. I opened two or three haphazard, and gazed vaguely into blank nothingness . . . But still no faintest gleam of knowledge of what I sought was borne in upon me.

* * * * * *

Then suddenly that same strange *influence* seemed to guide my hand that had directed my steps, and I turned away from all those multitudinous brass-knobbed drawers that faced me like unsolved enigmas—away to a tiny, obscure one in the left-hand corner, at the very top, almost hidden beneath the overhanging edge of the heavy old-fashioned piece of furniture.

It was locked; but the wood was rotting, and at my second rather vigorous pull the lock gave way.

I drew out the drawer, but it was empty, like the others, dust of many, many days, that had rolled itself gradually into soft, woolly, fluffy balls and oblongs being its only contents. Still I drew it out to its entire length. It was long, narrow, shallow, but nothing lay concealed within . . . Yet still my hand and eye seemed riveted to it, and I felt compelled to do what I then did; and that was to remove the drawer altogether from its groove, and scan the empty space at the back.

I did so, but could see nothing, the place was so confined and dark; but, inserting my hand, I felt suddenly and convincingly that I had at last found what I had been blindly forced to seek. The drawer was strangely shallow—shallower much than its outside appearance led one to suppose—and in the vacant, unsuspected space thus gained my hand closed on a long slight roll of paper.

With a strange feeling of standing on the brink of some added mystery, I drew it forth and gazed on it half fearfully.

The paper was yellow and stained and brittle with age; it was tied round with a somewhat broad band of rich satin ribbon, that had been doubtless once a neck-ribbon and bright-coloured, but from the same cause as the paper, it had faded to a sickly neutral tint; and lastly, the characters traced upon the outside of this somewhat flat roll of paper had become so faint, though of a reddish hue, as to be scarcely legible. But I carried it to the wide old casement window, my heart beating thickly, while a strange tremor of expectation thrilled me, and after a little I deciphered the following singular inscription—or rather, inscriptions, as there was writing on both sides of the small scroll.

"The Last *Will* and Prophetic Curse of Dorothea Eleanor Beresford, written and signed *with her blood* this day, April 27, 1687."

And on the other side—

"When he who in the far distant future shall find this paper first holds it in his hands, the final vengeance of the prophecy herein writ with my own hand, the curse that I lay upon the house of Beresford, will have begun to work."

With trembling, eager, and yet shrinking hands, I opened this document so strangely inscribed. All the feeling of mechanical action that had been so strong upon me had vanished; the subtle influence that had seemed to dominate and guide me had disappeared, leaving me as usual, only nervous and somewhat shaken.

Just as I had untied the fatal binding ribbon the search-party returned for me, and to say that there was now no corner of that eastern gable unexplored. So I told them to return to the inhabited part of the house, and that I should soon follow.

Yet I will confess that as I listened to their retreating footsteps, a slight feeling of apprehensive dread came over me for a moment; but I conquered it, and opened the strange secret I had disentombed.

The writing of the inner portion of the manuscript was much less faint and shadowy than the outer, and I should have read it with comparative ease, but for the odd, thin, spidery character of the handwriting, combined with unfamiliar, old-world spelling, which I shall not attempt to transcribe.

This singular mysterious document ran thus:—

"I, Dorothea Eleanor Beresford, wife of Sir Hugh John Beresfort, Squire of Deep-Dell Manor, and master of the wide vast Manor lands, in the parish of Cotham, barony of Kingswood, county of Daleshire, and within five miles of the city of Westerham, being a hopeless prisoner in this terrible chamber, and sentenced to the slow agony of death from starvation, by my aforesaid husband, Hugh John Beresford, as the reward and punishment for my crimes—first, my betrayal of himself; and, secondly, my murder of my lover in this very room, on believing him false to me, owing to the deliberate misrepresentations of my treacherous husband—do hereby declare that I leave the curse of my undying, vengeful spirit upon the house of Beresford; and do solemnly now prophecy, being of sound mind and clear understanding, the evil that will be in the latter days, when I and my time and times are forgotten, or are remembered but as a wild and baseless legend.

"The cloud shall gather slowly—very slowly, over this house

that is my murderer, and to which I am an alien, although I bear its name, which I have dishonoured. Slowly, but surely, it shall darken on all sides. Money and lands, honour and title shall go, one by one; and then, at last, the race shall die out too. And *this* is the time I choose for my final vengeance.

"The last of the House of Beresford will be a woman, lovely, and pure, and good, and sorrow-stricken. She shall live on till long past her shadowed youth, and she shall die when the chill breath of life's autumn begins to blow—die horribly, as if by witchcraft. The magic of the dead shall slay her; and *then* will the time of my vengeance be ripe.

"She will die and be buried, but she shall come again, Aye! in sooth, again; though none will guess, not even she herself, of this mystery and curse that I now foretell, and say shall be.

"She shall come again, lovelier even than before, with the beauty that lures men; and *my* spirit shall dwell in her, and she shall be false and wicked; crime shall she do, even as I have done. And when the measure of my guilt is doubled even in her, when the tragedy that these walls have seen is reproduced in dual shape in those distant days—then, and not till then, will the cup of my revenge be full, and at last I shall rest!

"I see it all with my dying eyes. I look into the future, and read it as if it were a book.

"Let none, forsooth, say hereafter Mistress Beresford died mad, and these are the ravings of one who perisheth with hunger and remorse for her crimes.

"I have no remorse, save for him whom I slew in my haste and hot wrath, believing him false. I would that I had slain him who now slayeth me; but my vengeance will be sure and full.

"And, behold! I will give this one sign in the fulness of time, that he who reads may know my words are about to be accomplished:—

"Let him who hears the music—not of earth—sound from the eastern gable, the music of the violin (*his* hated violin), take heed, and know that the end is at hand, and the prophecy about to be fulfilled!"

CHAPTER VI
WHAT WAS IT?

SUCH were the exact words of this most extraordinary and mysterious document that I had become so strangely possessed of.

I lost all count of time as I stood there, reading over and over again that eerie, startling prediction. The paper seemed to have a magnetic, horrible attraction for me. Of course it was all nonsense—wild, absurd rhapsody; the malevolent delirium of a brain strained to snapping-point by the weight of its own guilt, and the deadly, cruel, lingering nature of the punishment meted out.

What barbaric times they were in which that sinful Dorothea lived! When a husband could condemn a wife to—and carry out unmolested—so horrible a sentence, even though she had been wicked, superlatively wicked; even though she had, in a mad fit of ungovernable rage, taken a life . . . Still, a prisoner in this room, shut out from all possible means of escape—as the gulf below that decaying old casement was shudderingly deep—condemned to slow starvation; a woman, doubtless, young and strong and beautiful, with the life currents coursing like wine in her veins, to die thus, like a rat in a trap;—*did* she wait for that awful, agonizing death to steal upon her pang by pang? or did she add another to the black record of her crimes, and escape by the one door still left open to her—suicide? . . . History said not.

But even as the thought came over me, a breath of icy air seemed to sweep through the room, though the window was close shut and the weather wonderfully mild for December; and as I shivered, and glanced round with a sudden unspeakable dread, my ears caught, as it were, a faint rustling sound, and then, in a moment, *something* seemed to pass me by, close—quite close, for I felt the air fanned by that mystic presence, though my straining eyes saw nothing, and gazed but on vacancy . . . Yet *it* was there near me—quite near, horribly near—for an instant, that invisible, formless, soundless presence. And then, in another moment, I knew I was alone again . . . And, with the blood beating in my ears like the piston of a steam-engine, while a cold sweat of deadly terror burst on my brow, I stumbled from the room, still clutching that strange long-concealed paper in my trembling hands . . . With faltering, uneven footsteps I made my way back, rapidly as possible, to the inhabited part of the Manor, almost losing myself among those singularly intricate, winding curves and passages and stairways, that puzzled and distracted me in that first inexplicable rush of ghastly fright, making me irrationally feel as if I were caught in a maze of unearthly terror. And as I went, . . . suddenly there was borne to my ear, faint and low, but yet distinct and clear, the vibrating notes of the mystic violin! . . . Yes, away there behind me, in that farthest point of the eastern gable, sigh'd and wailed those phantom eerie strains!

* * * * * *

The short December daylight was swiftly waning as I gained the occupied portion of the house. I had been hours, though I knew it not, in that lone east wing, and now, with the growing dusk, that weird music filled me with inexpressible awe.

What inscrutable mystery was hidden beneath the roof-tree of the grey old Manor? I asked myself, as I approached the death-chamber, longing, yet half dreading to look once more on the sad, sweet face of Eunice Beresford, locked in the calm of its eternal repose.

But I need have had no fear; there had been no occult change in the dead. All was the same as when I last stood within the room in the early morning hours.

But as I gazed on that rigid, motionless form, hoping that the awful calm which always seems to reign in the presence of that dread, mysterious visitant might soothe and quiet my over-wrought nerves, the extraordinary realization of a portion—the earlier portion—of that weird, mystic prophecy I had that day discovered struck me with the force of a blow.

If but a coincidence, how tragically similar! The pomp and wealth and state of the house of Beresford had indeed departed. The baronetcy was now a thing of the past; the wide-stretching manorial lands had become alienated from the family; and the late proprietor's spendthrift grandfather, the last baronet, who had dishonoured and forfeited the title, had poured out money like water, leaving little more to his successor than the heritage of the old name, and a pile of mortgages.

Maxwell's father made a great effort to pay off some of these latter, almost swamped himself in the attempt, gave up struggling against adverse fate, drifted with the tide, and passed away, to make room in turn for his son—room in a house that could no longer be called their own, and with the small portion of the estate that remained to them mortgaged up to the hall-door. And when old Maxwell's time came, and he passed to "where, beyond these voices, there is peace," the race was virtually extinct.[52]

He, the only son of an only son, had for his only child a daughter, and when she died unwed, the name and family of Beresford died too; the house and lands passed into the possession of strangers, and that singular prophecy was thus oddly fulfilled.

---

[52] A line from *Idylls of the King*, "Guinevere", by Alfred, Lord Tennyson.

And were there not other and even more startling realizations of that hidden eerie writing? Had not Eunice's death been strange and mysterious? Had it not in some way been compassed or brought about, either by actual mystic contact with the dead, or else by an awful, inexplicable force or influence, some extraordinary *magnetism*, exercised by the dead, yet still *living*, *will* of that unknown guilty Dorothea?

Her body had been dust for centuries, but the thinking spirit, the mind,—that wondrous pervading, dominating, mysterious essence, force, power—call it what you will,—that exists in us all, and that really is *the* man or woman, apart from the poor decaying body; that mystic something that has share with the Infinite, being bounded by none of the finite laws that chain and cramp the physical nature; that possesses unlimited, immeasurable potentialities, and that is proof stronger than aught else we have of our immortality and kinship with the divine;—that occult *will-power* of Dorothea Beresford still had existence somewhere!! Had I not had proof of it a while ago in that distant terrible room?

And *it*, that indefinable, potent *it*, had foretold the manner of Eunice's death; foretold it while it was still shrouded in the misty, far-away future; and now it had come to pass.

Would—could the horrible supernatural sequel to that prophetic curse be wrought? I asked myself in dazed bewilderment, as the whole weird story appeared to spread itself out before me like a map, while I still stood in the silent presence of *her*, who seemed to have acquired suddenly a mystic individuality.

* * * * * *

And then again my thoughts reverted to that awful violin!

What was it?

Surely not a mere violin, nearly two hundred years old. Its actual history was strange; it seemed to have played a somewhat prominent part in the fortunes of the family to whom it belonged, being the favourite instrument, tradition said, of that stern, relentless, betrayed husband, who had loved devotedly till he found his love was outraged.

But it must have had some eerie dual life. It was a "familiar," an independent spirit, a creature! A lost, despairing soul was caged in its musical heart. It was *her* familiar—Dorothea's; she bent it to her will.

That strange, weird Cremona had come down as an heirloom in the Beresford family; but it had disappeared when they ceased to be; and now, *she*—that mysterious *she*—had possessed herself to it, to aid her in the spell of her demoniacal enchantments.

* * * * * *

I think, verily, my mind was a little unhinged by late gruesome experience, or I should not have perpetrated the folly of indulging in such ultra-wild imaginings. But the ordeal I had gone through in that desolate east wing had really tried me severely, and I could not shake off the effects for some time.

And even when my nerves did get tolerably calm, and I endeavoured to think out the whole singular mystery rationally and cohesively, I could arrive at no conclusion, but that some strange esoteric influence brooded over the house, in some way connected with that spirit of evil that had lived and died so horribly in the flesh beneath its roof in the long ago.

What that influence was I could not tell; unless some unsuspected phantom form of mesmerism—mesmeric power, exercised on living men by certain strong, peculiarly organized mental natures, whom death has claimed for its own, but whose subduing, dominant *will-power* remains active, eternal, unconquerable; a power, or force, that may be disseminated widely, although the world—even the scientific world—acknowledges it not, and may exercise—rarely consciously—in numberless cases, an unconscious, vital, supremely potent influence on the lives of those whose temperament renders them especially receptive of the magnetic current, whether emanating from the living or the dead; and who may be thus moulded by an invisible, unimagined force, working silently, mysteriously at the heart of their being—moulded for good or ill!

And possibly in this astounding problem which suddenly presented itself to me, in this dark and fearful enigma, might be discovered by him who held the key to the mystery a clue to much of the crime and sin and sorrow of the world that seems so greatly unaccountable!

* * * * * *

"My father's narrative ends abruptly with these reflections," continues Professor Dysart, folding up the papers in his hands, and looking earnestly at the two men, who had listened with such profound attention to the strange sequel of his story—"reflections that embody ideas which doubtless many will consider little short of the ravings of a madman, and would excuse in the present instance as being only wild, exaggerated fancies, engendered by the strange horror he had gone through. But I am inclined myself to think that there is more in that startling idea of the minds of the dead being still active, living, influencing media in our earthly life, unknown, unsuspected by us, than our physical science yet recognizes. Of course, I mean rare and peculiarly organized minds—minds that had the mesmeric power largely developed in life."

"Does it not recognize psychomachy?" says the barrister, with somewhat of a mocking smile; "at least, I think I have seen some such big, impressive word somewhere; and, doubtless, the conflict understood in that terribly high-sounding term means that between a distant-in-death dominating spirit and some poor living victim that writhes in its unnatural bonds, but can't escape."

"Ah, Fenton," retorts the Professor, with a remonstrating head-shake, "I fear you are a hopeless scoffer, and that your conversion is beyond my skill! Your rationalism—or, perhaps, I should rather say, materialism—must be indeed of a pronounced order if you are still unbelieving of psychical phenomena after the——"

"Don't mind him, Dysart," interrupts Cyril Raymond eagerly. "He only assumes that *rôle* to disguise the real depth of his conviction. No man could listen to so startling a revelation of a weird, mystical agency, influencing human life in so terrible a degree, without being greatly impressed. It has always been a theory of mine that the human mind does not die when the man dies. We bury the brain, certainly, with the body, and it becomes dust with the rest; but that is the physical mind, that has corporeity in the head; but the immaterial, divine spirit of that mind, the condensed, sublimated essence of the man's being, has surely separate existence. The soul is the immortal part of man, indestructible, unseen, eternal; but may it not also be the spirituality of his mind? It is hard not to think that the soul has kinship close and inseparable with the intellect, the imagination, the higher nature, that seems to have so little in common with materialism of any kind. I suppose it is the humanity so strong within us," continues the clergyman deprecatingly, "that cries out for a continuance of this mental life in the future state; that clings frantically to the idea of eternal *mind*-life, as well as soul. The body *must* become dust; but the thinking spirit surely has an existence apart from the breath."

"Yes," speaks the Professor, with thoughtful accent, "it is hard, so terribly hard, to believe that those great and glorious intellects that shed a lustre on the earth from time to time, and those lesser mind-lights—inferior to those giant ones, and yet how brilliant—that illuminate each generation here and there, become extinct at death, and are not for evermore; that there is no 'progression' through the countless ages; that intellectuality is at a standstill for everlasting."

"How pleasant is the *Swedenborgian* theory!" remarks Harvard Fenton, catching for a moment the dreamy spirit of the other two.[53] "How delightful if one could think that it shadowed forth, even ever so remotely, the life of the world to come—an ennobled, purified, incorruptible, perfected life—but still life, wonderfully like this in its *mental* developments."

"The fact is," answers the clergyman softly, with a distant, rapt look in his dark, earnest eyes, "we are too grossly earthly while clogged with these bonds of flesh to understand, to comprehend even dimly, the divine beatitude of a redeemed spirit admitted into the Eternal Presence, and permitted to join in the celestial choir. Such unimaginable, ineffable bliss is beyond and above our dull, finite comprehensions; and we try to clutch at any simulacrum of the only state of existence that we know."

---

[53] According to Emanuel Swedenborg, author of *Heaven and Hell*, on entering the spirit world, a person appears much as they were in life, but eventually each individual's inner nature becomes the whole of their being, and the outer self—what they did or said to fit in when alive—is shed. This takes place in an intermediate realm. Following this shedding of the outer self, each person enters Heaven or Hell depending on their true inner nature.

CHAPTER VII

AN *OPEN* COFFIN!

AFTER a slight pause Fenton questions the Professor as to what further steps his father took to sift the Manor House mystery.

"Surely he did not let it rest there. Did he not seek more strenuously to solve that strange enigma—a puzzle that must have meant but clever conjuring?" he continues energetically. "Of course, there was no real value to be attached to that hidden paper, purporting to be a prophecy; the realization of its sinister words were, it must be admitted, a series of marvellous coincidences, but nothing more, believe me. Nothing would persuade me to the contrary. And I think, Arnold, old friend, you could not have a better proof that the whole weird history may be read by the light of singular coincidence and jugglery combined, than that five-and-twenty years, as you tell us yourself, have passed away since Miss Beresford's mysterious death; and all those long years she is quietly sleeping in her grave, and the great and crowning acme of that dread, prophetic curse,—the point where wizardry steps in and declares that the limitations of the range of man's understanding shall be passed, the natural laws by which humanity is governed set at nought and defied—that life and death, in short, will become exchangeable terms—remains still unfulfilled. Eunice Beresford sleeps the sleep that knows no waking, and has not returned in sinful guise to earth, as the prophecy foretold."

"I know not whether she sleeps or wakes," responds the Professor, softly and very gravely, with a sudden shade of mingled reverence and doubt in his tones. "The last and almost strangest incident in this mystic, terrible story remains to be told. I don't blame you for being sceptical, Harvard; it all seems so horrible and unearthly. But we know little, as yet, of *will-power*, whether in life or death, and certainly not enough to say dogmatically such and such phenomena cannot be. Doubtless, what we call phenomena now, as Cyril said a while ago, will be looked upon as quite commonplace and matter-of-course in the latter ages of the world.

"But to return to what remains as yet the last, and, I think, *unfinished* chapter in this unique and startling history.

"A week subsequent to the events I have related, Eunice Beresford was interred in the family vault of the Beresfords, in the graveyard of the old church, scarcely more than half a mile from the Manor. Many Beresfords slept their last sleep in that gloomy chamber, but still it was not full. There was room for more, only there are none to fill it.

"Poor Maxwell's coffin looked painfully fresh when his daughter's was carried in and laid beside it. Only two years since, that time-sealing gateway had harshly grated open to receive him—that gate which none who enter as inmates may recross, we are told. And yet——

"On leaving the vault my father, who was chief, and, indeed, only mourner, noticed that something was slightly wrong with the gate; it would not quite close, and so could not be padlocked. He gave directions to have it put in order, and a few days later left Westerham, aged and decidedly broken in health by the maze of horror and mystery in which he had taken so prominent a part.

"That *he* should have been appointed to find that document, the existence of which none had dreamt of through all those long, long years—for so he regarded the singular compelling power that seemed to force him to its discovery—he looked upon, in his then nervous state, as in some way ominous or foreshadowing that he was either to make some fresh discovery, or be involved in some future complication of the not yet ended tragedy.

"He guarded that mysterious paper carefully, but kept it a secret locked in his own breast. He told none of what he had found. He loved and respected old Maxwell Beresford and his daughter, and he determined not to make them the subjects of wild, speculative, eerie gossip. If all ended there, as he prayed (though he scarcely ventured to hope it would be so at first, when the ghastly impression was fresh and subduing), why should any know of that weird prophetic curse that lay upon the house, and that in so many respects had been strangely accomplished?

"As to the awful manifestations which had been made to Eunice, none knew of them but himself; she had confided the events of that last terrible night to him alone, also the mystic revelation of the previous year when the violin had disappeared. The facts of its being marvellously restored, and as supernaturally again withdrawn at the moment of death, were known to Mrs. Hancock the faithful old housekeeper, who adored her mistress. The professional nurse, too, was aware of its final vanishing; but she was a prudent, sensible, practical-minded woman, who had no knowledge of, or faith in, esoteric powers outside the ordinary limitations of man's being. It was she, in fact, who had been the first to suggest 'trickery;' she felt neither awe nor fear, only indignation; and for the day or two that she remained, before returning to the London hospital, she made no mention to the three or four servants who were the sole other inmates of the great Manor House of what had occurred.

"And though Mrs. Hancock was inclined at first to believe that all sorts of witchcraft an black-magic had attended her dear Miss

Eunice's death—for she had heard the mysterious music on two or three occasions, and she heard it again the night after her mistress died—yet by carefully concealing all else from her, and by urgently insisting on trickery, my father at last induced her to accept this solution of what had terrified her. She was familiar, of course, as were all in the neighbourhood, with the legend that declared the Manor House to be haunted by the spirit of a woman who had committed murder beneath its roof in the olden time; but that was all.

"For the same reason that actuated my father, she promised to breathe no word of the strange things that had happened. She had loved and honoured the family she had served so long and so well, and it would have broken her kind old heart to have heard any member of it spoken of in terms of reproach or slight.

"And now, at last, to reach the final mystery—final, at least, *as yet.*

"More than a year passed away, and by degrees the terribly strong impression made on my father during his sojourn in Daleshire paled and faded to a certain extent, as things must and will, under the numbing influence of relentless time, that potent destroyer of all illusions and impressions, whether they be for good or ill.

"About this time he had business in Westerham, whither I accompanied him, being then a lad of nearly fifteen. And then, when this business was concluded, he thought, being so near, that he would like to look once again on the old house that enshrined so strange a story.

"We drove out to Cotham, and walked on to the Manor, but found it empty and deserted. No one remained in it even as caretaker; it was void of all human presence. He into whose hands it had passed on Maxwell Beresford's death, when the mortgages were foreclosed, and who had granted Eunice a home there for the last two months of her life, had as yet made no use of the property of which he had become possessed.

"Gaunt and desolate it looked, with its innumerable windows blank and barred and rayless. All those on the lower storeys being protected by outside shutters, only those diamond-latticed casements away in the quaint old gables caught the light and reflected it a little. Dreary it seemed in the extreme, left, as it were, to decay and moulder with the race that had lived an loved and died within its walls, and were now extinct.

"Even my inconsequent boyish heart felt chilled and depressed, I scarce knew why. A feeling of eeriness, almost of awe, stole over me, as we stood in silence outside the massive gates, which were securely fastened, and gazed away to where that great grey pile raised its ponderous bulk, just within sight of the high-road.

"Where were those who had looked out on the world from all those melancholy, sorrowing windows through the misty past—looked out in joy and grief, despair and ecstasy; with the ardent hopes of restless, fervid youth; with the disillusioned eyes of disappointed middle life, that has eaten eagerly of that sunny southern apple that mocks the thirsty one, and found but dust and ashes at its core? Or, again, where were those who had looked abroad thence, with the calm, contemplative eyes of age that had played its part in the drama of life, outside which it now stood contentedly, knowing it was but the preface, the prelude to the real play which will soon begin for all? Where were they all? I asked myself in vague bewilderment, losing myself in a strange, confused, meditative dream, unfamiliar to my young careless mind. But somehow, looking at that grey old house, and knowing even dimly of the strange shadow that silently brooded over it, and that, with suddenly quickened imagination, I almost fancied I saw, I seemed to myself to grow, even there and then, older and more thoughtful.

"After a little we turned from the gates and pursued our way through the sweet country lanes, to that graveyard not far distant. As my father could not enter the house, he would at least pay a last visit to the Beresfords' final resting-place; 'And then, doubtless,' as he said to me, as we walked between those perfumed hedges, 'we shall hear no more of the Manor House, or the dead race that owned it.'

"My father had told me very little of what had occurred at the time of Eunice Beresford's death. The restoration and final disappearance of the violin I was obliged to know, being in the house at the time, and seeing the mysterious violin with my own eyes."

"Ah! you saw it, Dysart! What did it look like?" interpolates Cyril Raymond quickly.

"Just like an ordinary fiddle," answers the Professor, "save that it looked old, very old, even to my ignorant child's eyes. It had a strange look of age about it, inexplicable, but undoubted, as if antiquity had set its own peculiar seal upon it, as indeed it had. But my father had told me nothing of the prophetic writing which he had discovered—I was too young to be trusted with such a confidence—neither had he told me anything of what Eunice had imparted to him with regard to that awful night in which her father visited her, and restored the violin. But yet I knew quite enough—being familiar with the legend of the haunting spirit, as known to the Westerham world—to feel there was something strange, weird, uncanny, about the house.

"We soon reached that historic old church, beautiful in its

old age, with its ivy-clad tower, and moss and lichen-grown walls that veiled so tenderly the decay that here was picturesque. It was a lovely old-fashioned graveyard, set on the slope of a hill facing the westering sun; not trim and pared and pruned with maddening, jarring precision. There was long lush grass waving above the lowlier sleeping places, unmarked by memorial stone; rich clover grass, in which sweet smelling wild-flowers bloomed luxuriantly and at will; and there were plenty of trees—lovely gnarled old oaks and beeches, as well as weeping ash and willow, and cypress and yew—through whose glorious foliage the sunlight fell in chequered radiance on those quite graves.

"You may wonder why I seem to rhapsodize about the country graveyard, and how I remember it so well; but it made a strong and lasting impression on me, which, all things considered, perhaps, is not very surprising.

"Near the centre of this abode of the dead there was a sort of fosse or moat, only the bottom was dry and gravelled instead of containing water. You descended to this perfectly circular sunken path by a rather long flight of steps; or you crossed to the centre of green that the path enclosed, and on which were some of the handsomest tombstones in the graveyard, by a pretty rustic bridge. But it was to that lower level we were bound, for within this circle were some eight or ten vaults, the burial-places of the few families of distinction in the neighbourhood. That of the Beresfords was one of the most important. All the vaults had large iron gateways, through the bars of which one could look into the space beyond. That which we sought was the third from the steps. We came to a standstill before it; the gate had been repaired and was securely padlocked.

"We stood and looked into the gloomy, silent chamber, with

faces close to those strong, unyielding bars. I looked vaguely straight before me at the piles of mouldering, dust-laden coffins, without any definite purpose in my gaze, and with a sense of dull depression, mingled with a feeling of bewilderment and confusion in my breast strange and unfamiliar. I seemed stupidly to stare at nothing through a dreamy haze of undefined trouble, and a sudden, astonished, excited exclamation of my father's startled and unnerved me . . . He had been looking, with twisted neck and straining eyes, round into the shadow of the right corner of the roomy vault, where rested the coffins of the lately dead.

" 'My God! what is it? Are my eyes deceiving me? Am I mad or dreaming? . . . Great God! surely—yes, surely, it is open! . . . No, it can't be; it is something in my sight!' he murmured in rapid, almost frenzied utterance; while I, scared, though I knew not what he meant, fell back against the tangled mass of ivy on the outer wall of the vault, with beating heart and starting eyes.

" 'Arnold, my son, come here; tell me what is this. Your eyes are young and strong, and will not play you false. Do you see something like a mass of tumbled white drapery away to the right there? . . . Do you see—do you think—that—that the last coffin left here is—is—is *open?*'

"The idea of an open coffin did not greatly appal me; or rather, perhaps, I should say, I was so enormously relieved to find that this was what had so startlingly affected my father, and not some fearful ghostly vision, some ghastly, spectral form, that I felt comparatively easy and courageous.

"I moved to the spot where he stood, and gazed as he directed; and after a moment or two, when my eyes again grew accustomed to the gloom, I saw that it was even as he said . . . Old Maxwell Beresford's coffin lay in that right corner in a niche of its own;

even there in the shadow the fresh deep red of the handsome velvet gleamed richly. On it stood Eunice's, covered in black; but across the lower portion of the coffin was thrown a heap of white linen that might be either sheet or shroud; and, on looking more intently, I saw that the coffin *was* open, as I could plainly discern the creamy tint of the satin lining.

"I told my father, and he seemed to me extraordinarily disturbed. Of course, I thought it was very strange and queer that the coffin should be open, especially if also the body were gone; and from where I stood, it appeared as if it were empty! But I had read and heard of such things being done before by wicked men, perhaps hoping to get a reward, or to steal something, or for some equally evil purpose. But why my father should be so terribly dismayed and aghast I, not having the clue, could not guess.

" 'It has begun!' I heard him mutter. 'That awful curse is real, active, living. And she, that sweet, pure, patient soul is the victim . . . Great heavens! what an inscrutable mystery it is! *Can* such a weird, ghastly horror be?'

"Wild and incoherent seemed to me his broken, murmured speech.

"We at once sought the guardian of the dead, the caretaker of that peaceful graveyard.

"The man was genuinely astonished, and even alarmed. He brought the keys, and in another moment we stood within that vaulted chamber, amidst the mouldering dust of the extinct race of Beresford, and gazed with awed, non-comprehending eyes at the singular and novel sight—a coffin open and empty among its fast-sealed brethren—a coffin that looked as if some one had lain down to sleep within its narrow space for a brief repose, and, awaking, had tossed the coverlets aside and gone forth from the silent companionship of the dead into the palpitating world of life around, having gained a new and strange experience.

"What was the meaning of it? Who had opened those jealously closed doors? Who had liberated the imprisoned inmate? We read of 'seeking for the living among the dead;' but here it was reversed, and we should be obliged to seek for the dead among the living![54]

"The dead have no volition of their own; where, then, was the senseless clay that had occupied that narrow bed?

"On examining the coffin it was quite apparent that the body must have been removed before even the very earliest stages of decomposition had set in, as it was sweet and pure as when fresh from the undertaker's hand. And, strangest marvel, the nails that had been driven home so surely to their mark, sealing the dead within so fast and safe for all time, were all in their places, none of them extracted!

"It was as if a mighty heave had thrust up the lid from the *inner* side, and thus the quiet inmate had gone free."

---

[54] Luke 24:5.

CHAPTER VIII

CONCLUSION OF THE PROFESSOR'S NARRATIVE

"THE man who was the then sentinel appointed to watch over those dreamless sleepers was astounded, even more so than ourselves. He could not account in any way for the disappearance, for, in cases where graves have been rifled for the purpose of theft, both body and coffin remain; an where it is designed to steal the body, the coffin goes too.

"The gate that had been out of order at the time of Miss Beresford's funeral had not been repaired for a month or more, but during the interval it had been securely fastened with a stout rope, which remained undisturbed, he knew, as once or twice a week he made the round of that sunken path, to keep it in order and see that all was right. Of course, he didn't take any particular notice of the interior of the vaults, having no reason to imagine it necessary; but anything wrong with the gates would have immediately attracted him.

"There had been no loiterers about the graveyard at that time, not at any time. It was quite different from the large cemeteries that are open to all, at all times; the gates here were always locked, except at service time, or when he and his men were at work among the graves, and even then they often locked themselves in. Any one wishing to visit the graveyard would have to apply to him for the key.

"My father remained silent, sunk, doubtless, in speechless amaze, knowing what he knew about that awful mystic prophecy, while the man exclaimed and explained; but after a little he roused himself. It was necessary, he thought—such, at least, I consider must have been the feeling that actuated him—that he should talk, and talk naturally; expressing indignation, anger, astonishment, at the sacrilege that had been committed in the removal of the dead; carefully doing and saying all that might avert suspicion (superstition is a plant of natural and gourd-like growth in the ignorant peasant mind) of any unholy, occult, weird influence having part in this mystery of disappearance.

"Thus they spoke for a while. Why should the body be stolen? There were no valuables buried with Miss Beresford; neither would the theft and retaining of the body be likely to induce a reward, as there were none to offer one—no relative, no one caring for this last scion of an extinct race, argued the man, who was both shrewd and sensible.

"Yes, my father agreed that this was very rational; but, still, in robbery for some purpose was to be found the only solution of this extraordinary problem. Doubtless it was in the interests of pathology this hideous desecration had been carried out. There were circumstances attendant on Miss Beresford's last illness and death, peculiar phases both of brain and nerve-power, that may have been heard of, and elicited overweening, irrepressible curiosity in some sacrilegious, scientific mind, that hesitated not even at crime to gratify that baleful craving.

"Such was the only possible and feasible mode of accounting for the singular fact of disappearance. And with this argument, a little above his head, the man seemed convinced, and my father's task here was over.

"Boy as I was, I could see what a terrible effort he made to keep up, and not give way to the natural human awe and dread that must have been strong upon him. The strain was great, he was ashen pale, and his limbs shook as if he had the ague.

"But still he did his best to spare those last two members of the old Beresford family all obloquy and injurious, wild, desperate surmises. He interviewed the proper authorities, laying his statement of the facts before them. The world would have to know the strange and horrible fact of Eunice Beresford's body having disappeared from its coffin; better that it should know it first through him; stamped with the peculiar impression he desired to give it.

"And now all was done that could be done by him. The authorities would take all proper steps to try to recover the body, communicating with him as success or the reverse attended their efforts, he, of course, bearing all expense. But I know now, as surely as if he had told me with his own faithful lips, that this was all done to give a false scent, as it were, to the world; to prevent the possibility of their imagining any mystery behind. Not, surely, that any could dream of what I am convinced he believed to be the reality of that awful disappearance.

"Was not this another startling step in the realization of that terrible wizard prophecy? 'She will die and be buried, but she shall come again, aye! in soothe, again,' " concluded Arnold Dysart dreamily.

* * * * * *

"It's marvellous and ghastly, Dysart; an out and out horrible story. A fellow feels completely bowled over, utterly floored, by such weird, terrible coincidences. But still, even with all that swelling pile of realized predictions, I feel morally convinced that they were but a chain of singular chance agreements with that devilish writing your father found," says the barrister earnestly. "And I am borne out somewhat in what you'll call my stubborn belief," he continues, in slow argumentative tones, "in its mystic, prophetic character, in my want of faith in the theory that the mesmeric power remains after the person who possessed it has passed into shadow-land; that the world is dominated and controlled, in some singular cases, by the living, active influence of the 'will-power' of certain strange, strong minds, largely possessing the magnetic current, that have passed away into the darkness, but whose spirit of Thought still is living potent and subduing somewhere. This is the theory you advocate, is it not—what Raymond believes, and what your story goes to prove? But I am borne out, as I say, in my incredulity by the fact that, notwithstanding the mass of evidence you have given us of the inexplicable concurrence of events—phenomenal events in some instances, like the mysterious music—yet that still, through all these years, the crowning point of the prophecy remains unfulfilled. I take it for granted, from your manner, that your story is at an end, and yet Eunice Beresford has *not come again.* Doubtless, the old Manor House has either been pulled down, thereby exorcising all indwelling evil spirits, or, still more likely, it has been restored and rejuvenated, and is now the abode of modern fashion that knows and cares nothing about the Beresfords, and who would laugh immoderately at the idea of anything so absurdly obsolete and old-fashioned as a ghostly presence sharing their home.

"Even when poor Miss Beresford died, comparatively late as is the date, superstition still lingered here and there; but since the diamond-wedding of our century with time, the world has grown infinitely more scientific—the one being a natural outcome of the other—and those lingering marsh-lights of superstition have been extinguished once and for all by the penetrating electric rays, etc. There is no longer any corner sufficiently dark for the traditional ghost to lurk in; all is swept and garnished, and pitilessly exposed to the searching rays of realism and rationalism."

"But, Fenton," exclaims the clergyman, almost impatiently, "how can you be so obtuse? The very scientific progress that you advance as an argument against Dysart's story, annihilates yourself, and leaves you nowhere. The matter under consideration is altogether appertaining to the domain of science—*most modern science*—and not, as you seem to imagine, to vulgar superstition. Surely, the weird and mystical tale we have listened to is not to be ranked as a mere 'ghost-story.' A supernatural episode, if you will; but I question greatly whether what we now call by this obscure and comprehensive term may not be looked upon as quite natural by our descendants, thanks to science. The science of thought, or 'will-power,' seems to me almost an illimitable field for speculation and discovery, and one which has been very little worked as yet. That man's marvellous mental spirit dies not with the breath, I feel assured. Perhaps, as a clergyman, you may think that I ought not to hold such theories, or, at least, ought not to confess them; but I do not see that they are in any way subversive of the faith which I profess and teach; on the contrary, I consider that faith, as a beacon-light, lighting us to those glorious and divine mysteries of our own immortal being; and that to seek to unravel a few of the occult threads of our spiritual nature, is no more displeasing to the Most High, who, in His beneficent love and mercy, has given us the grand, crowning, priceless blessing of intellect—intellect so soaring in its nature; that, though bound by the finite laws of human life, strives to grasp the Infinite—than He is angered at our wrestling secrets from Nature's storehouse.

"But have you quite finished, Arnold? Is your story at an end? Has the house of the Beresfords indeed undergone the transmutation Fenton suggests, and become the dwelling-place of wealth and fashion?"

"By a strange chance, Harvard is right in his conjecture," answers the Professor. "The Manor House *has* been restored, and is now the abode of wealth, though not exactly of rank and fashion. By rather what I call a coincidence, I know a little—a very little—indirectly, of its present occupiers, which seems to myself all the more singular, as I took no steps at any time to hear anything of the house. The impression made upon my boyhood by the mystery of the violin, followed by the disappearance of Miss Beresford's body from the family vault, naturally wore away, and became almost effaced with years. I had no clue, as I have already told you—knowing nothing of these"—pointing to the papers he had laid down on an adjacent table.

"My dear father died in less than a year from that day on which we made the discovery in old Cotham Church graveyard, his death accelerated, I verily believe, by the strain of mind and horror he had gone through, and by the weird secret he kept faithfully locked in his breast. Within a few months of his death, I know he received information from the Westerham authorities that all possible measures had been taken for the recovery of the missing remains of Miss Beresford, but without avail. He died before I was sixteen; I am now, as you fellows know, just forty, and until some nine or ten months ago, I never dreamed of the existence of these papers. I found them by chance, last autumn, in a private—I can scarcely call it secret—drawer of my father's writing-table, which I have retained for my own use. I thought they were quite valueless, and was about to burn them unread, when, on opening them carelessly for that purpose, the words 'Westerham' and 'the Manor House' caught my eye, and at once enchained it. With a rush came back all the strange, wild memories of my brief boyish associations with the Beresfords, and with eagerness I perused the memoranda my father had made of that singular episode of his life. Also the hidden prophetic writing which he had found, and which, read by the light of the occurrences he testified to, seems, I aver, in spite of Fenton's incredulity, to be the key to a terrible mystery!"

* * * * * *

"And what do you know of the present tenants of that uncanny Manor?" asks Fenton lazily. "Nothing, doubtless, eerie or uncommon; and I think I would venture to stake a small wager that these unknown people, whoever they may be, have experienced no unpleasant revelations of realized prophecies since their occupancy—eh, Dysart?"

"No, very possibly. All seems as prosaic and commonplace, according to what I have heard connected with the house and its inmates, as if they inhabited the latest atrocity in the way of the 'select villa residence' type that a modern builder can perpetrate.

"Some seven or eight years ago, the house having fallen into grievous decay—the man into whose hands it passed on Maxwell Beresford's death having either failed to find a tenant for it, or abstained from seeking one—it was purchased, with a large portion of the original estate, by a wealthy old cotton-spinner from Lancashire. He had the place put into thorough repair, I understand; transformed it into a stately mansion, modernized it as much as circumstances would allow; and there he lived, for some five years or so, in solitary grandeur. He was a widower, with a reprobate son; but, about three years ago, he married a lovely young creature—young enough to be his granddaughter, I believe. I know nothing either of husband or wife.

"The way in which I became acquainted with these facts is, that I became very intimate, some few years ago, with a soldier-cousin of this girl who afterward married Cotton; and he confided to me that he was then almost engaged to a sweet and beautiful girl, his step-uncle's daughter. He had loved her all her life, he declared, with a ring of passionate tenderness in his tones; but he feared they could not marry for some time, as he had nothing but his captain's pay, although he had large expectations from a wealthy uncle.

"A year or two later, I received a letter from him from Bengal, whither he had gone with his regiment some months previously; and to that letter there was a postscript, saying that the dream of his life was over and his heart broken; that, henceforth, his profession held for him his sole interest in life—a few noble, manly lines, showing the true, brave, faithful heart of the man, in which he mentioned the marriage of the girl he so devotedly loved (though with never a word of blame to her) to a cotton manufacturer and a millionaire, who lived a few miles out of Westerham—the girl's native city—in the old Manor House belonging to the dead and gone Beresford family.

"And though I had not then found those papers, yet even so the mention of the name excited a certain interest in my breast; and, in any later letters, I looked for any chance allusion that might tell me something of those unknown people who lived in the house to which tradition attached so tragic a story. But the details I have gathered are few and bald.

"The old man adores his young wife; their union is one of complete happiness, with not a shadow to mar it, save, perhaps, the reprobate son, who, however, has been long banished from his father's roof.

"The girl has apparently forgotten her lover, who is still in India; either that, or she prudently weighed 'love and money' in her heart-scales; love kicked the beam, and she married money, and is 'happy ever after.'

"I was truly sorry for Erncliffe; he is a thoroughly good fellow,

I know, a man of stainless rectitude and spotless honour, and with a strong element of chivalry in his unselfish nature. His one strong desire in his letters to me, I plainly saw, was to remove any injurious impression I or others might conceive of the girl who could so heartlessly throw him over when wealth came along; indirectly, he made all valid excuses for her, speaking of her father's strong propensity for speculation—how he had plunged so deeply lately into that fatal sea, and had almost failed to come up again, was very nearly sucked under for good and all; and hinting very broadly that it was to save her father from his terribly pressing pecuniary embarrassments that his lovely young cousin had sacrificed herself. I don't know; it may be so, of course, though I think the record of our marriage-market of to-day shows pretty clearly that England's fair young daughters are quite ready and willing to so sacrifice themselves on the cold altar of ambition. They offer up their beauty and youth, and honour and virtue, on the dark, unlovely shrine of an old man's gold, or a bad man's title and lands, as the case may be, and count it no deed of wondrous heroism, no act of self-abnegation. And yet we wonder at the important place which the Divorce Court holds in our midst to-day. We train our girls to consider 'a good settlement in life' the one thing desirable, attained whether, I am almost tempted to say, honestly or dishonestly; for such legal couplings—the holy word 'marriage' seems out of place in such a connection—*are* dishonest; in my mind, all marriages unhallowed by strong, true, pure love are vile,—we train our young womanhood so to think, as I say, and yet we dare to feel surprise and resentment at the result of our own teaching.

"But, to return to the Manor House. In spite of the utter prosaicality of these very modern central figures in the picture; in spite of the regilding and general rejuvenescence of the old, old frame in which that picture is set, yet I cannot help expecting new developments. I cannot but think that the world will hear again, in some way, of the mystic house! Perhaps it is still in the distant future; and yet that strange writing said that when 'he, who in the far-off days was predestined to find that hidden scroll, should hear the mysterious music, the final mystery of that weird prophetic curse should have begun!"

"Those wild, strange words, seeming to foretell that Eunice Beresford would live again and work out that curse, I look upon as a mere figure, or perhaps, rather, a phantasy of a disordered brain; but what I do believe is that that tragedy of the past foreshadows some terrible tragedy in the future, that will, in some way, link itself by similitude with that distant horror, and will be induced, or brought about, by some strange occult influence *in* the house, that is really the evil living 'will-power' of the dead and gone Dorothea!"

And with these words, Professor Dysart's narrative, and the discussion that ensued, and which took place in his rooms at Cambridge, comes to an end.

PART II

THE VARLEY MURDER CASE

"What nether-world gulf-whispers doth she hear,
In answering echoes from what planisphere,
Along the wind, along the estuary?"
DANTE GABRIEL ROSSETTI

CHAPTER IX
THE VERDICT

THEY are the winter assizes, and the court-house in the large, populous city of Westerham is crammed to suffocation. It is a trial for murder, and that chamber of justice is literally packed from floor to ceiling with human heads; not one square inch of room but is utilised; and human eyes—sympathetic, awe-struck eyes, eager, curious eyes, and hungrily excited eyes—gaze from every corner of the spacious building on the central figure, on that small, slight girl with the white, set, lovely, but inscrutable face, who stands in the dock.

The trial has lasted three days, and all the time that soft, girlish face has worn the same fixed, stony look—not so much a scared or terrified expression as an intense eagerness, held in fierce suppression; as if there was a horror behind those large, innocent blue eyes, ready to leap into them, but kept back by sheer force of will. But only the physiognomist sees all this; to the crowd it is a death-like, pale, fragile, sweet girl-face, worn with suspense and dread.

And now all these hundreds of eyes are momentarily averted from that isolated figure. The jury are slowly filing back into the court; the verdict—that mighty word of such terrible significance, on which depends the life or death of the human creature whose existence literally hangs upon the breath of those other few poor human creatures—is about to be pronounced, and a thrill of expectation runs through that densely packed throng; a murmurous wave seems to pass over it, like a summer breeze through foliage, leaving an intensity of stillness, a hushed, breathless silence behind. And the slender figure in the dock bends slightly forward, one small white hand grasping the rail in front, and the eagerness, at this supreme moment not to be repressed, looks from those great blue eyes, as they almost glare in frenzied doubt at these twelve arbiters of her fate.

She looks nowhere else, as she stands there, with a ray of wintry sunshine lighting up the deep gold of her hair. All these hundreds of human faces seem to have no meaning for her; only these twelve men, gifted with so fearful and unnatural a power, form her world. And yet, away in that corner to the left, separated somewhat from the crowd, sit two figures—a woman bowed with the weight of years, is it? or woe? A woman in whose agonized, worn, aged face there still lingers a something that instinctively makes one feel that she and the prisoner are connected by that closest of all ties, mother and child. The elderly man at her side is evidently her husband; his impatience and nervous anxiety know no bounds; his gaze is constantly turned to his daughter, as if to try to strengthen and support her through this terrible ordeal; but, strange, extraordinary phenomenon, though the mother's face is filled with a great fear and anguish, as if a horrified pain had got into those haggard eyes, and would not be expelled, yet never once are those eyes turned on the pitiful white face, on the slender girlish figure of the prisoner at the bar.

And now there is the authoritative cry of "Silence in the court!" although the silence is already so profound, so deep, that one could almost fancy one heard all these throbbing hearts beat as one gigantic pulse. These terrible twelve whisper together for a moment, and then the foreman speaks, speaks loudly enough; but the one listener whose fate depends upon his fiat does not seem to have heard, as she still stands, with head outstretched a little, and great eyes dilated, non-comprehending. But the crowd has heard, even to the furthermost corner of the building, and a sudden great and mighty shout fills that silent court-house, and escapes out through one or two open windows into the wintry air beyond, to the eager, curious, waiting throng outside. And another bursts forth, and is re-echoed by those outside the closed doors, and the air is rent on all sides by the cry, "Not Guilty!" Every little senseless urchin expends his small soul screaming those pregnant words; the fickle, sensation-seeking crowd, that would be just as much impressed and excited—nay, much more morbidly interested, if that last awful word had stood alone, without the merciful preceding negative; only then their enthusiasm in the cause of justice would have vented itself in awe-struck whispers, in gloomy ominous head-shakes,—shout themselves hoarse proclaiming the thrice blessed news. Caps are flung in the air by exuberant souls in the gallery, and fall on the heads of those below, who are vociferously called on to return the unconsciously acquired property.

And while still the doors are unopened, before the crowd yet begins to melt away, the meaning of the tumult dawns on the dazed brain of her who is the centre and cause of all this wild communication; the full meaning of that triumphant cry resounding on all sides reaches her; and for a moment her eyes close, and the willowy, pliant young form sways a little, as if she were about to faint. But only for a moment; the next, those lovely blue eyes open, with the strained expression gone; the whole face softens, as if some rigid tension of the muscles were suddenly relaxed, and a faint, shadowy, ghost-like smile, imperceptible to all but the gaoler standing near, plays round her lips for an instant, as her eyes seek, with an arrow-like precision—not the faces of those heart-stricken parents, now being congratulated by sympathizing friends and acquaintances on the result of the trial, but the face of a bronzed bearded man, who stands leaning against a pillar in an obscure corner of the court, who has thus stood each day, and all day, through the long-weary hours, just where her eye could reach, without having to turn her head, trying to sustain and cheer her by glances of faith and encouragement. But all through this last most terrible day, not once had she glanced at him; the faces of the judge and jury were all that her suspense-held eyes scanned; but now they go to him straight, swift, sure, and such a look springs into them as almost to glorify her face. It was fair enough before, beautiful exceedingly; but now it grows absolutely angelic, the incarnation of lovely confiding innocence.

How plaintively, how pathetically young she looks to be placed in so terrible a position.

"What is she but a child? God bless her sweet face!" murmurs many a rough man, as he takes a last look at her who has been the central figure in that tragic picture those three days. And yet, child as she looks, she has been a wife nearly four years, and is now a widow, just acquitted of her husband's murder!

And while the court slowly empties itself of its tired and talking throng, the father frantically embraces his child, and asks God to bless her, inveighing in incoherent excitement against the dogged wickedness and devilish suspicion of one or two cursed officials, who could impute such a crime to so young and innocent and trusting a creature; while the tall bronzed man holds both the little cold hands in a grip like steel, as he gazes down with irrepressible love on the white, wearied, but altogether beautiful face.

"I don't know how I lived through it, Leonard," she whispers, with sweet blue eyes raised fearlessly to his; "but," she adds in a lower whisper still, "your presence seemed to give me strength beyond my own."

And then other friends come crowding round, and the girl, the erstwhile prisoner at the bar for the blackest of all charges, is the heroine of the hour. Even the great and dignified judge, the representative of the law in its most mighty and terrible force, condescends, contrary to all precedent, to congratulate the fair young woman on her full and perfect acquittal from even the suspicion of so atrocious a crime. For the beautiful Mrs. Varley is a person of some distinction in the busy city of Westerham, and even so immaculate and unassailable a being as a Lord Chief Justice may unbend a little, without any great derogation from his lofty state, when loveliness and wealth go hand in hand . . . And then, at an entreating, compelling glance from those blue eyes, the frail, trembling woman who has remained strangely silent in the background toters forward with uncertain steps, and takes her daughter in her arms; but she does not kiss her; the worn face, out of which the horror has not yet been banished is turned away over the girl's shoulder, and her lips emit no sound.

Then as she releases herself from the arms that do not seek to detain her, she sinks fainting to the floor. For a moment a wild gleam of fright springs to the great blue eyes, but the next Mrs. Varley is kneeling by the unconscious woman, trying her best to revive and restore her.

"Poor dear mother!" she murmurs, in anxious solicitude. "This terrible day has tried her sorely. God grant she may not be seriously ill."

"And you, Muriel, my darling—if I may call you so once again?" whispers a man's voice in her ear.

"I, Leonard!" she answers, looking up at him with those childlike, innocent, trusting eyes. "Oh, I have——"

And though her lips say no more, those tell-tale eyes say as distinctly as tongue could utter that little word "you." And yet she is a new-made widow, with a murdered husband's blood crying out for vengeance.

CHAPTER X

TOLD BY A SPECIAL-PLEADER

"IS the trial actually concluded, Fenton? I drove here straight from the station, and the man said he believed it was over, and that she was acquitted; but I thought, surely, he must be wrong," questions Professor Dysart eagerly, as he hurriedly enters a private sitting-room in the "Royal Hotel," Westerham, where Harvard Fenton, Q.C., the famous special-pleader,—whose brilliant annihilation of the prosecuting counsel in the "Varley Murder Case," and after eloquent, indignant protest in favour of the hideously slandered accused, is at this moment the one absorbing subject of conversation at every dinner-table in Westerham,—is himself dining in solitary state.

But he chose this loneliness, refusing the judge's invitation, and that of his brethren of the Bar, because he expected Dysart, who has now arrived.

"Ah, Arnold, my dear fellow; I'm sorry you're late," he says now, rising and shaking hands heartily with the Professor. "I hoped you'd turn up this morning, as you appeared to have so strong a fancy to hear how it went, and I guessed it would not run beyond to-day."

"But I can't understand," said the Professor, vexation and disappointment mingling in his usually even, earnest tones, "how a case so serious, so tragic, was huddled up so quickly, so indecently quickly. Why, I thought it would last for many days!"

"My dear Dysart," says Fenton, with a laugh at the other's supreme disgust at the brief length of the trial just concluded, "it is not often that the law is censured for its swift movements; the tortoise, not the hare, is its prototype, I fear, in most instances. But the Varley case—an extremely interesting one, by the way; an interest radiating, of course, from the wondrously fascinating central figure—was not huddled or hurried in the slightest degree. The truth is, there was *no* case properly so-called. The real culprit, as every sane man must believe, was arrested and judged by a higher court than ours, while the brand of Cain was but freshly stamped upon his brow; the parricide went straight from his crime to his death. The case for the prosecution was simply nowhere from the first; it was either a piece of gross official blundering, or else fiendish personal malice—the latter most likely, the emanation of some jealous, spiteful woman's baleful whisper."

"Then you really think the wife was not guilty?" exclaims the Professor; and there is a tinge of—what is it?—in his tones. It sounds like incredulity, mingled with a sense of incompleteness.

Professor Dysart fully expected to hear that the beautiful Mrs. Varley was guilty of the terrible crime imputed to her, although Fenton's brilliant defence may have given her back to the world with a tolerably clean name. It is the way of barristers; *they must* know the truth; but "guilty" or "not guilty," makes no difference to them; they equally insist upon, and seek to prove (possibly by hints or innuendos against a person they know to be guiltless) the innocence of their client. It requires a very elastic conscience, or rather, none at all, as Arnold Dysart sometimes thinks, to make a really good barrister. And he now seems to feel an unreasonable sense of flatness, almost dejection, that the Westerham tragedy has ended so tamely. Surely, with his kind, gentle heart, he must have a strong motive, for allowing so morbid, so horrible a sentiment to have existence in his breast even for a moment; surely, he ought to rejoice that the fair young woman has been fully acquitted from even the shadow of so foul a suspicion. Murder is an awful word; and when bracketed with youth, and loveliness, and feminine weakness, and, above all, with what appears like sweet, trusting, confiding innocence, it is thrice terrible! But Professor Dysart has a motive, or, at least, thinks he has, for the peculiar attitude of his mind.

"Am I guilty? Is the unborn child guilty?" exclaims Fenton, with almost a tinge of enthusiastic defence in his accents, strange in one supposedly hardened by constantly looking on tragic misery, despair, and crime, through the ossifying medium of a legal lens.

* * * * * *

"Well, Harvard, I think you'll admit," exclaims the Professor, after a slight pause, occupied by him in preparing to share his friend's repast, and unburdening himself of overcoat, travelling-cap, muffler, etc.—for the weather is severe, and Arnold Dysart is not strong, besides having just come from a warm climate—"you'll admit that my words of a year and a half ago have been strangely verified. Do you not remember my saying that I felt convinced that the world would hear again, at no very distant date, of that weird old Manor House? And how tragically it has heard! At least, I know no particulars, only the bare, bald fact, that the master of the house has been murdered, foully and treacherously murdered. But why do I talk about my poor words; what do they signify? But if that woman had been guilty, Fenton, how startling would be the realization of the words of that mystic prophecy, 'When the tragedy these walls have seen is reproduced in dual shape in those distant days, then——' "

"Ah, exactly—in *dual* shape," interrupts Fenton, with somewhat of a mocking laugh. "My dear Dysart, do not let your naturally fertile and a trifle eerie imagination run away with you to fancy that the very ordinary murder, known to the world as 'The Varley

Poisoning Case,' in any way fulfils the conditions of that uncanny document your father found more than a quarter of a century ago. First of all, there is no *dual* crime!"

"Ah! not yet—not yet!" murmurs the Professor *sotto voce*.[55]

"And, secondly, if I remember aright, in that old legend of the Beresford Manor House, it was the lover was murdered, and not the husband. And I suppose you hardly think that the *rôle* of lover and husband are merged in one—at least, in the present instance. The wife loved the old man fondly, I am sure—they all bore witness to that effect—but in a nice granddaughterly way; she scarcely could ever have regarded him in the light of a lover, I should think. Besides, the lover that was, is very robustly alive, and——"

"The *lover!* What do you mean? What do you know of the lover?" interrupts the Professor eagerly.

"Well, a good deal, considering the brief period of our acquaintance; and a thorough good fellow he seems, as you said. It was he, in fact, who retained me for the defence. Dr. Hilliard, the lady's father, wished for——"

"Erncliffe back from India! Are you sure, Fenton? Captain Erncliffe?"

"Major now," answers the barrister laconically. "Back this six months," he adds, after a moment or two's pause, in which his attention is occupied by his plate.

"And, good God, man," cries the Professor, so energetically and suddenly as to slightly startle the imperturbable barrister, and cause him to spill a little of the wine with which he is in the act of filling his glass, "does not that very fact, that I didn't dream of, shake

55 *Sotto voce*: in a quiet voice, under the breath.

to its very foundation the structure of innocence that you seem to think so unassailable? Erncliffe returned six months ago, and three months later the old husband is mysteriously poisoned. What could look worse, knowing how matters were a few years ago between these two? How can you for a moment say that she should not be suspected? Why the most trusting, unsuspicious creature on earth should think that——"

"My dear Arnold, pray don't excite yourself! You are prejudiced—"

"Prejudiced!" interrupts the other impatiently. "Why should I be prejudiced? I know nothing of the young woman—never saw her in my life."

"No, of course; I don't mean individually prejudiced—that could not be possible, I think. If you *did* know her, you would feel at once how unjust your suspicions are—a loving, innocent, trusting child, with a face like an angel's. Why, look at me, an unbeliever by profession! For what lawyer, who is at all a success, or, at least, has plenty of business, can keep much faith in human nature? It is the seamy side that is for ever turned to him, until his eyes actually ache, looking at the ugly knots and many coloured tangle. Yet I believe in Muriel Varley's innocence as I do in the heavens above me!"

"Because you're a man as well as a lawyer, and are caught, like others, by the witchery of a face and winning wiles of manner," mutters the Professor scoffingly.

"You are prejudiced," reiterates Fenton, "by reason of your inclination to regard this tragedy as in some way a sequel to the strange history of the past, or rather, a realization in part of that wild prophecy discovered by your father. It is somewhat of a coincidence, perhaps, that there should have been a murder in the house about the time you seem to think that singular curse ought to be working out its final malevolence—though why it should be necessary that five or six-and-twenty years should elapse between Miss Beresford's death and the climax of accomplished vengeance I am at a loss to determine. But, unfortunately, murders are such commonplace events nowadays, are multiplying so terribly and mysteriously, that I think no significance whatever can be attached to the murder of old Varley at the Manor House, especially when we consider that it was the act of that wild reprobate son that you know of, and who committed the desperate deed under the pressure of enormous need of money. You see, this clear daylight of reality dispels the halo of weirdlike romance in which you are inclined to envelop the case," he said, leaning back in his chair and contemplating the Professor's somewhat distracted countenance with a calm smile of superior wisdom.

"Tell me about it, Fenton, like a good fellow," speaks the Professor, after a pause, in which he seems to have been weighing the barrister's words. "I may say I know nothing. Your few lines nearly two months ago, scrawled to me in Egypt, hardly told me more than that there had been a murder in the old Beresford Manor House, that the wife was supposed to have poisoned her husband, and that you were retained for the defence, and concluded by saying that the trial was to come off early in December. The one newspaper you sent me contained almost as barren an account as your own. It was strange that there should have been so meagre a report of the case before the coroner and magistrate—a case that the latter thought serious enough to send for trial; but, of course, that was the result of powerful interest. I made my arrangements accordingly. Of course, I don't mean to say that I should have come home purposely, but I intended returning about the beginning of the year. My Investigations of the old Buddhist rites and doctrines—the occult Buddhism studied by 'Initiates' in the first century, and from which some unbelievers are wicked and daring enough to say we draw out whole theory of Christianity—were almost completed for the present,—I hope to go again in a year or two,—and so I decided to come just a month sooner than I had determined, and be in time to hear the trial, in which I could not help feeling an enormous interest—very foolishly, of course, you think; and doubtless you are right. And now I arrive to find it over."

"I'd have dropped you a line to tell you the actual day appointed for its opening, but I didn't know where to write; your movements when abroad are generally so erratic," interpolates Fenton, as he lights a cigar and dreamily takes a few enjoying whiffs, lazily watching the while the faint puffs of curling blue smoke rising above his head.

"Won't you light up, old fellow?" he asks, after a minute or two's silent luxuriating in the divine soother.

Why is the use of nicotine virtually denied to women? Why must women be socially ostracised—at least, in England—considered unwomanly, fast, almost improper, if she is known to smoke even the mildest, most inoffensive of cigarettes? Men claim to have no special prerogative in any particular food or medicine. Why in the tobacco plant? And if, in extreme moderation, the use of it is admitted to be beneficial, in cases where the nerves require to be calmed and soothed, why is the sex in which the nervous, emotional, hysterical temper predominates to be excluded from this mystic healer? Women have brain-work—and arduous brain-work—to do as well as men, and yet the phrases so often used in regard to the latter—"He *must* smoke, you know, while he reads and writes;" or "A cigar helps him to think so much better;" or, "The luxury of a smoke is absolutely necessary after those long hours of study," would sound somewhat novel and strange in conjunction with the former.

Selfishness is essentially man's attribute, and what he wishes to keep to himself he manages to do in a large and lordly way. So, without actually formulating a decalogue of "Thou shalt," and "Thou shalt not," for his weaker fellow-worker in this weary world, he skilfully arranges it so that when women at all encroach upon these self-established privileges, if they venture to dispute the unwritten law of a divine, masculine monopoly in certain directions, they find matters made rather rough for them. It is men's opinion women really fear and value, not each other's, and with numberless women that opinion is a sort of *ukase* that they dare not defy.[56]

* * * * * *

"It's rather hard upon a special-pleader, Dysart, to expect him to turn *raconteur*. I haven't your gift that way, dear boy; and if I weren't very good-natured I'd send you to the newspapers. However, as you wish to have the story *vivâ voce*, I'll do my best for a while; and if I grow tired I'll turn you over to the *Westerham Comet*, which, *en parenthèse*, luxuriates more in lies than any other paper out."[57]

"Thank you, Fenton; you're a thorough brick, old man! A few words from you, and I'll feel master of the situation; whereas I might wade through half a dozen of these unreliable papers, and their conflicting statements would possibly leave me more obscure than ever," says the Professor, glancing up with a kindly smile in his dark, deep-set eyes, as between nervous, slender fingers he rolls a cigarette—the only form in which he conjugates the verb "to smoke."

"Well, you see," begins the barrister narratively, "somewhere about five months ago, just in the dead heat of the summer, old

---

56 *Ukase*: authoritative proclamation, decree.

57 *Vivâ voce*: by word of mouth. *En parenthèse*: in parenthesis.

Jacob Varley, the cotton manufacturer, who bought Manor House that had belonged to the Beresfords, fell ill. It was a sort of low fever, induced, the physicians stated, by the unusually high temperature of the season, accompanied by the excessive drought. You may remember that we had no rain for fully seven or eight weeks; though, of course, this must seem little to you, who chose to ruralize in arid, rainless Aden a year or two ago for nearly a whole summer, seeking vestiges of a lost civilization. I'd let the lost civilizations find themselves if they wanted, and be content with endeavouring to add ever so little to the civilization of to-day, which has still here and there enough lingering traces of primitive barbarism to justify a small crusade.

"When the 'record-seeker' of the future digs and delves amongst our remains, and discovers, perchance, a *gallows*, or possibly some wonderfully preserved document from which he may gather—if that scientific man of the future could even imagine anything so horrible—that men, in these vaunted days of high-pressure civilization, were actually endowed by Government with a licence to kill; that legalized human butchery was not alone allowed, but encouraged, enforced, and rewarded by the State,—I fear he will think that we were still but in a very early stage of evolution, but slowly casting off the slough of primeval ferocity, when bloodshed was the one grand ambition of undeveloped man; and that the other evidences he may find of our co-existent Chistianity—the records of war or legalized murder side by side with apparent proofs that the religion of 'love' and peace, and good will and charity to all men had taken deep root among us; that we believed in and worshipped the Christ of Nazareth, and yet spent our highest ingenuity, for which we received honour, distinction, reward, in fashioning devilish instruments, or discovering chemical combinations, that would be most deadly in their slaughter of our fellow-men, our brethren in that Christ whose one supernally lovely and divine spirit of teaching was 'to love one another;'—that future record-seeker of extinct civilizations will, I say, be so puzzled by this hideous, gigantic contradiction, that he will——"

"Harvard, my dear fellow, as you are great, be merciful; in your very desire to annihilate my pet pursuit, don't quite crush *me* beneath the weight of your eloquence. Besides, it would be a sad pity not to reserve the brilliant peroration that I am sure is brewing in your argumentative brain for some time when you are prosecuting counsel, and the defendant belongs to the hapless ranks of the 'killing no murder' species. Fire your heavy grape-shot, Fenton, at a responsible target, not at me. I am neither a soldier nor a clergyman, and, consequently, perhaps fail to be sufficiently impressed by the force of your reasoning; though I frankly admit that you seem to me altogether and utterly right in your views of 'war *versus* Christianity.' But, seriously, if I let you tackle this theme—one of your favourites, I know—you'll wander so far from the 'Varley Poisoning Case,' that you'll never find your way back again. He fell ill from the heat and the dry weather—there's your cue. Go ahead, old man, and don't stop to moralize."

CHAPTER XI

FROM THE "EVENING STAR"

FENTON laughs softly at the Professor's energetic interception of further digression, and meekly takes up the broken thread of narrative.

"It was a sort of intermittent fever; and the old man was better and worse, and all things were very uncertain. He was old, and some people said he could not recover. And through all this time of anxiety and suffering the young wife's devotion was lovely and untiring. She wore herself to a shadow in her constant attendance night and day upon the invalid; she could not bear that a strange hand should minister to her husband, and after a while he would take food or medicine from none other; she grieved terribly at the thought of losing him, it appears, her beautiful eyes often being red and swollen with weeping.

"Of course, the great mass of evidence in her favour was given by the servants at Varley Hall (so the old Manor House has been rechristened); in fact, with the exception of a few agitated words, respectively from Dr. Hilliard, her father, and Major Erncliffe, they were the only witnesses for the defence; and they one and all testified to her wonderful, loving devotion. Her own maid, Watson, gave a great deal of very important evidence with regard to the day of the murder and Richard Varley's hurried visit."

"The *day* of the murder! What do you mean by that?" questions the Professor quickly. "Was not the unfortunate man being slowly murdered all along by some of those insidious, stealthy, slow poisons?"

"Not at all. How did you get hold of that idea? No wonder you were prejudiced against the wife. Old Varley died of a tremendous dose of prussic acid, enough to kill a dozen men! The poison had been introduced into the sleeping-draught that was taken on the night of the day of the son's visit; but I have not reached that culminating point yet. Suddenly, after about two months of this fluctuating state, and when it seemed as if the old man must die, he took a marvellous change for the better; he grew stronger rapidly, and the physicians declared him good for another ten years at least.

"The young wife was half crazed with delight, she was so fond of him. All the servants testified to her laughing and crying together in hysterical joy at the thought of her 'dear old man,' as she called him, being spared to her a while longer. She went through the house singing, with radiant face, 'as happy as a Queen,' as they phrased it, unable to keep from speaking to every one of her great happiness in the beloved master's recovery.

"Then there was some slight imprudence committed. Old Varley went out driving too soon, over-fatigued himself, or something of the kind, got a trifling cold, was threatened by a slight relapse, but nothing at all of any consequence. He had to take to his bed again, but only, as it was expected, for three or four days.

"Then Richard Varley came down, and forced himself into the old man's presence, to try and wring money out of him by fair means or foul. He was an out and out rascal, as I suppose you know, and had been forbidden his father's house years ago; he had disgraced that good, honourable father's name more than once—gambler, cheat, blackleg, liar! Jacob Varley had been compelled to cast him off, and disown him as his son.

"When old Jacob married the beautiful Miss Hilliard four years ago, he executed a will, leaving his widow £15,000 a year and Varley Hall; a sum of £5000 to his son Richard Varley; and all the rest of his great wealth in charity. But a year ago, when he heard by chance what a superlatively tremendous ruffian Richard had grown of late, he made a new will, in all other respects the same as the former, save that the son's name was expunged therefrom.

"But Richard did not know this; he thought the first will still stood; and he came to Varley Hall that September day, I verily believe, with the avowed intention of endeavouring to wring some money out of his father, weakened and less resistant as he might prove from illness; but really with the fell determination to *do* for the old man, and secure at least the five thousand that he imagined still would be his on Jacob Varley's death. He was leaving England for good, he said; and I am convinced he came prepared to commit that desperate deed if opportunity favoured him.

"He forced himself into the good old man's presence, into his very bedroom, violently ejecting the young wife, who cried and clung to her husband, longing to remain and sustain him through the terrible ordeal; but she was banished, and then a stormy scene took place; old Varley, prostrated by recent illness, and still ailing, was yet firm and unyielding. He was torn by distress and agonizing memories, for he had loved this evil man with passionate, woman-like devotion in the early years of his innocent, promising youth—loved him even long after he had forfeited all right to that love; and though that faithful love had now turned to disgust, contempt, almost loathing, still to be obliged to repudiate that son gave him unutterable pain, for the old man was of a peculiarly generous, noble, honourable nature himself, I understand, and especially despised the vices so rampantly accentuated in his son. He was spent and exhausted when that interview was over; but yet he had not yielded to the imperious demands, the threats, the cursings, the wild, sinful, impotent ravings of the baulked, unrepentant prodigal. He told his son quietly, though his heart bled inwardly, that he had done with him for ever; that he was less to him than the stranger passing at his gates; that if he was actually in want he could have a hundred-pound note, which he tendered him. He would relieve his necessity, as he would respond to any other call upon his charity; but not another penny of his money should he ever touch.

"The son stamped and swore and raged, and tore the note into a thousand pieces, but the old man remained firm. Unhappily, he did not mention the change in his will; if he had chanced to do so the fatal culmination might never have been reached. If Richard Varley had been quite assured that he would in no way benefit by his father's death, he might not have utterly blackened his sin-stained soul with that last crowning guilt. But five thousand pounds is a large sum to a desperate man, who is conscienceless and pitiless, and he will risk much to gain it.

"He dashed from the room, his lips foul with curses, having managed, as I believe, to leave that fell agent of death behind him. The large, handsome dressing-room opened off the spacious bed-chamber; velvet curtains hung between, but were swept aside; and in his wild trampings to and fro, as he stormed and railed and swore at the poor old man, lying weak, trembling, defenceless, but unflinching on his bed, he may have caught up that night-draught from the little table at the side of the bed, unnoticed by the old man, who was too stricken by mental anguish at the unnatural scene to take much note of the details of the other's actions; and then, carrying the phial with him into the inner room out of sight, how easy, through one of the open windows (which would carry off the strange, strong odour), to empty out a portion of that innocent sedative, and substitute that deadly drug, afterwards replacing it as before. It was but a little bottle, that could be easily concealed in a man's hand, and none could guess of the change it had undergone.

"Shortly after he left the room he quitted the house. The vessel that he said he had taken a passage in for Melbourne was to sail from Liverpool at three o'clock in the morning. It was more than five when he left the Manor House—he was just barely in time.

"Less than a week later that vessel, *The Orinoco*, was reported to be lost with all on board, crew and passengers, not one saved! Richard Varley's name was entered in the sailing-books of the firm as having taken a passage in the ill-fated steamer; his name was also reported as amongst the lost. She foundered when only two days out; and what I firmly believe is, that Richard Varley intended landing at some distant port they would touch on their outward bound way, and coming back quietly to reap the reward of his guilt.

"But to hark back a little. Some two hours after he left Varley Hall it was discovered that the old man's desk had been forced open, and a roll of bank-notes and gold, amounting to nearly £1300 extracted therefrom. Old Varley was half-frantic, not with rage, but with humiliating grief and despair at having to call such a reprobate 'son.' But the young wife soothed and comforted, and poured the balm of her love and tenderness into those quivering, open wounds; and at last he grew calm, and it was hoped that he would not be thrown back seriously or very much the worse for the trial he had gone through.

"Watson, a thoroughly reliable woman, gave, as I said before, very important evidence connected with that day's and evening's proceedings. She was the last person, save the wife, to see the old man alive. She testified to being in her master's bedroom at half-past eleven o'clock. The household usually retired before eleven, but owing to the confusion consequent on Richard Varley's visit, and the discovery made after his departure, they were later, she said. But you may as well read the woman's own words. Hand me that *Evening Star*, on the table at your back. Thanks. Yes—here it is—'Jane Watson in the witness-box.' Well, I've told you all the earlier part; you don't want that again. This paper gives a very accurate, exhaustive report. Where's the bit I want? H'm—h'm! Ah, yes—this is it;" and Harvard Fenton hands the Professor the paper, his finger indicating the following paragraph in the maid's evidence in the special edition of the *Evening Star*, under the somewhat melodramatic heading—

"STARTLING EVIDENCE ABOUT THE MYSTERIOUS VARLEY HALL POISONING CASE.

'Jane Watson in the Witness-box.

"Watson then deposed that she was in her master's room at half-past eleven o'clock, when he seemed to have grown quite calm and tranquil again.

" 'The dear young mistress was sitting upon the bed beside him, reading to him, an' her hand clasped in his. They seemed as happy together as doves. They were like a picture,' continued the witness, with warm enthusiasm. 'He looked so lovin' at her, with his long white beard, as if she was all the world to him, an' he never could tire gazin' at her; an' she had a colour in her cheeks all that evenin', an' a light in her eyes that wasn't her way of late, an' made her look like a hangel. An' then, while I was still in the room, she stopped the readin' an' said—

" ' "It was terrible stupid of me, Jacob dear, not to get your cough-mixture renewed to-day. Both papa and Dr. Freeman said this mornin' you should continue it, but we've had such an upset that I forgot all about it. I trust the tiresome cough won't bother you much to-night. You've got nothin' but your composin' draught to take, an' I suppose you won't take it till the very last."

" ' "No, indeed, my pet," he answered; "an' I doubt I'll take it at all. I'm growin' better, thank God, and getin' independent of that horrible physic."

" ' "Oh, but Jacob," she cried, quite distressed-like, "your sleepin'-draught—surely you'll take that, dear; you may have no rest if you don't, after this terrible day especial."

" ' "I'll promise you, love, to take it if I can't sleep; but I'd rather let nature have a try first."

" ' "Very well, dear old man." she said as soft an' sweet as a lamb; "an' I'll get up an' give it to you, Jacob, if you just touch the bell." Mr. Varley would have no nurse sit up with him now that he was better.

" ' "Indeed, an' I'll do nothin' of the kind, my pet. You've had broken rest enough this good while back. If I want the stuff I'll take it myself. I am sure you ought to be for hatin' your old man, Murrie darlin', wearin' out his little girl's bright eyes."

" 'Them was the blessed old gentleman's very words, an' I'll never forget them. An' for all answer the dear young mistress just hugged an' kissed the master as fond as fond—God bless her sweet, kind heart! An' then she went on with the readin'—which it was the Bible—an' I left the room, an' shortly after every one in the house was in bed. Mrs. Varley slept in the dressin'-room, just off the master's room.

" 'An' then, somewhere about three o'clock in the mornin', we was all woke up by a terrible noise—a noise to haunt one to their dyin' day! There was first a hawful chokin' cry, an' then as if some hanimal clutched the bell, for it was like no mortal hand, the sound it made, so unnatural; an' the table with all the bottles an' glasses an' things that stood by the bedside was overturned with a great crash, as if some one was strugglin' fearful. An' then there were the most hawful screams from that poor young lamb that 'twas enough to kill her dead. She'd been woke up by the cry an' the bell, an' rushed into old Mr. Varley's room just in time to see him dyin' so fearful.

" 'An' her mother was there at the same moment, an' fainted right off; an' Edwards, his own man, who loved him true, flew down like lightnin'; an' I on his heels, though I were nearly dead with the fright of it. An' there was the mistress in her night-dress, a screamin' for the bare life, with her face as ghastly as a corpse; an' Mrs. Hilliard lyin' like one dead on the floor; an' the dear sainted old gentleman, half in the bed an' half out of it, with his poor face lookin' so wild an' dreadful like, an' a horrible white froth on his lips, an' the bell in one hand, an' the glass he'd drunk the physic from in the other. An' the first thing that struck Edwards an' me with such a deadly, hawful chill of fear, though we didn't know the meanin' of it then, was the sickenin', overpowerin' smell of bitter almonds!

" 'Then the mistress fainted dead away too; an' when the doctors came, they said he was quite gone, an' as how it was prussic-acid, an' that it must have been mixed with his medicine. But though they searched the house, not a sign of prussic-acid could they find. They—the imperent police, or detectives, or whatever they calls themselves—turned out every box, an' drawer, an' press, an' cupboard; all the lovely cabinets an' things that stands about in all the great drawin'-rooms, an' that have shelves or drawers or hidin'-places in them, they turned them all out. They hunted every room in the house that the family occupy, an' even some that they don't use, an' that is always shut up, like the "red parlour," an' the "blue drawin'-room;" but it was no good, nothin' could they find, which shows that Richard Varley must have brought it with him.

" 'Yes, Mrs. Hilliard took on hawful. She'd been stayin' with her daughter for a few days, an' she was there that last terrible night; an' whether it was the shock of old Mr. Varley's death, dyin' like that, an' she bein' the first to get there, but she's never been the same lady since—strange in herself, an' silent-like, an' wouldn't go next or nigh the house in all poor Mrs. Varley's trouble, do what they would. I think her mind's a bit gone; they say there's madness in her family.'

"This concluded Watson's evidence."

* * * * * *

"We had another most delightfully entertaining and irrepressible witness for the defence," continues the barrister, in a tone of retrospective enjoyment, when the Professor has finished reading with much interest Watson's evidence, during which time he (Fenton) has had a thoroughly restful, undisturbed smoke, lying back luxuriously in an American rocking-chair by a noble fire, and with a bottle of Louis Roederer at his elbow. "If she had been committed for contempt of court every time she was so threatened—and, indeed, I am afraid, deserved it—the time of incarceration might have been briefly stated in the phrase, 'for the term of her natural life.' She *was* droll, and she *did* take it out of the opposing counsel"—with a little amused laugh. "She was an elderly woman of the name of 'Page,' who had been Miss Hilliard's nurse, and who accompanied her to her new home as a sort of under-housekeeper.

"She had a doglike devotion to her young mistress, and could not contain her wrath against all officers of the law, from the police constable to the judge himself; she rated them all round with noble impartiality, and during the time she occupied the witness-box, she had the court indecorously convulsed with laughter, considering it was a murder case.

"They only reported one or two of her quaint speeches. She was too utterly impracticable; she would not answer questions, except when she chose and gave any amount of trouble; but they had wonderful patience with her, because she was rather an important witness.

"Let me see—it's not in that"—as the Professor involuntarily turns to the sheet before him. "I think it was in this morning's *Daily Mercury*;" and Fenton stretches out a lazy hand, and takes a paper from a table near, which he opens, and proceeds to read aloud the following paragraph:—

'Mrs. Page in the Witness-box.

"This witness was then sworn, and gave her name as Martha Page, and occupation as under-housekeeper at Varley Hall; but she then became irritatingly recalcitrant, ignoring the questions that were put to her, and insisting on making irrelevant and abusive remarks.

" 'I never did hold,' she proceeded to impart to the court, in a voluble and belligerent manner, 'with circustantal hevidence; it's downright heathenish in a Christian country to be made to hold your tongue when you is the only one as has somethin' to say. An' if it's convictions you want'—looking very fiercely at his lordship—'you'd have twice as many, only they wouldn't be the wrong people, if you let the prisoner speak; for if a body's not tellin' the truth they'll contradict themselves shameful at every hand's turn, for no one had a memory good enough to remember their own lies!' "

"By Jove! there's something in that," ejaculates the Professor, with a smile.

"The witness was several times called to order, but she declined to be admonished; and after answering a few questions in a very aggressive and unsatisfactory manner, she burst forth again, with emphatic energy—

" 'It would be the greatest mercy if you all got took yourselves, juries, an' justices, an' the lot of you, an' were shut up in a pen there for all the gapin', idle crowd to stare an' gibe at, an' then to be told the dreadfullest lies on, an' never to be let say one word; you wouldn't find it quite so pleasant then, I'm thinkin', for your lives to depend on the fancy of stupid, murderin' jurymen. Just think of Page there on a jury'—pointing to her luckless husband, who was coachman at the Hall, and stood in a group of other servants. 'An' why not he as well as another? Why, I wouldn't hang a cat, no, nor a canary-bird, on his opinion, much less a human creature! Rubbishy, ignorant lot,' she continued, in spite of a running fire of reprimand, being told to 'stand down,' and threatened with committal for contempt of court, besides stern, fierce cries of 'Order in the court!'—'who'd just think as little of sentencin' a man to death if they were in a bad humour, or wantin' to get home to their dinners, or were tired of the whole business, as I'd think of killin' slugs in a cabbage!'

"The witness, as already stated, was repeatedly threatened with committal for contempt; but she calmly disregarded all such suggestions, fillipping her fingers in a derisive fashion at his lordship, who could not repress a smile at the woman's absurd pugnacity.[58] At last, finding it quite hopeless to try to extract any information

[58] Filliping: holding a finger towards the palm of the hand with the thumb, then releasing it outwards suddenly to produce a snapping sound.

from her, save what she chose to impart—and this being chiefly her own sentiments with regard to the law and its officers—she was desired, though with reluctance, as she was an important witness, to 'stand down;' but she did not seem at all inclined to obey, and at last had to be almost forcibly ejected from the witness-box, amidst roars of laughter, and authoritative cries of 'Order!' Her last muttered words, as she was being vanquished, were audible to many, and were a final shaft cast at the police, against whom she appeared to entertain an unquenchable animosity—

" 'Mean, underhand, pryin' creatures, a reckonin' the very bits a body puts into their mouth! Just because they couldn't clap their dirty paws on the right man, death havin' caught hold of him first, and dragged him off to the devil, they must needs harrest a lady like my own dear, beautiful, blessed Miss Muriel, as wouldn't hurt a fly, the sweet, innocent lamb! I hates the very sight of them, I does!' "

* * * * * *

"Ah! they didn't report half of her racy speeches," concludes Fenton, as he throws down the paper with a laugh, in which the Professor joins. "Well, at any rate, Dysart, I think you'll have to knock under, and confess that your antagonistic attitude towards Mrs. Varley was utterly unjustified. She seems to me altogether in the light of a martyr and a very lovely one," he adds in a reflective tone.

"Yes, poor lady, she appears, indeed, deserving of all our best sympathy, though nothing could compensate her for the terrible ordeal she has undergone. To be suspected even for a day of such monstrosity, would be enough to crush for ever a sensitive nature. And yet I cannot help thinking how singular would have been the coincidence if she *had* been guilty; and how strangely it would have seemed like the beginning of the end of the 'weird of the Beresfords,' " murmurs the Professor in low, dreamy tones.

CHAPTER XII
THE EASTERN GABLE

"Dreams full oft are found, of real events
The forms and shadows."[59]

IT was just three weeks before the sacred, genial Christmastide that the trial was brought to an end—a trial which had electrified all Westerham, causing it to preen its dull and somewhat dingy feathers with a lively satisfaction at having gained an enviable notoriety, and being lifted, even for the proverbial "nine days," from the virtuous, but colourless ranks of the commonplace.

* * * * * *

The festival, though a very grey and sombre one in the Varley and Hilliard households, yet is not quite without its deep-toned consolation, that often finds vent in Dr. Hilliard's impulsive speech to Major Erncliffe, his step-nephew, who is much with him during this shadowed winter-time.

"Think, Leonard," he will cry, "what it would have been to have had our child, our Muriel, lying under sentence of death in Westerham gaol this holy Christmas season! And yet it might have been so. Many, as pure, as innocent, as guileless as she, have died on the scaffold—have had their lives sworn away by wretches who, to gratify some petty malice, some unsuspected devilish spite or jealousy, have called God to witness to their hell-spawned lies. Or, again, the thrice cursed system of circumstantial evidence,

---

[59] From the play *Ethwald: A Tragedy, in Five Acts* by Joanna Baillie.

corroborative testimony, call it what you will, has been too many for them; appearances have been against them, and have carried the day, and the innocent man dies, calling God and man to witness that he is murdered; and by-and-by the real culprit turns up—and yet the law has leaned no lesson."

Thus he often speaks, til the bronzed cheek of the soldier grows pale, and Mrs. Hilliard's grey face grows still greyer. All through this winter season she moves about her house as a woman in a dream. The shock has told upon her sadly; it seems as if she could not shake off the effects of it, though her health does not actually give way. She never goes out, never even once crossing her daughter's threshold, making the inclemency of the weather and her want of strength an excuse.

But she is strangely changed; a singular dumbness, coupled with what strikes you as an unsleeping watchfulness, has fallen upon her; her eyes, too, have caught an odd, nervous, apprehensive way of glancing, that makes one feel uncomfortable. A silent, dreary, brooding woman she has become in these latter days, and one is almost tempted to place some credence in the report of a strain of insanity in her blood.

Mrs. Varley spends the Christmas season in the profound solitude of her widowed home. But soon after another "New Year" has wrapped the poor old sin-stained, shivering earth in its hopeful young embrace, she goes away for a few weeks—a change that all declare she so sadly needs, and comes back early in March.

* * * * * *

Old Jacob Varley has been dead now more than five months, and his charming young widow must really not be allowed to immure herself so completely any longer. She has shown a wonderful respect and affection for his memory, considering the terrible position in which she was placed with regard to his mysterious death—a death now universally laid at the door of Richard Varley, that wild, bad man, who had gone to his long account with a father's blood red upon his sin-stained hands!!

* * * * * *

So Westerham society elects to accept Mrs. Varley as a "martyr," and designs to honour her as such. Old Jacob was a little, just a little, below the rank of standard that these Westerhamites have raised up for themselves; though, of course, money is an ample cloak that covers all sins of parvenu birth, etc. Still—well, Muriel Varley belongs to the mystic middleocracy, that tries to steer a difficult, and ofttimes unrecognized course between plutocracy, that it affects to despise as mere trade wealth, on the one hand, and aristocracy, that confounds its pretensions with those of its inferior neighbour, on the other; in short, Muriel hails from the professional classes, besides claiming on her father's side a very remote and distant kinship with the old and distinguished Beresford family, now extinct. And now that the offensive ingredient is removed—poor Jacob Varley, to whom a faint and subtle aroma of "cotton" still clung even in his retirement, and whose constant mislaying of the eighth alphabetical letter was an unceasing reminder of his low origin—now that she is a heroine and a martyr; above all, a martyr owning delightful Varley Hall, and fifteen thousand a year,—she is to be petted and made much of. If she had been equally a martyr, and shabby and shillingless, and yet audacious enough to be beautiful, Westerham society—the female portion of it, at least—would most probably have united in declaring that if she did not commit the crime imputed to her, she was, they felt convinced, quite capable of it.

As the first step in the "petting" process, the shining lights of

Westerham society call upon Muriel. A young and beautiful and wealthy widow must not be allowed to shut herself up in solitude; it would be really quite un-Christian-like to neglect her at such a time, especially when there are sundry sons and brothers in a chronic state of impecuniosity, whose interests must be studied, as well as the more advanced Christian principles of neighbourly love.

They all unite in avowing that Mrs. Varley is "as perfectly lovely as ever—more beautiful, in fact, than in the sunny, untroubled days of her girlhood; but that there is a strange, sad expression in her glorious eyes, a sort of look of haunting sorrow, mingled with a latent horror, that will remain until the coffin-lid covers them up for ever."

* * * * * *

But these people bore Muriel. She does not want to be patronized by the Westerham *élite*; she is proof against the manifold seductive influences of Westerham's *jeunesse dorée*; and her doors are often heartlessly closed against those heroes who would fain pluck the "golden apples" growing—oh, so tantalizingly!—in her garden.[60]

But she has one constant visitor during those early spring days who is never denied admittance—Leonard Erncliffe, who, in the right of a sort of cousinship, as well as of old friendship, presents himself at her gates, without fear of misconstruction in these watchful Westerham eyes. And even if they do read between the lines, what then? They will soon be presented with the no longer concealed book, writ so clear, that those who run may read; for it is tacitly understood between those two, though perhaps it has never been said in so many words, that when Muriel's year of mourning shall have expired, she and Leonard will become man

[60] *Jeunesse dorée*: gilded youth, wealthy and fashionable young people.

and wife. Poor fond, faithful, adoring Jacob Varley stretches from his grave a ghostly detaining hand that parts them just for this little space, and no longer; but after the shadowy hand may stretch in vain; it, and he to whom is belonged, and the love that lies buried with him, will be alike forgotten by his widow—are forgotten, one would almost say, save for that wistful sorrow in the lovely eyes, for Muriel "lives, and moves, and has her being" in Leonard Erncliffe's presence.[61]

He, passionately as he loves her, sometimes feels a strange thrill, a sort of dazed, shocked sensation, at the intensity of her feeling for himself, as if he were unconsciously dishonouring the old man's memory by allowing her to love him so devotedly, so entirely. He is a strictly honourable man; Professor Dysart judged him rightly. But, then, he is only a man, and madly, ardently in love with this beautiful young creature. So these quixotic glimpses of self-abnegation do not last long; and then, after all, he argues to himself, she did love her husband—she loved him truly and fondly. Had not he, Leonard, proof of it, in her untiring devotion to him during his illness?

"She is too noble and sweet a creature not to love devotedly any one who was so unsparingly good to her, as was old Varley," he murmurs; "but she loved him as she would a father, and all the ecstatic lover love is mine."

* * * * * *

And so the early spring weather passes away, and Easter is upon us unusually late this year—the last week in April.

Mrs. Varley has become marvellously charitable during those few months of her widowhood; she seems determined to be a "wise

[61] A reference to Acts 17:28.

steward" of her husband's great wealth; in fact, to treat it as if held in trust for the benefit of others. At Christmas, though she was not visible, immense donations of charity in ever shape were bestowed upon the poor of Westerham, and in the neighbourhood of her home; and now the Easter festival is to be alike celebrated; and blessings are called down upon her head in many homes of poverty. Muriel does not limit her almsgiving to the conventional "coal and blanket" business, perhaps accompanied by a small, very small, dole of money, and flanked by dubious aquatic soup.[62] No; she does things on a princely scale. Money she gives freely, lavishly; and that spacious Varley Hall kitchen cooks quantities of rich, good, nourishing food, that, steaming from the spit or oven, are sent round to these poor homes. She seems to taken an actual delight in giving to those miserable, half-famished wretches food such as they could never have hoped to taste again, even if they ever had done so in the past; to surprise them with these unexpected dainties, and see their looks of unalloyed, wondering amazement and joy, and hear their halting, abashed, but sincerest words of astonished gratitude.

On this Easter Saturday she is especially busy, taking an active part herself in the "distributions;" and when Leonard calls, he is told that she is in the housekeeper's-room, surrounded by a detachment of pensioners, and that he can either join her there or wait for her in her own peculiar sitting-room. He elects to wait; he feels hardly courageous enough—gallant Major though he is—to face all these uneducated eyes, that seem to make up in acuteness of gaze what they lack in brain-power.

"What an angel she is, my little Lady Bountiful, my beautiful,

[62] Coal and blanket funds provided coal and blankets to the poor.

tender-hearted Muriel!" he soliloquizes, as he restlessly roams up and down, man-like, with his hands in his pockets.

A perfectly lovely room is this boudoir or private sitting-room of Muriel's; everything that love could imagine, or money could procure, and that could contribute to his lovely young bride's delight and comfort, was placed in it by old Mr. Varley. But Leonard Erncliffe is now very familiar with it, and he walks up and down at first without noticing anything; then he takes up books, and throws them down again impatiently; stares at choice water-colours and rare porcelain that adorn the walls, and at statuettes and bronzes with lack-lustre eyes. Then, by-and-by, he makes the round of the room methodically, conscientiously, seemingly intent upon an exhaustive examination of each pretty trifle; but though he gazes most pertinaciously at all those fanciful ornamentations, his thoughts are far away, and instead of being the "*dilettante*" he seems, absorbed in the contemplation of a peculiar patterned blue-china bowl, or gravely weighing the merits of *cloisonné* enamel, priceless oriental jars, *repoussé* silver, hand-painted brackets, etc., he is straining his ears to catch the sound of a certain light footstep in the corridor without, an would ruthlessly consign bowls and brackets, fans and photographs, to everlasting oblivion, rather than miss the first glimpse of that sweet young face that will come smiling in to him—now—any moment—by-and-by, smiling under that badge of woe, that widow's cap, that seems such an anachronism on that girlish golden head.

But in the meantime he continues his aimless stock-taking of Muriel's artistic belongings. He has done more than half the room, and now comes to a standstill before a quaint old Japanese cabinet, rich in gold-work and black lacquer, which stands in a nook by the picturesque fireplace, with its antique brass grate and blue-and-white tiled hearth. There are two or three other cabinets in the room, but of lighter and more airy design—lovely Italian walnut, inlaid with amber, lapis-lazuli, etc.; but this of Japanese workmanship is more sombre. Its glass-protected shelves contain some beautiful specimens of "eggshell Sèvres," but the lower part is a solid panel and is always locked; never yet has Major Erncliffe seen it open till to-day. Now it stands ajar, and his blank gaze wanders over it unseeingly.

He is just about to turn away; his glance has strayed off, for the hundredth time, to the dainty little clock ticking away the lagging minutes on the mantelpiece, when his side-sight (if one may be pardoned the expression) catches the opening, and, urged by some impulse which he cannot understand, as curiosity forms no part in his mental composition, he steps forward and pulls open the almost closed door. There is not much to reward intrusive eyes; the cabinet is quite empty, save for a large, somewhat rusty door-key huddled up in one corner—not a very æsthetic object to be so sumptuously lodged!

Aimlessly Leonard takes it out, and swings it on one finger, as he completes his amateur inventory of his sweetheart's costly nic-nacs.

And still Muriel comes not. How tiresomely *exigeant* are those hungry deputations she is interviewing, he thinks impatiently,[63] as he at last subsides into a luxurious reclining chair, that must have been fashioned for the express purpose of wooing slumber for its votaries, as Major Erncliffe is seated in its downy depths but a few minutes—still unconsciously twirling that clumsy key that seems an anomaly amidst the airy, fragile prettiness, the artistic luxury of

---

[63] *Exigeant*: demanding.

Mrs. Varley's dainty sanctum—when all things round him become hazy and uncertain, the room is gradually fading from his gaze. He pulls himself together with a start; he is not sleepy! What absurdity! What could make him sleepy in the middle of the day? He never did such a thing in his life; his eyes even are not closed. But even as he denies the possibility, the same dim vagueness steals again over everything; the room and its objects imperceptibly dissolve, as it were, before the eyes he would swear are open; and this time he cannot come back to reality . . . He is out away upon a deserted staircase, unfamiliar; yet he instinctively knows he is still beneath the roof of Varley Hall, or rather, the two-hundred-year-old Manor House, re-christened, rejuvenated, restored by the millionaire. But, modernize it as he would, Jacob Varley could not altogether erase—though he might do his best—the seal of time from this old Tudor mansion; and that massive masonry, those many gables, and clustering chimneys, speak of a past in which he and his had no part. However, there were many improvements, which *are* decided improvements on those far-away days, when "comfort" was almost an unknown quantity; and other changes that set one's teeth on edge, from being such sheer and terrible anachronisms. The house had fallen much into decay when bought by old Varley; parts of it were considered almost unsafe; but he had architects and builders to overhaul it, and it was all put in thorough repair, with the exception of those low casement windowed rooms, lying away under the projecting eaves in some of these picturesque gables. These attics—as we moderns call them—were not wanting; there was a plethora of rooms in the great rambling house, and they were left to the mice and mildew, to the rats and dry-rot. And yet it is on the staircase leading to those unvisited distant chambers that Major Erncliffe finds himself, in his—what shall we call it?—waking dream.

How dim and gloomy it is, he thinks; surely it must be night. Yes, his only light along those quaint echoing passages, those abrupt curves, and sudden alternate ascents and descents—for this part of the Manor stands as it did in the olden time, and is full of those unexpected staircases, irregular levels, surprise closets, nooks, passages, that the builders of that epoch delighted in—the only gleam that illuminates the shrouding darkness, proceeds from a flickering candle carried by some one much in advance of him. He had not noticed this before; but now he sees that some one—a woman—is rapidly traversing these lonely corridors and stairs, and he is following her, though he knows not why he does so . . . Automatically he pursues that swiftly gliding form, as if compelled by some power outside his own, some invisible influence that he cannot resist . . . And now he gains somewhat on her, and there is less draught, the flame of the candle is steadier, does not flare so, and surely there is something familiar in that distant flitting figure—strangely familiar. It is—is it not?—yes, surely it is—Muriel! That dainty, graceful shape cannot be altogether disguised, even by the loose, floating, unfamiliar garment she wears. The gold of the rich burnished hair momentarily catches a gleam from the candle, and reflects the light with lustrous brightness. Yes, Muriel! and none other. His lips form her name, but no sound is emitted; again and again he tries to shout, to stop her hurried progress. Why need they be chasing thus mysteriously through the darkness? But his voice falls back in his chest with a hollow, murmuring whisper; his power of speech is gone, and he must only go on. He could not turn back, even if he would; he feels drawn forward as by a magnet!

And now she whom he is thus compelled to follow pauses before a closed door in the eastern gable. It is the most remote and distant point from the inhabited part of the house, being a sort of upper wing that extends over outer offices, and seems almost separate from the dwelling house. This particular room looks out upon a paved yard connected with the old laundry offices, and projects so much as to appear, from the outside, something like an excrescence growing on the outer wall.

Leonard, as he listens, hears a key inserted in the rusty lock, which turns with a dismal creak. What possesses Muriel? Where is she going? What is she doing, and at this hour of the night? And while he so thinks, she passes within the chamber, and the door, swinging from her hand, shuts with a dreary, echoing clang. When he reaches it, he fumbles some time with the lock before he can get it to open. When he does at last, and enters, a strange sight meets his gaze. At the end of the room, farthest from the door, is the wide old casement-window, and beneath it, kneeling on the dusty, decaying floor, is Muriel Varley, the candle on the ground beside her, and a large piece of the rotten old skirting-board displaced, while her slim white hand is groping in the aperture left. She does not seem to have heard him approach, though the door made such a noise. He walks over and stands beside her, but still she is unconscious of his presence; and, looking at her, now that he can see her face—the light from the candle being thrown upon it, and revealing its soft, sweet curves perfectly—he notices, with a sudden fear, that the great blue eyes are fixed and staring, that the whole face is strangely set and vacant; that it is, in fact, the face of a somnambulist! Muriel is asleep; has come to this desolate, unfrequented, remote part of the old Manor House in her sleep—for what purpose? Her waking wishes would never bring her here. She would be frightened, even in the daytime, to penetrate the fastnesses of this somewhat ruined old gable wing, said to be ghost-haunted; much less would she come in the stillness of night—alone! . . . What is she searching for in that rotten wainscot? And even as he so thinks, the little groping hand closes on something and is withdrawn.

He sees something like a glitter of glass, and, stepping forward to look better what the reward is of that mysterious midnight search, his foot touches that piece of dislodged wainscot, which is balanced on end against the wall. It falls with a crash, and, with a shrill scream, Muriel wakes; Leonard simultaneously catching her by the hand that holds that unseen something, with no intent of curiosity, but only the desire to reassure and comfort her by his loving proximity. But at that clasp she cries again—a cry of maddened, desperate fear; a convulsive shudder passes over her entire frame, and he sees, while glancing at that now awakened, intelligent face, the light of a hideous, awful horror thereon; eyes that look at him with—what is it?—hate, madness, despair, in their terrified gaze. His grasp of the hand that holds that something unknown tightens involuntarily. "*Never!* I will die first!" she mutters. Then, with a supreme effort, she wrenches herself free from his clasp, pushing him violently from her with the other hand, with a strange, new-born strength. He loses his balance, and staggers heavily against the window. The rotten woodwork cracks, groans, gapes. Leonard clutches convulsively at nothing! The whole space where the window was, and the crumbling wall beneath, are gone in a moment; there is a rush of cold night air, a sense of falling—falling through a great darkness! And, with this strange physical feeling, Major Erncliffe comes back to life and reality, and finds himself still reposing in Muriel's most seductive of lounging chairs, while Muriel herself is standing beside him, with a scared, startled look in her lovely face.

CHAPTER XIII
THE SHADOW OF THE STAIN

"MURIEL, my darling! Where have you come from? What have you been doing? What is the meaning of it all? Was it a dream, or a vision? I'd swear I wasn't asleep. And yet it was all so horrible!"

"What was horrible, Leonard?" asks Muriel, with pale and trembling lips. "You are talking strangely, and frightening me, dear. I have come in only this minute."

"But where were you?" he reiterates, gazing at her in a sort of blank, bewildered way.

"I was with some of the poor Westerham folk, first in Mrs. Parker's room, and then in the big kitchen. Didn't Marshall tell you? I was sorry to keep you waiting, Lennie love, but I thought you wouldn't mind for once. And such a number of poor creatures came flocking and crowding so eagerly. I saw them in detachments, and made their hearts glad to bursting by all the good things we had ready for them. How delicious it is to have plenty of money, for the mere sake of giving abundantly! The rapture, the astonished joy and gratitude, in those hard, toil-worn, half-starved faces was a priceless reward. There is no greater luxury in life, I think, that to be able to give, give, give." She speaks rapidly, nervously, as if she sought to distract him from what troubles him; and she partly succeeds; he smiles, and kisses her passionately.

"You are an angel, my dearest," he murmurs, "with a heart of gold. They have tired you, though, your troublesome pensioners; you look fagged and strangely pale"—looking lovingly and lingeringly at the exquisite young face so near his own.

"It is you who have made me pale, sir; you looked so odd and unnatural, dreaming there in restless trouble, with your eyes more than half open."

"My eyes open! I knew it—I wasn't asleep at all! What the deuce was it? It seemed more like 'mesmerism,' 'clairvoyance,' whatever you call it, than a dream. I have been bewitched, Muriel. I have been through some strange experience, dear, which has left a very unpleasant impression."

"You've had a bad dream, Leonard—simply this, and nothing more; or, perhaps, the old Manor House ghost has visited you, and laid her spell upon you. It's a woman, I believe."

"The ghost of the eastern gable, isn't it?" he says quickly, looking at her suddenly.

She shivers, as if smitten by a chill blast, and grows paler even than before. "East or west, I'm sure it doesn't matter. She'd be equally dreadful wherever she promenaded, provided she existed," she says, with a strained smile, and a great effort to appear gay and unconcerned.

"Oh yes, the east gable," continues Leonard, unheeding her words, his eyes looking away from her, distant and dreamy. "I've heard the legend scores of times, and her visible presence forebodes woe and disaster to the inmates. She murdered some one, I believe, a couple of centuries or so ago,—whether husband or lover, history is not quite certain,—murdered them somewhere in that eastern gable, and buried the body beneath the flooring; and she is compelled to haunt the scene of her crime, says superstition. Also tradition says that the blood of her victim gushed out upon her after that fatal stab, and that hair, face, and garments, are streaked and splashed with the ominous red! She was young and beautiful, and——Ah! perhaps, after all, it was she whom I saw in that extraordinary dream—vision—call it what you will;—yellow hair, floating white draperies, the midnight taper, all the legendary ghost paraphernalia complete, except the blood-stains, and—and yet——Good heavens! Muriel, my love, what a brute I am to frighten you out of your senses!" he says, as Mrs. Varley sways heavily against him, with closed eyes and ashy face. "My darling, it's all right! Look up, sweet! There's no one here but your own Leonard. Confound me for a drivelling idiot!" he exclaims, raining kisses on the soft, tender face, that resumes its sweet warm flesh tints thus fanned back to life. "I had a bad dream, as you say, my dearest; rather a strange dream than an evil one, by the way; and the fact of sleeping at all in the daytime—a misdemeanour of which I never yet was guilty—has unhinged me a little, that's all. We'll go away out of this," he added, looking round the room with an irrepressible slight shudder, "and forget all about it, won't we, pet?" he asked, smiling down reassuringly at the beautiful face resting so contentedly against his shoulder; and Muriel, recovered from her momentary faintness, looks back into his eyes with a wan, loving smile.

"Yes, Leonard, we'll go straight to the library, even though dinner is not yet served, and we will talk of these horrors no more," she whispers; and then she puts up those sweetest, ripest, loveliest lips, to kiss him of her own accord; and he, as he holds her close to his heart, in a passionate mute embrace, silently thanks God for the great blessing of her love, and vows that never again will he allude to that singular, unaccountable experience he has just been through (as he still refuses to believe it was a dream), or to the Manor House ghost.

His darling is a nervous creature, though she bore herself so wonderfully through that most terrible ordeal of a few months ago; but the fearful strain and tension she had undergone during the awful days of the trial, the supreme effort she made to keep up, and not seem frightened, has told upon her, of course, is doubtless coming against her now, and has made his "brave, dauntless Muriel," as he loved to call her in the olden days, timid, fearful, afraid of what she would have laughed at a while ago.

And so they leave the room together, and he never misses the large clumsy key that hung upon his finger when he fell into that strange visionary state, never remembers it at all, and consequently does not notice that it is gone. Also he does not remark what might perhaps strike a third person, if he were present, as somewhat singular—that Muriel asks him no questions as to his dream—what it was about, or what troubled him.

* * * * * *

The library at Varley Hall is the cosiest room in the house, and the whole suite—the great drawing-rooms, dining-room, and breakfast-room of the occupied portion of the old Manor—are alike deserted by the mistress during this period of her widowhood; she scarcely ever enters them, especially the first-named, save when obliged to receive formal ceremonial visits.

Since her husband's death she has almost lived in the library, having all her meals served there, and sitting there throughout the evening. The room has been always a favourite of hers, since she entered the house a bride more than four years ago. Her pleasant hours have been spent there. Old Jacob Varley had a library, as a natural adjunct of a millionaire, but he had little use of care for it. The retired cotton-spinner delighted rather in his massive dining-room and stately, gorgeous drawing-rooms, and saw nothing to admire within his room of books, save his "darling Murrie," whose lovely face so often shone there, like a rare and beauteous blossom, amidst its sombre surroundings, and whose love for the room and its contents the old man could not understand.

Perhaps Muriel is a wise woman in her generation, and, apart from her love of books and their vicinity, knows that she could not choose a more effective background for her radiant, shining beauty, than these oak-panelled walls, these polished ebony cases, massive oaken mantelpiece, dark-red velvet hangings, and few deep-tones Persian rugs scattered on the otherwise carpetless oak floor. Nowhere else did the rich deep gold of that amber head shine with a more glorious lustre, or the wondrous blue of those dark-fringed eyes look so intensely azure, or the perfect exquisite colouring of that lovely face show to such splendid advantage.

And sombre in hue as the room is, yet Leonard thinks it looks strangely attractive to-night, with a big bright fire burning in the great, wide, old-fashioned hearth, with its ingle nook recessed under the high mantelpiece; for end of April as it is, yet is grows extremely chilly with the declining day; a small octagon table drawn close to it, dainty with shimmering glass and glittering silver, choice hot-house flowers, and wax candles under rose-coloured shades, not yet lit; while to complete the picturesqueness of the interior, Muriel's favourite of favourites and prince of pets, "Rupert," a magnificent tawny-haired St. Bernard, lies stretched on the great fur rug in front of the fire.

The room, which is elliptical in form, is lit by one grand oriel window, entirely filling one end of the ellipse. The upper portion of this window is exquisite painted glass, on which are emblazoned the arms and heraldic devices of the noble family to which the house belonged through so many generations, but which is now extinct; and at certain times on bright days, according to the sun's position in the heavens, the room is glorified by slant streaks and dashes of richest colouring from that lovely stained glass.

To-night as Muriel and Leonard enter, the sun is fast sinking in the west, which the window faces. He is almost gone; the glory of the pageant is nearly over; in a few minutes the sky will be grey and cold and tintless; in a few more minutes the gloom of the advancing night will be marshalling its dusky forces in that rose-and-opal sky; but as yet it is all shining brightness, though the great pomp and blazonry of that royal departure is well-nigh past.

Leonard walks to the window to take a farewell look at the monarch of light, sinking into the purple of his kingly couch. He stands so for a few moments, and then turns just as the last tiny rim of the day-god is vanishing; he starts most unpleasantly, though he speaks no word; for there before him is Muriel, lying back in a low chair facing the window, with closed eyes (she is feeling somewhat weary after that touch of faintness), and it is as if a stream of blood were pouring over her. The pretty amber-head is streaked and splashed with the crimson tide; one soft cheek and little white hand are dyed with the same fell hue; while all down the dress is the same large splashing streak of red—blood-red!

Leonard catches his breath, and with difficulty represses an exclamation as he gazes, while the horrible legend he has been speaking of—the ghost of the Manor House murderess—rushes back on him with startling force. Never in all the times he has been in this room with Muriel has the light so chanced to fall on her through that beautiful crimson glass. It is gone, that strange appearance, even as he looks—gone with the dipping of that last little bit of sun below the horizon.

It was absurd of him to be so startled. The effect was singular and unpleasant, but to attach any importance to it is simply lunacy or superstition of the lowest possible order.

Still, scoff at himself as he may, it leaves a cold, nameless, apprehensive impression, in some way entangled with his dream or vision, that mars to an extent his enjoyment of that exquisite little *tête-à-tête* dinner with the woman whom he so passionately loves. An this is all the more annoying, as it is not often that he is thus indulged; for, cousin as well as lover though he is, yet Muriel is extremely careful that no tongues, be they ever so censorious, may speak her name lightly, or say that she failed in any way in the respect due to her husband's memory.

And although the world of Westerham may already guess how matters will arrange themselves after a little, yet, meanwhile, she is most cautious not to evoke unkind gossip; and, young and beautiful though she is, none have yet had the hardihood to whisper that Jacob Varley's widow is glad of her freedom, or that it came most opportunely.

CHAPTER XIV
AN OMINOUS WHISPER

THE months glide swiftly away; the spring ripens into loveliest summer, which, in turn, mellows into early autumn; and this, again, gives place to the "fall," as the fading of the year is so truly and poetically styled in the far west. It is the saddest time of all the year, when death and mourning are abroad in the land; nature grieving for her bright-hued children, for the radiance and the golden glory of their lovely lives, and will not be comforted. It is the time of all the year when hurrying humanity should, perforce, stand still a while and ponder; when our miserable mortality has no longer any excuse for not remembering that the autumn of *our* year will come too—is coming with rapid strides, however green and vivid may be the fleeting spring, however luxuriant and vari-coloured the brief, bounteous summer. Autumn is coming surely and steadily to all and each; the chill wind of its advancing breath is felt by many round us; the sad neutral tints of its unmistakable livery are assumed by friend after friend—the tired grey head, the bowed form and furrowed cheek, the faded eye and weary, weak, and halting step; and yet we take no warning; and the young, in the joyous, unheeding insolence of their youth, and the middle-aged, in the security and vigour of their maturity, alike disregard these signs and tokens of life's garnered year. *Their* barns are not yet full, nor half full; they are still quite empty. Why, the spring is not nearly over yet; and then there is the whole long, long summer, stretching away in the dim distance, which seems as if it would never end. And yet—it is over, and autumn is here; ay, and the winter of death, in a flash!

'Tis but yesterday, surely, that we were looking out on the tender green of our spring-time; and now, behold, they are the snows of the end! Yes; the late, late autumn, when death, and its twin-brother "decay," are all around one in nature's kingdom, is a very sad and solemn season. And at the very height of this dreary time, when youth and hope and promise seem far off in the past, and sorrow and desolation and a grave seem all that is real in this strange, mystic tangle which we call "life"—in the very last week in November Muriel Varley and Leonard Erncliffe become man and wife.

But the dull grey depression of this most melancholy month affects not the bride's shining beauty, dims not the sweetness of that exquisite face, which seems to have acquired a new transfigured loveliness since she has cast off the shadowing widow's cap, that outer seal of affliction which always seemed so incongruous on that young head. For though Muriel is more than four-and-twenty years of age, yet her face has the soft sweet freshness, the bright indescribable radiance, of early, innocent, buoyant youth, and those who see her for the first time find it almost impossible to imagine her a wife, and, above all, a widow, guessing her to have but reached the magic milestone of seventeen. And that one expression that sometimes seemed a little anomalous to that spirit of youth that sat on her brow, that startled look of fright or horror that dwelt in the great appealing blue eyes through the terrible time of the trial, and for months after, and that people said would never more depart from the lovely face, is almost effaced; and a great, ineffable content, a look as if she had at last gained her heart's desire, is her one dominant expression as she walks up the aisle of the dim old church on her father's arm, in the early misty dreariness of the November morning.

All things have been done decently and in order. None can say that she treated her husband's memory with the faintest shadow of disrespect, as just fourteen months have elapsed since his death.

The marriage, too, is the quietest imaginable, everything conducted with the strictest privacy. Muriel and her father walk to the church, scarcely half a mile from her home, in the raw dulness of the early day, the bride in her sober travelling-dress of seal brown; and there at the altar, Major Erncliffe, with the light of a great joy in his eyes, his unpleasant impressions of last April long forgotten, awaits them. No bridesmaids, no best man, no guests; Muriel has insisted on its being absolutely private, which delights Leonard, as he would have shrunk horribly from any outward show of merry-making or wedding festivities, partly from the great depth and strength of his love—he feels as if the conventional rejoicings and congratulations, etc., would have jarred detestably, marring the sweet, sacred holiness and happiness, too deep for words, of their union—partly, he would have considered it execrably bad taste, owing to the circumstances of old Varley's death.

Dr. Hilliard, however, would have wished it not quite so remarkably quiet. His daughter is doing no deed of which she need be ashamed. She is marrying a good and noble man who loves her devotedly, who has loved her since she was a mere child, and who has been her cousin and friend all her life—marrying him after a due and proper interval of mourning for the good old man who is gone. That he came to his death unfairly, mysteriously—a mystery that has never yet been actually cleared up—is certain, though, of course, all Westerham has accepted long ago as final, the belief that Richard Varley, the *vaurien* son, incensed by his father's marriage, and the possibility of the birth of a child, who would, he knew too fatally well, inherit all, and exclude himself from any possible share of his father's wealth, he having forfeited by his evil life all right and claim to an eldest son's portion, or any portion, when, fortunately, there was no entailed property, and goaded by a desperate present need of money, which the rifled desk and the disappearance of the £1300 proved beyond a doubt, committed that last and terrible crime. But the fact that there was such a crime perpetrated, through which his daughter had been such a terrible, innocent sufferer, was, in Dr. Hilliard's opinion, the very reason why the marriage should not be of this most clandestine character.

However, Muriel's and Leonard's united wishes overrule his, and perhaps it is as well; for by-and-by, when the ceremony is over, and the newly-married pair have driven straight from the church porch to the railway-station, *en route* for the continent, it begins to be whispered about Westerham that there has been one very strange fact—more than strange, indeed, extraordinary—connected with the wonderfully quiet wedding solemnized in the sickly early daylight of that November day, in that old country church distant from the city; and that was the unaccountable and most singular absence of the bride's mother. Mrs. Hilliard was not present at her daughter's wedding! And even her strange morbid distaste for going abroad of late, her peculiar and suddenly developed desire for utter seclusion, for which the plea of ill health is advanced, seems no valid excuse for acting thus.

It is generally known amongst her friends in Westerham that a great and terrible change has been wrought in her since the fearful shock which her nerves sustained fourteen months ago. She and her daughter were the first to reach that bedside after that awful cry. They had confronted each other and death in its most ghastly form, in that never-to-be-forgotten moment before Edwards or any of the rest of the awakened household reached the spot; and it was universally supposed that that awful conclusion to her last visit to Varley Hall had seriously undermined Mrs. Hilliard's health both of mind and body.

Never since that hour had she crossed her daughter's threshold, scarcely had she crossed her own. During the terrible time of the trial, she had held aloof in a strange, cowed, distracted manner, hardly glancing at her child during those awful days of suspense. And yet, when she was not actually ill, confined to her bed, it seemed strange, cruel, barbarous even, as some folks said, that she should have thus absented herself on an occasion like the present. The girl she had so idolized, the daughter she had adored, loved with a self-sacrificing, devoted love; whose lightest wish had been her law, in whose very being she had almost merged her own identity.

An absorbing love for her child had been, in short, Mrs. Hilliard's most marked individuality; and now this singular, unaccountable avoidance! And at last it began to be whispered by one or two ultra-suspicious, slanderous folk, with bated breath and ominous head-shakes, that perhaps Mrs. Hilliard had not been quite right in her head this long time back, though none suspected it, and that with this mental aberration her distaste, amounting to dislike in the beginning of the acquaintance, for old Jacob Varley returned with renewed strength. It may have grown on her in some wild, fanatical, vague way that she was appointed to sever the bond which she had been so very reluctant, years ago, should have ever been forged. For it was well known in Westerham that when old Varley, the retired cotton-spinner and millionaire, first came courting sweet Muriel Hilliard, Mrs. Hilliard had violently opposed even the idea of such a union, although she knew well the state of her husband's affairs just then—his great financial embarrassments, the heavy losses he had recently sustained, that threatened almost to crush him. For the clever, popular physician, who stood at the very top of his profession, whose fame and reputation were great, and his practice far and away the best in Westerham, was a daring, incurable, reckless speculator, which is nothing but being a gambler on a Titanic scale, whose rash and desperately wild investments, that more by good luck than anything else sometimes turned out wonderfully fortunate, almost broke his wife's heart with anxiety as to their result; to him the advent of Jacob Varley in such an unexpected guise seemed almost miraculous.

But the self-abnegating mother-heart felt only for her child. That loveliest girl of nineteen summers, in whose winsome beauty the mother had taken an almost sinful pride, was, in order to save her father, to be thrown away on an old man, more than old enough to be her grandfather, and not even a gentleman. It was unnatural, horrible! She for one would never countenance it. Her daughter, with her fair and gracious beauty, was to be defrauded of her woman's heritage of love. Money! What mattered money? Such sale and barter was disgraceful and wicked. Was her Muriel's young and lovely life to be shorn of all joy for the sake of sordid pelf?[64] No; let the three of them sink or swim together. Her husband might, very likely would, retrieve his losses; but at least let her girl have a fair chance of finding happiness.

So Mrs. Hilliard argued hotly and urgently, till she suddenly collapsed, on discovering that her daughter had quite taken her father's view of the case, at which the mother mutely marvelled, guessing as she did how matters were between Muriel and her soldier cousin; but she said no word of dissuasion after that; and by-and-by she became quite reconciled to Jacob Varley—indeed,

[64] Pelf: money, especially when acquired in a dishonourable way.

much more than reconciled; she grew apparently to respect and love the good old man, as she could hardly fail to do, seeing his great and dog-like devotion to her child.

But those who now spoke in dark whispers, suggested that possibly her mind may have been getting queer this long time; that her old feelings towards her daughter's husband may have revived and increased to giant-like growth, fed by the fatal fever of insanity; and that then, taking advantage of Richard Varley's hurried visit, and his desperate need of money, proved by the rifling of his father's desk, which was discovered some hours before the murder, she had, with the strange subtlety so often evinced by the insane, laid her plans so that the added crime of murder would be naturally imputed to the evil man who rushed from the house half frantic with rage and disappointment—rushed to his death, though he knew it not. But, bad as he was, perhaps drowned, Richard Varley had not this last and most terrible guilt to answer for; and that by-an-by, when "the sea gives up its dead," and the "secrets of all hearts are known," it will be found that though "few and evil were his days," yet that that erring soul was not red with his father's blood.

CHAPTER XV
A STARTLING LIKENESS

MONTHS pass away and the bride and bridegroom still remain abroad. Muriel is, in fact, reluctant to return at all, if it were possible for her to remain away. She candidly avows that Varley Hall has become hateful to her, and the thought of living there abhorrent. But at last she yields to her father's entreaties who,—bereft of both daughter and nephew, whom he loves as a son, he is indeed desolate,—yearns to have his child near him once more; and they return late in November, after just a year's absence. Leonard secretly rejoicing, though, for Muriel's sake, he has done his best to conceal his longing for home and England, and his weariness and distaste for foreign life. She had seemed so radiantly happy amidst these new scenes and surroundings; her love for himself and delight in his individual society so unbounded, so profound and tireless, that he hesitated to suggest a change that might mar or shadow the blissful heaven of their lives. But yet, when she herself proposed their home-coming, he is unfeignedly glad. And in the first excitement of the return, Muriel seems bright an joyous as ever.

They fill the house with guests for Christmas, chiefly Major Erncliffe's friends, as Muriel does not care much to cultivate the Westerham *élite*, who had elected to patronize her, and whom she had somewhat snubbed; and old Varley's few intimates she calmly ignores—men whose interests are centred in, and bounded by, the state of the money-market; whose talk was interlarded with strange cabalistic phrases, such as "Cotton is firm," etc., or, again speculations on the mystic fluctuations of "stock"—those erratic, inscrutable rises and falls that seem so like wizardry to the hapless uninitiated, and magic malign indeed when *it* suddenly collapses and engulfs the novice.

It—that indefinite *it*, that is nothing graspable or tangible; that is something, and that yet we are told is nothing; and that men who understand the mysteries surrounding that invisible sphinx-like goddess, who sits enthroned somewhere in the central core of the commercial world; who is not, and yet is;—men on 'Change, who are versed in the rites and ceremonies of this peculiar form of mammon worship, and who can mutter the proper incantation at the proper moment; men who, in short, are behind the scenes,—can make colossal fortunes in a few days, possibly hours, by the simple interchange of bits of paper, that have, if we are truly informed, neither value not meaning, and represent absolutely nothing.

No; old friends, whether her own or her first husband's, Muriel does not desire; but Major Erncliffe's receive warmest welcome, and she is the radiant, animating spirit of the party. She looks more gloriously lovely than ever, and her actual idolatry of her husband, continually evinced in word and glance and tone (unconsciously, for she would sensitively shrink from parading the strength of her affection), has lent to her face an infinite, almost pathetic tenderness, which spiritualizes her beauty, giving it the one finishing touch which makes it perfect.

In these strangers' eyes she seems the very incarnation of love itself—trusting, innocent, absolute love. They are also much struck by the remarkable resemblance she bears to the family with which she is so remotely connected; feature by feature she seems to reflect these dead and gone Beresfords, who appear to gaze down mournfully at these aliens in the home of their race, from the walls of the dim, shadowed picture-gallery. Especially is her wonderful likeness to the last of that dead race, the lovely, gentle Eunice Beresford, commented upon. That sweet, beautiful, tender face glowing upon the canvas, in the freshness of its winsome youth, and that other no less exquisite countenance in the flesh, are surely identical. Many think that this portrait must be Muriel's, and that for some pretty caprice, some arch, wild fancy, she arrayed herself in these old-world garments, and dressed her glorious hair in the fashion of nearly fifty years ago.

But one old gentleman who is among the guests, the representative of an old country family, who knew the Beresfords well, and whose memory can easily clear the half century, declares that the picture is indeed of the dead and gone Eunice, as he remembers its being painted; but that Mrs. Erncliffe now, in the glory and perfection of her beauteous womanhood, is almost an exact reflection of what Eunice Beresford was fifty years ago, before the blight fell that for ever shadowed her life and her beauty.

Thus singularly, in distant offshoots of families, do marvellous likenesses appear, or strange peculiarities of either mind or body crop up after long intervals, and are somewhat puzzling and incomprehensible.

Dr. Hilliard and Major Erncliffe have often noticed Muriel's remarkable resemblance to the Beresford family—judged, at least, by their presentments on the walls of the picture-gallery (which, of course, they had never imagined till Muriel had entered the house as mistress, some half-dozen years ago, not having before seen those portraits); but never have they seen it so accentuated as now.

The extraordinary likeness to Eunice Beresford, since Muriel's face assumed this later aspect of pathetic, tender love, seems to increase daily, and is sometimes almost startling in its astonishing vividness; and Arnold Dysart, who is one of the guests, takes a deep, unflagging interest in this strange fact.

He will stand before the picture in reverie long and profound; he studies it at all points—it is exquisitely painted by a master hand—taking note of every smallest detail of that lovely expressive face, expressive even in its perpetual wearing of one expression, which is all the artist—genius though he may be—can stamp upon the canvas. And then he will seek his hostess, and watch her intensely, though furtively. And sometimes a great strange eagerness, verging on amazement, dawns on his face, but is instantly repressed.

* * * * * *

He, scientist, psychologist and all, as he is, is voted a decided acquisition to the house-party. He is nothing of a kill-joy. Pleasant, cordial, genial, he enters into every little passing interest or amusement, with a quiet zest and earnestness almost wonderful in one whose thoughts so often wander in such inaccessible regions. He and Major Erncliffe are fast friends, and, but that Professor Dysart was absent from England at the time, Leonard would have confided to him the singular dream, or vision, he had in Muriel's boudoir in the April preceding his marriage. But that dream—for he had long ago come to the conclusion that it *was* a dream, strange and unaccountable, but still only a dream—has now almost faded from his memory, and he scarcely remembers it, and consequently never mentions it, much as they discuss all such phenomena; which is perhaps unfortunate, as Arnold Dysart might discern, at least, some strange prophetic warning in that peculiar vision—might discover in it the clue to some unsolved mystery.

All the other guests are delighted with the Professor, and declare that he in his own person does more to make a three weeks' visit to a country house in mid-winter—when the snow is a foot deep, and yet no chance of skating, from continual slight thaws followed by fresh snow-falls—a success than all the rest of them put together. And yet all that he does is to relate strange, eerie stories, weird tales, unearthly experiences that he had amassed from many sources, some from the very "Psychical Society" itself, and that all possess the one great and surpassing charm of being founded on absolute facts.

And each evening, as the hour grows late, the small brilliant group of men and women will forsake their dancing or charade playing, the billiard-room or music-room, and crowd round Arnold Dysart to listen, fascinated, while he tells some fresh singular story of "Mysticism," or "Dream-Science," or discusses some problem of the "Hidden Life."

And none seem more enthralled than Muriel. That instinctive craving all we poor mortals have to thin, or lessen ever so slightly, the density of the veil that hangs between the known and the unknown—a veil that we feel unconsciously is often lifted, but that our eyes are sealed so fast by earth as not to see it rise—is peculiarly accentuated in his wife's sensitive, highly-strung nature, thinks major Erncliffe, in his loving, almost foolish solicitude, as he watches the great eyes darken and dilate as she hangs, spellbound, upon the Professor's words.

Muriel has grown somewhat nervous lately, he thinks, apt to start suddenly, without any apparent cause, to shiver and look about her with a scared, hurried glance of dread. Dysart's mysticism does not agree with her, he thinks; but when he speaks so to Dr. Hilliard, his father-in-law, who is one of the Professor's warmest admirers—the clever physician, with a bias for brain-study, taking especial delight and interest in all brain and thought phenomena adduced by the occultist—he scoffs at the suggestion.

"Harm her, indeed!" he says. "Dysart's society would only do her and the world at large—the world of women especially—an immensity of good, by giving them something novel and interesting to think of. Nothing is so injurious to the mind of man or woman as to be compelled by circumstances to run in one of more certain regulation channels; to be obliged to think only in certain given directions; to be so situated in life, by the press of outward things, that when the mind wanders of itself, as a thinking, cultivated understanding must and will, into unfamiliar paths, other than those beaten, tiresome tracks prepared for it, the possessor of the weary errant will, that yearns and sickens for fresh mental pabulum, must, perforce, summon it from its little excursive exploration, and chain it once more to its old thought mill-wheel, lest those small rambles might unfit, or make grow absent, the weary brain for the monotonous work which it *must* do, the unbroken, undeviating path which it *must* follow. Yes," continues Dr. Hilliard, waxing energetic, "for men and women who have mind—that priceless and greatest of all good gifts—to be so let and hindered and hampered in their mental life, is, in truth, a misfortune and a misery. Of course, I speak only of cases where the mind chafes at the restraint put upon it, and rebelliously seeks to break its chains; and in such cases it would be almost better for the owner of that mind to let it have its freedom, as compulsory work, whether mental or physical, is never so well done as when the heart is in the labour.

"As to Muriel, you are much too anxious about her. My darling girl never seemed so bright and strong—wonderfully so, in the circumstances; and a little nervousness is only to be expected.

"I think Professor Dysart is an acquisition to your house-party, of whom you ought to be very proud, Leonard; he is the most interesting fellow that I have ever met. I often heard you speak of him, but never imagined he was a man of such immensely wide culture, and familiarity with subjects outside the ordinary range."

"Yes, sir; and it is this very familiarity with those mystic subjects that might make him a particularly dangerous companion for a sensitive, highly-organized nature. If Arnold Dysart were but a clever, skilful narrator of what we somewhat vulgarly term 'ghost stories,' more or less ingenious, I should only laugh at them and him, and any credulous minds who were impressed by his mental sleight-of-hand. Conjuring, whether by the finger or the tongue, would have little effect on me, and I should have still less sympathy with would-be converts to the impostor's creed. But round all Dysart tells us there palpitates the ever-visible halo of truth—weird, mystical truth—but still truth. And it is this fact which would have the telling, and possibly disastrous effect upon some natures.

"I'm very fond of Dysart, and, except yourself, uncle, there is no man for whom I have so great an affection; but, even apart from his startling psychical theories, his beliefs or religious views are strange and singular, and might possibly lead one whose faith was not extraordinarily strong and vigorous to falter, to question, to lose its hold on the sweet old satisfying creed that has hitherto upheld, and been all-sufficing. Heaven knows, I'm no sectarian or dogmatist, attaching, perhaps, too little value to special form, though, indeed, I have noble examples for any laxity I may evince in such matters. Wasn't it Gordon, our grandest and most heroic Christian soldier of these latter, or, indeed, any days, who received the Sacrament more than once in the Greek church, and wrote I believe to a Roman Catholic priest for his prayers?"

"And why not?" interpolates Dr. Hilliard quickly. "Are not the prayers of any good man, who believes in, reveres, adores the

God of the Christian, let his rite of worship be what it may, equally beneficial to the creature prayed for, and equally acceptable to Him to whom those prayers are addressed? I should be sorry to think otherwise; I should think myself guilty of unpardonable, sinful presumption, in assuming that mine, and mine only, was the form of worship tolerated by the Most High, especially when we recollect that nowhere in the sacred Book, least of all in the New Testament, is there laid down any fixed rule or command that is to regulate the manner or form of the creature's instinctive adoration of the Creator. And I have often thought that this is a point not sufficiently recognized or acknowledged by the believers in revealed religion. There is no formula of worship enjoined upon believing man in the inspired writings; there is no law for him to break, no statute for him to disobey. Consequently, how wicked, how heinously presumptuous it is of us to declare, '*Thus* shall ye worship, and be saved,' or 'Thus shall ye worship, and be eternally lost!' Pah! it's unwarrantable, sickening, blasphemous intolerance!" And Dr. Hilliard, who speaks with rapid, excited utterance, having touched on a subject on which he feels strongly, pauses for breath, thereby allowing Leonard to complete his more or less broken speech.

"Ah, yes, that's all very well, and I feel much with you; I abhor illiberalism of any kind, above all, in matters pertaining to religious conviction. But Dysart, you know, has steeped himself in, and absorbed many of these strange modern notions, that seem to me the outcome more of an unwholesome straining after some new sensation, something odd and singular, something that will excite a jaded fancy, rather than real, honest, downright belief. They are the feverish imaginations of a weakened, diseased brain—the brain of our nation, that, I fear, is fast leaving its virile stage behind, and entering that on which all great kingdoms must perforce pass through, before they reach the final one of decay and collapse . . . Superlative luxury, superlative immorality, and superlative infidelity, are the fatal three that indicate the decline and fall of nations. It has been so; and why not again? Other kingdoms have risen, culminated, and set; why not ours?

"Beyond a certain pinnacle of greatness man or nations cannot go; all that comes after must, in the mystic order of the trinity that pervades all things, be inferior . . . Incipiency, power, decay! forenoon, noon, afternoon! That land where it is always afternoon is a pleasant land, where live the lazy Lotus-eaters; but it is more the land of retrogression than advance. Are we entering it? . . . Under the brilliant, glittering mantle of our high-pressure civilization and supernal culture, are there the first faintest hints of the putrescence that will develop by-and-by? You think I speak wildly, uncle; perhaps I do; but I'm not caught by new-fangled ideas. I like to cling to the old things—above all, the old faith, that we have tested, and not found wanting, and that, after nearly nineteen hundred years, springs as green and fresh as it did on the first wondrous Easter morning.

"Dysart is the best fellow in the world, and, in spite of his strange theories, is, I believe, a thorough Christian—the two are quite compatible to a great intellect, a strong, comprehensive mind; but what I fear a little is, that to one not so endowed by nature, where the brain-power is weaker, and the imaginative faculties are much accentuated—a sensitive, nervous organism, in fact, like Muriel's—that there might be danger. She is so strangely fascinated by his mystical talk, and——"

"Ah, Leonard, take care, take care!" breaks in Dr. Hilliard, with a laugh; "don't blind yourself. I think it's Dysart the man you dread, after all, not Dysart the metaphysician. But, indeed, lad, you need have no fear. My little girl has no thought or care, I verily believe, for creature on this earth, save your own big, foolish self. Her old dad she just tolerates, and as to her mother——Well, that's an inscrutable mystery! The daughter'd be loving enough, I'd take my oath, if she were let. But—Rachel—I cannot understand her—the child she almost worshipped.

"I suppose you could have no slightest inkling of the reason of your aunt's extraordinary conduct, Leonard? She always loved you, so the marriage could not have displeased her; besides, the strange change of feeling to our girl set in long before. I seek in vain for a cause, and the only one that suggests itself to me is so horrible that I don't like to allow myself to dwell on it." And the elder man pushes back his hair with a nervous, tremulous gesture, as he somewhat narrowly scans the face of the younger.

"And that is——" speaks Major Erncliffe, with slow enunciation, gazing steadfastly into his uncle's eyes, while his bronzed cheek blanches slightly.

But at that moment Muriel and two or three of her lady guests enter the library, where the preceding conversation has taken place, and Leonard's half-uttered question remains unfinished and unanswered.

CHAPTER XVI
IN THE STILLNESS OF THE NIGHT

"I HAVE been just telling Professor Dysart," cries one of them, a bright, winsome girl of twenty, Leonard's younger sister and only very near relative: thirteen years younger than her brother, she has been considerably spoiled by him, and Muriel now is doing her best to complete the process. The girl's home has hitherto been with a rather austere maiden aunt, in whose charge she was left some fifteen years ago by her dying father; but in another year she will be twenty-one, and her own mistress, and Muriel declares that she must then reside with them altogether—"I have been just telling Professor Dysart," she exclaims gaily, "that he must give us his very best and most creepy story to-night—Christmas Eve, you know"—with a nod of the pretty roan head; "the traditional night for a ghost *séance*. What a weird unaccountable custom it is, by the way," she continues, with a pretty air of moralizing, "that links indissolubly superstitious horrors with the season of 'peace and good will!' It seems almost something of a paradox—doesn't it? Festivity and phantoms! However, the lamentable fact remains that we look for ghosts at Christmas, as surely as we look for plum-pudding. But isn't it shabby—I mean of Professor Dysart, not of the ghosts, poor things; they must pass their spectral existence in a perennial condition of shabbiness, for we have never yet heard even of the most advanced modern ghost having got its 'new clothes on.' "

"Nell, Nell, you bad child! You grow more incorrigible daily. When will you learn respect for anything or any one?" asks her brother, with an indulgent smile, while the others laugh at the arch girl's saucy jesting.

"Well, a shade is not 'any one;' and who respects shadows?" she retorts, with a roguish gleam in the bright, sparkling, hazel-grey eyes.

"But how has Professor Dysart won your disapprobation, Nell?" asks Muriel. "You have been loud in his praise hitherto; though why you are so eager for his stories, I can't imagine. While you are listening you are all creeps and shivers, and neglect none of the pantomime expressive of intense and fearful appreciation; and yet the last word has scarcely passed his lips, when you are as volatile as ever, almost chaffing the horrors you shuddered at a moment before."

"And why not?" argues Nell Erncliffe vehemently. "Take my word for it, Muriel, the best way to exorcise phantoms, whether real or imaginary, substance or shadow—let it be trouble, or only an intrusive spectre, whose *metier*, after all, is generally tolerably harmless—is to laugh at them.[65] Laugh long and loudly, believe in the efficacy of your own laughter, and they, the unpleasant visitants, will believe in it too, and will scurry away, and your fears along with them."

"Brava, Nell! you're growing almost as metaphysical as Dysart himself," laughs her uncle, Dr. Hilliard; and the girl, somewhat ashamed of her small outburst, colours, and goes on hastily—

"What I mean by Professor Dysart's being shabby is, when I asked him wouldn't he give us his very best to-night, he said—just fancy, how disappointing!—that he feared he had quite exhausted his small stock of real authentic mysteries; that a supply of genuine, unaccountable, weird stories was not, as I appeared to imagine, inexhaustible, but, on the contrary, extremely limited. Occultism and

[65] *Metier*: occupation.

the mystic problems of 'The Hidden Life' offered, he said, an immense field for discussion and argument, in which he would be happy to take a prominent part, and impart a portion of the small wisdom he has acquired; but if Mrs. Erncliffe—he especially dwelt on Mrs. Erncliffe—insisted on a story again to-night, he should fall back upon a very singular and startling experience of his own, or rather, perhaps, he should say his father's, though some of the extraordinary phenomena did come under his own observation as a boy; and that's what I call shabby of him. Every one knows when it comes to 'personal experience' how flat, stale, and unprofitable the story or anecdote is almost sure to prove. The very prefacing words, indicating that the 'ego' is responsible for the coming tale, impresses one with a damp chilliness and general depression which the result is almost inevitably sure to warrant."

"That couldn't be the case with Professor Dysart, I feel convinced," remarks Muriel decisively. "I should be rather inclined to think it will be quite the other way, and that the Professor's own experience will be quite the best thing in his repertoire. You deserve to be banished from the charmed circle to-night, Nell, for your shocking heresy and want of faith in our apostle of mysticism."

Muriel speaks lightly and laughingly; but her cheek is flushed, and Leonard fancies he detects an eagerness in her tone not habitual. And then his unlucky young sister, influenced by some malign spirit of mischief says, unconsciously, the very last thing she should say, and earns thereby her brother's great and silent wrath.

"Well, Muriel, if you have such great and perfect faith in the satisfying nature of 'personal' strange experiences, why don't you recount your own? I mean, of course"—with a half-frightened catch in her breath, on noticing the sudden, horrible scowl on Leonard's face, and the wild, strange terror that flashes out on Muriel's, vanishing almost instantly, but leaving a great and singular pallor behind—"the intimate personal knowledge of ghosts, and the somewhat irrational, startling habits of that 'peculiar people' that you must have acquired during your long residence here at Varley Hall. Every one knows that the house is reputed to be haunted; and surely you must have seen or heard something. In fact"—with a little nervous laugh, for the girl is beginning to be startled, the look in her sister-in-law's face is so strange—"I sometimes think you must be a ghost yourself—the ghost of Eunice Beresford. You are so absurdly like her picture; and if——"

* * * * * *

But the girl's silly words end abruptly. There is a wild little strangled cry from Muriel, who steps backwards with an ashen face, and both hands thrown out in front of her, as if warding off some physical or mental horror, her eyes gazing, as it were, on something that the others cannot see!

Her husband and father both rush to her side, but the sudden movement seems to rouse her. She starts and looks around dazedly, and then sinks into a low chair, sobbing softly, also muttering strangely, though her words seem to have no meaning for the ears they reach.

"I know it—I have been guessing it this long time . . . She and I are one! . . . What does it mean, that dreadful mystery? . . . That picture! Yes; that picture. I have whispered the secret to it, and it has not denied it . . . It looks at me, and I look at it and speak to it, and yet we are the same . . . Eunice and I—not two, but one! . . . And there's another—a third. I feel and know she's often near me . . . She! Who is that she? Tell me who she is?"—with a sudden gesture of imploring appeal to the two distracted men, who gaze at her in astonished non-comprehension.

This last is the only sentence they have clearly heard, the rest being too muffled and indistinct; owing to her face being buried in her hands; and now it seems as if she were gone a little mad. Whom is she talking of?

"An influence in the air, that seems to draw you, and compel you, and that you cannot fight against; and she and *it* are one . . . I told it to the picture; but it only said, with a sorrowful moan, 'We all three are one.' "

And she lapses back into the low, pitiful sobbing; and the men look at her, and at each other, and Leonard whispers the familiar, trenchant phrase—

"I told you so."

Then after a little they all leave her to her husband, whom she seems to wish to be alone with. And a few hours later, when they meet at dinner, Muriel seems brilliant, radiant, joyous as ever; though Leonard cannot help fancying, in his intense anxiety, that there is a feverish restlessness, eagerness, and strange, nervous watchfulness under her assumed gaiety. But Doctor Hilliard tells him he may make his mind easy; that attacks of nervousness or hysteria are quite natural in Muriel's present state of health.

And when Leonard argues, with a troubled face, that it wasn't mere hysteria, but that it quite seemed as if his darling's mind was wandering for that few minutes in the library, his uncle smiles reassuringly, saying—

"It was simply a fantastic fancy that took hold of her for a moment, my dear boy, believe me. She has been hearing much of her likeness to that picture lately; and then naughty Nell's wild words about her being the ghost of that pictured Eunice struck her, in her present weakened, nervous state, with a strange weird thrill, and overcame her a little. She confessed as much to me an hour or two ago. Perhaps you were right, and that Dysart's mysticism is not very good for her just now. It is as well, possibly, that he has come to the end of his repertoire. I don't fancy we'll find his 'own experience' very terrifying. You see, Nell has inoculated me with her pessimistic views in that direction."

And Doctor Hilliard laughs cheerfully as he turns to give his arm to the lady committed to his charge, on hearing the magic formula, "Dinner is served," solemnly pronounced by the stately, dignified butler, who, on the strength of having lived last in a nobleman's family, feels somewhat patronizingly towards his present employers; while Leonard mutters *sotto voce*—

"His own experience, or anybody else's, shall not be told, if I can prevent it."

* * * * * *

But Major Erncliffe's wishes are overruled.

By-and-by, when his guests gather round Professor Dysart, in full expectation of receiving at his hands, or rather, from his lips, the pleasure they have almost grown to regard as habitual, and their prescriptive right, none are so urgent as Muriel that he should recount the strange experience he spoke of to Nell Erncliffe earlier in the day; and though her husband does his best to combat her entreaties, without being actually uncourteous to Dysart and the others, he cannot forbid the narration of the incident, whatever it may be. And so, comforting himself with the belief that doubtless Nell and her uncle were right, and that the forthcoming horrors will prove to be of a tame and milk-and-watery type, he adjourns to the billiard-room with one or two men who have no very pronounced taste for the mystical. And the last thing he hears, as he leaves the room, is his wife's voice, saying to a lady near her—these two are seated in a somewhat shadowed corner some little distance from the brilliant, animated group near the fire—

"It is sure to be something good. His father was a wonderful traveller—Desmond Dysart, the celebrated archæologist, you know; and, doubtless, this is some marvellous experience of his in some wild, distant land."

And then he hears no more, for the door closes behind him; but Arnold Dysart caught these last few words, and he smiles strangely as he says—

"No, Mrs. Erncliffe, my story has nothing to do with foreign lands; it is, rather, very near home—so near, in fact, as to be *in* your home! Yes, ladies and gentlemen,: he said, looking round on the slightly astonished faces of the Major's guests, "the story I propose to tell, with Mrs. Erncliffe's permission—indeed, she has been the most urgent that I should relate this weird and singular episode in my father's life—is altogether connected with this old Manor House of the Beresford family, under whose roof you are now assembled, and treats of the last two representatives of that now extinct race; especially of the good, sweet, and lovely Eunice, whose portrait you know so well, and to which our charming hostess bears so astonishing a resemblance."

Nell glances with frightened eyes at her sister-in-law, remembering the scene in the library a few hours ago. Muriel is deadly pale, with something of a rigid, fixed look in the soft, beautiful face, but otherwise she makes no sign of being affected by the Professor's words, and the girl hopes that all is right, though she feels regretful now at having helped to urge him to tell this tale, that she is sure "is not going to be a bit nice." "It's not good form of Professor Dysart," she thinks a wee shade resentfully, "to sit down coolly to tell horrible stories about one's own house;"

and she shivers unpleasantly, and glances round her with a new-born feeling of dread that is decidedly disagreeable.

"It's very possible that you may have heard, Mrs. Erncliffe," resumed Arnold Dysart, apparently glancing at Muriel for the first time since he began to speak, though he has furtively kept a keen watch upon her slightest variation of expression; but, unfortunately, she is in the shadow, and he cannot see her as clearly as he would wish—"it is very possible that you may have heard of the weird and terrible ordeal that Eunice Beresford passed through on this night some six or seven and twenty years ago; of the awful manifestation that was made to her on that Christmas Eve, and the strange, incomprehensible phenomena of the mystic violin. Perchance you have even heard the unearthly music of that spectral violin sound from the eastern gable—that terrible gable, that enshrines so mysterious and deadly a secret; a secret that——"

But the Professor's sentence remains unfinished, and his story untold, much to the chagrin of some present; for suddenly there is a shrill, wild, terrified cry, and the next instant Muriel lies prone and unconscious on the carpet, and scared confusion and distress reigns where all had seemed tranquil and serene.

She is carried to her room, and there remains insensible for an hour or more, to Leonard's startled dismay; while her father, in spite of his professional coolness and familiarity with all species of nervous seizure, cannot altogether disguise his anxiety.

When she does recover consciousness she appears to them wandering and incoherent, muttering in the same wild, unmeaning way as in the library in the afternoon—

"The secret of the gable! Has it *two* secrets? . . . How did he know of it? . . . The ghost of the eastern gable; that's what people say; but never the *secret*; and yet . . . he never could have guessed *that!* . . . That awful night, all those years ago. Yes, I seem to have a faint memory of it, as across a great gulf of time, as one hazily remembers the things of a dream. Perhaps it was a dream! . . . *I* and Eunice . . . one and the same! . . . How could such a terrible thing be? And yet . . . I feel it is . . . And the violin! . . . Two or three times I woke in the middle of the night and heard a violin playing; oh, so far away it seemed; and yet it was clear and distinct, as if in the next room; and I said I was sure that it was somewhere in the house; but Jacob laughed, and called me a little goose, and said it was some young fellow walking out home from Westerham, and playing as he went for company."

* * * * * *

So she murmurs on for a little while, and Leonard's heart grows cold and sick with fear; they seem so like the ravings of insanity or delirium. But Dr. Hilliard feels more easy now that she has recovered from her prolonged swoon. Her nerves are terribly shaken, evidently; but still he hopes that all will be well. After a time she grows quite quiet and rational; but she is strangely silent, and there is a feverish, restless light in the great shining azure eyes that he does not like.

Tranquil, refreshing sleep is the best medicine for her, and he determines that she shall have it artificially, as there is not much chance of her winning natural slumber to-night. And so, reluctantly, he calls the magic chloral to his aid—that sorcerer that is so terrible a foe when we get to know him well, so sweet a friend while still comparatively a stranger—and just before two o'clock she falls into a deep, profound sleep.

After watching half an hour longer, and all seeming calm and peaceful, Dr. Hilliard—anxious father though he is—weary and worn-out with his arduous professional duties in Westerham, whence he went and came out to Varley Hall two or three times that day, and knowing that he had a fatiguing day before him on the morrow, even though it be Christmas Day, having been sent for to visit a patient who lives some fifteen miles away, and to whom he must ride or drive, as no train will run to-morrow, makes up his mind to snatch a few hours' rest. His room is in the same corridor, but a few yards off, and so he shall be quite within call.

Leonard declares his intention of not lying down all night; he will remain where he is, active, waking, watchful.

He is not quite alone in his vigil, as Mrs. Page, good soul, Muriel's old nurse, the recalcitrant witness at the trial, is comfortably ensconced in an armchair by the fire; but she has been tranquilly slumbering for nearly an hour, and her gentle, whispering snores are the only sounds that break the intense stillness that seems to reign all round him, as, seated in the shadowed room, after the doctor's departure, Leonard looks about, with a little feeling of loneliness, or eeriness—which is it? And yet how absurd! In this handsome, luxurious, familiar room, with its glowing red fire and shaded lamp, with his sleeping wife and sleeping servant so near, how could he possibly feel either?

He gives himself a little shake, tosses off a glass of green Chartreuse, and then opens a book that lies at his elbow; but whether it is that he finds the book (a volume of Herbert Spencer belonging to the Professor) dull, or that the Chartreuse is more soporific in its effects than he imagined, it is but little past three o'clock when he, too, falls heavily asleep, weary with intense anxiety and watching. And for anther hour no sound save the soft breathing of the many sleepers, in their various chambers, breaks the profound stillness in that great old echoing mansion.

* * * * * *

But about four o'clock, just when the winter night is at its very darkest, through those wide, lofty corridors, those great staircases, those spacious chambers, come stealing, soft and low, yet vibratingly clear and distinct, the notes of a violin—horribly, supernaturally distinct, in contrast with the apparent distance the sound has to travel!

And that mystic music sighs, and sobs, and plains, and sometimes shrieks through the thick gloom of the night; now dying away among the massive timbers of the great old Manor House roof; now swelling in murmurous cadence, and seeming to fill with unearthly harmony all the air around.

And of those many sleepers three or four waken and hear those awful, mysterious strains; and those few, with one exception, cower and shiver in the darkness, and draw up the bed-clothes over their heads, and feel faint with terror as they remember Professor Dysart's allusion to the ghostly violin and the eastern gable, and think with horror that, to-morrow being Christmas Day, they can't possibly leave this terrible house till the day after. Yet *how* are they to endure another night under its haunted roof?

* * * * * *

But that one exception is Professor Dysart himself. He, too, wakes and hears that phantom music; but coupled with the natural human awe of all things unearthly, of any startling and unaccustomed manifestation of the occult spiritual powers that surround us, any tiniest temporary rift in the thick cloud of materialisation that shuts our earthly eyes and ears to the mysteries that encompass us—blent with this involuntary shrinking dread is a great and eager interest and curiosity . . . He alone knows something of the meaning of the mystery of that weird music. He has never expected to hear it with his own ears, as he has never expected to be a guest in this strange, mystical old house, that he knows to have so startling a history; and yet how singularly things come to pass.

* * * * * *

He does now what his father did a quarter of a century before: he springs from his bed, and goes to the door of his room to hearken to that wild, wailing sound. Out into the long corridor he gazes, with eyes dilated with an eager awe . . . Nothing to be seen; . . . darkness profound, inscrutable; only that terrible unearthly music filling all the air, sobbing, sighing, moaning—now at your ear, though soft and low; now more distant; anon creeping and stealing in regions far away above one's head . . . Away! Ah yes, away in that remote eastern gable . . . That is the point from which the sounds proceed, concludes the Professor, as he softly paces along the corridor in the impenetrable gloom that is only faintly broken by the ray of light from his open door.

Is it a sign, he wonders, with a shuddering thrill of excitement, that the prophetic curse is working? . . . And then again he thinks, do Major Erncliffe and his wife hear that supernatural music, and how do they regard it? Is any one waking in all that vast space within those grey old walls but himself?

He moves along, feeling his way to the end of the long corridor in which his room is situated, and then at right angles with it, is the corridor in which are the apartments which the Erncliffes occupy. Gazing along its shadowed length, he sees one small stream of light piercing the intense darkness; it is from Dr. Hilliard's room, where the tired physician is sleeping with open door, fearing he may be summoned to his daughter's side. But neither he nor any one else appears to be disturbed by those eerie strains; and the Professor retraces his steps lingeringly, brave man as he is, and possessed by almost a devouring curiosity with regard to that phantom music, that awful ghostly violin and its mystic player. Still, like his father six and twenty years before, he has not courage enough to seek to run it to earth, to penetrate the fastnesses of that eastern gable.

PART III

THE PROPHECY FULFILLED

"Our birth is but a sleep and a forgetting;
The soul that rises with us (our Life's star)
Hath had elsewhere its setting,
And cometh from afar."

WILLIAM WORDSWORTH

CHAPTER XVII

THE MANOR HOUSE PHANTOM AGAIN VISIBLE

AMONG these startled sleepers was Nell Erncliffe, and none were more terrified than the darling, saucy girl. Yet she does not venture to mention the subject to her brother, when she finds by furtive, well-directed questioning that he knows nothing of the extraordinary phenomenon of the night. For, by a strange coincidence, the two who are really concerned in the weird manifestation of that unearthly music heard it not. Leonard, in the first sleep of exhaustion, after great mental anxiety, did not wake; and Muriel, sleeping the sleep induced by the narcotic, was unconscious of all. Neither is Dr. Hilliard aware of anything singular having occurred in the night. And of the few who did hear, and trembled as they heard, none cared to enlighten these three, who appear to be the chief actors in this uncanny Manor House drama. The fact of Muriel being still ill and invisible closes these people's lips, but they will talk among themselves. And those who did not hear the phantom strains of that ghostly violin, are told of it by those who did. And though inclined at first to be incredulous, and ascribe it to excited fancy engendered by the Professor's strange introduction to the tale which he had been about to tell last night, when Mrs. Erncliffe had been so suddenly and oddly smitten with mysterious illness, still the united and persistent testimony of these three or four at last has its weight; and a more miserable Christmas Day is rarely spent than that passed in Varley Hall by those unfortunate guests, compelled by decency to remain for another twenty-four hours, yet thinking the morrow will never come, when they will have a fair and valid excuse for departure on account of their hostess's indisposition.

With quaking hearts they seek their respective rooms at night, and little sleep visits their eyelids; but the hours of darkness bring no weird manifestation on their dusky wings, and those who were inclined to be sceptical are slightly sceptical again. But still they one and all bid a relieved, though outwardly regretful, farewell to the Major, with much expression of concern and anxious solicitude on his wife's behalf, and much inward gratitude that she has given them this delightful loophole of escape.

He does not ask them to remain; he feels that it would be a mockery, and that they would detect the insincerity of his expression if he had. He is honest and true, and void of the social veneer of society hypocrisy. He is only anxious for them to be gone, that he may have nothing to distract his time and thoughts from Muriel, and he does not express himself to the contrary.

He somewhat grudgingly tells his sister that she "can remain if she likes," which cannot be construed into a very warm and pressing invitation. But the truth is, he feels rather resentfully towards poor innocent Nell, as being the "first cause" of his darling's strange attack. Only for her unbridled tongue, he thinks, with a good deal of exasperation and much injustice, Muriel might never have been so smitten.

But the girl does not take advantage of this reluctantly given permission to stay. No one is more anxious to get away than pretty grey-eyed Nell, who deserves a little pity for this gloomy, "horrible," as she dubs it, termination, to her joyously anticipated visit. The soft bright cheeks are pale, and the witching eyes have contracted a scared, terrified expression, since she heard that awful music.

"No; I'll go at once with the others, Leonard dear," she declares, with nervous precipitancy. "Poor dear auntie will be lonely; it's the first time I've been away from her for more than a week together."

(Ah! Nell, Nell, you shameless little hypocrite! were you not calmly contemplating but the other day deserting the same poor aunt for good and all in a year's time, and making your home here at the Hall?) "I'll come back again when darling Muriel is better;" though inwardly registering a solemn vow never to enter the gates of this fearful Manor House again. "I dare say I should be only in the way now," she concludes lamely and hurriedly, feeling that her affection for "darling Muriel" is not very ardently displayed by insisting on rushing off immediately her sister-in-law and cousin falls ill.

And so there is a general stampede; every one departs, and the only person who wishes, and would give much to remain a little while longer, is obliged to go with the rest. Yes; Professor Dysart lingers after the others have made their adieus, hoping that Major Erncliffe might possibly ask him to prolong his visit. He thinks it would not be very unnatural for him to do so, seeing that Leonard is alone now, save for his father-in-law coming and going when he can. But there is little chance of it; for if Leonard felt resentment against his sister, how much more warmly indignant does he feel with the Professor, to whom he attributes altogether the cloud that has descended on his home! He tries hard to disguise his sentiments, in memory of his former regard for Dysart; but he cannot completely banish a certain coldness of manner. And so, regretfully, the Professor, too, packs his portmanteau, and is off from the ill-fated house.

* * * * * *

After a little, Muriel is able to leave her bed; but she moves about in a strange, dull, spiritless way; and as the weeks pass on, and the New Year shivers in its early babyhood, an indefinite languor and depression, both of mind and body—which is, perhaps, not very unnatural in the circumstances—steals over her. Doubtless, when the expected heir to the united Varley and Erncliffe fortunes (the Major is a rich man since his uncle's death) is born, Muriel will be herself again. So reason Leonard and Dr. Hilliard, and so speaks Dr. Freeman.

And in the meantime she grows more and more depressed, nervous, gloomy, taking no delight in her usual occupations, refusing altogether to go out of doors; spending nearly all her time reclining on a couch in her dressing-room, in a sort of brooding melancholy.

Leonard gets uneasy and miserable. Though Muriel might be languid and weakly, why this strange morbidity of mind which evidences itself so plainly in the sad, dreary expression of the erstwhile bright face, now so wan and almost haggard; in the lovely azure eyes, which have since that Christmas Eve again contracted something of that singular frightened look so apparent in the first days of her widowhood; in the gloomy silence in which she wraps herself, and out of which, when spoken to, she comes with a start, and a glance of fearful appeal, showing that her thoughts have been far away? And the only change from this condition is when the mind, instead of seeming distressingly pre-occupied and absorbed, is sunk in a sort of lethargic torpor, akin to that which holds her body; when speech and thought seem alike impossible, and she lies as if in a waking sleep, indifferent to all around her.

Yes, Leonard is perfectly wretched. He has one of the first physicians down from London, in consultation with her father and Dr. Freeman; and the great man departs, after urbanely pocketing his thirty-guinea fee, assuring Major Erncliffe that he may make his mind quite easy; he need not be at all anxious, such cases are not very uncommon. The nervous system certainly wants tone; it seems as if the patient has received some mental shock, that, in her present condition, preys perhaps unduly on her mind; but when a certain happy event has taken place, Mrs. Erncliffe, he feels quite positive, will regain all her sweet, serene healthfulness, both of mind and of body.

* * * * * *

And it seems as if he was a true prophet—at least, for a while . . . About the middle of February a little daughter is born to Muriel; and almost from that hour she seems a new being. A rapturous love for the tiny creature—her Leonard's child—fills her soul, and banishes all gloom and nervous depression . . . Buoyant, exultant, joyous, she grows well marvellously fast—much too fast, as is said later. When baby is a month old, never has woman seemed brighter, happier, healthier, both in mind and in body.

But when baby is nearly two months old, there has come a change. Not that there is a return to the despondent, lethargic state; rather, she is possessed by a restless, feverish excitement that seems to increase each day. A nervous watchfulness, that amounts sometimes to an unaccountable sense of apparent anxious expectancy and apprehensive dread, takes the place of the singular brooding absorption of a few months back; her eyes wear the expression of one who does not sleep, or whose sleep is broken, disturbed, and unrefreshing; and once or twice as the weeks pass on, Major Erncliffe is startled and distressed, on being awakened by a slight noise in his room in the dead of night, to find his wife moving aimlessly about the chamber, fast asleep!

He got her back to bed each time without waking her; but this somnambulistic tendency somewhat frightens him. He does not know how often it may have been repeated without his knowledge, as in the usual way he is a very heavy sleeper, and wonders much how the trifling sound on these two occasions—merely the opening of a drawer—had aroused him. He speaks to Dr. Freeman, without saying anything to Muriel, fearing it might alarm her to hear that she walks in her sleep.

And it is then the medical man delivers himself of the opinion that he is afraid Mrs. Erncliffe has got well too quickly, that possibly she has made too free, and that it is now coming against her; that the nerves are much disordered, and great care will be needed in the future; that the very best thing Major Erncliffe could do would be to take her away for a change of air and scene, as soon as the weather settles a little.

"Not abroad—no; a vigorous, bracing upland air is what would be most likely to blow the nervous mists away. What would you say to a tour through the northern Highlands? More easily reached than Switzerland, less fatigue, and quite as beneficial. Of course, St. Moritz and Pontresina in the Engadine are the fashion; but, for my part, I consider 'Far Lochaber' quite as good a tonic." continues Dr. Freeman urgently. "In the meantime, Major, you must contrive to keep Mrs. Erncliffe's mind tranquil, happy, gently amused, if possible; above all, to avoid anything that might disturb, excite, irritate, or, worst of all, frighten, etc."

And the very day after this long conversation with the doctor, who knows her constitution thoroughly, Major Erncliffe hears quite accidentally what may possibly have reached his wife's ears long before, and have caused or increased, in her present weakened, unsettled health, the strange nervous symptoms which so alarm and distress him. He hears—what detestable, absurd gossip it is! he thinks vindictively—that the Manor House ghost has been making herself unpleasantly conspicuous of late. For years she has been more or less of an intangible personage, believed in profoundly, as an uncomfortable, incontrovertible fact, but a shadowy, impalpable one, that has made its presence known to the present generation by sound only, and not by sight. Sundry strange, unaccountable noises have been occasionally reported as proceeding from the haunted eastern gable. Doubtless they existed in imagination only; but when this mental condition—so often but a very uncertain blessing—does exist amongst the lower classes at all, it is apt to take the form of superstition. And here in Varley Hall, there is at least valid excuse for all belief in startling phenomena; for is there not a legendary family ghost on hand (undoubtedly a mark, sign, seal, and token of respectability, though perhaps hardly an agreeable one), ready to be trotted out—would it be more harmonious to say *glided?*—descriptively, as occasion warrants, to appal the unwary stranger?

Three or four new servants, in addition to the old and numerous staff, have been engaged of late at the Hall, and, whether it is that, being strangers to the district and, hearing the tale of wonder for the first time, their imaginations, excited by novelty, are more prolific than those of the others, who are nearly all Westerham born and familiar with the legend from their earliest years, or whether they really saw and heard what they describe, none can say positively; but, be it as it may, Leonard hears to-day for the first time—the day his little daughter is two months old, and just a clear fortnight before Easter—that within the last six weeks the spectral lady has been seen on two or three occasions in the distance, on the stairs leading to the eastern gable. Once it was from outside she was visible; the gliding phantom form carrying a light, swiftly passing one of the staircase windows. It was nearly two o'clock in the morning, and the terrified servant advancing in stealthy fashion through the shrubbery, who had been indulging in unlicensed freedom, staying out without permission, trusting to the faith and friendship of a fellow-domestic for ingress at unlawful hours, was suddenly conscience-smitten, and regarding the unearthly apparition as a direct judgment for their offence, turned and fled precipitately, not daring to venture near the house again till the reassuring daylight embraced all things in its friendly, honest, mystery-killing clasp. Leonard is wild with distress and anger when he hears these reports.

"Confound them for a pack of beastly idiots!" he mutters in hot wrath. "What tremendous craven duffers they are! And what evil may not their wild, superstitious folly have already wrought? Muriel is almost sure to have heard something of these absurd tales, and in her present excitable state they would prey on her, and be Heaven knows how injurious. Look at the cautions Freeman gave me yesterday. And what am I to do? I dare not speak of the subject, to scoff at and deride it as it deserves, and laugh my darling out of any credence in their fantastic imaginings, because, by some most inconceivable good-luck, she may not have yet heard. And I shall not soon forget what a detestable ass I made of myself two years ago, when I insisted on detailing to her my ridiculous dream, when this same troublesome spectral lady, by the way, condescended to interview me in sleep-land." Major Erncliffe has long since come to regard that somewhat peculiar circumstance as a dream—strange, realistic, unaccountable, but still, only a dream. "Why, my dearest nearly fainted then; and now it might kill her to speak of it. And yet, unless she has caught some whisper of this confounded report, what is making her so odd and queer, and altogether unlike herself?"

* * * * * *

Yes, just a fortnight before Easter, Leonard Erncliffe makes the unpleasant discovery of the legendary lady's renewed predilection for making herself visible in the old Manor House. In the ghost theory itself he has not one whit of faith, summarily dismissing the problem when presented for discussion in terse phrase as "all rot!" Yet he cannot but recollect that his singular dream made a strong and disagreeable impression at the time, and as the days go by he finds himself haunted pertinaciously by the memory of that dream, which is all the stranger as he had quite forgotten it during those long months of love and unalloyed happiness. And now, as he tries to recollect it, he finds that the first part is clear and distinct in his memory, but the latter is almost completely faded and blurred. He again finds himself even wondering, did his dream reveal to him anything like the real eastern gable as it exists, or was it, as is the way with dreams, but a fancy picture, or possibly an effort of the mind to reproduce something he had read and long forgotten? We all know how thoughts, memories, associations, countless serried ranks of pictures, more vivid than ever glowed on any canvas, are packed away, unknown to us, in that vast silent picture-gallery, that wondrously mysterious storehouse as well as workshop—the brain of man.

Though more than four months resident in and master of Varley Hall, Leonard has never taken the trouble to verify this point, to decide the topographical accuracy or inaccuracy of his dream. And why? For the simple reason that the dream itself had entirely escaped his memory, and the eastern—or western gable, for that matter, presented no attractions that would warrant an exploring expedition. No one goes near them, and neither does he; the approach to the former, especially, being shut out from the rest of the house by a heavy swing baize door, which no one has the curiosity—or the courage, if we come to that, always excepting Leonard—to cross.

But now his thoughts are constantly reverting to that odd dream, recalling it by degrees, bit by bit, each little forgotten circumstance, save quite towards the end, which ever eludes him;

and suddenly it smites him, with a strange shuddering chill of remembrance, that the face of the Manor House phantom, as seen by him in the eastern gable of dreamland, was the face of his Muriel! The next moment he pulls himself together with a slightly contemptuous laugh at his weakness. Is it possible those superstitious lunatics of servants have actually infected him with some of their insane imaginings? He will think no more of the whole absurd subject. The very proof that *his* was but the wildest dream, without meaning or motive, is evidenced by its ridiculous contradictoriness. He dreamed of the Manor House ghost, which, perhaps, was not very unnatural, seeing that he had heard the legend so often; and, with the charming consistency of dreams, the mystic lady wore his darling's face—which, again, for a dream, was all as it should be; for was not Muriel's sweet face imprinted on his heart, the only face on earth for him? If he had dreamt of an angel, that celestial vision would have worn his loved one's aspect.

He'll think of it no more, but devote himself to watching over his beloved wife, devising little distractions for her, if possible; trying to amuse and enliven, and also to soothe that highly-strung nervous nature, with the knowledge of his all-protecting, tender, abiding love.

And his efforts are rewarded with success, for during the next fortnight Muriel gains, to a great extent, her normal calm, bright cheerfulness and evenness of manner. The excitement and anxious restlessness and watchfulness gradually subside, and her utter delight and happiness in her little daughter, her supreme passion of love for baby Hilda, seems to increase each day.

And so Leonard grows to feel once more intensely happy; he adores his wife and idolizes his child. Life has no more to give him. His cup is full of joy and sweetness unutterable, no "fennel floats" therein. And a great glad peace and thankfulness reign in his breast as the holy Easter season again comes round.

"May will be here in another week now," he reflects with pleasure. "And Muriel is so much stronger, and baby such a little brick—happy, healthy, handsome" (at two-and-a-half months old! But, after all, why not, with such a perfectly lovely mother?), "never crying, always jolly—that we may be off on our Highland tour as soon as we like. And, by Jove! I'll not be in a hurry to get back this time. Let Uncle Hilliard join us if he can't get along without his daughter; but I think Varley Hall will have seen the last of us as residents the day we start north. We shan't live here again. My pet disliked the idea of coming back to if from Italy, and it evidently does not agree with her. Perhaps it *is* a bit uncanny! At any rate, the dear girl has such terribly disagreeable associations with it, since poor old Varley's death, that none can wonder at her shrinking from it.

"I'll let the place. One ought easily to get a good tenant—*new* people, of course, anxious to try to obtain the halo of a little antiquity, and hoping that even a faint borrowed reflection might dimly illumine them by residing in an old ancestral mansion.[66] Cads, most likely; but if they pay the rent, what need we care? Old Jacob Varley would have been called a 'cad' by some hypercritical folk, I suppose; but, in spite of his '*cotton*' and his '*h's*,' the dear old chap had the soul of a true and high-minded gentleman.

"We'll buy a snug nest in Devonshire or Cornwall, and we might have a little box in Scotland also, or, perhaps, the west of Ireland. We've money enough to keep half a dozen places going. Let the old man come to us if he feels lonely; aunt Hilliard certainly is not a very lively companion of late. I can't think what's come

[66] *New* people: those with money that has been earned, not inherited.

to her; never saw a woman so changed! Morbid and gloomy, seems as if she'd something on her mind, unless the mind itself is touched; looks uncommonly like it, I must say. I believe her grandmother died in a madhouse. The strangest symptom in her case is how she seems to have lost all affection for Muriel, the girl she almost worshipped."

And so his musings wander off from one subject to another; but the dominant feeling in his breast on this Easter Saturday morning, is a serene content and happiness, a tranquil joy, which is all the sweeter from being coupled with an inexpressible feeling of relief from the anxious strain and uneasiness that have possessed him for weeks.

CHAPTER XVIII
REALIZATION OF THE VISION

NEVER was Muriel brighter, sweeter, or more radiant than she is all through the hours of this lovely spring day. She has rapturously caught at the idea of the Highland trip; they will go "as soon as possible," she declares energetically—"in another week or two, at farthest—and not come back for months and months. It will be twice as delicious as going through the tiresome, beaten track of continental travel. I did it twice with poor dear Jacob, and once with you, love, and I am sick of it. And, Lennie darling, we shall not confine ourselves to the prosaic mainland, but have a yacht and go cruising about among those northern lakes and islets. I think I should like to live on the water, and make a regular mermaid of baby Hilda.

"Yes, we will have a yacht, dear, and visit all those delightful, out-of-the-way island nooks that must be so exquisitely wild, picturesque, and, above all, unhackneyed, judging by Mr. Black's charming books. Perhaps we'll create our darling another 'Princess,' if not of 'Thule,' of some remote, lonely, lovely region, away in those northern seas."

So she plans, and laughs and jests, and is apparently altogether her own gay, girlish, lighthearted self. And the twilight falls upon the land, and night, with his gloomy cohorts, takes possession of the darkling sky; and, by-and-by, sleep and silence brood over the earth's dark breast, and the old Manor House is hushed in the soft stillness of repose.

And the hours pass on in the strange unconsciousness of slumber, so mysterious an element of our being, in which we seem to lead a dual life; and the second hour after midnight has just rung out upon the silent air from the clock in the new stables, when Leonard wakes suddenly in his luxurious bedchamber.

Vague, sweet, misty, are the first half-roused thoughts. Nothing startled him, nothing disturbs him, as he lies in lazy contentment for a few moments, gazing sleepily at the light—for since Muriel's illness they have burned a night lamp—the shadowed rays of which dimly illuminate the large, handsome room. Then, with a gentle sigh of serene satisfaction, he turns round to go to sleep again; but as he turns, his drowsy, half-closed eyes fall upon the space at his side, which is blank and empty!

For a moment he looks with a stupid, noncomprehending stare at the vacant place, where Muriel was sleeping so calmly and sweetly, more than two hours ago, when he came to bed; then, with a rush, he remembers her sleep-walking proclivities. In an instant his mind is vividly awake and alert, and he jumps out of bed. Where is she? She is not in the room, and the door is carefully closed as it was—nothing seems disturbed. How softly she went, or how heavily he must have slept, he thinks, as he hurriedly throws on some clothes. Where can she have gone? She never yet left the room in her sleep—at least, not to his knowledge. What terrible accident may not happen to her in that helpless, somnambulistic state, in that great, rambling house? And a cold moisture of apprehensive dread bursts on his brow.

Then, in the act of lighting one of the candles standing in fanciful bronze and silver filigree candlesticks on the dressing-table, he notices that the other is gone, and he grows swiftly restful, easy, assured. How foolish he has been to be so alarmed! Of course, his darling woke, and grew fidgety about little Hilda, and, without disturbing him, slipped away to pay a nocturnal visit to the nursery, fearing the little precious creature might perhaps have vanished in a fairy-car, etc.—to assure herself, in fact, of the well-being of her baby. She has done so on one or two occasions, since her small daughter has been separated from her at night—a step on which the doctor insisted more than a month ago. So, with a fairly tranquil heart, Leonard leaves the room, and seeks the night-nursery near at hand, meditating but a gentle reproof on the loving folly that thus induces Muriel to run the risk of serious cold, out of her warm bed, but half-clad; and these spring nights are chilly. If she must know how the little one fares during the silent hours, why not let him go and see?

And so thinking, he steps softly into the shadowed room where his little girl is sleeping. A night-lamp burns here also, and its dim light reveals to him the nurse and her charge both fast asleep, the little one in her own pretty crib at nurse's side. But it also shows him that there is no third presence in the room, and a sudden cold clutch of fear grasps his heart in icy bonds. Where is Muriel? Where is he to seek for her, when he has failed to find her here?

For a moment or two he stands irresolute by the crib, looking down lovingly on the tiny rose-leaf face; then, with an irresistible impulse, he stoops and touches the tender velvet cheek lightly with his lips, while an unconscious gush of prayer for the welfare of the little helpless creature, so inexpressibly dear to him, wells straight from his heart.

Then, again taking up the light, he turns to renew his search for his—as he now feels—sleeping wife! And, with a strange and singular foreboding, premonition, instinct—which is it?—he involuntarily takes his way to the back staircase of the disused upper storeys that leads to the *eastern gable*.

Yes; it is as it were some mysterious influence, not his own will, that guides his steps thus. Never yet has he set foot upon this stairway, as it is quite removed from the occupied portion of the house; and it is with a sort of dazed shock that he now finds himself quickly ascending these dreary, unfamiliar, and yet at the same time startlingly familiar stairs—familiar, inasmuch as they are the stairs of his dream.

Every turn, every curve, every sudden, unexpected ascent and descent, are horribly, unnaturally familiar. These remote, lonely passages that he traverses so swiftly now, and that echo so dismally to his tread, he has never been through in the flesh before; but his spirit-feet have trod them, and their fantastic, intricate windings are indelibly impressed upon his memory.

All is exactly as it was two years ago, when that extraordinary dream or vision revealed to him an unknown region, and incidents still hidden behind the veil of the future; for is he not now, as in that singular dream, hastening through the darkness and silence of the olden, unchanged part of the Manor House, stepping swiftly through the night's stillness in pursuit of some one—only in his dream, he knew not whom he followed, or why?

And still, on he goes unerringly, with a wildly beating heart, while a feeling of awe and mystery grows upon him, mingled with a dread expectancy. He feels as if he were groping for the key to some mystic cipher—groping for the light through gloom impenetrable; as if he were just hovering on the confines of some unfathomed abyss, into which he may plunge at any step. The light may be glorious beyond that gulf, but he cannot know, and sees only the darkness of the way.

* * * * * *

And now an overwhelming impression comes on him suddenly, with the certainty of conviction, that the shrouding veil that hangs between the known and the unknown is about to be lifted for him to-night. And he pauses, with a shuddering gasp, and a half-formed resolve to relinquish his task and retrace his steps. He has even forgotten why he is here; forgotten his dream, forgotten Muriel. All reality seems swallowed up in this strange, new, inexplicable, brooding sense of awe. Fear—actual fear—for the first time in his life, blanches the cheek of the brave soldier, and palsies his strong limbs. It is the haunted, unhallowed air of this lonely eastern gable that is affecting his nerves, he thinks, trying to shake off the strange influence that weighs on him so eerily. He will go back. What folly has brought him here? But just as he has made this resolution, an indefinite breath of sound is wafted to his abnormally sharpened ears, a something that breaks the terrible stillness with faintest echo. It might be a distant footfall, a shutting door, a voice's instant murmur. But, whatever it is, it breaks for a moment the weird spell which has held him. He remembers Muriel and her danger, and, with suddenly quickened vitality, dashes round the curve near which he has been hesitating; and with the hasty motion, and, perhaps, some sudden draught, the candle in his hand flares brightly and goes out, and he is alone in this desolate, haunted gable, in complete darkness!

And with this horror, his momentarily renewed courage and fearlessness fade. He has no matches, no possible means of striking a light. He has very nearly reached the farthest point in this eerie east wing of the Manor House; to retrace his steps in that profound obscurity is well-nigh impossible, with all those extraordinary turns and irregular levels. To remain here—*here!*—through the remaining hours of darkness, till the returning blessed rays of earliest dawn lighten ever so dimly those gaunt, ghost-like windows, seems all that is left to him; and yet, how can he do it, with this weird sense of horror, of some impending awful revelation, again growing strong upon him? He is too far removed from the inhabited part of the house for his wildest cries to bring any one to his aid; besides, even if he were heard, none would venture near this haunted wing, and any startling sounds proceeding from it would be attributed to the phantom, whose royal prerogative is vested in this her kingdom.

And as he thus stands in helpless, fearful dismay, staring with wild, straining eyes into the thick darkness before him, it is suddenly lifted slightly, grows less dense and oppressive; a faint lightening of the shrouding gloom becomes palpable, at what seems the far end of a long, narrow corridor.

He watches the growing light with fascinated eyes. It gets stronger, though still but weak and uncertain, and seems as if it were advancing from the right-hand of this long passage, at one end of which he stands. *What* is it? *Who* carries it? . . . He fights against the supernatural dread that threatens to overcome him. Is he about to behold the ghost of the Manor House gable?

And even as he asks himself this question, the figure bearing the light glides into sight, and for a moment he feels faint and weak with an unearthly terror; the next he is moving softly, slowly along that shadowed passage, with all his fears of the last ten minutes vanished, moving in pursuit of that mysterious presence, for even at that distance, in that uncertain groping duskiness, he plainly saw that the moving form was no phantom, but his own beloved wife—Muriel!

She is evidently asleep, and he must follow her to guard her. To wake her suddenly, and *here*, in such startling circumstances, might kill her! What must he do? And what brings her here? What associations can she possibly have with this shunned portion of the house, to induce her to visit it in sleep? And so he follows with softened steps and a wondering, anxious heart; he dreads lest his hushed footfalls may rouse that sleeping swiftly-moving figure.

She has turned the last angle now in this strange old record of a sixteenth century builder's wild caprices. She is out of sight, and he steps more quickly through the returned darkness, the rays from that distant solitary candle not piercing the gloom sufficiently to dispel it, when carried at right angles to this narrow corridor. He hastens, because he fears Muriel may take some sudden winding turn he knows not of, and begin her dangerous descent without his vigilant, loving care ready to save her from possible peril.

She is evidently strangely familiar with this banned portion of the Manor House. She must have approached this extreme point of the eastern gable by some unguessed passage connecting it with the western gable, which, though unused, has not the evil reputation attaching to this dreary east wing. There may be some intricate winding way on ahead, which will lead her back again to the west side of the house, and so he dreads to lose the faint ghost-like flicker of that far-off light, for losing that, he loses all!

He has forgotten his dream completely, and how strangely it is being fulfilled. All his faculties are concentrated in the one absorbing idea to watch over Muriel, and protect her from harm.

And now, as he almost gains at the end of this long gallery or passage, he hears a sound as of a key inserted in a somewhat creaking rusty lock, and as he quickly turns the corner, he is just in time to see that gliding figure, with its fluttering white draperies and floating yellow hair, pass within an open door, which swings slowly to again, with a low, melancholy clang, leaving him for the second time in absolute darkness; but he feels no fear now.

Thank God, Muriel has entered a room from which there

scarcely can be—owing to its position with regard to the outer wall—any other mode of egress. Thus he will gain on her gently, and without alarming or waking her—unless that wretched door has already done so—and will be able to lead her back with infinite tenderness and care the way he has come.

And so thinking, he gropes his way to the door, which is but a few yards off. It is a minute or so before it yields to his touch, and when it does, it emits a rasping sound which causes Leonard to swear inwardly.

Then he steps softly within the chamber, and a strange sight meets his astonished gaze. It is an exact reproduction of his dream, though he recollects it not now.

At the end of the room farthest from the door, just beneath the old casement window, kneels Muriel on the dusty, decaying floor. She has removed a long piece of the rotting skirting-board, and in the vacancy left she is searching eagerly for something with trembling, groping hand. What does she seek? And for the first time to-night, a feeling of curiosity, mingled with a nameless apprehension, enters Major Erncliffe's breast. He crosses the room softly, and noiselessly stands beside her.

And now he can see her face clearly, the candle at her side revealing its every line distinctly; but when he looks on that exquisite face, set and stony in the fixed glare of the somnambulist, the new-born curiosity almost dies, while a great pity and love contend for the mastery in his heart . . . His darling! How sad it is to see her thus; it is almost like—like—madness! and he shudders horribly as he remembers the taint of insanity in her family. Her great-grandmother died mad! Well, that is far off; but, then, her mother has become decidedly odd lately, and—but he's a fool; *this* is only sleep-walking! And as he thinks so, the little groping hand closes at last on something in the darkness of that aperture, and is withdrawn.

He fancies he sees a glitter of glass, and makes an involuntary movement to look closer, to see better what this strangely hidden object can be. But as he moves, his foot inadvertently touches that piece of rotting, displaced wainscot, which leans angle-wise against the wall.—Was it not so in that mystic vision, though he has never remembered clearly quite up to this point?—It falls with a crash, and with the sudden sound Muriel wakes, with a strangled cry of fright, glancing round her with wild, scared eyes.

Leonard seizes her hand, with loving, soothing words. His sole thought is to reassure her, to comfort her with the knowledge of his protecting presence, feeling how intensely terrified she will feel to find herself in this eerie haunted gable in the dead of the night; but his grasp is laid unthinkingly on the hand that holds that concealed something! And, with a frenzied look on the face that has swiftly grown horribly awake, conscious, and filled with a desperate, defiant fear, Muriel screams again—a wild, ghastly scream of mingled grief and terror; her eyes glare into his, with an awful, hideous horror in their depths . . . His grasp involuntarily tightens on that hand he holds . . . A light of maddening rage—despair—which is it?—sweeps over the beautiful face he loves so well.

"*Never!* You or I shall die first!" she mutters, with rigid lips. Then, with a sudden supreme effort, she wrenches herself free from his clasp, pushing him at the same time violently from her, with a singular new-born strength. Simultaneously, a small phial falling to the ground, there is a crash as of broken glass, and immediately a penetrating, clinging smell of "bitter almonds." He, all unprepared, loses his balance, sways, and staggers heavily against the window; the old decayed wood-work cracks, splits, gapes!—he clutches frantically, convulsively at nothing! . . . The whole space where the window was, and the mouldering wall beneath, are gone in a moment! . . . There is a rush of cold night air . . . And *one* figure stands alone, within that desolate haunted chamber—immovable—petrified—a frozen, awful horror on the ashen face!

CHAPTER XIX
THE WAIL OF A LITTLE CHILD

"LEONARD!" she gasps, with the force of a shriek; but the single word falls with but a hissing murmur on the silent air. And, in answer, a faint dull thud is borne to her frenzied, straining ear, resounding from those cruel flagged depths so far below! . . . "Both!" she whispers to herself, as she crouches to the floor, still glaring fearfully at that blank, terrible space, through which he who is her very life has gone forth for ever . . . "*Both!*" she repeats, in that same strange, awful whisper. "*With the same hand!*"—holding out that small right hand, and gazing at it as if it were some fiend apart; while the dawning light of madness gradually steals into those fixed blue eyes . . . "*He* drank it, and I saw him die! Those eyes—those eyes—they will be with me through all eternity! . . . Jacob—Jacob—forgive—forgive!"—in wild appeal, suddenly throwing herself on her knees, with outstretched hands, as if imploring pardon from some invisible presence.

And there, in the dim further end of the room, surely there can be discerned a vague shadowy form, gliding through the gloom; an impalpable simulacrum of humanity; a phantom shape; but a woman's shape! For was it not here, in this very chamber, the two-century's-old murder took place? Is it not here that the long-buried secret lay hid?

But the frantic gaze of madness sees the spirit of a murdered husband in that awful something, that glides nearer, still more near!

"Torment me not!" she moans. "I am guilty—yes, guilty—guilty—guilty! . . . You have come for me. You bring the odour of the grave. My place is ready, but not with you! No—no, I say—

not with you! . . . I cannot come! . . . See! his hands are fleshless, and his head a skull! . . . He comes closer—closer!"

*　*　*　*　*　*

The appalled eyes, burning with the fire of insanity, glare horribly at that floating unearthly form, now past her, and fading again into the nothingness from which it seemed to evolve itself.

"Save me! save me!" she shrieks, cowering back, and covering her face with her hands.

*　*　*　*　*　*

"*He* calls me!" she murmurs, after a moment or two's pause, letting her hands drop to her sides, and lifting her face, full of a new-born joy and peace.

She has forgotten the ghastly presence which has vanished; forgotten him whose avenging spirit she thought had come for her. She remembers only her love, that infinite and fatal love, which has been the destroyer of a soul that would have been pure and white and fair but for the deadly, blighting influence of an unconquerable, deathless passion, which was allowed to master and conquer and kill, where it ought to have sweetened and hallowed and ennobled. In so much can our crowning virtues be turned into our most crushing, soul-slaying vices.

"He calls me—I hear his voice! Yes, Lennie darling, I am coming!"—moving slowly across to that black, yawning void where the wall and window were, and through which the night-wind rushes in unchecked. "It is sweet and soft and cool down there among the daisies and pink clover by the old stile . . . I am nearly always first at the trysting-place, Lennie; you are often a laggard, sir; but you got the start of me this time . . . No, love, you need have no fear; I will be as true as death; no one shall ever come between us; I am yours and you are mine, for ever and ever! Go to India, if you must; but I will be no 'false Imogen.' Your spirit will not need to come 'to bear me to the tomb,' a bride!"

She is once again, in fancy, innocent Muriel Hilliard, before she was tempted by the old man's wealth.

"Yes, Leonard, we will go immediately, in a few days. I hate this house; there is a shadow of evil upon it! We will sail away into those northern, unknown seas, and make our darling baby an ocean princess."

She pauses, as if hearkening to a soundless voice.

"You are ready, dear, and waiting? So am I. We will go at once, and together. Thank God! always together."

A smile of bliss unspeakable flits over the lovely insane face. There is a flutter of white drapery through that gaping void, and the room is empty of all human presence, while in a moment another dull, hollow thud echoes faintly from below! And the stars in the chill April sky look down from their wondrous heights of calm and tranquil serenity, and make no sign. Nature never makes a sign, but is always unresponsive, cruelly, stoically, indifferent, when helpless man is at his hour of direst need and peril.

> "How strikingly the course of nature tells,
> By its light heed of human suffering,
> That it was fashioned for a happier world!"[67]

And then, into that awful, soul-curdling silence that has suddenly fallen on this fearful, accursed room, steal, with weird and whispering breath, the notes of a violin! At first so faint, so shadowy, so unreal—as if it were the distant, dying echo of a forgotten harmony—that it scarcely disturbs or breaks that terrible, brooding stillness.

[67] From 'Absalom' by Nathaniel Parker Willis.

And yet one feels instinctively that these unearthly, mystic vibrations, that are but as yet the suggestion of sound, rather than sound itself and are consequently infinitely more horrible and impressive, laden with supernatural awe, reach not from afar, but are ever here—*here*, in the portion of space enclosed within these fatal walls! Yes, here is the invisible dwelling-place of that mysterious phantom violin!

And now that wailing whisper swells into wild, surging, terrible strains. Like no music ever heard on earth is this, that throbs and pants and pulsates like some caged, frantic creature, in such vehement, fierce clangour, through this doomed chamber of the eastern gable.

Louder, faster, wilder it grows, till all heaven and earth seems to have resolved itself into this one sense of crushing, ghastly, maddening sound! But through all the demoniacal horror of the music may be heard an ever-recurring note of triumph; as if a weird, malignant exultation shrieked its hellish joy throughout this terrible, unearthly "dance of Death."

* * * * * *

But suddenly the measure changes, as if another phantom hand evoked the strains, laden with a mysterious, awful pathos, that now sigh and sob through the desolate room. Saturated with an unutterable despair and woe, weighed with a burden of inexplicable, unending sorrow, the mystic violin breathes its last weird, unearthly harmonies.

By degrees, the moaning, dirge-like lament becomes fainter and fainter, gradually dying away into a thrilling, whispering breath. Less and less it grows, like broken, inarticulate, far-away sobs of dying anguish, and at last all is still.

* * * * * *

And again, as silence falls once more upon the room, that shadowy, phantasmal shape evolves itself from misty vagueness, and glides across the floor of this doubly fated chamber.

The twin tragedy has been enacted within its shuddering walls. Will the haunting spirit of evil be at last content, and rest?

Into the light of the solitary flaring candle that awful thing floats. There is a momentary vision of streaming yellow hair, a rigid dead face, and flowing white robes, through which the wall beyond is visible; it is, as it were, a ghastly shadow, or presentment, on which Death has set his seal, of *her* who has just gone forth into the silent night.

* * * * * *

Closer still to the light it comes!

* * * * * *

Ah! the very spirit of murder itself! Yellow hair, white, dead face, and whiter garments, all streaked and splashed with the fell crimson tide . . . The stream of blood, still warm and wet and flowing, is the curse she has carried through the centuries! . . . That terrible prophecy has been, indeed, fulfilled . . . That awful curse is now complete . . . The crime of the long-forgotten past *has* been reproduced in "dual shape;" for she in whom the guilty Dorothea chose to accomplish her vengeance—whether really only to Muriel Hilliard, or actually, by some incomprehensible mystery, Eunice Beresford, clad in new robes of flesh—has, in truth, worked it out to its ghastly end.

The old husband was murdered for the lover's sake; and now, though not intentionally, the lover, who was also a husband, has been slain by the same small white hand! . . . The crime of suicide has even repeated itself in this fell chamber.

* * * * * *

The cup of horrors is full . . . The weird of the Beresfords is at last fulfilled. And now, will this haunting spirit be laid? Will that formless presence of evil, that active, living, dominating 'will-power' of the dead cease to subdue, and magnetize, and force to sin the helpless living—those who have been possibly unconsciously influenced and compelled to crime by this terrible, unearthly power, or force, dwelling unthought of in their midst?

* * * * * *

The fearful thing again fades into a formless, misty shadow, which slowly vanishes, and as it does so, a low, mocking, demoniac laugh rings eerily through the chamber, and all is still again . . . Stillness deep and profound as that of the grave . . . Stillness that is broken in another part of that great desolate mansion by the shrill, wailing cry of a very little child, the sobbing, wild, unconscious lament of a young baby, who wakes in the heart of the night's silence with a yearning cry of unknown sorrow—a mysterious, sudden, wailing grief, which the watchful nurse soothes and calms and comforts; and the tiny creature drops off asleep again with a pitiful catching of the frail little breath, and all is still once more!

What did that atom of humanity mourn? Did it know, by some divine, wondrous instinct, past man's finite understanding, of what has happened in the brooding darkness of this fatal night? Did it wail and yearn and cry for the two who have gone forth and left it alone,—left it to make its solitary pilgrimage across life's barren wastes, bereft of those who were its natural protectors?

"An infant crying in the night,
And with no language but a cry."

But our grosser mortality cannot interpret the cry; and, perchance, the babe left fatherless and motherless, within a brief half hour, mourns the two out there under the silent stars, lying almost side by side in the awful stillness of death—with mangled, bleeding bodies, and on one face a great and hideous horror, as if the shock received before death annulled the fear and agony of the death itself; while on the other still lingers the terrible smile of unmistakable insanity!

* * * * * *

An awful, ghastly sight for the sweet, rose-coloured spring dawn to find out by-an-by, and reveal to a horrified world.

* * * * * *

But still a stranger, of not more awful sight, is that which meets the astonished gaze a few hours later, when she who was Muriel Erncliffe is laid upon her bed for the last time, with tortured limbs composed for their final rest.

The face is totally uninjured; but it is no longer the face of the beautiful, brilliant young creature, who has been in such rapid succession Muriel Hilliard, Muriel Varley, and Muriel Erncliffe; it is the face of a middle-aged, nay, rather an elderly woman—a woman not far from fifty years old; a woman with a sad, sweet, patient face—a face that was lovely exceedingly in its far-away youth; a face strangely like that of *her* who went out through that terrible gable window into the night's darkness, only grown old, quite old, and faded, and weary, and sorrow-stricken. The golden hair is grey, and the milk-white skin is lined and withered.

The face that lies upon the pillow in Muriel Erncliffe's luxurious bed-chamber is *not* Muriel's, but—that of *Eunice Beresford*, who died six and twenty years before!

* * * * * *

Yes, even Eunice! startling and mystical as seems the swift, unaccountable transformation.

* * * * * *

And though the ghastly horror in that awful distant room—horror quickly succeeded by *madness*, combined with terror and despair—might suddenly bleach these amber tresses, and dull those wondrous azure eyes, even shrivelling the soft skin; yet, how has that unmistakable look of *age*, that look of having lived a long and shadowed life, come down and set its seal upon the bright young beauty, the passionate, ardent life of Muriel Erncliffe?

A chastened, holy look of sainted resignation to an unhappy fate is the characteristic of the face we now gaze upon, so widely different from the radiant, joyous, intensely living, youthful aspect of her whose strange history has ended here so mysteriously.

* * * * * *

Is it even a proof incontrovertible that that weird, terrible writing, that mystic prophecy, has been in *every* part fulfilled? or is it only another marvellous, incomprehensible coincidence? thinks Professor Dysart, as he stands and gazes, with appalled eyes, and a great awe in his breast, at the extraordinary phenomena before him . . . The mysterious change in the dead woman astounds and confuses the other onlookers, filling them with a startled, fearful dismay; but to him who holds the weird key to this mystery and tragedy; to him who *saw* with his own living eyes Eunice Beresford lying dying, and Eunice Beresford lying dead, and now, after all those years, looks upon the same picture, a climax of mystified horror is reached past comprehension!

* * * * * *

But whether Eunice Beresford really *did* live again, through some awful mystery of being that we cannot yet even hope to touch in thought, in the guise of Muriel Hilliard, and worked in her new presentment the horrible, unearthly curse laid upon her and her house by the sinful Dorothea; or whether all these phenomenal points of agreement with the hidden writing, discovered by Desmond Dysart, the Professor's father, a quarter of a century before, were but a series of weird and ghastly coincidences,—still the one great and unalterable fact remains, that the "will-power"—the dead, yet still occultly *living* will—of Dorothea Beresford, remained active and dominant through the centuries, exercising a mysterious, unsuspected, magnetizing influence on the living, subduing and compelling them to certain predestined ends.

And that this mystic, awful force, power, influence—call it what you will—of the minds of the dead, may surround us, though we guess it not, and may be a mighty, potent, unconquerable factor in our life-history, in the world's history—above all, in the history of what appears like inexplicable crime—still remains a problem to be solved by science.

CHAPTER XX

MISERRIMA![68]

ONE last tableau in this record of mysterious and terrible tragedy.

* * * * * *

Some few weeks later a woman, with weak, uneven steps, ceaselessly paces a padded room in a certain private lunatic asylum not far from Westerham.

Night and day she is watched, her attendants being regularly changed every few hours, so that they may never sleep at their post; though, even if alone for a space, it would be hard to imagine how she could injure herself, guarded as she is from the possibility of secreting any object that might be used as a weapon. But the insane are possessed of an extraordinary, an incredible cunning—cunning that often baffles the highest intellectual intelligence; and so it is thought wise to take all precaution.

See her as she walks untiringly to and fro—to and fro; slight, frail, bent, with snow-white hair, though her years scarcely number more than half a century, and wan and haggard face . . . Now she raises her head, and there, plainly visible across the front of the throat, is a terrible wound, not yet quite healed—a frightful gash that just missed being fatal. Is it any wonder that they watch her as they do?

* * * * * *

Now hark! She speaks, and the burden of her speech is always the same.

---

68 Miserrima: pitiable, wretched.

"I saw her! I saw her put it into the night-draught. I stood at the open. door and saw her. She did not know I was there, and she forgot the looking-glass. I never guessed what it was until afterwards. I smelt the bitter almonds, strong—so strong, but never dreamed of wrong. How could I? My child—my own child—whom I nursed at my breast—whom I loved and worshipped more than I did my God—a murderess! And then to keep this awful secret always locked in my bosom; for I must never, never betray her. But I can't; I feel it is driving me mad—mad—mad! Sometimes I feel that my mind is nearly gone, and that I must cry it aloud. I feel the madness, the insane desire to tell—to tell what I alone know—stealing over me. And it will be so if I live. But I won't live—I won't run the risk of letting slip that terrible thing! And when I am dead, her guilty secret will be safe, it will be buried with me . . . I'd do it at once, at once, but I am a coward, a miserable, trembling coward! . . . My child, my own and only child! O God! a murderess! . . . I will die to save her from betrayal, but I will never look upon her face again!"

And so, with a moaning, terrible sob, the heartbreaking monologue ceases, only to recommence a few minutes later, with the reiteration of insanity, and but slight deviation of expression.

And thus, poor unhappy Mrs. Hilliard passes the remnant of her days in unending lament for her daughter's sin; but she does not know, and will never know, the awful termination of the tragedy . . . The events of that fatal Easter Eve are hidden from her by the cloud that has mercifully come down and obscured her understanding. For by a strange and weird coincidence, on the same night, at the same hour that her daughter died, mad and a suicide, she, for that daughter's sake (the instinct of love and the struggling effort to defend the creature loved still lingering strong and faithful when all else was growing dark), feeling the insanity overcoming her, made, with the last flicker of departing reason, the determined and desperate attempt upon her life of which we see the cruel mark. It was not quite successful; but when she awoke from the stupor of unconsciousness that lay upon her many days, her mind was wholly gone.

* * * * * *

And thus this tale of crime and sorrow and mystery which we have followed "to the bitter end," proves once again how terribly true are the awful words from the sacred Book, "The wages of sin is death."[69]

---

[69] Romans 6:23.

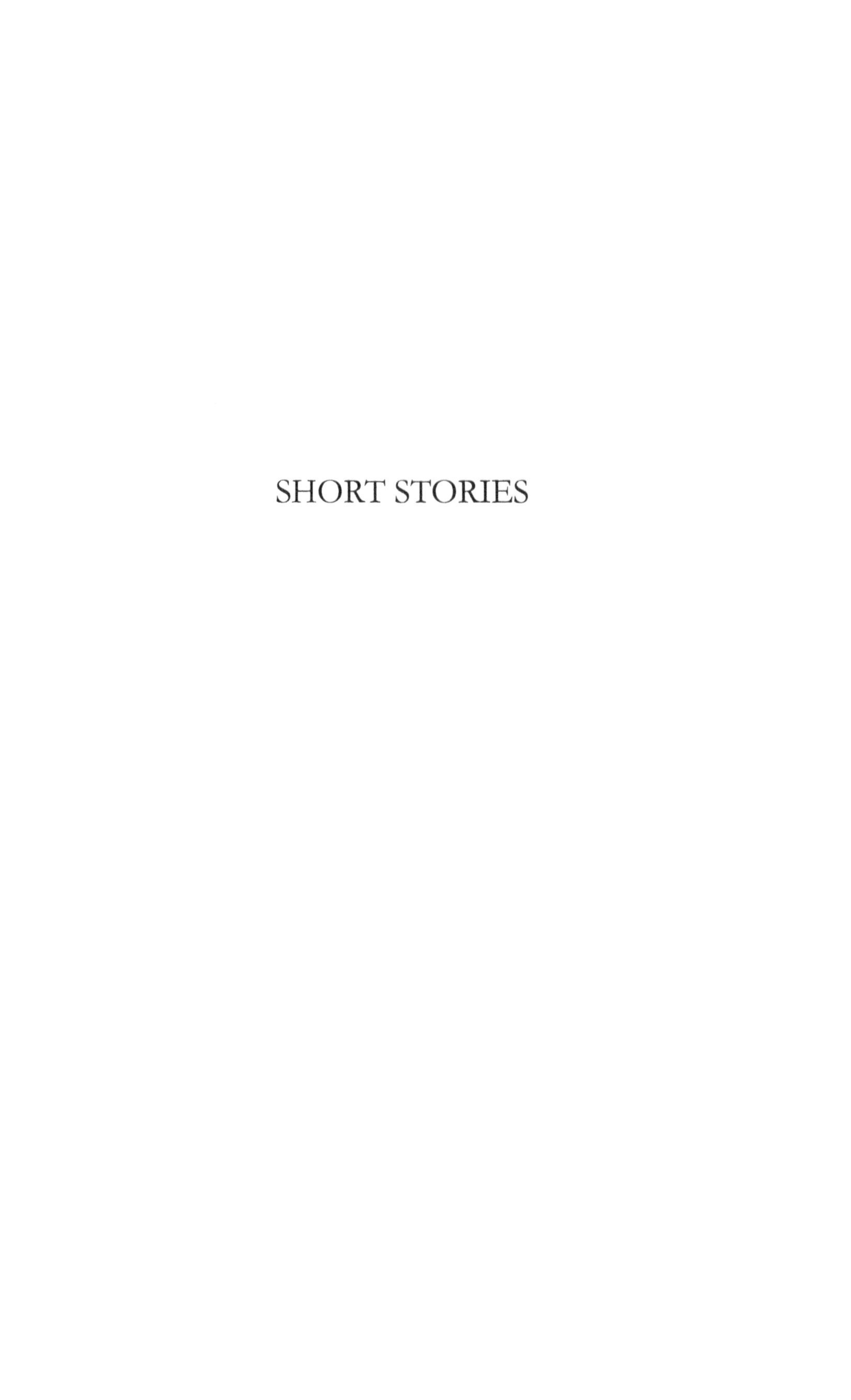

SHORT STORIES

SO INNOCENT

The Idler, Volume 28, October 1905.

HOW pretty and innocent she looked as she stood toying with the handle-bar of her machine—the rosy lip pouting, the great childish eyes wearing an anxious, expectant look as she scanned the crowd pouring out of the big hall.

She was evidently watching and waiting for someone. What had brought her to the meeting? She must have been infinitely bored. She was but a child—a child playing at being grown up. A delightfully unconventional child too; she had addressed him once or twice during slight pauses between the speeches, smiling as she did so, and showing the most enchanting dimples.

And above all—what had brought her into the little railed-off pew reserved for members of the Press?

So Glover, of the *Western Light*, reflected, as he slowly emerged from the hall leading his bicycle. Bicycles were permitted to representatives of the Press and accommodation provided for them (to Glover his machine was almost a necessity owing to a slight lameness), but where had this pretty school-girl hidden hers? There had been a packed meeting. The spacious "Park Hall," Cardiff, was filled to overflowing. A bye-election was in progress, and the town was in great excitement. Almost invariably a Liberal seat, it had been a severe blow to the party, when, at the General Election, two years before, a Conservative had been returned. But now, the seat was again vacant, and it was hoped that a great victory was in store for the Liberal candidate, who was very popular. Every effort was made to ensure his success—though some pessimists opined that the present was such a peculiarly strong Conservative

Government, that the Radicals had no chance, and that a Liberal-Unionist was the best Cardiff could hope for. A great man, a noted speaker, an eminent politician had come down from London expressly to address the meeting attended by two or three minor, but shining lights. The meeting should have taken place at night, but the great man had to return to London by the evening train, so it was held in the afternoon.

Glover had arrived rather late, proceedings had commenced, and the hall was already crowded. As he made his way to the reporters' railed-in benches, he was surprised to see seated among the somewhat dingy followers of his craft the girl with the big wondering eyes. "How the deuce did she come into this *galère*?" was his mental soliloquy as he took his seat, which happened to be next to the pretty intruder, and produced his pencil and note-book.[70] He furtively watched her when opportunity offered. It was evidently all very novel to her, and after a little, very wearying. She made no pretence of listening to the speeches, but amused herself by watching the eager, animated crowd, and doubtless admiring the many pretty toilettes. He caught her casting many wondering glances at himself and his fellow-scribes, especially regarding one lady worker with curiosity, mingled, as it seemed to him, with a fine disdain.

Doubtless she could not imagine what strange rites they were performing, scribbling in hot haste these extraordinary hieroglyphics, instead of sitting up straight, and listening and looking about them, like everyone else. Then, by-and-by, she began to yawn and fidget a little. Once, he was certain she was falling asleep, and he began

---

[70] *Galère*: a group of people having a common interest, particularly one of undesirable people.

to wonder would she, like a child, make a pillow of his shoulder! She was unconsciously leaning over close—so very close to him. It would be a decidedly awkward situation for him, and he was just beginning to tremble at the prospect when she, suddenly roused, sat up. Appearing to remember something, she commenced to search diligently in various pockets of the natty little coat she wore, which provided her with several of these receptacles—outside breast-pocket, inside ditto, and two hip-pockets. Each was carefully examined without result, then, as a last resource, the skirt-pocket was tried, and he heard a triumphant little chuckle of satisfaction, as she produced a small box of chocolate creams.

At the next pause, she offered him the box with the shyest sort of smile, and a whispered, "Do take one; they're so good." Not to hurt her feelings he took one. After this, she seemed to regard him in the light of an ally and confidant, and at the next pause she whispered with a charming pout, "When will that tiresome man be done?" indicating the platform and the great speaker of the occasion. "He ought to be weary of hearing himself talk. How stupid it all is! not a bit of fun anywhere," she said, gazing into Glover's face with wide, childish eyes of discontent, as if she thought he ought to provide some amusement for her. The next moment saucy dimples were playing hide-and-seek in the lovely mignonne face, as she murmured some laughing remark anent one of the audience. Certainly a most fascinating, unconventional child; and Fred Glover began to fear that his notes would suffer if he allowed himself to get too interested in his pretty neighbour.

By-and-by, after the usual votes of thanks being proposed, seconded, responded to, &c., the meeting came to an end; not, however, before two or three speakers on the other side essayed to get a hearing. One or two were quickly silenced, but another, by sheer dint of persistence, got himself listened to, in spite of groans, and made a very clear sarcastic speech. All this caused delay, and though carriages had been ordered for five it was nearly six o'clock when the hall began to empty itself.

Glover turned aside for a moment, to say a few words to one or two of his *confrères*—representatives of country papers who had come some distance, the meeting being an important one. When he looked round, pretty "Miss Innocence," as he mentally termed the girl who sat next to him, had disappeared. So she must have had some friend in the reporters' seats. Slowly emerging to the street with his bicycle, he saw her as described a page or two back. She was evidently watching for someone who had not yet turned up, although the crowd was thinning fast, and the hall would soon be empty. She did not appear to see or notice him, all her attention being concentrated on the principal entrance, through which the last of the audience were issuing. But he felt privileged to address her after her late friendliness, and she did look so pretty and forlorn. Many curious and admiring glances were cast at her, as she stood by the kerb holding her bicycle, and eagerly scanning the faces of the departing throng.

He approached, removing his cap.

"You look worried; I fear you are waiting for someone who has not turned up. Can I make any inquiry for you?"

She turned to him with a start and a little smile of recognition.

"Oh! I didn't hope to see you again," with a childish familiarity that somehow pleased him hugely. "Thank you, you're so kind," she continued. "It's papa I am waiting for, and I am afraid he has forgotten all about me. It was he brought me to that horrid meeting. I am so sorry I came. He put me to sit there with all you people who wrote; he said I'd be safe there with the Press. I saw no press."

Glover found it hard to maintain a decent gravity of countenance at this added proof of his new friend's guilelessness.

"Papa had to go away to see someone, he said. If he could he'd come back for me, and take me to sit with him; but if not, he'd be sure to find me at the entrance, and I was to wait for him. Now, I don't know what to do. He'll be so angry if I go home without him; besides, I'm rather afraid. It's a long way, all up beyond Penylan," or some such word it sounded to Glover, who was not long in Cardiff and knew little of the surrounding district. "It's such a lonely way too, and I don't often ride by myself," she continued.

"It's nearly six o'clock, and will soon be growing dark," responded Glover, glancing up at the still bright October sky. "Can I inquire if your father is still in the hall? He may have left some message for you with the doorkeeper."

"Oh! thank you; you are clever to think of that; but, no," struck by a sudden thought, "if you will hold my wheel a moment I'll run in and look for myself. It's the quickest way. He might be there and you would not know him; I can ask the man."

As she spoke she was gone, and for fully five minutes Glover waited holding the two bicycles while the last stragglers from the meeting made their way into the wide, handsome Crockherbtown thoroughfare.

When she reappeared, he knew by her face she had been unsuccessful. She evidently with difficulty kept back her tears, and Glover felt bitterly resentful against the unknown parent, who could be so careless of his pretty daughter's comfort and convenience.

"He's not there and there's no message. He's gone off and forgotten all about me," she said, with a suspicious quaver in her voice. "I would not mind so much, for, of course, I do ride alone sometimes," she continued confidentially, after a successful effort to gulp down the tears that for an instant had nearly overmastered her, making the childish eyes more childlike and appealing as they gazed at him with humid glance; "but I have had such a nasty dream three times lately—last night was the third time. I dreamed I was thrown from my machine away on some lonely road where nobody ever seemed to pass. I was badly hurt and could not stir, and there I lay, and no one came though I called for help, until it was growing dark, when I heard wicked men whispering behind the hedge, and I knew they were robbers, and I was so terrified I fainted. That was my dream," she concluded in an awe-struck voice.

"A sufficiently alarming one," responded Glover, with ready sympathy. "I am not surprised at your shrinking from riding alone with the memory of it so fresh upon you. You must permit me to see you home; a spin in the fresh air will do me a world of good after being stifled in the hall."

Her face lit up at his words with such a relieved, delighted smile, the happy roguish dimples chasing each other in glee, as she cried, "Oh, it's too good of you. I *am* so glad. How can I thank you?" The next instant her face fell. "But perhaps papa will be angry. You see, though you're so kind I don't know you; besides, I ought not to trouble a stranger."

"But you must not consider me a stranger any longer," eagerly interrupted the young man. "Tell your father that Glover, of the *Western Light*, took care of you, and he'll know it was all right—you know he said you were safe with the Press," he added, with a lightsome laugh as he hunted in his pockets for a card.

"Of the *Western Light*?" repeated the girl with a radiant smile. "That's the name of your ship, of course?" interrogatively.

"Ship?" echoed Glover, as he gazed at her for a moment, not comprehending.

"Yes," cried the girl; "papa's a captain, you know, and if you're a captain too, or even only a mate, he'll be so interested."

And then, Glover interrupted her with another laugh, not quite so genial this time. Somehow, he resented the idea of being supposed to be a seafaring man; but he suddenly remembered that Cardiff was a city of captains, the shipping element and interests predominating, so it was a very natural mistake of the girl's, who apparently claimed kinship with the sons of Neptune.

At last he found a card, and presented it to her, explaining that he was on the staff of the newspaper called *The Western Light*. As they were thus speaking, a solitary figure issued from the hall, ran down the steps, and passed them walking quickly. It was the somewhat austere, uncompromising-looking young woman who sat amongst the reporters. She did not appear to notice the figures in the roadway.

The girl gazed after her with a half-curious, half-contemptuous glance.

"Who is she?" she said. "She looks very cross, and rather shabby; she wrote all the time, too."

"That is Miss Benson, who reports for the *Daily Leader*, and is dead against us," answered Glover, with a laugh of satirical enjoyment this time.

"She's on a newspaper too?" queried the girl in surprised tones.

He nodded affirmatively.

"And where is she off to now in such a hurry?"

"To write up her notes, I presume," he responded, with an uneasy qualm that he too should be doing the same for his office. However, a quick run through the fresh air would brighten up his faculties, and his work would be all the better for it; besides, it would be brutal to leave this young girl till he saw her safely home, especially when she had a presentiment of danger.

"To write up her notes?" she questioned, as she prepared to mount. "Why, do you know her; does she get many letters?"

"Oh, I didn't mean that sort of note," he answered, smiling at her. "I mean the notes she has taken of the meeting. How she will pitch into us," he continued reflectively. "All the brilliant and good pointes made by our speakers will be suppressed or slurred over, and that one little speech made by Dawes, on the other side, will be reported in full. A woman journalist takes the palm for being bitter and unjust, and where politics are concerned she positively has no conscience."

But he pulled himself up, when he saw the big wondering eyes gazing at him in a puzzled way. The girl knew as little of journalism as she did of politics—he was talking over her head. His new friend, though captivatingly sweet and pretty, was, he feared, intellectually a failure. But the girl was a mere child of seventeen at the outside. She could ride at any rate, was his next reflection as, having proceeded at a decorous pace up Park Place, she suddenly shot ahead as they left the houses behind, and looking back with arch, laughing glance, called out, "Let's have a race!" and on they flew, the road each moment becoming more rural. At first, it seemed to Glover, who was not at all sure of his topography, as if they were making for the suburb of Cathays, but a sudden sweep to the right on the part of his leader, brought them into a region with which he was as yet unacquainted. The still, peaceful country seemed to be all round them; they might have been miles from a town.

He felt refreshed and invigorated. The girl slackened speed for a moment until he came abreast.

"Isn't it grand?" she cried exultantly. "I do love cycling."

"What a splendid rider you are!" he responded enthusiastically, gazing with admiring eyes at the flushed, radiant face. "I wish we could often have a spin together—it is so exhilarating."

"It is better than stuffy old meetings. Now, catch me, if you can," with a roguish daring glance, as she again shot ahead.

She skimmed over the ground like a swallow. Glover did his best, but still the distance between them widened. The slight lameness alluded to interfered with his very rapid pedalling, so, after a spurt, he put his feet up on the rests, and glided down a slight descent in dreamy rapture. As he watched the racing figure ahead, it shot round a sudden curve and disappeared. He thought he heard a faint cry. All his enjoyment vanished as he remembered the dream the girl had told him of. Had she met with an accident? He pedalled wildly forward, shouting as he advanced, but he heard no response, then, slowing, he cautiously rounded the corner and saw his conjecture was right. The pretty girl sat huddled up at the side of the road, where she had evidently been flung from her machine. She was nervously crying, and was dusty and scared-looking. Glover was off in a moment, trying to console her, and to find out if she were hurt.

"Oh! I knew it would come—I dreamt it three times!" she sobbed.

"But are you hurt, or only shaken?" he questioned.

"My ankle is sprained. I suppose I'll never walk again," with a fresh outburst of hysterical sobs.

And then he saw that one pretty foot was stretched out in a rather helpless manner.

He attempted to take her foot in his hand to discover the injury, but she screamed with pain.

"I trust it's not sprained," he said; "there's no sign of swelling.

Let me take off the shoe and examine it. I know a good deal about sprains."

But she would not have the shoe removed. She allowed him, however, to bind his handkerchief round the instep where the pain seemed to centre.

Then she attempted to rise, with his support, but sank back again. She could not rest on the foot. What a distressing predicament it was, he thought, as he gazed distractedly at the forlorn young figure, seated in the dust, her face now buried in her handkerchief, he form convulsed. Her bicycle was useless to her—they were still far from her home—what was to be done? There was no cottage near to which he could carry her. Why had she been so reckless and daring, when she had had so strange a warning, he thought parenthetically, with a momentary feeling of irritation; but this was soon swallowed up in his intense sympathy and anxiety for the girl, who looked at him now with troubled eyes.

"I can't sit here all night," she said dolorously. "And it would be no use to let you go home and tell them—poor mother would be so frightened, besides, they could not help me; we have no carriage."

"No! no!" interrupted Glover. "You must let me carry you to the nearest cottage—I suppose there's one somewhere about—and then I'll go back to town for a cab; it's the only thing to do."

"You couldn't carry me to the nearest cottage, even if I'd let you," she said, with the pallid ghost of a smile flitting over the woe-begone face, "as the nearest cottage happens to be that pretty little place we passed, nearly three miles back, the one you admired. You know we saw no dwelling since. No," she continued, growing more calm and composed as he became more perplexed. "The only thing I can think of is, to let you go back to that pretty cottage. I know the people, they are very civil and decent; they have a nice low donkey cart, and the man would drive me home. Of course, papa would pay him for his trouble. I am awfully sorry to be such a nuisance to you, but think what it would be for me if I were alone. I don't even know how I'll bear it now when you're gone. I'm sure I shall cry the whole time, I'll be so terrified; every moment expecting to see a big wicked man climb over there, like my dream!" pointing to a five-barred gate on the other side of the road.

Glover did his best to reassure her. She had hit on a capital plan, he told her. "My wheel will take me there in no time, and when I tell them to send the cart, I'll race back to you to keep you company. It's quite light still, and I'll not be more than ten minutes," he urged.

"Ah, yes, you must be more than ten minutes. I know the distance better than you do. However, you'll be as quick as you can, and I'll try to be brave," attempting another little smile.

"Have you any paper with pictures about you, that might amuse me, and keep me from thinking? Any little magazine even without pictures? I'd try to read though I don't care much for reading, but it would make the time seem shorter."

He hunted wildly and hopelessly in all his pockets, feeling savage with himself, for not being provided with literature for such an emergency. Her face fell, as she saw the search was vain.

"Nothing at all!" she said, in disappointed tones. Then, seeing some loose sheets of paper in his hand, held together at one corner, which he had unearthed from his breast-pocket in his frantic search:—

"What's that?" she said, stretching up a detaining hand.

"Oh, these are only my notes of the meeting," he answered, not handing them over.

"The meeting we've just been at?" she asked. He nodded

affirmatively. "Oh, give them to me!" she pleaded. "They'll be better than nothing. I don't listen to the speeches much, but now, I'll try to read, and improve my mind. I know nothing of politics, but that will teach me a little, and I'll be able to talk to papa about the meeting, and he'll be surprised."

"But this is shorthand," he interpolated with regret in his voice. "You could make nothing of it."

"*Shorthand!*" she repeated with curiosity and interest in her tones. "I have often heard of shorthand, and longed to see it—do let me look!" coaxingly.

He handed over the fluttering papers, delighted to have anything to interest her.

"Oh, how funny," she exclaimed. "How I should like to learn shorthand! Perhaps you'll teach me some day?" looking up at him with a glance that made the young man's heart beat quickly and his pulses throb with a sudden novel and pleasurable excitement. "I'll study this; it will help me to forget the pain, and the loneliness while you're away."

Then he turned to his machine, and as he was about to mount she said:—

"I want you to do one little thing for me, and that is to ring your bell at intervals as you go. It won't seem so dreadfully solitary, as long as I can hear you ever so faintly."

"Yes," he said, catching up her idea, "and when I ring it on my way back you'll know I am nearer to you at every tinkle."

"Exactly," she said, with a sudden bright smile that made her look quite herself again.

But when he was actually off and turned to wave his hand, the sweet eyes were again humid, gazing after him with a mournful desolation in their depths.

"Cheer up! I'll be back in no time," he shouted, and then vanished round the corner of the road by which he came, ringing his bell as he went.

The girl sat quite motionless, making no attempt to look at the papers on her lap, but listening intently. The bell sounded fainter this time, still she did not move. Her whole being seemed to be concentrated in the act of listening. Again the bell tinkled—more distantly—again—still farther off—the next time it was scarcely distinguishable, strain her hearing as she would.

There was a sudden and extraordinary change in the listener. She sprang to her feet with the strangest triumphant little laugh, untied the handkerchief that bound her instep, and hung it on the hedge in a conspicuous spot, with another ripple of laughter, in which lurked a derisive echo. The girl's whole aspect seemed altered. The face, no longer childish and wondering, wore a keen, clever look in spite of its youthful prettiness; the figure alert, and businesslike, no longer suggested a young person bent on amusement, but an individual accustomed to serious occupation and with now a definite, important aim to accomplish. With a quick, deft movement, she shook and flicked the roadside dust from her neat serge costume. Then, snatching up the papers, which she had placed on the ground while unbandaging her injured foot, she gave a swift and comprehensive glance through them to see if any portion of the report was missing. No, all was there.

With an amused smile, she slipped the precious notes into the breast-pocket of her coat, raised her prostrate wheel, mounted, and started off down the road at a rate as swift and reckless as before. A slight curve disclosed a cottage, not more than five minutes' walk from where the supposed accident had taken place, but poor Glover, unfamiliar with the district, did not know this, and had been sent in the other direction to leave the field free for this unscrupulous young woman's singular proceedings.

On and on she went, not slackening her pace until she emerged into Castle Road, and from that into the stately main thoroughfare of the handsome suburb of Roath, close to the infirmary pile of buildings, then—sharply to the right towards Cardiff; and soon she was speeding through Crockherbtown's spacious thoroughfare past the "Park Hall," so lately left, on into Queen's Street, then past the "Castle," and at slackened speed, she turned into Mary Street, the great business centre of the city. Down the wide busy street she cautiously wheeled, steering her way scientifically amongst tram-cars, 'buses and vehicles of all descriptions, past the offices of the *Western Light*, at which she glanced with a momentary smile, on, nearly to the lower end of the great bustling thoroughfare, when she dismounted before a large and handsome building, on which might be read the legend, *The Daily Leader.*

Taking her wheel into one of the inner passages, she left it, and raced up many flights of stairs, with apparently familiar feet, but just as she reached the landing outside the sub-editor's sanctum, a lady emerged from one of the three doors, which she closed behind her. It was the same somewhat austere-looking woman who had sat amongst the other reporters at the meeting. The new arrival flew at her and hugged her frantically, while she laughed—and laughed—softly but ecstatically; and then, for all explanation of her somewhat mad behaviour, she dived into her breast-pocket and produced poor Glover's notes! Then the elder and sober-minded individual's gravity gave way, and she joined in her junior's mirth, murmuring the words:—

"Oh, Mollie! Mollie! So you actually were successful; you have won your wager after all!"

A week or two later, when all the fuss and excitement of the election was over, Fred Glover received one morning a small packet directed to his office. On his opening it, he discovered his unlucky notes. The packet bore a London postmark, but there was no address. On an accompanying sheet of paper, written in a firm characteristic hand, were the words:—

"Borrowed, and now returned with thanks."

And then lower down:—

"You know, 'where politics are concerned, a woman journalist has positively no conscience.' "

THE TRANSFIGURATION OF LETTICE WILLOUGHBY

The Novel Magazine, Volume 2, March 1906.

THE Hon. Greville Newcome was a rising young politician. Some two years before the incident recorded in the following pages, he had been elected member for Blackmore, a manufacturing town, thriving and populous, with a large Irish contingent among its grimy workers.

For many years the town had been represented by a man holding opposite views of a very advanced type, and the return of the Hon. Greville Newcome was bitterly resented by a certain section of the community.

The Hon. Greville Newcome was not twelve months in the house before he had made his mark, and now at the end of two years he was spoken of by some as "the coming man." And this was all the more to his credit, as he was completely without influence in the political world. All he gained as yet he had won entirely off his own bat; but he began to see that there might be a big future waiting for him had he someone in power to push him on.

And now it seemed as if he might have that influence, if he put out his hand to take—a wife!

The Attorney-General looked with an eye of marked favour upon the Hon. Greville. He had been heard to speak of him in the highest terms, and seemed to think that the young man had a promising political career before him—and the third daughter of the Attorney-General, the youngest and her father's favourite, was still unmarried.

Quite apart from his high official post, Sir Francis Willoughby had wide parliamentary influence; he was much valued by the Government, and it was possible, even probable, that a son-in-law of his, if proved to be a thoroughly efficient man, might get a seat in the Cabinet.

His mother advocated the match. "With Lettice Willoughby for your wife," she said, "you'll be a made man, my dear boy; the girl has a fortune, but that is of little consequence as compared with what her father's influence can do for you; and I am sure she likes you, Greville, though she is so quiet and self-restrained."

"Poor little Letty," and there was a sound of pitying contempt in his tones, "can she like or dislike, love or hate? Is she capable of any feeling but an overpowering, shrinking timidity, and absurd nervousness and cowardice? No, mother, I don't think I can do it. It's not that I want great beauty (the girl's pretty enough, I'll allow), or wit, or accomplishments—intellectuality and social gifts would be a great boon in a wife, especially in the wife of a political leader, if such a position should ever be mine—but I *do* want a little character, a creature with some individuality, not a colourless little creep-mouse that is frightened at its own shadow."

"I think, my dear Greville, you take a wrong, or, at least, a much exaggerated view of Lettice Willoughby's character. She is certainly not like the modern young woman; but, if I were a man, I should consider it quite refreshing to meet such a girl at the present day, so modest and——"

"Modesty and reserve are all right; no one prizes such virtues more than I do, and I hate a forward woman; but I don't want a limp creature without any backbone for a wife—with no decision of character, who could never make up her mind about anything—even whether she liked golf or tennis the better—who starts when you speak to her, hesitates and stammers when she responds, and never advances an opinion of her own. Besides, these ultra-timid, cowardly people are sure to be intensely selfish. Cowardice, whether moral or physical, is the outcome of selfishness."

"Well, Greville, you're very obstinate, and in my opinion unfairly prejudiced against Miss Willoughby. As for the extremity of shy embarrassment you speak of, neither your sisters nor I have seen it, nor have I heard it commented on by others; so that I would argue that this is a sure sign that you have won her affections, and that, being a true, modest woman, and being uncertain of your sentiments with regard to her, she feels nervous in your presence, half-ashamed of her own heart, knowing that she has given her love unsought."

"Oh, mother dear, you are giving reins to your imagination, and it's cantering wildly away with you," laughed the young M.P., though he flushed a little at her suggestion.

"And I did hope," continued the Viscountess with a sigh, "that next month, when the Willoughbys go to Blackmore—you know Sir Francis is about to visit his brother"—the Attorney-General's brother was one of the largest employers of labour in Blackmore—"that you would be a good deal thrown together, with more opportunities of getting intimate with Lettice Willoughby than in this huge, busy London, and that matters might arrange themselves, as I so fervently wish."

"I am not sure that I shall turn up at Blackmore during the Willoughbys' stay. I want to recruit a little, and am thinking of running over to Norway for a few days' salmon fishing," yawned the Hon. Greville, plainly evincing that he was getting tired of the discussion.

"Why, I thought that there were certain meetings arranged at which you had engaged to speak during the recess, and then I know our great friend, Lady De-La-Hunt, is purposely putting off her grand local ball, so as to be able to secure the presence of the 'Hon. Member,' " with a fond, proud little laugh.

"The 'Hon. Member' has made the place too hot to hold him," said a voice at the door, as Greville's elder sister entered the room, newspaper in hand. "Have none of you seen the evening paper?" she continued. "They have been burning you in effigy at Blackmore last night. Greville! I told you that your speech in the House the other evening would raise a hornets' nest about your ears."

"The scoundrels! The ungrateful scoundrels!" muttered her brother with frowning brow, while his mother echoed in distressed, nervous tones:

"Burning him in effigy! Oh, Eleanor, is it possible? And he has been *so* popular with his constituents. My dear boy, I am so thankful you are going to Norway, you must not think of going near Blackmore till all irritated feeling subsides."

"Why, that's the very reason I'll turn up there as soon as I possibly can. If I went to Norway after this, they'd say I was skulking and afraid of them, the rascally renegades. What a thankless, treacherous lot the masses are, taking them in the lump, and so fickle! But it was ever so—the grandest reformers the world has ever known have been crowned to-day, and kicked, mayhap killed, to-morrow! The idol of the people this hour—the next, the same mob shouting itself hoarse: 'Away with him-away with him!' "

"Well, Greville, you have only yourself to thank for this change of front," said Eleanor. "I can't say I'm very much surprised—a hot-headed set of men like they are—and your speech was bitterly sarcastic."

"I've the courage of my opinions, I'm proud to say, and the

Blackmore lot knew them at the time they elected me. Look at the way I worked at the Labour Question last year, taking the men's side altogether against the employers—they thought they could not make enough of me then, and I gained much for them, and *this* is their gratitude! Not that I mind that sort of thing," with a scornful flick of his hand towards the newspaper on his sister's knee. "It's an excuse for rowdy horse-play, and making a blaze; 'twill be forgotten as soon as the flare-up fades, and ten to one I'll get a big reception in a fortnight's time when I go down there. Anyhow, I must take the risk."

*　　*　　*　　*　　*　　*

Three weeks later Blackmore was *en fête*, and the leading and popular figure at all the assemblies was that of Greville Newcome.[71] The honours were divided between Sir Francis Willoughby and the Member for Blackmore.

Greville had apparently been a true prophet when he said that the resentful spirit would fizzle out with the last flicker of his effigy flare. He had been given a thoroughly hearty reception and warm welcome by men of all shades of political opinion. His speeches had been applauded to the echo, and altogether he seemed more popular than ever; only on one or two occasions were a few impotent hisses heard amidst deafening cheering, and only one dissentient, sullen voice was raised at the most crowded of the meetings.

The fortnight of gay doings flew by quickly, and now had come the last day of the Willoughbys' stay at Blackmore. Sir Francis and Greville Newcome were due in London on the morrow when Parliament was reassembling after the recess, and this was the

---

[71] *En fête*: in a festive mood, holding festivities.

evening of Lady De-La-Hunt's ball, which she had purposely postponed till the last, so that it might be at once the farewell and the most brilliant function of the fortnight's festivities.

Sir Francis left rather early with his brother, the iron-master; the Attorney-General was feeling somewhat fatigued; besides, the brothers had matters of importance to discuss. But Lettice remained behind with her aunt and cousin.

During the fortnight, Greville had seen a good deal of the girl, but never alone; and though he thought of his mother's words from time to time, still he had no reason to alter his opinion of Lettice Willoughby's character; rather, in fact, were his views strengthened.

Somehow, she appeared to him absent and distrait as well as shy; the usual timidity of manner was flanked by an unfamiliar mental absorption which conspired to give her a more confused and nervous air than was her wont. It sometimes struck him that she wanted to say something to him, and that moral cowardice would not let her speak.

"What a frightened little soul it is!" he thought to himself, with a sort of indulgent pity, as he found himself reverting to his mother's suggestion that Lettice loved him and that this fact made her embarrassed in his presence.

But could this account for the added peculiarity of her manner since they came to Blackmore? He caught her sometimes watching him, when she thought she was unobserved, but he could not flatter himself that there was anything of sentiment in her regard—she seemed more animated by anxiety.

She had been very quiet all this evening—danced little, saying she was tired; and yet she refused to leave with her father—her aunt and cousin were staying and she would remain, too, she said. But her aunt and cousin were devoted to bridge, and to the room set apart for its delights Mrs. Willoughby had gravitated soon after her arrival.

Letty abhorred bridge and yet she decided to stay, which seemed odd, Greville thought, when she would not dance.

He had two dances with her early in the evening, and the only remark that she originated was to ask him when he was leaving!

He masked his surprise and said that he supposed he should have to see the thing out, Lady De-La-Hunt being so old and kind a friend of his.

The house was situated in a handsome square near the outskirts of the city. It was a corner house, and the room used as a ballroom had four large windows—two looking out on the quiet square, and two on a dull, respectable, somewhat gloomy street.

Those two windows looking on the square seemed to have a strange attraction for Lettice Willoughby. Greville noticed that she was constantly near one or the other of them; hidden by the sweeping folds of the silken curtains, she would remain gazing out in an odd, abstracted manner for quite a long time, on one or two occasions even stepping out on to the iron balcony where he once suddenly joined her, feeling a little curious as to her proceedings.

She had not heard his approach, owing to the sounds of music and laughter and the rhythmic feet of the dancers, and he had time to notice that she did not seem at all in rapt contemplation of the night—her eyes were not turned skyward, but seemed fixed on the shadowed path encircling the square.

Following her steady gaze, Greville thought he saw a dusky, moving figure hugging the railings. It might have been but a waving tree branch, yet instantly the unworthy thought was born in his breast, that, perhaps, Lettice had a lover—not in her own sphere—some clandestine entanglement of which she was ashamed, and that it was this fact, and the constant fear of discovery, which made her nervousness and timidity of manner so pronounced.

Her present action confirmed the wild, inchoate thought, for, turning a little, she saw him, and started distressingly, with difficulty repressing a cry. And then, pale to the lips, she insisted in almost a frenzy of—haste—awkwardness—fear—what was it?—on returning into the ballroom, almost pushing him before her to the window in her eagerness to get through.

"Oh, do go in, please, and let me in! No, you go first," as he drew aside to let her pass. "I have a perfect horror of these balconies," she panted, "one so often reads of their collapsing, and this is an old house and it may be quite insecure."

"Another proof of the girl's absurd cowardice; only, she was content enough to stay till I came," he murmured to himself. "There's someone out there she does not want me to see. Miss Letty is sly as well as chicken-hearted," he mused, a strange feeling of indignation smouldering in his breast as if he resented the idea of the imaginary lover. "Odd, how the mean vices hang together—cowardice—selfishness—deceit—hypocrisy; and yet the girl is so pretty, and has such a sweet, frank, open face that it is hard to believe that she is sly as well as shy."

But he watched her and he saw that in a short time after the balcony incident she stole behind the curtains to the other window looking on to the square, and when he saw her face again she looked pale and troubled.

He could not imagine why she had remained; she evidently took no enjoyment in the brilliant scene around her.

What was on the girl's mind? Greville wondered; and, somehow, though she had decidedly fallen in his esteem since the balcony episode, yet the girl intruded herself more into his thoughts than at any time since he first met her, and, singularly enough, his mother's words were constantly recurring to his memory to-night

It was getting on to three and the ballroom was appreciably emptying, when Lettice Willoughby, who had suddenly emerged from the silken *portières* leading to an inner room, touched his arm and said rapidly, in a nervous tone, as if she feared her request might seem a strange one:

"Mr. Newcome, will you please be so very kind as to take me home at once—I am not at all well—and—and I know my aunt and Dora are so devoted to bridge that they will not be persuaded to leave for hours yet."

Greville was amazed, but betrayed no surprise.

"Delighted, Miss Willoughby, to be at your service—but, if you are not well, should I not inform Mrs. Willoughby?"—in a more concerned tone, as, observing the girl more closely, he saw that she was remarkably pale, and that there was a slight twitching in the muscles of the mouth, bespeaking nervous tension. "Poor little scared girl! She's as timid as a frightened hare. What mess has she got herself into? Perhaps the fellow—for there's a man in it, I'd swear—has threatened to tell her father, or is bullying her for money," was his unspoken, lightning-like reflection, as she responded with a touch of impatience:

"Oh, I'm not actually ill, I should be sorry to spoil their evening, but I'm sick of all this froth and glitter"—with a little comprehensive wave of the small hand.

"I fear your aunt's carriage may not yet have arrived, I will go and see," Greville murmured.

"Oh, I don't want the carriage—I—it—I'd suffocate in the carriage," she stammered quickly, with a little gasp between her words. "We'll go home in a hansom, if you don't mind—it's—it's a fine, warm night and the air will do me good—there's one just outside the square, please secure it." And she turned swiftly towards the staircase, while Greville felt more astonished than ever.

If the proposal of a long drive in a hansom in the small hours of the morning had come from any girl but Lettice Willoughby, he would have considered it a daring challenge to a very pronounced flirtation! But the girl was so pre-occupied that she was evidently unconscious that her suggestion might be open to misconstruction. "I have missed her from the ballroom for the last half hour or so. Where's she been? Watching from some other window, apparently, else how should she know about the hansom?" he reflected, as he went to do her bidding.

He returned immediately, steering straight for the cloakroom, where, though he had been but a moment gone, she was waiting for him—"why was she in such a fever of haste?"—her pretty pink wrap and soft, fleecy hood making her look still paler.

But though so colourless and with that look of nervous tension about the mouth, yet, in Greville's eyes, she was more attractive than he had ever seen her. There was more character and purpose in the face, the eyes wore a look of mingled expectancy and determination, and the nervous, timid manner that was habitual to her seemed to have fallen from her; dominated by some stronger feeling she had forgotten to be shy.

But once they were seated in the hansom all sign of flurry or haste vanished. She sat calm, motionless almost as a statue, and silent as one.

She would not allow the glass to be put down. "Let us leave it up," she said to Greville—"the night is so warm it will be pleasanter." And though again surprised (she was treating him to a series of surprises) he obeyed her without comment.

She sat very forward, almost on the edge of the seat, throwing him completely into the shade, and would have been a somewhat conspicuous figure, as seen from the street, owing to her brilliant pink wrappings, had there been wayfarers abroad. But the streets were deserted at that hour. Still, it was odd her doing so; she was always such a shrinking, reserved girl.

Greville began to feel that he would be compelled to reconstruct his pre-conceived ideas of Lettice Willoughby.

But though they were thrown in this strangely intimate fashion, alone together, and at the girl's request, he could not flatter himself that any desire for his society had impelled her suggestion. In fact, he had to admit to himself, with a faint flavour of humiliation, that, once they were seated in the hansom, she seemed to become oblivious to his very existence.

Two or three remarks of his remained unanswered. She did not even seem to hear him and never turned her eyes in his direction. Those same soft, full-brown eyes, generally so quiet and rather dreamy-looking, were now wide open, bright with a somewhat feverish lustre; intent in their gaze, as they seemed to try to pierce the gloom on either side.

His remarks were not very profound, and were suggested by a peculiar, mournful cry, or whistle, that seemed to come from amongst the trees in the square just as they entered the hansom.

"A curlew's cry, I fancy," observed Greville, glancing skywards. "Such a wailing, eerie note! Odd to hear it now, on so calm and fine a morning—it really is morning, you know, though the daylight hasn't arrived"— with a little laugh. But Lettice made no reply.

The hansom sharply turned the corner into the quiet, dull street, over which some of Lady De-La-Hunt's windows looked, and when they had proceeded about half-way along its sombre length the cry was repeated, with close and startling suddenness and plaintive stillness.

"Yes, certainly a curlew; we're in for a storm, though as yet there seems no indication of it to our duller faculties, but these birds are reliable weather prophets."

Again Miss Willoughby was silent.

"She might at least have vouchsafed me the courtesy of a response, however brief," thought Greville, offended, and determined not to speak again.

And when, on turning into another street, still darker and gloomier than the last, the cry was repeated, he said nothing, though this time it struck him there was more of a human note in the off, eerie sound, and he thought he discerned a woman's figure moving quickly in the shadows of the houses, at least, he saw the flutter as of a skirt. But to his astonishment, Lettice, who sat immovable and whose eyes seemed straining to pierce the darkness, muttered in a strange, tense whisper, what sounded like: "It's the signal!"

He stared at the rigid figure, sitting so oddly forward, non-comprehending, only filled with the same thought that had leapt to his mind on the balcony, when he fancied he saw the skulking figure beneath the trees—a clandestine love affair!

But, before he could ask her what she meant, an object came hurtling through the air from the side path. Straight into the hansom it was flung with unerring aim and force. It fell on Letty's lap, on the pink bravery of fleecy wraps, under which her pretty, bare arms were loosely crossed—a large, square, brown paper parcel it appeared in the flashing moment his gaze rested upon it.

The next instant, before Greville had realised what happened, the girl had risen impetuously to her feet, and with all her strength (a strength wonderful and new-born) had flung the strange missile (heavy as a large stone) far out into the darkness.

She did not scream, or faint, or even start, or exclaim, but only acted instantly, fearlessly, with lightning-like rapidity of thought and deed! This girl who was a *coward* and who had no presence of mind or decision of character!

The driver had instinctively lashed his horse to a gallop; in two or three seconds they had covered a hundred yards and more. Letty was still standing with outstretched arms, as she had thrown the thing from her, her face ghastly pale; but no sound issued from her tight-locked lips—the watching soul that had dwelt in her eyes had fled to her ears, she was one acute note of listening.

"Why did you throw it away?" came in a hasty, fault-finding tone from Greville. "We don't know what it was; I should have liked to——"

And then—a great roar and rumble filled the night—there was a sound of rending earth and shivering glass, the ground shook beneath the flying feet of the horse, which now bolted and raced blindly on, the hansom swaying wildly from side to side, the driver in his panic having dropped the reins.

Greville Newcome knew, in that awed and awful moment, that Lettice Willoughby, the little, frightened, creep-mouse girl, had saved his life at the risk of her own! He, not dreaming of danger, would have examined that deadly missile. She, for his sake brave, with every nerve strung, every sense alert, had cast it out instantly.

The bomb had burst and played havoc with the street, which it tore up, shattering all adjacent windows, but injuring none, save him who had flung the ball of death, and who, not contemplating its being returned so promptly to the street, had lingered for those few seconds, watching the retreating hansom, and now lay mutilated and unconscious on the pavement.

And Letty, whose noble act had been even greater heroism than Grenville yet suspected, sank back on the cushions with a great sigh of relief, and the simple cry which gave away her secret"

"Oh, thank God—thank God, I was with you! I knew something was coming, but I didn't know *how* or in *what* shape it would come."

And the Hon. Grenville went down on his knees in the runaway hansom and bared his head in reverence before the girl he had so slightingly regarded, had so utterly failed to appreciate, as he kissed her hands and the folds of her pretty gown, again and again, in a passion, not alone of gratitude and admiration, but of stinging remorse, self-reproach, and self-abasement.

"Oh, Lettice, Lettice, can you ever forgive me?" he murmured, hardly conscious of his words. "I am a craven and a cad, you've saved my life and I don't deserve it, least of all at your hands. You're a heroine, my darling, with a magnificent courage, and angel of fearlessness and unselfishness—and I—am a fool, a vile-tongued—aye, and a vile-minded brute!"—in quick contrition, as he remembered his late unworthy suspicion of some compromising love affair.

And then he saw that the pretty, round, white arms were bruised and swollen (one so severely hurt that she had to wear it in a sling for days) where the hideous thing had crashed down upon them.

Possibly the soft bed of Lettice Willoughby's lap and arms had delayed the explosion by a few seconds—and yet those soft, tender arms, tingling with pain, had been strong to save him!

Letty did not understand his half-wild words—they had no meaning for her ears, save that she was conscious of a singing at her heart when he caressed her hands and called her "darling"; besides, she was too agitated to take in any new impression just then.

An awful peril had been averted—a ghastly catastrophe escaped; they were still in a position sufficiently alarming in the rocking, swaying hansom, and then the reaction from the great strain had set in and she felt numb and dumb and could only murmur again:

"Thank God, oh, thank God, it's past and *you* are safe!"

The racing, terrified horse was soon brought to a stand by some members of the crowd, rushing from all directions to the scene of that widely heard explosion. And later on that night, or rather morning, when they had reached the safe shelter of her uncle's home, Greville drew the confession from Letty that she had faced the danger deliberately—that she had intentionally confronted an unknown peril, in the hope that her presence might possibly avert a threatened and premeditated attack.

The cool courage and wonderful presence of mind were not merely, then, a noble height of heroism to which a timid woman must rise on sudden impulse in exceptional and unexpected circumstances; her line of action that evening had been altogether planned and of set purpose; therefore, her bravery and extraordinary fortitude were ten times as great as if they had been born on the spur of the moment.

"Yes," she confessed, "I knew they meant to harm you. I've been fearing something all through the fortnight owing to their burning you in effigy last month, and I thought you were rash to come here so soon.

"Last night," she continued, "when we were leaving the Empire Theatre, we had to wait quite a long time in that outer corridor for the carriage. Aunt was impatient and pressed on with me to the entrance, where there was quite a crowd, and as we stood there, looking out into the dim street, I heard a voice to the left, where a group of men—like working men—were standing, say quite clearly, but softly: 'Is he here to-night?' And at once something told me they meant *you*. 'No,' said another, and then some bad language, 'but, if he were, this is no place—there's too many about.'

" 'That's always your cry, Jim, I believe you're funking it,' said another voice. 'The fortnight's just up and the job's not done.' 'It would have been done long since, but he's never alone, always a lot of other toffs with him, an' sometimes wimmen, and I don't want to hurt no one else if I can help it.' More bad language, and then: 'You're too downy a chap for this business.[72] We've took the oath and we've got to keep it.' 'An' so we will,' broke in the other voice. 'I'm only waiting for a good chance, an' to-morra night after Lady De-La-Hunt's ball'll see his light turned out, or my name's not——'

" 'Hush, no names, you fool!' said another voice that had not yet spoken; 'but mind, that's the last night, an' if you fail you know the reward,' with a gruff laugh.

"It was only by the greatest straining I could hear, they spoke so softly," panted the poor, pretty heroine, looking anything but heroic now as she blushed and cried alternately between nervous strain and the terrible embarrassment that had seized her as the conviction forced itself upon her that she had, by her noble, altruistic act, given away her jealously-guarded secret. For no woman who did not love a man—and love him devotedly—would have voluntarily placed herself in such awful peril.

"I didn't know what to do," she sobbed, completely breaking down. "I was afraid, if I told my father or my uncle, that they'd at once tell the police and that the men, out of sheer revenge, would

---

[72] Downy: sympathetic.

be more desperate and determined, and if I told *you* I thought you'd think it was all 'bluff,' as you said once before, and that you'd insist on facing the danger alone. So I made up my mind to try to stay with you; and I thought, if the man was a bit soft-hearted, not liking to hurt others as he said, that seeing me would stay his hand.

"That's the reason I asked you to take me home, and chose a hansom, and sat forward, so that he might see me. I thought, if I could stave over to-night, and prevent him by my presence doing his wicked deed, that you'd be gone to-morrow morning (to-day, as it is now), and, once in London, I'd tell you all about it, and you'd inform the police of the conspiracy."

"But your action was the action of an angel, my darling!" (All conventionalities were at an end for ever between these two, and Greville spoke from the depths of a surcharged heart). "A divine selflessness inspired you. How had you—a soft, little, gentle, tender girl—the bravery—the almost superhuman bravery—to sit there calmly facing an unknown danger, approaching you knew not in what form, or from what quarter?"

"Oh! I only thought of shooting," she replied in childish phraseology. "I never dreamt of *that* horror!"—closing her eyes and trembling pitifully, symptoms that were not apparent when the danger was present and the time for action had arrived.

"I thought if they saw me clearly—the pink showed up well, you know—and by sitting forward I cast you into the shadow, that they would not have the heart to shoot a girl. And besides, I hoped that they might believe that they had missed *you* and that I was alone, and that they'd go back and watch for you, as they had been watching in the square all the evening—which I guessed—and I watched them. And then again, I thought, if it was to be a bullet for me—well—a bullet would be often a great mercy as compared with the anguishing deaths many people have to die peaceably in their beds, and—and—after all, I could be better spared from the world than you."

And the words rose to the inner door of Greville's lips, though he tactfully refrained from uttering them: "Greater love hath no man than this, that a man lay down his life for his friend."[73]

And at this point we will ring down the curtain. Greville's deep abasement of shame and remorse, his keen, almost agonising pangs of love and gratitude, the love that sprang into vivid, instantaneous life in the flying hansom, and, gourd-like, grew with amazing swiftness, are too sacred to be gazed on, to be analysed and dissected with the literary pruning knife.

Suffice it to say, that the singing that had commenced in Letty's heart amid all the whirl of danger in the runaway cab grew to a great, grand psalm of joy and beatitude, and that these two were happier than either had ever hoped to be in this world.

Greville Newcome, ever after, held his mother's opinion in greater reverence. For she, with her woman's shrewd, true insight, had penetrated beneath the surface of the other woman's nature, and had divined what we now see was correct—that Lettice Willoughby had secretly fallen in love with her son, and that the ultra-shyness and timidity he railed at were the outcome of the embarrassment felt by the pure, proud, innocent girl, when in the company of the man to whom she had given her love "unasked, unsought."

Though, when Viscountess Newcome affirmed this to be her conviction, she little knew by what heights and depths that love was to be tested, or how startling would be the transfiguration of Lettice Willoughby!

[73] John 15:13, though the original text ends 'friends'.

THE RED SKIRT

The Pall Mall Magazine, Volume 38, September 1906.

MAY Palliser was crossing the large meadow. It was a lovely autumn day; and, clad in her rich crimson gown, she made a brilliant spot of colour in the middle-distance, against a background of ambers and russets.

Old John Palliser, though only a farmer, was a wealthy man, and he had grudged nothing where his only daughter was concerned. So May had received a high-class education, had been to college, and taken her degree; and had also graduated in the physical schools—had gone in for the culture of muscle as well as mind.

May had been to the nearest market town, three miles away, and, preferring walking to cycling, was now strolling slowly homewards across the fields. She chose to walk because she could better indulge in meditation than when steering her wheel along the high-road; and as she crossed the large meadow she was sunk in deep and pleasant thought—and, for all her modernity of mind and body, still the subject of her reverie was only—the old, old story.

May, the athlete and the B.A., and the champion golf, cricket, and hockey player of the district, was only thinking of her—lover. How stupid and ordinary it sounds!—just like an old-fashioned girl!

But then, it must be said in extenuation of May Palliser's weakness that her lover was not quite ordinary. At least, she did not think so, for he was a poet!—"One of the minor poets," as he used to say himself in sad musical cadence, with a far-away look in his fine dark eyes; "a very minor poet!"—the savage critics insisted on the adverb, and the still more heartless and silly stupid public confirmed their dictum.

But May knew nothing of the argot of the literary hub, of the under-currents and cross-currents which are always in motion. A poet seemed to her a creature almost godlike—worthy to be deified, that is, when poetry went hand in hand with beauty and nobility of countenance, a nobility that was only a reflex of the character. This she knew, for was not his verse (and he read much of it to her) full of the grandest sentiments? He was a man, she felt, to do great deeds.

As she looked at him sometimes when he was expounding his poetry to her, and noted him shake back the mass of somewhat long, waving hair, his handsome eyes fierce or soft, according to the emotion portrayed—seeing him thus, she could imagine his leading a "forlorn hope," inciting and rousing a mass of inert people to great and noble action, an apostle, a crusader, a righter or wrongs—above all, a champion and defender of women and children. Yes, she did a good deal of idealising, in spite of her twentieth-century upbringing, as she strolled on slowly, oblivious of all outer things, her sunshade, matching her dress, held low down over her face, shutting out an extended view, even if she raised her eyes. Yes, Percy Wyndall was a great poet, and a great man also, with noble and heroic impulses, and he loved—her.

This was the climax of her musings. She knew he did, though he had not yet declared himself—knew it by a thousand signs. How glad she felt now that she had given no serious encouragement to her brother's chum Jack Desmond, when out at Ted's Californian ranch last year! "Jack is a fine fellow, and a good fellow, but he is inclined to epitomise all poetry as 'rot,' " she murmured to herself; "and though muscle, which he possesses in perfection, is a grand thing, still, muscle and mind is grander." Here a terrific savage bellow roused her from her idyllic reverie. There, right in her path, not fifty yards off, was an angry young bull, fiercely lashing his sides with his tail. Her unfortunate gown and sunshade had apparently got on his nerves—for, as he was still fairly young, he had not been considered dangerous, and as yet had made no bad record for himself. But now he was evidently bent on making amends for past amiability. He roared and bellowed again and again, filling the welkin with furious clamour as he fiercely pawed the ground in front of him, preparatory to lowering his head for the charge. But after the first dazed moment May's presence of mind was restored, and though really alarmed, indeed horribly frightened—what woman would not be?—she instantly decided on a plan of action. Instead of turning to flee, as would be the natural instinct, and which equally naturally would precipitate the bull's rush, she made a little dash towards ramping "Taurus," then, having somewhat diminished the distance between them, she flung towards him, with all her strength, her open parasol.

Having thus, as she guessed, both astonished him for a few moments and diverted his attention, she made a swift, wild race to the nearest tree: there were several here and there in this large meadow, but distances apart, with plenty of open between. Attempt to leave the field she dare not, though more than three-fourths of her way across, as it happened that in the side to which she was nearest there was, as she knew well, a large gap in the hedge, through which the bull could rush nearly as easily as herself, and a narrow steep lane lay beyond, bare of tree or cabin or shelter of any kind. The other three sides were quite dim and distant, the meadow was so extensive.

In a trice, thanks partly to her Californian experience, partly to her muscle training, she was safely up the tree, ensconced in the fork of a great overhanging bough, and from her elevated position was able to note the effect of her somewhat daring strategy. The bull had been slightly astounded, and thrown out of his reckoning by his victim taking the aggressive. This delayed his rush; but when she flung the sunshade, he instantly accepted the challenge, and promptly tore it to shreds; he was trampling on the last fragments with snorts of rage, and in another moment, before she was well settled in her stronghold, he came careering direct to the tree.

He ramped round in impotent rage, lashing his sides, tearing up the ground. It was a difficult and perilous position, one sufficient to try the nerves of the strongest-minded woman. If she slipped from her giddy perch (and the very fear of doing so would make one's brain reel a little), she would soon be made mince-meat of—witness the parasol; but May kept quite cool, and tried to think out some plan of escape. Surely she was not condemned to remain a prisoner till the men came to take the bull in! It was now only four o'clock p.m., and they might not come to the field in the morning till five or six o'clock. All those hours perched in a tree, with that savage sentinel waiting below! But, no, of course—how foolish she was! They would miss her at home,—at least, her father might think that she had stayed with her aunt at Clayton, the market town, and not get fidgety about her till after nine or so; but Percy—(she only called him "Percy" to herself, and blushed as she did so, even there in the tree)—he would be wearying for her return. He told her this morning, when she was leaving, that to pass the time, which would seem so long in her absence, he would drive over to Sunny Beach for a good swim, and perhaps go for a row; but he had doubtless returned long since, and would be sure to come and meet her.

Then she let her gaze wander round about. She had a good view from her eyrie, but there was no one in sight; down to earth dropped her eyes again, and almost simultaneously she gave a little exclamation. A few yards off, lying amongst the lush grass, she saw a length of new rope. What brought it there? What a strange coincidence! It looked as if Taurus, after all, had been a suspect—that he had been secured, but with a fairly long feeding-range, and that he had broken loose from his restraint. "Oh, if I only had it!" she murmured excitedly, with bright eyes fixed longingly on the treasure so far out of reach. It was near another tree, a more branchy tree than hers, not so straight a stem, an oak, with great outspreading boughs, easier to climb, more comfortable to abide in. She continued to gaze at the coveted article.

"I think I could manage if I could only get it. I'm sure I could make the running noose—I saw them do it so often; besides, Jack Desmond taught me, and showed me how to throw it."

Her reminiscences were of her last year's Californian visit, when, during her six months' stay on her brother's ranch, she had often seen the cowboys using the lasso in securing either wild horses or obstreperous cattle; and she was actually contemplating turning her Wild West experiences to account—and tackling Taurus! He was getting tired somewhat of playing sentinel, and was now browsing a short way off.

She heard the clock of the village church strike five—a whole hour in the tree, and it seemed like half a day, and still not a soul in sight.

Might she venture to try to secure that rope? It was not in his direction, and, if she got so far, she'd mount that other tree. She could rest a little there, at any rate; here, she had to stand all the time. It was a risk, of course—if he saw her he'd be after her like a shot; but she was very fleet of foot and courageous, and, as some would say, venturesome. "Besides," and she smiled a pallid little smile, "I have another small trick up my sleeve for him if he comes." And, so saying, she cautiously began to divest herself of her skirt—rather a difficult and dangerous proceeding standing as she was in a narrow fork of a tree.

Having successfully accomplished the feat, she slid noiselessly down the trunk, the skirt hanging over her arm ready for emergency.

However, she did not need to use it as a weapon of defence. She had intended to fling it at the bull if he came for her, as she did the sunshade; but she had secured her prize, a fine long rope, reached the other tree, and was just preparing to climb it, before the grazing tyrant had an inkling of her acts. Then, with a bellow, he came thundering across the intervening space; but May was safe and snug up aloft before he arrived, and looked down with calm contempt on her bellicose adversary, as she hung, not the flag of truce, but the flag of defiance, namely, the offending red skirt, on an adjacent bough, and sat down in a quite cosy aerial armchair to try if she could remember how to make the running noose, whilst Taurus, lulled to a sense of security by his prisoner's quietude, and tempted beyond his strength by the succulent clover growing in rich profusion around, again began to graze, in ever-widening circles.

Then she leant forward from her leafy retreat to take stock of Taurus and the field in general, and to her delight and immense relief she saw her lover, the poet, looking over the near hedge. The hedge was rather low; he was a tall man; she could see his head and shoulders quite distinctly. The dear fellow was remarkably pale: had he been worrying about her? He seemed to be watching her tree. Had he been there some time? she asked herself. Of course, no—how silly of her! If he knew of her wretched predicament, he would have come at once to her aid.

"Oh, Mr. Wyndall, I am so glad!" she cried joyously. "I have been a prisoner here these two hours."

He did not start at the sound of her voice, or even appear surprised to see her face looking out at him from her leafy turret; which seemed to her odd—as if he knew she was there. Also he did not respond in words to her appeal—at least, she did not hear his voice—but in vociferous pantomime he evidently urged her to try to escape, beckoning to her wildly, and then pointing energetically to the distant browsing tyrant, as if insisting on his remoteness and preoccupation, and that now was her time. But before she could adjust that confusing mental problem of Percy's propinquity yet aloofness, an apt illustration of "Thou art so near, and yet so far," her attention was suddenly and violently called off in another direction.

From her lofty look-out she espied, to her horror, a small child, a little girl, advancing leisurely across the field, unsuspicious of danger—perhaps too young to appreciate danger even if she saw it. For a moment May was dumb, frozen with wild, distracting thought as to how to avert the catastrophe that seemed impending. The child was right in line with the bull; the latter was turned sideways, and did not yet see the newcomer.

Then the girl burst out in staccato notes of urgent appeal. "Oh, Mr. Wyndall, the child! Don't you see the child? Save it!—oh, save it! I am helpless here. Rush down the lane to the gap, for the love of Heaven, and if you dash in there you'll be in time to snatch her up."

She shouted this in clear, trenchant tones that ought to have carried much farther than where the poet stood; but he did not seem to have heard, as his answer was, "May! May! my darling, come—come at once—now—while you have a chance—make no delay! There's a spot you can squeeze through here with my help."

On hearing the words, "May, my darling," a great wave of joy for a moment flooded the girl's being. In his anxiety for her he had given himself away—betrayed his secret; but the next instant a cold hand clutched her heart. He offered his help—yes, at the *safe* side of the hedge. Why did he not come to her? The bull might not mind him; there was no objectionable red in his get-up to inflame the creature's temper; and, in any case, he was a man and her lover. But the child was the only thing now to be thought of. Percy must save the little one; and in trumpet tones she shouted, "The child! for God's sake save the child!"—standing out on an overhanging branch as she spoke, and pointing with straight, outstretched arm to the small advancing figure, now well within the poet's range of vision; and Taurus, hearing the voice so clear and penetrating, raised his head, took in the situation, and bellowed furiously.

And in that moment's pregnant pause after that fierce challenge May Palliser heard quite distinctly words that chilled her very soul, and appalled her by their callous cruelty and cowardice: "Nonsense! Never mind the child—now's your time! The brute's attention will be diverted to it. Make a rush here to me, dear. I dare not enter the field, you know; it would only infuriate him still more."

For a moment May was almost numb with pain and bewilderment. Such words, such action, from the man she had so idealised—the man she had allowed herself to love, the poet, with his noble sentiments, his lofty, transcendental imaginings! A great wave of repulsion rushed over her—a sense of acute shame for him, of humiliating shame for herself that she could have felt attracted by a craven.

From that instant she spurned him, even in thought. She would grieve over the shattering of her idol by-and-by; now was the time for action.

Her mind worked, though her idol lay prone in the dust. All these thoughts, consequent on her sudden violent disillusion and revulsion of feeling, had flown like lightning through her brain, but she never lost her presence of mind. After that instant's sense of dazed shock, she had decided on a plan of action.

"Well, if you're inhuman, I'm not," she shouted back, a cold note of contempt and defiance vibrating in her tones. "I'll save the child, or perish in the attempt," she muttered grimly, with clenched teeth; and at the same moment she wildly shook and waved the red skirt that hung on the outstretching branch, guessing and rightly, that this would act as a magnet to the bull, and draw him off from the little girl, on whom he seemed preparing to charge.

Tossing his tail and his horns aloft, with another bellow he made a dash for the tree; but May was quick to draw the red flag of defiance to safety, though still she continued to dangle and wave it well within his sight, but out of reach. She might want it more than ever yet.

And again came the voice from the hedge in frenzied amaze and expostulation. "For Heaven's sake, what's that move for? What possessed you? You've lost your chance now. The brute will ramp round worse than ever."

And then, with a snort of rage, ere the words had died away, the "brute" was off to the hedge at a gallop to investigate the voice, and the speaker was racing for dear life up the lane, shouting, as he glanced terrified behind him, fearing that "Taurus" might perhaps leap the hedge—not being well acquainted with bulls and their little ways—"May! May! for God's sake, do nothing rash! I'm going for help."

And May Palliser, her nerves all one jangle of bitter pain an mortification, looked after the fleeing figure, disdain in her eyes, though her heart was heavy and sore within her, while a sense of loss and desolation seemed to animate her whole being—the loss of an ideal. Then she took quick action. The bull had returned, having seemingly forgotten the child, who, paralysed with fear since the alarming bellow, had never moved hand or foot.

Now the intrepid girl crept out on that great overhanging branch with the rope coiled round her arm to watch her opportunity. She had hung the red badge of courage in a conspicuous position, to get the bull as near to the tree as possible—this was her object. It was a daring and dangerous experiment. It spoke well for Miss Palliser's nerves that when that living battering-ram rushed at and crashed against the tree, she lay low, and clung with a vice-like grip to her branch, and did not even quiver. The angry beast only hurt himself. He did not seem to approve of that violent impact. He shook his head and stood for a moment or two as though a little dazed, and May was quick to take advantage of the momentary weakness and cessation of hostilities. Raising herself on her branch as noiselessly as possible, and steadying herself by clasping her left arm round an adjacent bough, she took careful aim. Poising the right for a moment in mid-air, she flung the lasso, with a murmured prayer for help, and—yes—actually—yes, she had secured her prisoner! She had expected at least to have to make two or three attempts, but the creature being stationary and a little stupid had much minimised her difficulties. But when the noose began to tighten, and he realised that *he* was now a prisoner, then indeed he waxed furious. He dashed, and strained, and struggled to be free, and only that the girl had been quick to take advantage of that first moment's inaction, and twisted the rope swiftly and deftly round a strong limb of the tree, it must have slipped from her grasp. He bellowed, and tore up the turf, dashing from side to side, as far as the rope would let him.

It was a terrifying sight, but still May kept her presence of mind. Do what she would, putting out all her strength, which was not inconsiderable, she could not secure the creature so tightly to the trunk of the tree that he would not still have plenty of range to attack her, wherever she might attempt to descend. For a minute or two she felt beaten. Having succeeded in making him captive, that she should remain a prisoner too was insufferable. She had one last card, and she would play it on chance, the merest chance, of being successful.

Poising herself, she waited for her opportunity, and down went the skirt with unerring aim, extinguisher-fashion, over his head. She had pinned the band together; the wide, flounced, fluffy tail fell easily over head and horns, and lay in soft, shrouding folds around the creature's neck. There was no outlet from the upper side; Taurus was practically blindfolded and helpless till he succeeded in tearing off his bandage. But almost before the curtain had well fallen—in the first moment of the animal's amazement and stupefaction at this added insult—May, the intrepid, the ready-witted, had slid from her perilous position, and was already racing madly towards the cowering child. She snatched it up, and in another moment was through the gap, and rushing down the country lane in the opposite direction to that in which the poet fled nearly a quarter of an hour before.

She looked back once at her prisoner: her poor pretty skirt would soon be in ribbons. Taurus had his horns and part of his head through, and was roaring like a mad thing. On she dashed, a little farther. When she reached the top of the lane, where it branched off directly into the village, and had no longer any reason to dread pursuit, she stopped, and gazed back on the scene at once of her victory and her humiliation—the humiliation, none deeper, of bitter disillusion. The bull was free at last, and was capering—waltzing, as it seemed at her present distance—about the field in circles, with the red skirt floating in graceful folds round his neck and over his back, with long fringed ends dangling round his feet. To see him thus, caparisoned, as it were, in the colour that infuriated him—the badge of battle—was inexpressibly ludicrous; but no smile dispelled the sombre shadow that lay on May's face. Then, shifting her glance from the field, she saw three figures, advancing towards the gap in the hedge, from the other end of the lane. Two, evidently, were farm labourers sent to her rescue, and in the third figure she recognised Percy Wyndall.

Just as she was about to turn into the village street, she heard a faint cry, and looking back one more, she saw one figure racing back wildly the way he had come, with hands upraised in terror or appeal. Percy had taken one glance within the field, and seeing the fearsome spectacle of the bedizened bull, he had fled for all he was worth; and at that sight, a faint, cynical smile crept round the girl's lips for a moment, but it did not lighten the sorrow in the eyes.

She had just buried her love-dream—her romance—her idyll, whatever word we choose by which to describe a young woman's first love-affair, and of course, it hurt.

Two days later, when Percy Wyndall, not having been able to see her in the interval, and having no inkling of her change of sentiment, proposed to her by letter, she smiled the same little cold disdainful smile, as, after reading it twice over deliberately, she dropped it into the heart of the fire, and wrote a refusal, so icily polite, that its chill even penetrated the thick hide of the poet's self-esteem, and he felt nearly as humiliated as the bull!

Miss Palliser mentally blessed that belligerent, as she doubtless might never have discovered the poet's true character till too late, but for the interpretation vouchsafed through the adventure with Taurus.